Praise for the novels of Patricia Falvey

The Girls of Ennismore

"Falvey, adept at combining vivid historical detail and rich char-
acterization, brings closure to Rose's and Victoria's amorous
predicaments with brio and simplicity as the women eventually
reunite in friendship."
—*Publishers Weekly*

"An evocative, heartfelt story of how the bond of female friendship can survive and thrive through adversity. Beautifully drawn,
full of rich historical detail, and with a truest Irish sense of
place, I was seduced from page one."
—Kate Kerrigan, *New York Times* bestselling author of
Ellis Island

"An engaging narrative of class differences, sibling
entanglements, inheritance of grand Irish estates, and the
potential loss of them, finding home, finding love, all set against
the turbulent 1916 Easter Uprising in Ireland. A complex and
enjoyable read."
—Susan Vreeland, *New York Times* bestselling author of *Girl in
Hyacinth Blue*

Please turn the page for more outstanding praise!

The Girls of Ennismore

"Two friends, born of vastly different worlds, dare to defy convention and the strict bindings of societal class in Falvey's latest novel. Rich in authentic historical and Irish detail, *The Girls of Ennismore* is a compelling story of love, duty, and reinvention, highlighting the vast rewards—or grave consequences—of following one's heart. Fans of *Downton Abbey* will devour this sweeping tale."
—Kristina McMorris, *New York Times* bestselling author of *Sold on a Monday*

The Titanic Sisters

"Falvey delivers the enchanting saga of two Irish sisters who board the *Titanic* with dreams of new lives in New York City. . . . Falvey does a good job capturing the girls' excitement at leaving Ireland for New York, and of showing Nora's gradual recovery of her memories. This new chapter of *Titanic* lore is worth plunging into."
—*Publishers Weekly*

"Falvey's engrossing historical novel charts the paths of two sisters as they journey from Ireland to early 1900's America. . . . With sharply drawn characters and shifting landscapes, Falvey's drama deftly explores the sisters' life-altering transformations and relationships as they come into their own."
—*Booklist*

The Famine Orphans

Books by Patricia Falvey

THE YELLOW HOUSE

THE LINEN QUEEN

THE GIRLS OF ENNISMORE*

THE TITANIC SISTERS*

THE FAMINE ORPHANS*

*Published by Kensington Publishing Corporation

The Famine Orphans

PATRICIA FALVEY

KENSINGTON
PUBLISHING CORP.
kensingtonbooks.com

In memory of the Famine Orphans from Newry and other Irish Workhouses who sailed to Australia in 1848–1850, and forged lives there for themselves and their descendants.

Part One

Famine
1845

COME HERE TO ME 'TIL I TELL YOU A STORY—

I'm an old woman now and I want to get it all down before I die. You might think I've already forgotten much of it, but you'd be wrong. Like all Irish stories, this one has woven the light and dark threads of joy and sorrow into a shawl of memory that has wrapped around my heart and will never let go. It is not only *my* story but the story of all the young girls who lived it with me.

It began one day in the summer of 1845 when my wee brother, Christy, came running into our cottage holding what looked like a ball of black slime in his two hands. He was white in the face, his eyes bulging as if he'd seen a ghost. He choked out his words.

"The potatoes, Ma, look at them. They're rotten."

Ma spun around from the washbasin. "Och, Christy, don't be joking us." She moved closer and let out a gasp. "What the devil is that in your hands? Take it outside this minute."

Four-year-old Maeve edged closer to him.

"Phew, it smells!" she said, wrinkling her nose.

Da came in right behind Christy, a pained look on his face.

"'Tis no joke, Mary," he said, slumping down in the armchair beside the turf fire. "There's a powerful blight on the crop."

He nodded at Christy. "Take that muck outside and wash your hands at the well before you come back in."

Christy shuffled off. Maeve and I looked from Ma to Da, neither of us daring to say a word.

"Och maybe it's just on that one tract," Ma whispered, "surely it's not the whole crop."

Da sighed. "Ah, but it is, Mary. Jimmy Fox and Bandy Hughes were just over here telling me the same thing. Their fields are full of rot. Not a healthy potato left in the ground."

Ma made a sign of the cross. "Please God it's only this crop. We've seen this before. Your own da used to talk about it. Remember that time years ago they were afraid they'd all starve? But the next crop came in healthy."

Da shook his head. "Pray all you want, Mary. But I don't think God will spare us this time."

When the first crop came in healthy the following spring, we began to think Da had been wrong. We breathed a sigh of relief and went on about our business as if the blight of the previous year had never happened. But Da wasn't wrong. Within a few months it returned, even more widespread than before. By the end of 1846, nearly every potato crop in the land was ruined, and the dreaded word "famine" rose from a whisper to a roar that was carried on the wind across the island of Ireland.

Like other tenant farmers, our family was dependent on the potato crop for our livelihood. For as long as I can recall Da had rented a few acres of land from Mr. Charles Smythe, who owned a powerful amount of land in Upper Killeavy in South Armagh where I was born. It was a common arrangement all over Ireland for men like my da to work as a laborer in the landlord's fields for a small wage and the chance to lease a bit of ground where he could grow enough crops to feed his family and sell any spare produce for a small amount of money that went towards the rent. It might only be an acre or two, and the land might not be the most fertile, but having a patch of land to call his own brought pride to the hearts of men like Da, whose ancestors had been chased from their land by a succession of invaders. Every year Da

planted potatoes. There was room, as well, for cabbage and turnips and for chickens and maybe a cow or a pig if, like Da, you
had the spirit for it. But it was the potatoes that were our salva-
tion. Even with just a small patch of land, a man could grow enough
to feed his family year-round and leave them well-nourished even
if there was no meat on the table.

I loved growing up on our wee farm, playing among the green
fields of Upper Killeavy and round the foothills of Slieve Gullion
mountain. Ours was a happy family, although a small one by Irish
standards—the oldest was my brother Paddy, then myself, then
came Christy, followed by wee Maeve. Da was hardworking and
well respected, but Ma was the heart of the family. She was a
great one for listening to other people's sorrows. In those days
our cottage was often filled with people—neighbors and strangers
alike—while the teakettle bubbled constantly on the turf fire.
Ma had been born in nearby Newry town into a family of thriving
Protestant shopkeepers who disowned her when she married Da.
She had, in their minds, committed two unforgivable sins—one,
she had married beneath her station and, two, she had converted
to Catholicism. But Ma had taken well to life on the farm, and
the neighbors slowly came to admire her and seek her advice, including help with letters and such. Unlike many of them she
could read and write. She taught Da and the rest of us to do the
same.

It never crossed my mind that my life would change—I
thought the carefree, happy days would go on forever. But I was
wrong. After that first day when Christy brought the rotting potatoes into our cottage, everything changed. Soon the stores we'd
filled with the only healthy crop of 1846 were empty again. Over
the remainder of that year, and on into the next, we sold the pig,
then the cow, and eventually the chickens, so we could get
money to help pay our rent. All our neighbors were in the same
boat as ourselves. What made our situation more desperate was
that there were crops like wheat and barley and corn growing in

the landlords' fields but they were no good to us since we weren't allowed to touch them. They were saved for export to the English mainland and beyond.

What I remember most about that time was the months after months of hunger. It was nothing like the vague pang of hunger you'd get sometimes but forget as soon as you were distracted from it. This hunger was like a ravenous demon that clawed ceaselessly at my belly, even during sleep. I bore it silently as did all of us except wee Maeve, whose wailing quieted to a whimper as her strength ebbed away. We buried her in September of 1847.

A week later, my brother Paddy announced he was leaving for England. A normally quiet lad, he stood facing us, twirling his cap in his hands, and made a speech I think he'd been practicing for days.

"I've got to go," he began, ignoring Ma's cries. "I can stay here no longer watching this suffering. I know I have hardly any money, but I still have my strength. I intend to get work on one of the merchant boats leaving Newry Docks in exchange for a free passage to Liverpool. I can haul heavy sacks as well as any man—better even." He gave a shy smile. "There's bound to be plenty of work to be had over there and, when I've enough saved, I'll come back. By then, please God, the famine will have eased," he said, pausing and gazing into each of our faces, "and if it hasn't—well, we'll have money for the fare to sail away from this cursed place!"

He was not to be talked out of his plan.

When we thought things couldn't get worse, Mr. Smythe arrived on a cold October morning, to warn us he would have to put us out of our cottage if Da couldn't pay the back rent he owed on his lease.

"I'm sorry things have to be this way, Mick," he said as he accepted a cup of tea from Ma. He went on talking in a rush of words about every tenant being behind on rent and the big increases in Poor Law taxes he was having to pay for the new Newry Workhouse that had been built just a few years before.

"You see, the rate is based on the amount of ground I own, including your wee patch, Mick, as well as on your cottage. And without the rents from you and your neighbors I'll have no choice but to tear all the cottages down."

He gave a heavy sigh as if he was expecting sympathy, but none of us said a word.

All that night Ma and Da and the neighbors sat in the kitchen, drinking tea and talking about what to do, while I sat in the corner with my arm around Christy. "Where will we go?" they repeated over and over. "We've no money to pay the rent we owe, let alone enough to emigrate."

No one mentioned the workhouse. For as long as I could remember I knew that all over Ireland people had a terrible fear of workhouses. Da had often said he'd rather die than ever go to one of them places. "Once you're in there, they break your spirit and you're condemned to a life of poverty," he used to say, "and you end up buried in a pauper's grave." I used to shudder when he talked about it, though never did I think we'd one day be facing that possibility. But we had nowhere else to turn. Ma's relations had not spoken to her since her marriage to Da and, even if they had relented, my parents would have been too proud to ask them for help. In the end even Da agreed the workhouse was our only choice.

Early on the morning when Mr. Smythe's agents were due to come with their crowbars and knock down our cottage, we hitched our old pony to the cart, filled it with our meager possessions, and set out for Newry Workhouse. Ma said she couldn't bear to stay and watch our home destroyed, nor would she make a show of herself crying and begging to be let stay on like some of our neighbors had done. I was grateful we hadn't lingered, but as we walked away, I fought the urge to look back just one more time at my childhood home.

We were not alone that morning. People just like ourselves—starving people who'd been put off their land—crowded the road that led from Slieve Gullion mountain down to Newry town like a procession of weary ghosts. It was mid-November, and a bitter wind blew scattered flakes of snow against our faces. Even though we had left in the dimness of early morning, the day seemed to draw in so fast that we lost the daylight in no time. In the darkness our old pony stumbled and collapsed into a ditch. No amount of coaxing could get her to stand up again.

We unhooked the cart and went on our way, pushing it in front of us. But it was soon clear that the four of us hadn't the strength to push it for the rest of the journey. If Paddy had still been with us, we might have succeeded, but he wasn't and there was no point wishing things were different. In the end we left it, and all our possessions with it, on the side of the road.

Ma brushed away tears. "At least some other poor *craturs* might get some good out of them," she whispered.

The effort of trying to push the cart seemed to have taken all the strength out of her and she looked ready to collapse. I rushed towards her and took her by the arm to steady her.

When at last the outline of Newry Workhouse came into sight in the dim distance Da suddenly stopped and begged us to go on without him.

"You'll stand a better chance of them letting you in without me," he said. "They save what little pity they have for women and children."

Ma and I stopped dead in our tracks and stared at him. I put my face close to his. I wanted to shout at him. Tell him he had no business leaving us now. But even in the dim light I could see the tears shining in his eyes and my throat squeezed shut against any words of anger. I looked at Ma. Surely she could talk sense into him. But, instead, she drew him into her arms, put her head on his shoulder, and wept aloud. Wee Christy clung to her skirts and sobbed. They stood like that for a long time until Da pushed them gently away and turned to me.

"Look after them, Kate," he said. "You're a big girl now, strong and with a good head on your shoulders."

I pushed down the protest that wanted to explode from me. What was the point of arguing? Ma had already forgiven him. I nodded. "I'll try my best, Da," I said.

He sighed. "Go on now, there's the girl. I'll come for you soon."

I took Christy's hand and told Ma, who by then was in a bad way and could hardly walk, to lean on me. Together we climbed the hill to Newry Workhouse. The year was 1847 and I was fifteen years old.

Part Two

Workhouse
1848

Six months to the day after we arrived at the workhouse, I turned sixteen. It was the first birthday I could remember when there'd been no celebration at all. Even in those early years of the famine Ma had managed to find the ingredients for a currant cake with white icing, and she'd brought it to the table, lit with a wee candle, and Maeve and Christy and Paddy all cheered while Ma smiled and Da looked at me with tears in his eyes. Now, as I sat beside Ma on the straw pallet where she lay, I tried to picture every detail of those moments before they faded away from my memory for good.

A sudden May storm turned the sky black and set the dormitory windows rattling while rain pelted like bullets against the panes. Ma began to cough and I moved closer to her to try and keep her warm. I thought back to that November evening when Ma and Christy and I joined the queue outside the workhouse. A storm had been raging that night as well, but we were so numb with hunger and grief that we scarcely noticed it. Ma could barely stand up and Christy clung to me. I knew I would have to be the one to take charge as I had promised Da that I would.

People pressed around us, gaunt-faced and wide-eyed. Some hardly looked human at all, their skeletal bodies so shrunken I could hardly tell the men from the women. I turned away from them, swallowing hard, and pushed Ma and Christy forward. We had long ago abandoned our belongings, leaving us only the rags we stood up in. It struck me then that maybe we looked just as bad as everybody else.

It's a *quare* thing to realize that when you're close to starvation nothing matters to you in the whole world—not power, not pride, not shame—nothing except food. And it was the specter of starvation, like a sudden insanity, that drove me to steer Ma and Christy through the growing tide of people to the front door of the building, into the big open lantern-lit room and right up to a severe-looking man who turned out to be the master of the workhouse himself. I don't know where I found the strength but I spilled out our story in a torrent of hysterical and disconnected words. The stern expression on his face never changed and, looking back on it, I think he was overwhelmed with the scene in front of him, but he let us through. The only time Ma came to her senses was when a matron tried to wrest Christy out of my grasp, explaining that boys had to be separated from the women. Ma's eyes burned as she screamed at her. Like the master, the overwhelmed matron had waved us on through, though she called after us.

"I'll be back for him in the morning!"

As I sat lost in memory, there was a sudden commotion outside the dormitory door and I left Ma to see what it was. As I drew closer, I heard laughter. I must be imagining things, I thought. Laughter was a rare thing to hear in a place like this. The door opened and young Mary Timmins poked her blond, curly head in.

"Ah, good, Kate, you're awake so. You left the dining hall early and were afeard you might be asleep."

I stared at her, wondering what she was on about. Mary turned behind her and opened the door wide.

"Come on in, girls, she's awake."

I stood aside and in marched a half dozen young girls wearing workhouse shifts, each one carrying a candle. They formed a circle around me and began singing "Happy Birthday!"

I thought I must be dreaming. Surely this was not Mary Timmins and the other young girls I'd been teaching to read and write for the past few months? Surely it was a chorus of angels, their thin, frail voices serenading me—or maybe they were ghosts! Many of the women in the dormitory sat up from their pallets, rubbing their eyes. Then Matron O'Hare appeared, smiling in a way I had never seen her do before.

"Happy birthday, Kate Gilvarry," she said. "The girls here wanted to let you know how much they appreciate all you've done teaching them to read and write."

Mary Timmins took something from her pocket and handed it to me with a shy smile.

"'Tis the best we could do, Kate!"

I looked down at the piece of white cardboard, cut and folded like a greeting card, and covered with wee drawings and each girl's signature in colored ink. The girls crowded around me and started speaking all at once.

"We've signed our names like you taught us, Kate."

"That's my wee drawing. D'you like it?"

"Sorry we don't have any cake."

"Matron helped us."

I looked around at them, at their gaunt, thin faces and their wide, innocent eyes and I fought back sudden tears. I reached out and hugged each of them.

"'Tis the best birthday celebration I've ever had," I said.

I felt a hand on my shoulder and turned around to see Ma, smiling at me.

"Isn't this a grand thing, darling?" she whispered. "You always said you wanted to be a teacher, so you did."

I didn't sleep that night. The storm had long ago let up and the place was quiet except for the occasional coughing or sighing of the women lying on the straw pallets. I lay next to Ma as I had done every night since we'd arrived. I had cried after the girls left—cried for them, cried for myself, cried for Ireland, and for all the poor souls who had fled to America and Canada, and for all the poor souls who had perished before they could flee. When my tears ran dry, I prayed. I prayed for wee Maeve in heaven, and for Paddy somewhere across the sea, and for Da, wherever he might be. Then I prayed for Christy, who was all alone with the other boys in a separate wing of the workhouse, and for Ma, who lay peacefully beside me on the bed. Then I made a pledge to God, aloud for anyone to hear, that I would get out of this place, that I would find Paddy and Da and take all of us home, wherever that might be.

During the first weeks after we arrived at the workhouse, we were given food three times a day—stirabout with milk for breakfast, bread and tea for supper and, for the main midday meal, meat and vegetables. But, like everywhere else in Ireland, there were no potatoes. One woman told us that they still served them when she had come into the workhouse the year before.

"Sure I thought it was a miracle," she recalled, gazing wistfully into the distance. "I looked at them in such wonder. There were some inmates who gulped them down with their two hands and others who hid them under their smocks or in their pockets. Them's the ones were severely punished when they were caught." She shook her head at the memory, then smiled. "Ah, but I ate them slowly, reverently like, as if taking Communion, enjoying the taste and smell and feel of them. Ah, it was grand, so it was!"

But it had been too good to last. The potatoes disappeared. The stores were empty, and the workhouse guardians were unable to find more to buy. Meat became scarcer, too, and all the while the inmate population continued to grow—from four hundred when we'd arrived to over one thousand in a matter of months. Now, all we got at midday was a bowl of watery soup. We were grateful for it, of course, but as I watched Ma grow thinner, her complexion turn sallow and her eyes more deadened, I was determined not to let her give up hope.

Besides the scarcity of food, money also grew short in the workhouse. Schoolmasters and -mistresses brought on to teach the children were sacked or set to other tasks. That was when I volunteered to teach Mary Timmins and the others to read and write. The class had been filled at first, but eventually dwindled to the half dozen who refused to listen to those who said they were wasting their time.

"What good will knowing how to read and write do you when you're kicking up daisies beyond in the paupers' graveyard?"

I hadn't realized how easy it was to lose hope in a place like this. The girls who dropped out were put to the task of picking oakum. They sat all day ripping apart old hunks of rope with blistered fingers and teasing out the fibers, which were then sold to shipbuilders who mixed them with tar to seal the lining of wooden ships. How could they have chosen to spend their time doing that over trying to improve themselves for the future? Why would they do such a thing? Slowly, the answer became clear to me. They didn't believe they had any future beyond this place. After that, it took every bit of strength I had to keep up the hopes of the remaining girls—and my own, as well.

About two months after my birthday, Matron came through the dining hall one lunchtime, tapped on the shoulders of about two dozen girls, myself included, and told us to come with her. We gave each other puzzled looks and some of the girls began firing questions at Matron.

"Where are we going? Why? Have we done something wrong?"

The rules at the workhouse were so strict we were always terrified of breaking them. Punishment was harsh—at best, flogging, at worst, being thrown out onto the street.

"I'm not after stealing anything, Matron," said Patsy Toner, a short girl my age, with a booming voice that belied her size. She had wild, tousled red hair, green eyes, a ruddy complexion and a vocabulary that would have made a sailor proud. I knew little about her background but I'd heard she'd been a street urchin in Newry before coming to the workhouse. Like most of the other girls, I stayed clear of her for fear of inviting a torrent of abuse from her sharp tongue.

Matron paused and turned around to the string of girls following her in a disorderly procession.

"You've done nothing wrong, girls," she said. "Master Dunne wants to introduce you to a visitor who has something important to tell you. Now stop talking and hurry up."

We followed her down two sets of stairs and through a door marked "Board Room." We filed in behind her and sat down on the two rows of chairs she pointed to. We were quiet now, looking around at the grandeur of the room with its polished floor and portraits of stern-looking men hanging on the paneled walls. I supposed they were the workhouse guardians and this was where they held their meetings. In front of us was a stage on which stood a long, polished wooden table behind which were placed five high-backed, upholstered chairs. We shifted uneasily in our seats and waited. The door opened and Mr. Dunne, the workhouse master, strode in.

Some of the girls, including Mary, jumped to their feet and curtsied.

"Will you stop making shows of yourselves," said Patsy in a loud whisper. "He's not the bloody Pope!"

Matron turned around. "Quiet!" she hissed.

Master Dunne ignored us as he climbed onto the stage and sat down in the middle chair. He was followed by a sallow-faced man in a brown coat two sizes too big for him. He was middle-aged, balding, and had a long, sharp nose. He sat down next to Master Dunne, pulled out a large handkerchief and blew his nose lustily. He never looked at us either. I began to wonder why Matron had bothered to bring us.

Master Dunne signaled to Matron, who climbed hurriedly onto the stage and sat down on the other side of him, looking anxious. Master Dunne still had not looked at us but nodded towards Matron. She stood up and cleared her throat.

"Girls," she began in a timid voice.

"Louder, Mrs. O'Hare," shouted Master Dunne.

She flushed and started again. "Girls, you all know Master

Dunne beside me." Mary Timmins began to clap but Matron froze her with a stare. "He has called you here to meet our visitor." She nodded towards the newcomer. "This is Mr. Begley, who has come all the way from Dublin to speak to you today. He has news that will be very important to your futures so please pay close attention."

Matron sat down and Mr. Begley stood up.

"Er, ladies," he began before interrupting himself with a mighty sneeze. He blew his nose again, this time at a greater volume than before. "As Matron O'Hare has suggested, I have some news of great importance to all of you."

His voice was so extraordinarily high-pitched that some of the girls began to giggle.

"I have been appointed by the English government and the Board of Guardian Overseers to acquaint you with a program that will greatly affect your futures."

"Bloody Brit," whispered Patsy.

"For several months now the British Government, under the direction of Lord Earl Grey, has been developing a program which will give young women like yourselves the chance to become domestic servants on the continent of Australia." As if anxious to get through his speech he began to talk more quickly and as he did the girls grew quiet. Some of them clutched each other's hands. One or two began to weep and I knew they were afraid that they were going to be thrown out of the workhouse. I was worried about the same thing myself. But then Mr. Begley said something that shone a new light on things. We didn't have to go!

"Lord Grey is the British secretary of state for the colonies, including Australia, and has worked out this program with the Australian authorities and your Board of Guardians. The program is totally voluntary, but if you wish to go, your passage from Ireland to Australia will be paid for, you will be outfitted with new clothes, and guaranteed jobs in the best possible establishments in New South Wales. You will also be paid the going wage for your work."

He stopped and gave what I supposed passed for a smile and waited. The room was silent. If he was expecting applause, he would have been waiting a long time. Master Dunne, finally looking directly at us, stood up and began to speak in his deep, commanding voice. He was clearly annoyed.

"Yes, the program is voluntary, but not all of you will be suitable. Besides being between the ages of fourteen and nineteen years, you will have to be of upright moral character, industrious, and able to at least speak English. The ability to read and write in English is highly desirable."

Mary Timmins turned to smile at me.

"Furthermore, you will need to have a sponsor who will attest that you meet all these requirements before you will be accepted. Those of you who are accepted will be expected to be a credit to Newry Workhouse. Finally, I want to say that this is a wonderful opportunity being offered to you not only by the British and Australian governments but by the guardians of this workhouse who will be paying for your clothes and transportation to Dublin. I hope you are all extremely grateful."

He turned to Matron. "Matron O'Hare will try to answer your questions and give you more details."

With that he climbed down from the stage and nodded for Mr. Begley to join him. Together they walked out of the room looking straight ahead.

When they had gone, the girls erupted.

"Where's Australia, Matron? Is it far?"

"When will we be going?"

"When will we get our new clothes?"

"What's the catch, Matron? Sure the English would never give us anything for free."

"Could my sister go, too, and maybe my ma?"

"Who'll pick the girls to go?"

"I wouldn't trust that oul' feller, Begley, farther than I could throw him. I didn't like the cut of his jib at all," said Patsy to anyone who'd listen as Matron escorted us from the room and gathered us in the hall.

"I'm afraid I don't have all the answers," Matron said, "but I will find out all I can. In the meantime, go and get ready for supper. I'll meet you afterwards and explain as much as I am able."

At supper I told Ma about Mr. Begley and what he had said.

"He tried to make it sound as if they were doing all of this out of the goodness of their hearts," I said, "but most of us didn't believe him. Patsy Toner said there had to be a catch."

Ma smiled. "Patsy never has a good word to say about anyone. You know that."

"Aye, but plenty of the rest of us think she might be right. We'll know more when we meet with Matron later."

Ma said nothing so I hurried on.

"Anyway, Ma, catch or no catch, I'll not be leaving here without you and Christy."

Finally, Ma spoke. "I wouldn't be too hasty, Kate. It might be the best thing that could happen to you."

Before I could reply, Matron tapped me on the shoulder and signaled me to join her and the other girls in the now empty dining hall.

When we were settled, Matron pulled up a chair and sat in front of us so she was eye level.

"I expect you are all very anxious to hear more about the scheme Mr. Begley proposed," she began. "Firstly, you should know that it's already begun. Two ships carrying girls from workhouses in Ulster left for Australia, one in June, called the *Earl Grey*, and the second, called the *Roman Emperor*, earlier this month."

"And what happened to them? Did they arrive safe? And do they all have jobs like Mr. Begley said?"

Matron took a deep breath.

"They haven't arrived in Australia yet," she said. "The journey takes three to four months."

You could have heard a pin drop, then the silence was followed by a rush of exclamations.

"Three months? My God, that's longer than it takes to sail to America!"

"Where in God's name is this Australia anyway?"

Patsy Toner piped up. "And when will our lot leave?"

"You're scheduled to sail next month, in August," said Matron, "on a ship called the *Sabine*."

"So we'll still not know by then how the others got on," said Patsy, determined to make her point. "We won't even get word by the time we leave. If it takes three months for them to get there, then it will take another three months to get a letter back. That means November, at the earliest, and by then we'll either be in Australia or swimming with the feckin' fishes at the bottom of the ocean!"

Several girls gasped. I could see Matron was growing exasperated.

"Look," she said, "I know no more than you do. I'm just doing my job!" She hesitated, looked pointedly at Patsy, and then added, "And keep in mind only those girls who meet all the requirements will be selected to go!"

Patsy fell silent. It was clear Matron was sending her a message that she might not be chosen. I felt a pang of pity for her.

Matron turned to the subject of clothes. I supposed she thought she would be on safer ground.

"As Master Dunne said, you'll each be getting your own travel box with new clothes and other articles to take with you." She took a piece of paper out of her pocket. "Let's see now, I have a list of the items here." She cleared her throat.

"Six shifts; six pairs of stockings; two pairs of shoes; two dresses; two short wrappers and two night wrappers; two flannel and two cotton petticoats; one worsted shawl and a cloak."

Matron looked up and smiled. "There will be an assortment of other items like handkerchiefs, linen collars, aprons, sheets, nightcaps and a pair of stays."

Several girls giggled at the mention of stays.

"And there'll be hygiene items, and needles and thread and maybe some scraps of cotton or calico. And you'll also each get a bonnet to wear when you arrive."

She smiled again. "That's it, I think. Oh, and one more item; Episcopalian and Catholic girls will each get a prayer book and a Bible, and Presbyterians will each get a psalm book and Bible."

"Jesus, we never get past religion, do we?" muttered Patsy.

Matron stood up. "That's all you need to know for now, I think. All of you here meet the age requirements, and most of you can at least speak English." She looked directly at me. "And thanks to Kate here, some of you can also read and write in English." She paused, and added, "What remains to be reviewed is your suitability for domestic service. That means you have good habits, work hard, are honest and"—this time she looked directly at Patsy Toner—"not given to talking back to your betters!"

Mary Timmins caught up with me as I made my way back to the dormitory. She looked up at me, her blue eyes wide. "Would they really let me go?" she asked. "I'm only fourteen. I know they said I'd qualify. Will you be going?"

I thought of my conversation with Ma. I'd told her I wasn't going, and I meant it. But I didn't want to hold Mary back. "I don't know yet," was all I said.

"Oh, Kate, I want to go but I'm afeard. Patsy said we might all drown. But I don't want to stay here without you!"

I looked at her. Yes, Mary was fourteen, but with her small frame and innocent ways, she was more like a ten-year-old. She'd been an only child—born to her mother late in life. From what she'd told me, I gathered she'd had a very sheltered upbringing. Her parents almost never let her out of their sight. I thought to myself that she'd been more smothered than sheltered. Her parents had died early on when the famine came, and Mary had been left alone for days in the cottage with their bodies until a neighbor found her and brought her to the workhouse. She was a sweet, innocent girl who I often thought belonged in a convent. I could understand her fears. Didn't we all feel the same way?

I patted Mary's arm. "Try not to worry yourself, Mary," I said.

Over the next few nights, I sat awake beside Ma as she sweated with a fever. For weeks now dysentery had been spreading through the workhouse population. To his credit, Master Dunne had ordered new privies to be built to accommodate the increased demands of the growing inmate count, which now totaled thirteen hundred. But it made little difference. Cholera, typhoid and chest ailments were also cutting through the population at an alarming rate, sending more poor souls to the infirmary, some of them never to return.

I was fortunate that I had not yet caught any sickness, but Ma had already been poorly when we arrived and she had little strength and, I think, less will to fight back. No amount of coaxing could get her to swallow the watery soup I offered her.

"You have to keep up your strength, Ma," I pleaded. "I need you to get well. How else am I going to get you and Christy out of here and back with Da and Paddy?"

Ma shook her head. "You know your da is never coming back, Kate. If he was alive, he'd have been here to fetch us by now. It's been almost a year."

"Don't talk like that, Ma," I said.

Deep down I knew she was right. I'd had nightmares where I saw Da lying dead in a ditch. But I had to stay strong for Ma. I had to stop her from giving up hope.

"Maybe he followed Paddy over to England and the two of them are earning money hand over fist. And when they have enough saved sure they'll be back for us in no time."

Ma's dull eyes lit up for just a moment and she smiled. "Ah, you were always a girl with a great imagination, so you were. My wee dreamer."

I began to cry. Ma reached out and stroked my long hair.

"Such lovely hair," she murmured, "the same as mine was at your age. 'Titian,' they used to call it."

I'd been told often that I was the spitting image of Ma and it pleased me to no end. I was tall, like her, with the same reddish-brown hair and hazel eyes. I looked into Ma's eyes now and shuddered. They were unusually bright, but it was not the light that made them shine—it was the raging fever.

"Go to Australia, love," she whispered. "It's what I want, and what your da would want. Don't let this famine curse our entire family. I want you to smile again, you always had the sunniest of smiles. God is giving you this chance. Take it."

She lay back down on the straw bed and as I mopped her forehead with a damp cloth she drifted off into sleep.

The next day Father Burns, the Catholic workhouse chaplain, sat next to me in a corner of the dining hall.

"Your ma's in a bad way, Kate," he said.

I nodded, unable to find words. I studied his solemn face. How many hundreds of times, I wondered, had he had this conversation with the relatives of sick inmates?

"She can't die," I said, holding back tears. "She and Christy are all I have left in this world."

Father Burns put his hand on my arm. "God has a plan for each of us, Kate, and you must trust Him to know what's best for you."

"Best? How can losing half my family to famine and ending up in this workhouse with my ma dying be best for me?"

"It's not for us to question—"

My anger exploded. "Question, Father? You know what I question? I question whether such a creature as God even exists, but if He does, I've no notion of trusting Him or His plan!"

I knew what I was saying was blasphemy but at that moment I didn't care.

Father Burns silently bowed his head.

Later that night I knelt beside Ma as she drifted in and out of consciousness and watched Father Burns perform the last rites. Some of the women in the dormitory sat up to watch but most of them lay on their straw pallets without moving. I supposed, like me, they'd seen this ritual often enough over the months, that it had ceased to have meaning. One more poor soul heading for the paupers' graveyard! The door opened and Matron came in holding Christy by the hand. I scrambled to my feet and ran to him, pulling him close. He looked up at me with wide, unblinking eyes that seemed too big for his wizened wee face. I'd caught a few glimpses of him over the months as he marched with the other boys out of the schoolroom, just as I was coming in to teach the girls. Workhouse rules were strict on keeping us all separated regardless of family connection. After a while, just a glimpse of him was enough to reassure me that he was alright.

He struggled out of my grasp and backed up to Matron.

"Do you not know me, Christy?" I said in alarm. "Surely you haven't forgotten me?"

"Go on now, Christy, there's a good lad," said Matron. "I'll be waiting for you just outside."

I took his hand and led him to where Ma lay. Father Burns nodded towards him. "Hello, Christy, would you like to kiss your ma goodbye, son?"

But Christy didn't move. He stood still in the dim light looking off into the distance. Part of me wanted to shove him towards Ma, to shout at him that this was his mother, and she was dying, but I did neither. How was I to know what was going on in the child's head or what he'd suffered through already? I sighed. He had become a stranger to us, and we to him.

Father Burns finished his prayers, anointed Ma's forehead, kissed the stole around his neck, and placed it in a box along with the holy oils and a crucifix.

"She's at peace now, Kate. May God have mercy on her soul."

Standing, he took Christy by the arm and led him out of the

room. I was left to keep vigil over Ma. I must have dozed off for a time for when I awoke the sun had risen and I was alone.

I got up and went to find Matron.

"I want to go to Australia," I said.

Two days before we were to leave for the journey to Australia the travel boxes we had been promised had still not arrived. We'd been on pins and needles for days waiting for them, trying to ignore Patsy Toner's constant taunts that we'd been lied to.

"Sure they thought we were stupid as well as poor," she said. "And they were right. You were all codded by their promises. I kept telling you it was too good to be true!"

"Stop it, Patsy," one of the girls retorted. "Just because you weren't picked to go doesn't mean you should be spoiling it for the rest of us!"

I understood Patsy's bitterness. A week earlier, Matron told her she would not be going. That night I heard her sobbing in the corner of the dormitory. She cursed at me to leave her alone when I went over and knelt beside her pallet.

"I'm sorry, Patsy," I whispered. "I really thought you'd be coming with us. I can talk to Matron if you like. See if she'll change her mind . . ."

Patsy sat upright. "Don't be bothering your head, miss," she said. "What makes you think I wanted to go with you lot, anyway?"

"Ah, now, Patsy. Of course you wanted to go. Who wouldn't? And besides, I've noticed how you've been behaving better the last couple of weeks and you even got Father Burns to sign a reference for you, and . . ."

Patsy burst into a new round of tears, burying her head in her hands. Her shoulders slumped and all the life seemed to drain out of her. "'Tis my own fault," she sobbed, "me and my vulgar mouth. I can't let go of it. The anger, I mean. It's what's got me this far."

I didn't know much about Patsy's life before she came to the workhouse, but from what some of the other girls told me it was a hard one. They said her ma died when she was twelve and her da had disappeared, leaving her to fend for herself, living in a run-down part of Newry, surviving on scraps and handouts and what she could steal. Poor Patsy, she had hardly stood a chance in life even before the famine. She, of all people, deserved to go. I decided to speak to Matron no matter what Patsy said.

Matron was sympathetic. "I tried to get her in," she said.

"And Master Dunne said no?"

Matron shook her head. "No, he would have been delighted to see the back of her because she's so disruptive, but it turned out one of the Board of Guardians knew her by name and reputation and refused to let them spend one penny on her. So, Master Dunne's hands were tied." She sighed. "We've got our final list of girls now and there's no changing it."

The travel boxes finally arrived on the eve of our departure. There was pandemonium as each of us crowded into the administrative building on the ground floor and snatched them from the men who were carrying them in. The "boxes" were wooden chests, two feet long by fourteen inches high and wide, with our names painted on the lids. When I found the chest with my name etched on it, I knelt and traced the letters with my fingers, then unlocked it with the key Matron had given me. I carefully raised the lid and inhaled the rich, earthy smell of the wood. I lifted out a white bonnet which lay on top of the pile of contents and stroked its crimson ribbons. Someone had embroidered my name on it in silk thread. I had never seen anything so fine. I imagined Ma wearing such a bonnet, its frilled edges framing her lovely face. I fought back tears as I hugged it to my chest. All around me girls knelt, unlocking their boxes, and pulling out the contents, squealing as they examined each item and then laid it on the floor. It was the dresses that caused the most excitement. One by one, the girls stood up, holding the garments against themselves, and spun around, their frail bodies as thin as candle sticks. The sadness that had begun to overtake me faded under the spell of their laughter.

"Can you imagine us parading around Australia in the likes of such finery?" cried one girl.

"Aye," said another, "and so many boys admiring us, we'd be spoiled for choice."

Another girl chimed in. "Was I telling you my uncle Niall was in Australia for two years? He says there's animals and birds there the likes of which we've never seen in Ireland, and Christmas is the hottest time of the year, and there's more boys there than you could shake a stick at, and all of them gorgeous looking!"

The girls all squealed with laughter as Matron fussed about, trying to check off the contents of each box to make sure everything was in order. She clapped her hands to get attention but finally gave up, sank down on the floor in the middle of us and waited for the excitement to die down.

Matron eventually announced it was time for everyone to go up to bed. Yawning, they trailed out, leaving the boxes in a neat pile near the front door as she had directed. I noticed there was a box sitting by itself in a corner. I walked over to examine it. The name "Patricia Riley" was carved clearly on the lid. Patricia was one of the girls who'd been in my reading and writing class. I realized I hadn't seen her with the others.

"Where's Patricia?" I asked.

"She's gone," Matron said. "Her relations came for her yesterday. They are bringing Patricia and her brother back with them to America."

I looked from Matron to the travel box and back.

"So, we have one more box than we need," I said.

She nodded. "Yes. Seems a shame to let it go to waste, doesn't it?"

"Yes, it does," I said.

Looking back, it was as well that the travel boxes arrived when they did. For a while it took my mind off the journey ahead of me the next day. But when I lay down that night on the straw pallet I had shared with Ma, I began to weep. I could still feel her presence beside me. Often in the night I would hear her voice or inhale her scent and I'd wake up expecting her to be there. That night my sense of her was even stronger. I was leaving her. Not only her, but Da and Paddy and Maeve, and of course, Christy. I was filled with guilt over leaving him behind. How could I do that? No matter what Ma had said I was still abandoning him. I eventually gathered the courage to go and see him, and Matron agreed to arrange it. He was as distant as he had been the night Ma died, pulling away from me as I tried to embrace him. It was as if the wee lad had already come to terms with the idea that he was alone in the world. He said nothing as I told him I was leaving. And still nothing when I told him I would be back for him one day.

I lay there, that last night in the workhouse, recalling as much detail as I could of my happy childhood days on the farm at the foot of Slieve Gullion mountain. There would be time enough tomorrow to worry about the future, about what awaited me beyond this place, beyond this land, beyond this only life I had ever known.

The next morning, I awoke and dressed in the darkness and tiptoed out of the dormitory. I joined the other girls in the administrative building and waited for Matron to come and tell us what to do. No one spoke. At last, she arrived and led us outside into the chilly, pre-dawn August morning and lined us up, two by two. The sharp bite of cold air shocked my senses awake. I was reminded of early country mornings on the farm when I went out to collect the eggs. But something was amiss. There was no sound. Not a bird was singing in the pre-dawn blackness. The world was silent.

We, too, were silent as we walked, shivering, down the hill from the workhouse to where horse-drawn carts waited to take us to Dublin. As we walked, I recalled another silent, ghostly procession back on that November morning when my family and neighbors walked down from Slieve Gullion mountain, leaving everything we knew behind us. We remained silent now as we climbed onto the carts and turned our faces to stare out over the shadowed land that had been our home.

Our small procession of carts began its journey south in the pre-dawn hours of Sunday, August 20th, 1848. There was no sound from any of the girls, or from Matron, who sat beside me. In time, a weak sun rose on the eastern horizon, its shadowed light painting the trees and bushes along the roadside in dark, ghostly shapes. I shivered and pulled my cloak tighter around me. The silence was pierced by a pack of crows that suddenly appeared and hovered above us, cawing and squawking, as if in scorn. My granny used to say crows were a bad sign—a sign of trouble on its way. I almost laughed—weren't they a bit late showing up now? Our troubles had started years ago. After the famine and the workhouse, what worse troubles could there be in store? No matter, I was glad when they flew away to annoy some other poor *craturs*.

The rising sun brought warmth, but still my teeth chattered as if it were the middle of winter. I shoved my fists deep into the pockets of my cloak. Matron, who was traveling with us as far as Kingstown Port in Dublin, had said the journey would take about eight hours, "although you never know what trouble we might meet on the way." I shrugged. She was only echoing the Irish habit of not waiting for trouble but going out to meet it. So far, we were making good progress as we trundled along paved roads. We passed Dundalk, a town about ten miles from our farm, which I visited often with my da on Fair days, to buy or sell a cow or sell our small harvest of vegetables. The memory warmed me briefly. We continued south to Drogheda, where English troops, led by Oliver Cromwell, laid siege in the 1600s. I let my imagination take me back to evenings in our cottage where our neighbors recalled tales of that time passed down through generations. Every Irish Catholic child knew the stories of Cromwell's brutal deeds, including the worst one of all when he locked the doors of St. Peter's Church in Drogheda, as hundreds of townspeople and clergy sheltered inside, and ordered it burned to the ground. After Drogheda we turned southeast towards the village of Swords and onward to Dublin. Paved roads gave way to rutted, twisting lanes, some so narrow I was sure the carts would get stuck. At least it isn't raining, I thought.

I'd tempted fate. Suddenly, a huge dark cloud appeared and rain poured down mercilessly, soaking our cloaks, and trickling down our necks as we bent our heads against the torrent.

"Jesus, I'm drenched!" cried one of the girls.

"Will you whish't," cried another, "sure you'll hardly melt."

More voices joined the chorus, some protesting, others complaining, while somebody in the cart behind ours began singing a silly song. "Rain, rain go away. Come again another day!"

It stopped as suddenly as it started, and an hour later I had begun to dry out. But I could do nothing to ease the stiffness in my hands and feet and I prayed for the journey to be over. From the position of the sun, I guessed it was nearly noontime. Others must have been thinking the same thing because a chorus of voices chanting the Angelus prayer suddenly filled the air around me. "Hail Mary, full of Grace, the Lord be with thee . . ." The chorus grew in sound and strength until I had the sensation of being swallowed up in something bigger than myself. I beat my chest furiously. Never in all the years of saying the Angelus prayer when the church bells rang at noon each day had I felt like this. I forgot about my damp clothes and my aching body, and an unexpected joy filled me.

Once the girls had found their voices, they began to sing. At first it was just one or two of them, but as others joined in it swelled to a chorus that filled the air with anthems celebrating Ireland's revolutionary history—"The Minstrel Boy," "A Nation Once Again," "The Wearing of the Green"—all songs I'd known since childhood. I sang out as loudly as the others, sending words of defiance slicing through the air. Exhausted and cleansed, we fell silent. Then a lone, halting, childlike voice from the cart behind us pierced the silence:

"I'll tell me ma, when I go home,
The boys won't leave the girls alone,
They pulled my hair and stole my comb,
But that's alright, 'til I go home.
She is handsome, she is pretty,
She is the Belle of Belfast City,
She is a-courting one, two, three,
Please won't you tell me who is she?"

I recognized the traditional children's song at once. Like almost every child in Ulster, I had danced in circles and clapped my hands and chanted the words over and over, making up some of them as we went along. Now, I joyfully joined in with the lone singer. Soon the air was filled not with defiance but with the joy and exuberance of childhood, as every girl in our little procession and Matron O'Hare sang and clapped their hands and did not stop until we reached the Port of Kingstown.

At last, we arrived at the docks where we were to board a steamship that would take us across the Irish Sea to the Port of Plymouth, England. I climbed down from the cart, my rubbery legs threatening to give way under me, and stood with the others while Matron handed documents and bank notes to a red-faced inspector sucking on a pipe.

"How many have ye?" he barked, eyeing us suspiciously.

"Twenty-nine," said Matron, nervously.

He raised a fat finger and began counting us, reminding me of a slow-witted child as he mouthed the numbers aloud.

"I'd say there's thirty of ye," he said, glaring at Matron, "not counting yourself, missus."

She grew flustered. "No, I'm not traveling, sir," she began and then stopped herself, her face turning crimson. "Oh, you're right, sir," she stuttered. "We added one at the last minute. Patricia Riley—her name should be on the list. Yes, that makes thirty."

I held my breath. In her confusion, Matron must have forgotten that, by silent agreement, she and I had arranged for Patsy

Toner to replace Patricia Riley, whose relations had rescued her from the workhouse two days before we left.

The man looked at her as if she was the slow-witted one.

"Where's your master? All the other workhouses sent their masters to settle the count and the fees due. Who are you, at all?"

Matron's cheeks turned an even brighter crimson.

"Master Dunne was taken ill," she offered, "and I was sent instead. I'm the Newry Workhouse matron, Mrs. O'Hare."

I heard a snigger from behind me and turned to see Patsy Toner.

"I'm Patricia Riley, so I am," Patsy declared, "big as life and twice as ugly!"

I hadn't noticed Patsy when we set out that morning. I was too preoccupied by my own feelings. But now, as I looked at her, I wondered if Matron and I had done the right thing. Any place she landed she seemed to cause trouble. I wondered, too, if she was at all grateful.

The inspector stared at Patsy, then at Matron, grunted and waved us on.

As we made our way towards the steamer, I was shocked to see dozens of young girls crammed together on the dock. I realized they were orphans like us. I hadn't stopped to think that the Earl Grey scheme could have been offered to workhouses in both the northern and southern part of the country. Many of the girls prattled away, some speaking in English, some in Irish. Others were quiet, as older people, who I took to be relations, hugged them, weeping and keening as if they were witnessing a wake—which I supposed in a way they were. They might never see these girls again, so they might as well be dead, I thought.

Matron guided us to the crowd of girls and told us to line up. She moved along our little queue touching each of us gently, tears in her eyes.

"I'll be leaving you now," she said, "there'll be other matrons escorting you the rest of the journey all the way to Australia. Be a credit to the Newry Workhouse now and set a good example for the other girls you meet."

She turned away but Mary Timmins sprang out of the line and clutched her on the arm.

"Don't leave us, miss!" she cried.

"Och, now, wee Mary, don't be taking on," said Matron as she guided her towards me. "Sure Kate's here, she'll look after you, won't you, Kate?"

In a flash of memory, I saw Da telling me to look after Ma and Christy the day we arrived at the workhouse, and I wanted to protest the way I had wanted to back then. But the sight of Mary's tortured face silenced me.

"I will, Matron," I said to her back as she walked away.

The line of girls edged forward and soon I was looking up at an enormous boat. A "steamer packet" someone had called it; others called it a "decker" and I could see why as I looked up at the railings that surrounded a huge, open deck. I had never seen the likes of it. Gingerly, I climbed up a row of metal steps, Mary holding on to me from behind with trembling hands. Once on deck, we were shoved forward by the tide of girls pressing in around us. I was afraid I might suffocate. I pushed my way towards the outside railing, pulling Mary behind me. At last, I managed to find a space for us, wedged against the railing, and I stood, taking in gulps of air, my heart beating loudly in my chest.

"It's alright, Mary," I said, "just breathe in the fresh air."

I focused my eyes on the docks, watching hordes of people, some in tattered clothes, clambering onto the ship now that the orphans had all boarded. I realized many of them were escaping from famine, as well, desperate to be anywhere but in Ireland. Parents, children, wives, and friends standing on the docks pressed into the ship waving goodbye, looking as forlorn as those on board. To stay or go—there was no peace or happiness to be found in either choice. I realized we were all orphans in some way, whether we lost parents or lost our country, or both. We were no different.

Matron had told us that it would be an overnight journey on the steamer. As I looked around, my fears rose. Where would we sleep? There would be no room to lie down anywhere. We'd have to sleep standing up. And there was no food. We had long ago eaten the meagre ration of bread Matron had given us when we started out that morning. Why didn't Matron warn us? I realized then maybe she had no more idea than the rest of us. And the master and Mr. Begley wouldn't have told us—all they'd wanted was to get rid of us from the workhouse—they certainly wouldn't have wanted to scare us into staying. I wondered what other horrors they'd left out of the rosy picture they'd painted for us.

As the steamer moved slowly down the canal, steam pouring from its two huge chimneys, I leaned over the railing. It was mid-afternoon, and the sun was high in the sky, as we pulled out into the Irish Sea. I watched the coast of Ireland grow small but wept no tears. I felt nothing—not hunger, regret, sadness, fear nor hope—I was numb.

I yearned to sink down to the floor of the deck but we were so tightly wedged together there was no room. I stood, hoping the swaying of the boat would lull me to sleep. And for a while I entered a limbo somewhere between sleep and wakefulness where fractured dreams sped before my eyes, images of children playing at the foot of Slieve Gullion mountain; Ma pushing an iron skillet into the turf fire; the candlelit face of Mary Timmins singing "Happy Birthday." I shot awake. My life had just passed before me. Was I about to die? I wiped away what I thought were tears until I realized the moisture was rain. I must have slept longer than I thought, for it was dark now. In Ireland, August evenings were light until eleven o'clock, so it must be gone midnight.

In the darkness the sounds around me grew more intense. Waves lashing against the boat sounded like thunder, while winds whistled like the high-pitched wails of banshees. The boat began to roll, dipping down close to the surface of the sea and then righting itself, then dipping again so far that waves began to splash over us. Girls screamed and I heard Mary, who was huddled beside me, vomit over the railing. My own stomach began to churn and I fought to keep down the bile that seared my throat.

"I'm afeard, Kate," Mary whispered. "Are we going to drown?"

I was glad I couldn't see her face as I lied to her.

"Not at all, Mary. I'll keep us from harm."

Driven by a now furious wind, the rain grew sharp as glass on my cheeks and drenched my clothes. I put both my hands up to my head in a futile effort to stop my bonnet flying away. Looking back on it, it was a silly thing to have done. But at that moment it was the only thing left in my control. The bonnet, with its crimson velvet ribbons, was the loveliest thing I had ever owned. Nothing, not even this demonic storm, was going to take it from me. I had lost enough.

It was late evening the next day when the steamer shunted to a stop at Baltic Wharf in Plymouth, England. As I looked across the harbor all I could make out in the dim light was the outline of a huge building that looked like a prison barracks or maybe another workhouse. I began to tremble with fear and confusion. Had we just left one workhouse only to be condemned to another? Had Matron and the master and Mr. Begley from Dublin told us a pack of lies? Had Patsy Toner been right? I wanted to cry out but I was shoved forward by the tide of girls pressing in around me, aware of Mary's hand like a vise on my arm. I couldn't let her see my fear. I swallowed hard and followed the other girls down the steps from the ferry. We must have been a pitiful sight, our drenched cloaks, some stained by vomit, our eyes half-closed from exhaustion, as one by one we staggered onto dry land.

A stern-looking woman marched up and down the dock barking orders.

"Line up now, two by two," she shouted, her English accent slicing crisply through the air. "You will wait to be inspected. Have your papers out and handy. After inspection we'll be going to the depot over there." She pointed to the large building I had first spied. "That's the Plymouth emigration depot where you're going to stay the night. It will be your last night on dry land. Tomorrow you will board the ship that will take you to Australia."

Although the last thing I wanted after my journey on the steamer was to board another ship, I breathed a sigh of relief. We were bound for Australia, after all. "Thanks be to God," I whispered.

The woman kept on talking but the rest of her words were lost to me. As a wave of relief washed over me, all I wanted to do was sleep. I was dead on my feet. I would have slept right there on the wharf if I could have. Wearily, I picked up my bundle, and taking Mary's arm, followed the procession down the dock.

Mary hardly let go of me as we lined up to be inspected. She stuttered out her name, her hand shaking as she gave her health certificate and other papers to the Inspector—a grim-faced man who shouted at us to pay attention and keep the line straight. The woman who had met us at the steamer flitted about, repeating her orders in English, and asking those of us who had a smattering of Irish to translate to the girls who were native speakers and who looked totally confused. I felt sorry for them. The ordeal was frightening enough even when you understood English. As Mary and I turned away, the girl behind us moved up close to the inspector, almost shouting at him in a tongue I'd never heard. I knew some Irish words but I didn't understand what this girl was saying at all. I turned back around and recognized her. It was Patsy. What on earth was she doing? I watched the Inspector throw his arms up and wave her on.

"Stupid *eejit* thought I was speaking Irish," she said to me, her face creased in a wide grin. "I didn't trust meself to remember me name's now Riley and not Toner, at all. I couldn't risk being thrown out on me arse before I even set foot in Australia!"

"What was it you were speaking then?" I asked, confused.

Her grin widened. "Gibberish!"

As we lined up, a bone-chilling cold settled on all of us and we huddled together in the queue for warmth, our damp clothes clinging to our bodies.

After the inspections we were led into the emigration depot, where we were met by a man who introduced himself as Doctor Harte. He told us he was the doctor who would be sailing with us on the ship to Australia and would be responsible for our health and safety. At any other time, I would have paid close attention to him—to his looks and manner and everything he said—but I was so tired I hardly took in any of his words. What I did remember was he ordered that each of us should be given baths before we went to the dormitory in the depot.

The water was only lukewarm but, after the dreadful ordeal on the steamer, it was like I'd gone to heaven.

Part Three

Voyage
1848

The next morning, I awoke to the sound of a crow tapping on the window of the dormitory where we had slept. I rubbed my eyes and looked over at Mary. She was still fast asleep, her blond hair a halo of curls around her head. She looked like an angel. I tiptoed over to the window and gazed out. The harbor stretched out into the distance but I focused on the area straight across from the emigration depot where we had disembarked from the steamer. I could see no sign of it—maybe it was back in Dublin by now. I pushed away a faint yearning that began to tug at my heart. What was the use of looking back? What was done, was done, and I needed to look to the future—if not with joy, then at least with determination to make the best of it.

I turned my attention to the street below the window. Men and women hurried back and forth. Well-dressed women held on to their bonnets as a strong wind picked up. Young boys carrying newspapers and parcels darted through the throngs. Hard-looking men in drab-colored shirts and trousers wheeled carts full of boxes, roughly pushing pedestrians aside. I wondered what was in the boxes and where the men were going with them. Could it be it was cargo they were taking to a ship? I leaned closer to the window and peered from side to side and far out into the harbor. To my surprise it was filled with sailing vessels, such a beautiful sight it could have been a painting. Could they all be going to Australia? How would I know which one was ours? My curiosity mounted and I looked around at Mary. She was still asleep. Maybe I had time to just run outside before she awoke.

I dressed quickly, my clothes still damp from the night before, and threw my cloak around my shoulders. With a last glance at Mary, I slipped out of the room and hurried down to the ground floor of the building and out onto the street. A stiff breeze caught my hair, and it began to fly in all directions, and I wished I had my bonnet. The night before, Matron had ordered us to store our bonnets in our travel boxes, saying we'd have no need of them until we arrived in Australia. I decided to follow a man who was wheeling a cart loaded with boxes. Maybe he is going to our ship, I thought, and fell into step behind him. Awake and alert now, I was suddenly dying to see this vessel that was to take us to Australia. I picked up my pace, trying not to lose sight of him as I pushed through the crowds. The smells of fish, some fresh, some rotten, almost overpowered me. A man wheeling a cart filled with squealing pigs startled me so much I had to stop and regain my breath. For a moment an unexpected excitement filled me, and I forgot about the journey that lay ahead. I watched him descend to the pier where our steamer had been docked and transfer the contents of his cart into a small boat. I was disappointed. He was not going to our vessel after all. I caught up with the man wheeling the pig cart and followed him further down the dock where two sailors waited in a small boat to herd the pigs aboard.

I watched as the sailors began rowing out into the harbor. I raised my hand to shade my eyes from the sudden sunlight that was burning its way through the morning fog. I saw the crew pull up their oars and float alongside a sailing ship and begin transferring their cargo to sailors aboard it. I moved as close to the water's edge as I could. From this distance I could make out three tall masts around which sails were furled. I swallowed hard. Was *that* the vessel I would be spending the next three months aboard? From where I stood it appeared to be no more than one hundred feet long and only about a third as wide. Surely it was much too small for a journey such as that. In a panic, I tugged on the sleeve of a roughly dressed man standing near me who was peering at the ships through a telescope.

"Excuse me, sir," I said, pointing at the vessel, "Is that the *Sabine*, the ship that's going to Australia?'

He hesitated for a moment, eyeing me up and down, then gave me a wide grin, displaying blackened teeth. He turned the telescope towards where I pointed.

"Aye, young lass," he said, "that's the *Sabine*. She'll be setting sail soon, bound for Van Dieman's Land, she and a few more of the ships out there. Popular place, Van Dieman's Land!"

He reached out to give me the telescope but I turned and raced back the way I had come. Bile rose in my throat, and I struggled to keep it at bay. Van Dieman's Land, I knew, was a part of Australia. It was where many Irishmen were sent by the English government as prisoners. Such deportations were the subject of songs that my neighbors and my da often sang during winter nights around the fire. How had I not made the connection before? Were we not just orphans, but prisoners? What was to become of us?

I raced back into the customs building and fled up the stairs and into the dormitory looking for Mary.

"Mary," I cried, "Mary, where are you? We must leave now! We can't go on that ship!"

But Mary was nowhere to be seen. I spun around, just as the English matron appeared in the doorway!

"So, you have decided to return, miss?" she said, her face grim. "You left your young friend in a terrible state when she realized you were gone. We had a beastly time settling her down. How could you be so irresponsible? Where have you been?"

"I—I just went out for some air, and—" I began.

"It doesn't matter," she interrupted me sharply. "You will come with me this instant. You have missed breakfast and it serves you right! We will go straight to the ship."

She grasped my arm roughly, her fingernails sinking into my flesh. "I shall be keeping a close eye on you, Kathleen Gilvarry, mark my words!"

Back down on the dock, the orphan girls stood looking out at the ship I had seen earlier. I joined them, with Mary in tow. Suddenly Patsy came up behind me and touched me on the arm.

"Where in Jesus's name have you been?" she said, her tone accusatory. "You were nowhere to be found at breakfast." She nodded towards Mary. "I had to take charge of herself. She was having a conniption. She said you left her alone. And I always thought you were the reliable one, not a hooligan the likes of me."

I couldn't summon the strength to explain. Instead, I said, "What happened to your hair, Patsy?"

Her long unruly locks had been cut short as a boy's.

Patsy scowled and put her hand up to her head.

"That feckin' doctor thought I might have lice, and ordered it cut off. Bastard! If I'd known—"

She was interrupted by the English matron's sharp voice. "Move along now!"

I turned from Patsy to look again at the ship. The fog had cleared to expose bright sunshine and I could see it more clearly than before. The mast and rigging and furled sails rose skyward from the deck. Sailors scrambled up and down the masts and scuttled along crossbars, securing and tightening the sails. The three masts with the crossbars reminded me of three huge crucifixes like the ones in the pictures of the Stations of the Cross we had to kneel in front of every Good Friday, and without thinking I made a quick sign of the cross. On the deck more sailors were hauling cargo up from the small tenders that wobbled unsteadily next to the hull. The din of the girls' chatter died down and they stood, open-mouthed, watching the scene before them.

"'Tis awful small, so it is," said one of them. "What class of a boat is it at all?"

"How in God's name would we be able to live on that thing for three months?" said another. "Sure 'tis no longer than our village football pitch and not even half as wide."

I didn't dare bring up my fear that we were going to be prisoners. I'd tried to explain it to Mary as we rushed along towards the dock. But she'd said nothing. The poor wee *cratur* was in shock. Besides there was no chance of escape now, with the matron watching us like a hawk.

Mary, Patsy and I were in the first group to be ushered into a small skiff. We sat stiffly as two crewmen rowed towards the ship. Doctor Harte, who'd introduced himself the night before, joined us. Mary trembled as I held on to her, cursing myself for having put her in such a state. Matron O'Hare back in Newry would have been very disappointed in me.

When it came time to board the ship, Mary refused to move, holding up the whole group. Doctor Harte tried to reassure her, but she became hysterical. It didn't help that Patsy began cursing her.

"Will you move your bloody arse, Mary," she spat, "or you'll tip over the fecking boat and we'll all be drowned. Is it back to picking oakum you want to go? For that's what's waiting for you beyond in Newry!"

Doctor Harte glared at Patsy. "You go first then, miss," he said, "set an example for the rest."

Patsy glared back at him and stuck out her chin. "Just watch me!" she said.

But she didn't move, and I could see by her face she was as frightened as the rest of us. We all waited, and grudgingly, cursing under her breath, she gathered up her skirts and stepped up on the platform that had been lowered. She shook off the crewman who attempted to help her out of the boat.

"Get away with you, you *eejit*. I don't need your bloody help."

After that, the others followed her timidly—some praying aloud, some crying. Two girls with red faces and strong Belfast accents joined arms and jumped out of the skiff together. One waved at the sailors on the deck who were watching us with curiosity.

"Hi ya, lads," she shouted, "can't wait to make your acquaintance."

Mary and I were the last to board. Doctor Harte took one of her arms and I the other and we gently coaxed her onward. "Promise you won't leave me again, Kate," she said, her voice trembling. "If you do, I'll surely die."

At last, we were all boarded. Doctor Harte lined everyone up on the middle deck and checked off our names in an official-looking book. When he was satisfied that we were all accounted for, he looked up and smiled—a shy, gentle gesture.

"Well, I'm glad to say we didn't misplace any of you." He nodded towards the matron and her assistant who stood with her. "Thank you, ladies, for your vigilance in watching over our young charges." He turned back to us. "Come," he continued, "the matrons will show you to your sleeping quarters and will pass out your supplies. You will each receive your own bolster and blanket for your bed, some eating utensils, a tin plate and mug, and a sponge and brick of soap to bathe with each morning. When you have settled in, you will return to the deck and I will talk to you about how your days will be structured during our coming voyage."

His calm voice was reassuring and Mary's grip on my arm relaxed slightly. But I was still uneasy. I couldn't get the idea of Van Dieman's Land out of my head. I didn't know if my fears were justified. I would just have to wait and see.

We lined up again waiting for the matron to tell us where to go next.

"My name is Mrs. Buckley," she began, "and that is how you will address me from now on." She turned and pointed to an older, portly woman with red cheeks and an equally red nose. "This is my sub-matron, Mrs. Phoebe Clark. You will be in our charge for the duration of this voyage. You will follow our orders without question, otherwise you will be reported to Doctor Harte and subjected to whatever punishment he sees fit." She took a deep breath and went on. "Doctor Harte is the ship's surgeon, and as such is second-in-command, reporting only to the captain. He has other duties, of course. Besides looking out for you girls he must tend to the sick among the paying passengers and the crew. There is an infirmary on the ship and he oversees it. He is also responsible for making sure the ship is kept immaculately clean so that disease does not spread." She wrinkled her nose. "Diseases like typhus and dysentery, whooping cough and heat stroke, pneumonia, ulcerated tongues . . ."

Doctor Harte put up his hand to silence her.

"Therefore, you must follow both his orders and mine to the letter," she finished lamely.

I stole a glance at the doctor, whose face reddened before he turned away. When I looked back, Mrs. Buckley was giving me what Ma would have called the "evil eye." I was already in her bad books.

"This is the middle deck where your lessons will take place. Now, follow me!" she commanded, and began to walk, straight-backed and brisk, along the deck. I wondered how she kept her footing so well. I was already stumbling as the ship swayed gently to and fro in the harbor. She led us down a flight of steps to a lower deck. "This is the orlop deck," she said, "where you will attend to your hygiene. You will also be responsible for its cleanliness. You will take your meals in the hold. You are forbidden to go on the top main deck—that is where our paying passengers are located and they certainly would not wish to mix with the likes of you."

She signaled to a nearby sailor. "Open it up!"

I wondered what she was doing. Surely this was a cargo hold— were we to be sleeping and eating amongst the sacks of flour, or God forbid the crates of live pigs, goats and chickens that I had watched being loaded on to the ship from the supply boats docked alongside? I bit my tongue and watched with dread as two sailors slid a long piece of wood free of two handles and lifted the cover of the hatch.

"When I call your names," barked Mrs. Buckley, you will descend into your sleeping area by the ladder. There you will find berths which have been assigned to you. You will not question your berth assignments, nor may you ask to change them."

A dull panic arose in me and muffled her voice. I fought to control myself for young Mary's sake. Eventually, her words burst through my consciousness loud and clear.

"The hatch will be locked down each evening at half-past eight and stay locked until it is opened again at five in the morning. This is for your safety. We already have many sailors aboard, as well as civilian passengers. It is the responsibility of myself and my assistant, as well as that of Doctor Harte, to deliver you to Australia unmolested!"

A low murmur arose from the girls in the queue, and the Belfast girls behind me tittered aloud, but no one, not even Patsy Toner, spoke up. Mrs. Buckley had done her job putting the fear of God in us. Docile as sheep, we followed the assistant matron through the hatch opening.

I stepped off the ladder into a dim, low-ceilinged room, lit only by candle lamps which swung from the ceiling. The room was long and narrow, and the walls lined with rows of open shelves, one above the other, each large enough to fit one person. I gasped. Was this where we were to sleep? I felt suffocated at the thought. A stale smell filled the room, putting me in mind of the old shed at the back of our cottage where Da used to store sacks of potatoes and turnips through the winter. And even though the hatch cover was open, no air moved through the space. My mouth and throat were suddenly as parched as if I was standing in the middle of a hot desert.

I breathed a sigh of relief when I saw that Mary had been assigned the berth above me. I was not so relieved to see that Patsy was in a bottom berth directly next to me, but I shrugged. There'd not been so much as a peep out of her since we'd climbed aboard. Maybe she'd had a sudden conversion into a model young woman, I thought, but I'd believe it when I saw it. We set about making up our beds, laying the bolsters and blankets over straw mattresses in each berth, securing our utensils, cups and plates in burlap bags provided for that purpose and hanging them from nails in the ceiling. The soap, sponges and towels we slid beneath the bolsters. The night before, our travel boxes were opened and we were instructed to take out just the items we would need for the journey—two shifts, two dresses and a shawl—there would be no room for any other belongings. I had folded my cloak and laid my bonnet gently on top of it and closed the lid. By now, our travel boxes had been stowed away somewhere on the ship and we had no access to them. Even if we had, there was nowhere to put them. It occurred to me then that even a prison cell might have more room.

A few girls who said they were Protestants complained about being made to sleep among Catholics, but Mrs. Buckley silenced them at once, reminding them that under no circumstances would the berth assignments be changed. Before we returned to the deck, we sat down at a long, wooden table where we were given a meal of cabbage broth, a biscuit and water. I devoured it quickly, draining the last drops of water, unconcerned about table manners. Afterwards I looked around, embarrassed, but all the girls knew what starvation had felt like. No one was about to judge anyone else on that score.

When we were finished, we returned to the middle deck and sat in a circle, our eyes fixed on Doctor Harte. I was suddenly aware of his soft, calm voice, so unlike Mrs. Buckley's bark. He was about two inches taller than me, with a slight build, wavy brown hair that curled around his collar, and startling blue eyes. He had a kindly way about him, like a new, young priest might have had before being toughened by the endless hardships of his impoverished flock. I thought he might be somewhere in his twenties. I wondered idly if he was married. No, I thought, if he had a wife at home, he would hardly have left her to journey across an ocean supervising a group of orphans like us. I almost pitied him for the responsibility he now had for this group of girls. I wondered how and why he had found himself in this position. Surely no one with any common sense would take it on.

"You always see the good in everybody, Kate . . ." I heard Ma's words in my head. "Be careful, darling, it could get you in trouble someday."

I smiled. "It's alright, Ma," I told her silently. "I'll be careful, but I think I'll give this one the benefit of the doubt."

When I came back to reality, Doctor Harte was explaining how we would pass each day during the voyage. We would start with a sponge bath each morning.

"But you will be fully clothed!" interrupted Mrs. Buckley.

The girls around me gasped.

"And how would we be managing that?" piped up Patsy. "We'd have to be bloody contortionists!"

The Belfast girls laughed aloud.

"Good on ya, Patsy," one called out.

"Matron's afeard we might be molested!" shouted the other.

Dr. Harte held up his hand for silence, ignoring a glowering Mrs. Buckley. The bath would be followed by breakfast, he continued. He explained that we would be broken into smaller groups to take our meals. Then we would have jobs to do—scrubbing the deck, washing our utensils, airing our blankets and washing our clothes.

"Jesus," said Patsy, "if I'd wanted to be a fecking skivvy I'd have stayed in Newry."

Doctor Harte tried to suppress a grin and quickly turned the subject to lessons. There were to be reading and writing lessons, English language lessons for the girls who spoke only Irish and lessons in domestic service to prepare us for our future jobs in Australia.

"Each Sunday you will be free to attend a religious service of your choice," he said, "and in the evenings you may entertain yourselves with songs or dancing."

One of the Belfast girls let out a snort.

"I can show yez all how to do the cancan!" she called, lifting her skirt and swirling it above her knees.

It was then that I finally believed that the Earl Grey scheme was going to be good to its promises. I felt a great weight lifted off me as my earlier fears ebbed. I smiled at Mary, who sat beside me, and squeezed her hand.

"We're going to be grand, Mary," I said.

Later that night when we were locked down in the hold, I fought to keep my spirits up. It was so dark, I felt as if I was lying in a coffin. Some of the girls wept openly and wee Mary climbed down from her bunk and squeezed in beside me. I let her stay.

The groaning of the hatch cover startled me. It seemed I had only just fallen asleep after long hours of lying awake in between nightmares. I realized it must be morning. I looked over at Mary, fast asleep beside me. It seemed a shame to wake her, but I knew I couldn't leave her there, not after her reaction back at the emigration depot. I tapped her on the shoulder, climbed out of the berth and groped around on the floor to find the nearest bucket that now served as a chamber pot. In the dimness I heard, rather than saw, girls rousing from sleep, yawning and stretching. Beside me Patsy stood, a bucket in hand.

"Where d'ya think we're supposed to empty these?" she snapped. "Or do we wait 'til they overflow and drown us in our sleep?"

I shrugged. "I should think we'll have to empty them over the deck railing into the sea."

At that moment the older sub-matron, who had told us to call her Phoebe—"This Mrs. Clark business gives me the pip," she'd said, "makes me sound as old as Methuselah"—made her way towards us, lighting the candle lamps as she went, and swatting the girls who were still asleep.

"Up with you now, girls," she shouted, cheery as a blackbird. "Take your buckets with you and your wash things. You'll be wanting a bath but make sure you hurry it up if you don't want to miss breakfast."

She finished her rounds and clapped her hands, ignoring the grumbling and occasional curses from the sleepy girls.

"Right-oh, up the ladder ya go, and don't spill your buckets on the girls coming up behind ya!" The thought seemed to amuse her and she let out a loud guffaw. "And mind what Matron told ya about keeping your clothes on. We don't want the sailors getting ideas, do we?"

"How the feck are we supposed to do that?" grumbled Patsy as she climbed up the ladder behind me. "We'd have to twist ourselves like bloody monkeys on a tightrope!"

Phoebe, apparently blessed with perfect hearing, laughed again. "It will be a sight to behold, I'm sure! Hurry up now."

I was expecting to see tin baths like the one we had at home but was puzzled to see only a few metal buckets lined up along the open deck beside the railing. The only privacy was a length of canvas about two feet high which created a makeshift fence that had been set up to conceal the buckets. Phoebe stood directing two crew members who filled them with seawater. Unsure what to do, I finally sank down on the deck beside a bucket, wearing only my shift, and began to wash my arms and legs, wincing as the coarse sponge and lye soap stung my skin. I signaled to Mary to do the same. I was aware of the crew watching me from the upper deck with a mixture of scorn, amusement and curiosity. I tried not to look at them as I slid the sponge under my shift to clean myself as best I could. I thought of the old tin bath Ma used to fill up every Saturday night in our warm kitchen. Paddy, as the oldest, always went first, and wee Maeve went last, complaining that the water was now cold and dirty. How innocent a time that was. Shame was foreign to me in those days. Now, with the sailors staring down at me, I was suddenly ashamed of my body. I stood up, my shift dripping wet and clinging to me, snatched up my sponge and soap and towel and made as quickly as I could for the safety of the hold.

Breakfast was a bowl of gruel, a hard biscuit, water and milk. That first morning the gruel ran out before the latecomers arrived. Mrs. Buckley would have none of their complaining.

"This will teach you discipline," she snapped, holding up her hand to silence them. "You must learn to follow a strict schedule. There will be no time for sleeping late or lingering while you bathe. Discipline is the first lesson you must learn if you are to be useful in domestic service."

Doctor Harte approached us. "Thank you, Mrs. Buckley," he said, and sat down on an upturned barrel in front of us.

"As I told you yesterday," he began, "there are many lessons you will be required to learn during this voyage. Mrs. Buckley is correct—discipline is a most important one."

Mrs. Buckley pursed her lips in what I supposed was a smile.

"Self-satisfied bitch!" whispered Patsy.

Doctor Harte continued speaking. "I have spent a lot of time laying out a plan for training you in the skills you will need to be successful in your future. I am anxious that you not only secure a position in service when you reach Australia, but that you are able to maintain such position. To guarantee that, you must prove that you are an asset to the household. Yes, speaking, reading, and writing in English will be highly desirable in helping you secure a position, but characteristics such as discipline, personal cleanliness, timeliness, willingness to follow orders and an agreeable disposition will be even more important in maintaining it. And of course, you must practice household skills like cleaning, washing, polishing, meal preparation and serving."

He smiled boyishly as a few groans greeted these last words.

"Fear not, girls," he went on, "I have also set aside time in my plan for some leisure pursuits. It won't be all dull labor."

He stood up. "For the rest of the day, do as Mrs. Buckley and her assistant bid you and tomorrow we will begin lessons in earnest."

He started to walk away and then turned back to look at us. "Oh, and tomorrow, weather permitting, we set sail for Australia!"

That night I tossed and turned, wondering what the future would bring. Tomorrow we would set out for Australia. The idea both terrified and excited me. We were sailing out into an open ocean, miles and miles of nothing but water. What if there were gales and storms, such rain and winds as we'd never seen the likes of? Would they be worse by far than the storm on the Irish Sea? Would the ship stay afloat, or would we all be tossed into the cold, black ocean? Would we survive such a journey? And if we did, what would await us on shore when we finally landed?

My fears gave way to brighter thoughts. Maybe Australia would be like a paradise, with beautiful flowers and birds. I pictured men and women and children gathered on a golden shore, their hands outstretched in greeting. They would prepare a banquet for our arrival, with foods we'd never seen in Ireland—delicious, colorful fruits and vegetables, and mouthwatering meats and breads. And we'd eat to our heart's content, and the supply of food would never run out.

I was in the middle of such a daydream when the ship's bell sounded and I knew the sailors would be opening the hatch any minute. Mary had slept in her own bed so I jumped up and stood, anxious to be one of the first on deck, able to watch the ship sail out into the channel and towards the open sea.

I hurried through my bath, then rushed down to the hold where I stowed my wash things and changed out of my wet shift. Then I retraced my steps up the ladder, stumbling in my excitement and climbed up to the top deck, praying no one would notice me. Doctor Harte and Mrs. Buckley had warned us that we were forbidden to go on the top deck and we would be punished if we were caught doing so. Sailors rushed in every direction around the ship, adjusting ropes and unfurling sails, clearing objects from the decks, securing the hatches, and shouting commands at each other using unfamiliar phrases. Seafaring language, I supposed. Some of it hardly sounded like English at all. They paid little attention to me. I had lodged myself in a corner between two upturned rowboats, hoping that no one would find me and haul me back to the hold. I had deliberately skipped breakfast, even though I was afraid I'd regret it later. But I didn't want to miss seeing the ship begin to sail.

The sun cut through the morning fog and I felt its warm rays on my face but I felt no breeze. I already understood that without wind the ship could not move and I was filled with disappointment. Would we be stuck here another day? I didn't understand what was happening as I watched sailors row a small boat away from the ship, carrying what looked like an anchor attached to a rope which trailed behind it. The other end of the rope appeared to be connected to the ship's wheel. At some distance away, the rowboat stopped and the sailors dropped the anchor and rope into the water, and I heard the cry, "Man the capstan." I looked down at the ship's wheel as four sailors began furiously turning its wooden handles, slowly winding in the line. As they did so, the ship began to move, as if we were being towed forward by the anchor. Down on the pier people had gathered to watch the ship leave, shading their eyes against the sun. A roar went up when we began to move. Children jumped gleefully up and down, waving at us. I waved back and smiled. I chanced a look behind me. By now the deck was filled with passengers. I had not been aware of them before but now I saw well-dressed men and women, some with young children in tow. I assumed they spent their time in their cabins or on the top deck. I shrugged and turned back to watch the sailors. The rope was now fully reeled in and the wind had strengthened.

"Raise anchor!" came the cry, followed by "Hoist the sails!" Men began scurrying up the rope rigging to adjust the sails. The noise was deafening as the wind filled them, causing them to billow like bed sheets drying on a clothesline. I waited, holding my breath. Soon a flock of seagulls crowded the sky above us and, as if it were a signal, the ship began to move again, the wind carrying us farther down the channel. I held tightly to the railings as the crowd on the pier and everyone on deck began cheering more loudly than before. We were on our way.

I made a note of the date in my mind—August 24th, 1848—
the day my life would change forever. As I watched the shoreline
slip away, I was overcome with sadness. It was an English shore I
was leaving, but my beloved Ireland lay just beyond it to the west.
My breath rose and fell in long sighs, my eyes were wet with
tears and I felt physically sick. With every minute that passed I
was moving farther and farther away from my homeland. I saw
images of Ma and Da and my brothers and little Maeve; I saw the
slopes of Slieve Gullion mountain; wee lambs gamboling on
green grass; turf bogs and hedges scarlet with fuchsia; our family
cottage surrounded by stone walls; and I heard the music of fiddles wafting over the fields on a summer evening.

A noise from behind startled me. It was Patsy. I wanted to
shout at her to leave me alone. Instead, I fixed my gaze ahead.

"Well, good riddance to bloody Ireland," she said. "I hope I
never set foot there again."

I said nothing, although I heard a catch in her voice. Poor
Patsy, I thought. She had known only poverty, struggles, and
worse, while, despite the famine, I was leaving behind memories
of a once happy life. At this moment, I didn't know which of us
was better off.

It didn't take long for us to discover the reality of life on a sailing ship. Mary was one of the first to get seasick. Within hours
she was down below, writhing in her berth, clutching a bucket.
Soon others joined her in the hold. Three days later, just as we
were getting our last sight of England at Land's End, every one
of us lay exhausted in our berths.

Doctor Harte tried to reassure us that seasickness was to be
expected at first, but that we would soon get used to the motion
of the ship beneath our feet. Nobody, not even I, believed him.
He even walked up and down past the berths showing us how to
place our feet wide apart.

"Watch how the sailors do it!" he said.

"Jesus, Mary and Joseph," Patsy groaned, in between vomiting into her bucket, "haven't the feckin' English punished us enough? Bad cess to all of them! Who knows what other torment they have in store?"

It didn't help matters that Phoebe seemed to take great delight in Patsy's distress.

"If you think you're in a bad way now, miss, just wait 'til tomorrow when we'll finally be out in the open sea. Sailing down the English Channel was child's play," she said, "compared to being knocked on your arse by waves the height of houses lashing the boat."

Patsy vomited again and lay back groaning.

As one by one we all succumbed to illness, the smell in the hold became unbearable. Sailors were sent to empty our buckets and rinse the floors, but it did little to relieve the foul stench of vomit and human waste. This new stench combined with the already awful smell of the wet stone and gravel ballast that was stored beneath the floorboards. Very few of us were able to hold up our heads without swooning, let alone climb the ladder up to the deck to get some air. Mrs. Buckley did not appear in the hold at all and Phoebe spent as little time there as possible. It was Doctor Harte who overruled the matrons and ordered the hatch to be left open during the day. But at night when we were locked down, the air became suffocating.

Unlike the matrons, it was Doctor Harte who regularly came each day down to the hold, stopping at each berth to reassure us that we would be well soon, and to try to tempt us with broth.

"Am I going to die, Doctor?"

"No, you are most certainly not!" he replied, as he was asked the same question repeatedly, "but you must try to eat."

I couldn't help but admire his patience and his kind manner. I wondered if he had sisters at home. If he did, I was sure they would be very fond of him. I didn't have much experience with doctors—I had always been a healthy child—but from what I'd heard they were pompous and gruff—nothing like our Doctor Harte. I realized how lucky we were to have the likes of him watching out for us.

Now, as we sailed out into the Atlantic Ocean, I thought back to all the horrors of the last few days—the long, exhausting ride on the cart to Dublin, the nightmare on the steamer to Plymouth, the fear that we were going to be prisoners in Plymouth or, even worse, in Van Dieman's Land—it seemed as if a lifetime had passed. I tried not to even think of the earlier horrors—the famine itself, losing wee Maeve and Paddy and Da, and then my dear, sweet Ma and leaving poor Christy behind. I didn't even have the strength to cry. I turned over, buried my head beneath my blanket, and willed myself to sleep.

The sickness passed eventually, just as Doctor Harte had promised, and our daily routine, as laid out that first day, was put into practice. All the orphans were divided into groups, or "messes" as they were called on a ship. Our mess consisted of myself, Patsy and Mary, which pleased me since we all knew each other, and I was not separated from Mary. But to my dismay, the two disruptive girls from Belfast, Sheila Hughes and Lizzie McShane, were included. They could have been sisters they looked so alike. Both were dark-haired, pale-skinned and stoutly built. Sheila was the more aggressive of the two, always ready to pick a physical fight, while Lizzie used her sharp tongue as a weapon. They'd worked together in a wet linen mill in Belfast before losing their jobs—they never said how—and entering a workhouse. I didn't think pairing them with Patsy was a good idea at all since they would likely encourage one another in mischief. Rounding out our number was a girl from County Kerry in the southwest of Ireland named Bridie O'Sullivan. She was a big, shy, country girl who only spoke a word or two of English, spending most of her time saying her prayers out loud and blessing herself, much to the disgust of Patsy and the Belfast girls.

Doctor Harte had assigned one orphan from each mess to be in charge. I was picked to oversee ours. My job was to go to the kitchen, or "galley" as it was called, located on the orlop deck, three times a day to fetch the food from the cook and bring it down to the others in the hold. Meals operated on a tight schedule and I was responsible for ensuring our food was picked up and eaten on time so the next mess could take our places. My annoyance about this assignment faded when I realized that it would give me something else to think about besides homesickness.

The first morning I nervously made my way to the galley at eight o'clock. It resembled a small shed built in the middle of the deck. Inside, a bin about four feet wide and two feet high had been filled with sand and on top of that a fire lit where the cooking was done, while pots sat steaming on iron tripods. Except for the sand, I was reminded of the turf fires in Irish kitchens, but here there was no chimney for the smoke to escape, just a hole in the roof.

I had a fit of coughing and Doctor Harte suddenly appeared beside me looking concerned.

"Are you alright, Miss Gilvarry?" he said.

I found my breath. "Yes. It's just the smoke."

He smiled, and I noticed the dimples in his cheeks. I realized I had never been this physically close to him and I stepped back nervously.

"Yes, I often wonder how the poor cooks stand it."

All business, he signaled the cook, who brought a variety of food over to the counter, including gruel, bread and milk, and waited while he inspected each item. Then he looked up and nodded while the cook returned to his fireplace.

"I intend to inspect each meal before it is served. I want to make sure that no corners are cut, and you get the rations you are entitled to. So, we shall meet again at dinner."

He smiled, gave me a little bow, and left.

Somewhat bemused, I watched him go, then I turned to the counter wondering how I was going to maneuver all this food back down to the hold.

At one o'clock and again at six, I made my way to the galley to collect beef, rice and beans, biscuits with molasses, and water for dinner and, later, tea and bread called "duff" made from flour and raisins. Doctor Harte, good to his word, appeared by my side on both occasions, inspecting each item and checking it off in a notebook.

By the third day, I was growing more comfortable in my new role. With the help of Mary, I was able to get the meals delivered to the mess in two round trips. I had enlisted Mary as much to build her confidence as to help me. She glowed with pride when I complimented her and I was pleased I had thought of it. Little did I know this would be the first bone of contention in the mess.

"If ya were lookin' for a body to help you, instead of that Mary one who's afraid of her own shadow, why didn't ya pick that big lump there?" said Lizzie McShane one night at teatime, nodding towards Bridie, who sat silently at the end of the table. "Sure, she could lift a whole cow," Lizzie continued, "let alone a wee jug of milk."

Sheila Hughes joined in. "You're right there, Lizzie," she said, grinning, "but be the size of her I'd say she might devour our meal along with her own before she even got down here."

"Aye, and us sitting waiting with our tongues hanging out!" said Patsy.

All three of them cackled like witches. I glared at them.

"Stop that," I said. "Bridie doesn't even know what you're saying about her. It's not very kind."

Lizzie widened her eyes. "Ooh, listen to that, girls," she said, looking at Sheila and Patsy, "it's not very kind," she finished, mimicking me. "Sure the big *culchie* has no notion what I'm after saying."

Mary turned pale and put her head down. I didn't know who I was angrier with—Lizzie, Sheila and Patsy for their meanness, or

Mary for not standing up for herself. I got up and started collecting the dishes, hoping to ease the situation, but out of nowhere Bridie sprang from her seat and set upon Lizzie, thumping her soundly around the head and shoulders.

"Stop it now!" I shouted, but nobody listened. Patsy jumped in to help Lizzie, while Sheila lunged at Bridie with a metal fork.

"Get away, or I'll stick ya with this, ya big ugly pig," she hissed.

I turned to Mary. "Get Mrs. Buckley. Now, Mary!"

She fled up the ladder.

I stood, shouting myself hoarse but they refused to stop fighting.

For the first time I was relieved to see Mrs. Buckley appear, Phoebe behind her.

"What is the meaning of this?" Mrs. Buckley barked. "Stop it at once or I'll call the captain and have you put in irons!"

At that moment several girls from the mess following ours arrived to have their tea. They stood gaping at the scene in front of them. Slowly, Sheila dropped the fork and Bridie backed away from Lizzie. I opened my mouth to explain.

"I'm sorry, Mrs. Buckley," I began, "I tried to stop them, but—"

She held up her hand to silence me.

"I do not want to hear what you have to say, Miss Gilvarry! I advised Doctor Harte that you were the wrong person to put in charge of your group, but he didn't listen. You have shown your lack of responsibility on more than one occasion." Her eyes narrowed. "Don't think I didn't see you on the top deck the day we sailed from Plymouth. I reported you to Doctor Harte but he made excuses for you." She sighed. "Now he will see I was right all along!"

"But . . ." I began, indignant that she was blaming me.

"No 'buts'!" she said. "I will be reporting all of you to Doctor Harte and it will be up to him whether or not he reports this outrageous behavior to the captain."

"If he has the guts to do it," murmured Phoebe.

Mrs. Buckley ignored her. "All of you will remain down here for the rest of the evening, and instead of going to breakfast tomorrow, you will report to Doctor Harte at first bell. That is all."

She looked at the plates and mugs on the table, then at the group of girls from the next mess who waited open-mouthed. "And clear this table up, Miss Gilvarry, so these girls may have their meals."

With that she signaled Phoebe and together they climbed the ladder and closed the hatch behind them.

The next morning the members of our mess stood in a circle around Doctor Harte, Mrs. Buckley and Phoebe. My stomach growled with hunger from missing breakfast, but that didn't bother me as much as my feeling of shame for having let him down. Mrs. Buckley recited our sins to him, a triumphant look on her flushed face. Then she pointed at me.

"I would recommend, Doctor, that you choose someone else to oversee the mess, or better yet assign her to a different group. Miss Gilvarry has shown herself on many occasions to be unreliable and a rule-breaker. If you remember, I have tried to warn you of this—"

She stopped abruptly when the doctor raised his hand for silence.

"Thank you, Mrs. Buckley. That will be all. And for goodness' sake get these girls some breakfast. I will speak to Miss Gilvarry alone."

He took me by the arm and led me away while Mrs. Buckley glowered after him.

"Let's go to the upper deck," he said curtly.

"But . . . I thought we weren't allowed up there," I said.

He turned to me. "No, you are not, but I understand that has not stopped you in the past."

A deep flush crept from my neck to my cheeks. I didn't reply. Instead, I followed him up the steps to the upper deck, ignoring the stares of passengers and sailors. He led me over to the railing, where he stood looking out at the sea, lost in thought. I waited.

He turned to face me at last. "I have tried to give you the benefit of the doubt, Miss Gilvarry," he began, his voice calm, "despite what Mrs. Buckley has reported to me, but this incident is
the most serious yet."

I froze, wondering what was coming next.

"In fairness I would like to hear your side of the story."

I took a deep breath, and, my voice shaking, recounted what
had happened the night before. "There was nothing I could
do to stop them once the fight began and so I sent Mary for
Mrs. Buckley," I finished, my voice fading almost in a whisper.

He listened attentively, nodding now and then. When I had
finished, he looked away from me and out to sea.

"As I thought," he murmured. "I did not believe you were the
instigator, even though Mrs. Buckley insinuated that you were."
He finally turned to look at me. "But you must understand that
Mrs. Buckley is my right hand on this voyage. I look to her and
Mrs. Clark to manage all of you girls, maintaining discipline
while I look after your health and welfare. As such I cannot in
good conscience keep ignoring her recommendations." He sighed
and I tried to avoid his eyes. "Therefore, you will no longer oversee your mess. I shall put Lizzie McShane in charge in your
place, while young Mary can continue as her assistant—"

"But Lizzie's the one who started the fight!" I protested.
"She's the last one who should be in charge of anything!"

I tried to hold my temper in check.

I thought I saw a flicker of a smile and I opened my mouth to
protest some more, but he cut me off.

"Miss Gilvarry," he said, "I understand your reaction. But I am
guessing that a little responsibility and recognition may be just
the thing Miss Lizzie McShane needs at this point in her life.
With her current attitude and behavior, she stands little chance
of securing a domestic position in Australia. Hopefully she will
thank me later."

He took my elbow and led me away from the railing and towards the stairs to the lower deck. Then he turned to me with a

broad, boyish smile. "I don't expect Mrs. Buckley will be too happy with my decision either!"

As I'd expected, Lizzie had a grand time letting me know she was in charge, bossing me around, firing orders at me at every turn. Poor Mary was caught in the middle.

"I'm sorry, Kate," she said over and over.

One evening I took her aside. "Listen, Mary, you've nothing to be sorry for. Lizzie's within her rights to give the rest of us orders. It's her job to keep the mess running smoothly."

"But—she tortures you every chance she gets," Mary began, her big blue eyes blurred with tears.

I smiled. "Don't worry, Mary, she'll get tired of it soon. I can cope with whatever insults she sends my way and so can you. Haven't we both been tortured far worse since the famine began? Surely the sharp words of a mill girl from Belfast can't do us much harm after all we've survived already?" I put my arm around her. "Just do everything Lizzie says and you'll be grand. She'd be lost without your help. Hold your head up high. Remember, we promised to make our Matron O'Hare proud!"

She nodded. "I'll do my best, Kate," she said solemnly.

Freed from my mess responsibilities, I joined the other girls in the task of keeping our areas clean, following Doctor Harte's orders to the tee. Each morning, after breakfast, we swept our sleeping quarters, tidied the berths and slid the dining tables against the walls out of the way. Mattresses were turned and the bedding, when necessary, was brought up to the deck to air out. The most back-breaking work was getting down on our knees every morning to scrape the deck free of refuse and other waste, then scour it with holystones and sand. We finished by mopping it until it gleamed. Fortunately, these tasks became easier once the bout of seasickness among the orphans had slowed down.

At eleven o'clock our lessons began. In those first days it was pleasant enough, sitting on the deck, the weather mild, the sea calm. At first, Doctor Harte stopped by to observe our lessons but, as time went on, left us to the mercy of Mrs. Buckley and Phoebe. I had wondered how he could possibly observe our lessons, check on our meals and inspect our hold and deck for cleanliness, while at the same time caring for sick children and injured sailors. It was almost as if he could be in two places at once. I soon realized the answer was his disciplined schedule and ability to work very hard. My admiration for him grew, along with my amusement, when I saw him one day striding about the deck swinging a portable stove that reminded me of a censer that priests and altar boys swung on a chain to dispense incense at Mass. Except, in this case, Doctor Harte was dispensing a vapor of vinegar and chloride of zinc to fumigate the ship.

Based on my experience teaching at the workhouse, I was immediately assigned to teach Bridie the basics of English. She proved to be such a quick learner I suspected she knew more English than she let on. Mary was assigned to teach writing to Patsy, Lizzie and Sheila. She was nervous at first, particularly when the three of them treated the lessons as a joke, but in time Lizzie began paying attention and the others followed suit. Had Doctor Harte been right about Lizzie, I wondered?

After a break for the midday meal, lessons resumed in the early afternoon. Mrs. Buckley looked on while Phoebe attempted to train us in the basics of domestic service—everything from how to set knives, forks, spoons and dishes on a table, to how servants were organized in wealthy houses from butler down to scullery maid. Surprisingly, when I tried to translate what we were being told to Bridie she laughed and indicated she knew all about such matters. We all had, me included, assumed since she was a farm girl living out in the countryside and far from any town, she would have little idea of how the wealthy lived. But I hadn't stopped to think she might have lived close to a manor house, which would often be called "The Big House" and, like many girls living nearby, had worked at times in such places. Instead, it was the likes of the rest of us from the towns who were mostly ignorant of such matters. It was a lesson not to rush to judgment—a lesson that might serve me well in the future.

Except for Patsy, our group was skilled at sewing and embroidery and were encouraged to make samples of our work using needles, thread and remnants of fabric which had apparently been donated to us by the good ladies of Plymouth. Phoebe said it would be good to show our skills to possible employers when we arrived in Australia. We all nodded, while Patsy muttered something I couldn't hear under her breath.

Patsy's attitude didn't improve as the days went on. She sat sullenly watching us do our sewing or embroidery, refusing even to lift a needle. Not surprisingly, Lizzie and Sheila were both skilled with a needle given their pasts working in a linen mill and with mothers who'd been seamstresses. Bridie said she'd been the one to make all the family's clothes before the famine came. Mary's mother had taught her to embroider, and while I didn't really like sewing, I was proficient enough, remembering what my mother had taught me.

Patsy was the odd one out. I realized she'd probably never had anyone to teach her. One night after supper I approached her about it. At first, she didn't want to listen, but I persisted.

"Maybe you can learn something else besides sewing?" I suggested.

"Like what?" she retorted.

"Well, how about baking bread? Maybe the cook would let you learn from him? I can talk to Doctor Harte . . ."

"*I can talk to Doctor Harte,*" Patsy said, imitating me. "*I'm his pet, and he'll do anything I ask him.*"

My face reddened. "That's not fair, Patsy. I'm only trying to help."

I said no more about it until one day after the sewing lesson Patsy said, "I suppose I'd be better off burning the arse off myself over a fire beyond in the galley than out here watching yez sitting in a circle with your needles like a group of bloody nuns in a convent. Next, you'll be chanting prayers while you're sewing like that *eejit* Bridie!"

It was Patsy's way of asking me to help. Within a week she was happily up to her elbows in flour and joking with the cook!

The training class in what the matrons called "etiquette" was undertaken by Mrs. Buckley herself. At first, she appeared oblivious to the reactions of the girls as she launched into a lecture on "society's rules of conduct." Bridie looked mystified, while Patsy, Lizzie and Sheila rolled their eyes and grinned, elbowing each other in the ribs.

"Oh aye," said Sheila, "I always comport meself with me nose in the air." She sniffed loudly as if on the hunt for a bad smell.

"And I'm all for the social graces," said Lizzie, "particularly when I'm lifting me skirts for some oul' baron."

"Aye," put in Patsy, "sure isn't it good etiquette to treat them all the same, never mind who they are—lord, bishop or beggar— we still have to keep up our standards!"

The three of them doubled over laughing. Even Bridie joined in, while Mary blushed to the roots of her hair. Phoebe grinned behind Mrs. Buckley's back and a few sailors came close to see what all the laughter was about.

For her part, Mrs. Buckley drew her lips into a prim line, rose from her chair and stalked away, muttering about "Irish heathens." She was no doubt on her way to complain to Doctor Harte. I thought about going after her to apologize for the other girls, but I suppressed the urge. I realized, perhaps for the first time in my life, that I didn't have to be responsible for the behavior of everyone around me.

And so the first days on board the *Sabine* passed pleasantly enough. The weather was warm and the white-capped sea tranquil. There was no land in sight and we had yet to see another ship. Flocks of seagulls followed us, wheeling against a cloudless sky. With little else to divert me, I focused my attention on the ship, my new home. I had begun to take comfort in the predictability of the ship's bells ringing to signal changes of the watch and alert passengers to meals. I enjoyed watching the sailors as they climbed the masts, adjusting sails and greasing cables, or jumping to attention at the orders the captain shouted through a horn from the forecastle on the top deck. I watched them as they sat in the evenings mending canvas sails with long needles or broke into song while enjoying their daily ration of rum.

I looked forward to Sundays when we would assemble on the deck to listen to a psalm or other reading and a sermon given by the captain, or sometimes by Doctor Harte. But my favorite time was evening when, for an hour before lockdown in the hold, many of the orphans gathered to sing and dance. One of the girls had brought a tin whistle with her and played lilting jigs while girls danced in ancient formations on the wooden deck. When they tired of dancing, some would sing. Bridie, it turned out, had a beautiful voice. She sang songs in Irish, some joyful, some haunting, but all of which carried a bittersweet sadness. Sailors often paused to listen, while some first-class passengers came out of their cabins to peer down to the orlop deck. From the first day we set sail from Plymouth I had begun keeping a diary, recording each date, the weather, and brief details of life on board. I was glad I had thought of it. It would have been easy to lose track of time or the days of the week. Every day on the ship so far had been identical to the one before, all of them melting into an indistinct fog of memory. The diary was how I knew that it was exactly thirteen days since leaving England that we first saw land. There was great excitement among the orphans early that evening when we caught sight of hills rising out of the sea in the distance. Such was our excitement that Doctor Harte gave in to our pleas and granted us a reprieve from our curfew.

"An hour more, only, girls," he said, trying to sound firm, but his smile betrayed him. "You realize that is not Australia you are seeing. We still have a very long way to go. What you are seeing is the island of Madeira off the coast of Spain. It's a group of four small islands called an 'archipelago,' and while it's off the coast of Spain it was settled by the Portuguese some four hundred years ago. It's . . ."

Doctor Harte launched into a geography lesson but he was cut short by the girls crowded around him, yelling questions all at once. He shrugged good-naturedly.

"Spain, is it? I think I heard tell of the place one time."

"Isn't that where the Armada came from—the ships that wrecked on the west coast of Ireland? Some say many of us are half-Spanish!"

"To think we'd live to see the likes of such a place."

"How far is it from England?"

"It's taken us thirteen days since we sailed from Plymouth," I piped up, "but I couldn't tell you how far. It all depends on how fast we were traveling."

Doctor Harte smiled directly at me and I couldn't hold back a blush.

"Miss Gilvarry is correct," he said. "We've covered almost fifteen hundred miles as the crow flies. We were blessed with a good wind and calm seas. Let's hope the rest of our journey continues so well."

He handed me his telescope. "Here," he said, "this will help you see it better. Pass it around to the others." I put it up to my eye, adjusted it and watched as Madeira came into focus. Little by little, a green landscape unfolded dotted by small white cottages. A herd of cows clustered around a barn waiting for evening milking. I swallowed hard as old memories came flooding back. I passed the telescope to Mary and she passed it to another girl in turn. Everyone had a chance to see what I saw and I wondered if their reaction would be the same as mine.

We watched in awe as the sun began to set over the island. It was like no sunset we had ever seen in Ireland. The sky and clouds exploded in a profusion of bright greens, blues, yellow, purples and golds, all blended in a magnificent display.

"God is a wonderful artist, isn't He?" whispered Doctor Harte from over my shoulder.

All I could do was nod. My eyes filled with tears and my throat tightened. I wondered then how I could have ever questioned God's existence. I was relieved, almost thankful, when dusk fell and all any of us could see were the twinkling lights shining from the cottage windows.

"Will we be stopping there tomorrow, sir?" called a girl.

"No. We won't. We are well provisioned for the moment."

There were groans of disappointment. I was a little let down myself but I realized later that maybe stepping on land would only make us dwell on how far away from home we had traveled and would make it harder for us to get back on the ship.

That night we carried our excitement with us down to the sleeping quarters. Normally, everyone was quiet once they had climbed into their berths and the lanterns were dimmed. But tonight, the girls prattled away. Seeing land for the first time in two weeks had enlivened and excited some of them while leaving others, like myself, pensive and disturbed. The reality of our situation had finally hit home.

"Fifteen hundred miles," said Mary. "Sure the length of Ireland is only about three hundred miles. That means we've sailed it five times over."

"That's true, Mary," I said, "the world is a big place."

"Aye," said Lizzie, "and here we were thinking Ireland was the whole world." She laughed. "What a crowd of *eejits* we were to believe it!"

One girl down the row began to cry. "What's going to happen to us?" she sobbed. "I wish I was back home."

More girls began sobbing quietly, their wretched groans rising around the room in a wave of despair. I held back my own tears. What good would giving in to such melancholy do? The turn in the girls' mood made me uneasy. How on earth were we to survive the rest of the voyage if this bout of homesickness took over? For once I was grateful for Patsy's sharp tongue.

"Jesus, Mary and Joseph," she called out in the darkness, "will yez whish't. Sure you'd think yez were sailing into hell itself. Do yez not remember the hell you just left behind—famine, poverty, disease? Is that what you want to go back to? Well, not me. I'd rather take my chances with the divil himself than go back to that torture! So shut your traps and go to sleep."

Lizzie began to clap. "Good on ya, Patsy," she called out. "Sure I for one would rather dance with whatever divil waits for me in Australia than go back to Belfast and suffocate in that bloody linen mill."

The crying eventually lessened, replaced by soft snores and sighs as one by one the girls fell into an exhausted sleep. As I lay in the darkness unable to fall asleep, I envied the others the sweet relief that sleep had brought them. I tried to focus my mind on happy thoughts—imagining a beautiful, golden world awaiting me at the end of my journey. I recalled our workhouse chaplain, Father Burns, encouraging me to have faith in God's plan for me. At the time, all I could think of was how God had been punishing me and my family. How could I hope for something better from Him in the future? Now, I realized, that no matter what had happened to me in the past I would need faith to see me through whatever lay ahead.

By the next morning the melancholy of the night before had lifted. The girls went about their duties and lessons, although, if not with their earlier enthusiasm, at least with a steady composure. The matrons didn't seem to notice the shift but Doctor Harte watched the girls with unusual interest. When afternoon lessons were over and he asked me to walk with him to the top deck, I had an idea what he wanted to talk about.

"Miss Gilvarry, is there something amiss with the girls today? I can't put my finger on it, but something seems different in their attitudes."

"Yes, Doctor," I said. "Last night after seeing land for the first time, many of them were overtaken by homesickness. It's hard to explain why, but—"

He held up his hand. "You have no need to explain. I was afraid it might affect them this way, which is why I was glad we never set foot on land. It would have been hard to get them back on the ship." He sighed. "I had a similar reaction when I made this same voyage last year. It was my first time away from England and when I saw Madeira, beautiful though it was, I was suddenly homesick for my own little corner of the world."

I was unsure how to answer him. "And where in England are you from?" I ventured, hoping I was not being too forward.

"My family is from Devon on the southwest shore of England. A beautiful place to grow up. I spent much of my boyhood exploring the rocks and beaches looking for caves and evidence of shipwrecks." He chuckled. "I suppose even then I was fascinated with the sea."

A faraway look came over his face and I wanted to know more. "Is that why you took this voyage?"

He glanced up as if he had forgotten I was there. "Voyage? Oh yes, this one and the one last year. I suppose I was running away from what life appeared to have planned for me. You see, my father was a successful Harley Street specialist in London, treating rich ladies with nervous conditions. As the only son, I was expected to follow in his footsteps and, for a while, I did. But I soon tired of it. Out of loyalty and obligation, I stayed until I could endure it no more." He grinned. "And yes, I was not just bored. I yearned for adventure. So when I came across an advertisement for a ship's surgeon on a ship sailing for Australia, I seized on it."

His expression turned solemn again. "There were no orphans on that first ship, but there were many poor immigrants, and I realized how much more useful I could be to people like these, than merely prescribing laudanum to rich ladies in distress. While still in England I began to study scientific papers advancing the theory that disease may well be spread by unsanitary conditions. And when I saw how dirty that ship was I realized I might be able to make a difference by making hygiene a priority to minimize disease."

He shrugged. "Not many doctors agree with me, my father among them."

"What happened when you returned home after the first voyage?" I asked.

He grinned again. "Ah, well, despite my father's ire, I knew I couldn't stay. So, I immediately signed on to the *Sabine*. Of course, I had somewhat underestimated the challenge of maintaining order amongst dozens of young ladies, each, it seems, with a mind of her own!"

He smiled. "And what about you, Kate? Tell me about your childhood."

I felt myself blush. Had he called me by my first name? Surely he hadn't meant to. Surely it meant nothing.

"Em . . . I grew up on a farm," I began, "at the foot of a lovely mountain named Slieve Gullion."

I forgot my earlier shyness and found myself describing my memories—childhood laughter in the fields on late summer evenings; the lilt of fiddles around turf fires on winter nights; waking to the cries of newborn lambs on spring mornings—all tumbling out of me, each upon another. When I realized what I had been doing, I stopped abruptly.

"I'm sorry . . ." I began.

He raised his arm as if to touch me, then pulled back. He turned away and cleared his throat.

"We'll be coming up on the Canary Islands in a few more days," he said, his tone suddenly formal. "The islands lie off the coast of North Africa. I have spoken to the captain and he assures me we will not be putting into port at Tenerife. But, still, I hope the sight of more land doesn't have a negative effect on the girls." He looked at me, and I could see the anxiety and something else I couldn't explain in his eyes.

"I can't say how they'll be affected," I said, "but I think it won't be as bad as last night. Hopefully, they will have made peace with the idea that this experience is real and there is no turning back. It was really homesickness that they, we, were all feeling but had not dwelled on until now."

He smiled. "Thank you, Miss Gilvarry. I think you are right."

If he was going to say more, he was stopped when the ship's bell rang, signaling passengers and crew to tea.

An unexpected nervousness came over me, and I backed away from him. "There's the bell for tea. I'd better hurry."

He gave me a small bow. "Yes, of course."

When I reached the mess, I hoped no one would notice my flushed face or flustered expression. But I should have known better.

"Well now, here comes the doctor's pet!" said Sheila.

"Aye, look at the red face of her. I'd say she has a notion for him, wouldn't you agree, Patsy?" asked Lizzie.

Patsy looked at me. "Och, this one was Matron's pet back in the workhouse. She'd make you think butter wouldn't melt in her mouth. But I think she might be a dark horse, don't you, girls?"

Bridie and Mary said nothing, while the other three burst out laughing. I put my head down to hide the wave of crimson that was spreading across my face.

The ship continued her voyage south, enjoying favorable winds and fine weather. Just three days after passing Madeira, as Doctor Harte had predicted, we passed the Canary Islands. Though in the middle of our lessons, our group stood up and peered out to sea, shading our eyes from the sun.

"Them's the Canaries," said Phoebe, who had also made this voyage before. "Funny name for a place, ain't it?"

Some of the girls giggled, and I knew I'd guessed right about their no longer being upset by the sight of land. In fact, the occasion seemed to lift their spirits along with their curiosity, particularly when Phoebe told them that by looking hard enough they might see Africa.

"Africa? You're codding us," said Patsy.

Doctor Harte appeared behind Phoebe's shoulder.

"Mrs. Clark is correct," he began. "Even though the islands are owned by Spain, they lie only sixty or so miles west of Morocco, in Africa."

We all stared intensely towards the islands, trying to take in the fact that we had reached a new continent.

"Will we be sailing closer?" I asked. "I'd love to see Africa."

The others nodded.

Doctor Harte shook his head. "No," he said, "and we will not be stopping at any of the islands. In fact, I expect the captain will already have ordered the crew to begin heading west towards Brazil so we can take advantage of the trade winds. Soon we will be passing yet another continent, South America!"

There was a collective gasp.

"I wish I'd paid more attention to geography," muttered Lizzie, "but at the time I thought it was bloody useless. Why would I ever be needing to know about places I'd never see. Lot of good it would have done me at the linen mill!"

"Aye," agreed Sheila, "but now . . ."

"It's a shame we're not stopping, just the same," put in Mary shyly. "It would have been grand to see it."

Doctor Harte nodded. "Maybe so, Miss Timmins, but you might change your mind when I tell you that Canary Islands in Spanish means 'islands of the dogs!' When the early explorers went ashore, they were apparently met by packs of very large, wild dogs!"

Lizzie and Sheila started howling like wolves and all of us, including Phoebe and Doctor Harte, took up the chorus. I smiled as I watched the girls, awed at how easily their emotions had swung from melancholy to mirth. Here, on this floating island of a ship, suspended in a new and strange reality, nothing in our past experiences could be counted on to predict the future. Just like our ship, we were at the mercy of temperamental winds, weather and fate. As I realized how little control of the future any of us aboard possessed, I suddenly felt lighter and freer than ever before.

"Come quick!" Patsy shouted at the rest of us. She was standing at the ship's railing waving her arm like mad. "You'll never believe your eyes!"

It was a beautiful, warm, sunny afternoon a few days after we passed the Canary Islands and were sailing southwest towards the Brazilian coast. We had almost finished our sewing lesson when she suddenly appeared, dusting flour from her apron, and raced to the starboard side of the ship. Her insistent shouts roused all of us, and we jumped up and ran to where she stood.

I shaded my eyes from the sun as I peered out to sea. Then I saw them—scores of fish flying out of the water and gliding above the sea's surface, their fins spread out like the wings of a bird, their tails pulsing up and down. I watched in awe as more of them appeared, skimming along the sea surface before rising to join the others in the air.

"What in the name of God?" muttered Lizzie from behind me. "What class of a creature are they, at all?"

Phoebe came up behind us. "Will you girls get back to your work before Mrs. Buckley sees you!" she called. "Or . . ." She didn't finish her sentence. Instead, she clapped her hand to her mouth, her eyes wide.

Suddenly Patsy pointed to the sky. A flock of birds, black, with enormous wings, had gathered, hovering over the flying fish. "Them fish are in for it now, so they are," she exclaimed. "Just look at them fellers waiting to pounce!"

We stood rooted to the spot. As Patsy had predicted the birds suddenly swept down, their plumage reflecting purple in the sunlight, their heads thrust forward exposing swollen, scarlet throats. Beaks wide open they dived headlong, straight as bullets, onto the unsuspecting fish and in one single swift movement plucked them out of the air and flew aloft, the captured fish dangling from their maws.

Even after the birds left and the remaining fish had disappeared below the waves, we did not move. What we had witnessed was nature in all its naked ruthlessness. The birds were only doing what was needed to survive. The fish were now most likely preying on smaller fish deep in the ocean. It was the logical order of things. I thought back to the famine—how God-fearing people had stolen food for themselves and their children. We all possessed the same instincts to survive. As I finally turned my back on the sea, I wondered what perils awaited me on this journey, and what unthinkable steps I might be willing to take to survive them? As the ship swayed beneath me, I felt the edges of my once firm beliefs start to crumble.

Later that night, for the first time in days, Mary crawled into my berth beside me. All evening she had been paler than usual and I could see that the events of the day had unsettled her. Lizzie, Sheila and Patsy had talked excitedly about what they had seen, arguing as to whether the birds or the fish had been the victors in the contest—in the way they might have argued about a favorite village sports team. Even Bridie had joined in excitedly with the others in halting English. But Mary had remained silent.

As she curled up next to me, I put my hand on her shoulder to reassure her. I'd hoped she was settling in and gaining confidence as the voyage progressed, particularly after I noticed she had caught the eye of a young sailor. He was a lad of about sixteen, fresh-faced, with brown, curly hair, and I caught them exchanging smiles. One day I saw him run over to her to help gather up some bread she had dropped on the deck on her way down to the mess and the two of them had blushed crimson. I kept an eye on her, knowing she, or more likely the lad, could get into trouble if Mrs. Buckley caught on. But it seemed to have gone no further than smiles and blushes.

I realized now that she was still fragile. A sudden anger

gripped me. She should never have been allowed to go with the rest of us. Fourteen was far too young to cope with all these changes, particularly for a gentle, naïve girl like Mary, who'd been sheltered her whole life. The violence between the birds and the fish she'd witnessed today had obviously upset her more than the rest of us. Although I had grown up on a farm, its raw violence had even unsettled me. What must it have been like for her? I made up my mind to keep a closer watch on her in the coming days.

Eventually the rocking of the boat beneath us lulled her into sleep but I was not so lucky. I lay awake, my thoughts racing and, much as I tried, I could not seem to shake a sense of foreboding.

Over the following days the temperature grew ever warmer. When we complained, Doctor Harte said it was because we were in what he called the "tropical zone."

"We've crossed the Tropic of Cancer," he said. "The captain must follow the trade winds as we sail south. The better the winds, the faster our journey will be." He gave me a solemn look. "I fear the heat will get more intense as we progress towards the equator."

"We're a long way from Ireland," I murmured.

He smiled. "Yes, Miss Gilvarry, we are. And once we pass the equator we'll be in the Southern Hemisphere or, as some might describe it, at the bottom of the world. It will be nothing like you have seen before; even the stars will be different."

I shrugged. "Almost everything I've seen so far has been new and strange," I said, "so why would crossing the equator be any different?"

A day later we passed a group of islands called Cape Verde. It appeared we had changed course to catch the trade winds, this time bearing away from Brazil and back to the southeast towards Africa. I wondered how the captain and his men plotted the ship's course—after all, we were in the middle of a vast ocean, without even visible landmarks most of the time. Was it by the stars, instruments, maps, or just memory? I guessed Doctor Harte had some explanation. I knew he had made this voyage once before as a ship's surgeon, but with no orphans to care for. I wished I had the courage to ask him to explain, but doing such a thing would amount to what Ma would have called "bold behavior." Still, I amused myself by imagining sitting close to him in his cabin while he spread out large maps in front of us and patiently answered my questions in his soft, gentle voice.

When we passed Cape Verde, the girls pointed out the granite cliffs rising from the sea. The islands looked bleak and menacing. In answer to the girls' questions, Doctor Harte said that the main island was sparsely populated and added that it had once been a stopping place for slave ships. He was met with blank stares. This was another subject I wished he would explain to me.

When our voyage started, I imagined it would be a long, boring journey with nothing to look at but a huge, flat ocean, and maybe a few birds. But I had been wrong. The ocean, it turned out, was teeming with creatures of all shapes and sizes. Besides the flying fish, we had learned to identify porpoises, dolphins, sharks and mackerel, and were told we would soon see whales, the biggest sea creatures of all. And each day, birds of every shape and color flew around the ship—some landing on the decks for a while, some following us for miles at a time, their calls rising above the wind.

And then there were the animals that were occasionally brought up on deck from cargo—cows, goats, sheep, and chickens and pigs—our dinners paraded before us. I was used to seeing animals slaughtered on our farm, but the town girls among us turned green at the sight, vowing not to touch a bite of it. Their vows weakened, though, in the face of hunger when ghostly memories of famine loomed.

More welcome on board were the dozens of cats who roamed freely. Their job was to keep down the population of rats and mice which infested the grain cargo and the bilge—sand and gravel shoveled into the belly of the ship to keep her weighted down in windstorms.

A few of the sailors adopted newborn kittens as their own special pets, but for the most part passengers and crew ignored them. One day, however, Mary appeared for afternoon lessons cuddling a tiny black and white kitten with bright eyes and soft fur. She confessed to me that the young sailor, whose name was Jamie, had given it to her.

"It's just a few weeks old," she said, "isn't it beautiful?"

"Yes, but you can't keep it Mary," I said, alarmed. "Mrs. Buckley won't let you. I'm sure it's against the rules."

Mary looked at me with wide eyes. "But can't you talk to her, Kate?"

"Me?" I exclaimed. "You forget she hates the sight of me. I try to keep out of her way as much as I can."

"But Doctor Harte doesn't hate you," she said, "and he has the final say. Please, Kate?"

I didn't promise her that I would do as she asked, but something about the joy that lit up her usually solemn face, tugged at my heart. I made up my mind to talk to him. And, as I knew he would, he said yes.

As the heat intensified, tempers among the girls began to flare. They argued and criticized one another over matters of no consequence—shouting at someone for touching their belongings, accusing others of stealing things that turned out to be merely misplaced, complaining that the person in charge of their mess had cheated them out of their proper ration of food. The worst arguments broke out over water. The heat had left all of us extremely thirsty and led to much pushing and shoving at mealtimes to get to the water jugs first. Even Mrs. Buckley's threats did little to curb the situation.

It was around that time that many of the girls began menstruating. For some, it was their first experience, while for others, like me, it had begun before the famine, but stopped again during those dreadful days of hunger. I felt for those who had no previous knowledge of such things. At least Ma had been there to explain what was happening to me and reassure me it was perfectly natural. Those other poor creatures were overcome with alarm. Many were sure they were going to die. Neither Mrs. Buckley nor Phoebe offered any explanation, let alone sympathy.

"Here," shouted Phoebe sharply, as she moved through the sleeping quarters passing out small towels, "you're to put these between your legs and you're to wash them out and reuse them. We don't have any to spare, so you're not to be throwing them overboard when you're finished with them. And will you stop your crying and whinging." She let out a cackle. "Aye, you'll have the rest of your lives to get used to it."

I was filled with anger as I listened, and I wasn't alone. Soon some of the older girls began shouting at Phoebe.

"You're a coldhearted witch, so you are!"

"Sure that one has no heart at all! She's as bad as that Mrs. Buckley. Bad cess to them."

"God will get even with you one day, you cruel oul' bitch."

Phoebe said nothing as she stalked away.

Then, without a word to each other, the rest of us went over to each sobbing girl to console her.

"It's alright, love, sure we'll help you."

"I know it's an awful shock when it first happens to you. I was the same meself but, thanks be to God, Mammy explained it all."

"Just ask me about anything you don't understand."

I kept a close watch on Mary, but her "monthlies" did not occur. I wasn't surprised. She was still an undernourished fourteen-year-old. I *was* surprised, though, when I realized Lizzie's had not yet started again. After all, she was eighteen, or so she said. In truth I thought she was a little older. She would not have been the only one lying about her age.

Later that night, in my head I replayed the scenes of girls comforting each other. Suddenly, all the earlier arguments and mistrust had disappeared, and in its place a new bond had surfaced among the orphans. Of course, we already shared the common bonds of hunger and hardship, of famine, loss, and of being thrust out into the world on a journey into the unknown, but this was a different kind of bond, not one based on shared experiences, but on the very essence of shared womanhood.

I finally realized that while nothing which had occurred on this journey was predictable, all of it was necessary to prepare us for the future.

As the *Sabine* sailed south, hugging the coast of Africa, we began to believe we would die of the heat. By day, we cast off as much of our clothing as allowed, including aprons, petticoats and undergarments. We would have discarded our shoes, but our feet would have been scorched on the blazing-hot deck. We begged to be allowed to take our bonnets out of our travel boxes, but Mrs. Buckley wouldn't hear of it saying they must be kept clean for our arrival in Sydney. So we soaked our handkerchiefs in water and draped them on our heads and around our necks in a futile effort to protect ourselves from the broiling, ruthless sun. Our pale arms and legs turned a vivid red and then erupted in angry, painful blisters. Doctor Harte instructed the matrons to rub calamine lotion on them, but it did little good. Finally, he ordered lessons moved from the deck down to the sleeping quarters, ensuring the hatches were left open for air to circulate. But that was almost worse than being on deck. The heavy, stale air threatened to suffocate us. All our energy drained out and finally all lessons were called off. We moved about in slow motion, with no interest in eating. All we wanted was water!

Over Mrs. Buckley's strong objections, Doctor Harte finally ordered our usual curfew to be extended until the heat subsided. The first evening, after supper, I went back up on deck. The heat remained, but at least the merciless sun disappeared. I watched its majestic display of oranges, reds and violets as it sank below the horizon, turning the sky on fire, and wondered how something so beautiful could inflict such cruelty.

"Spectacular, isn't it?" Doctor Harte appeared beside me.

I nodded. "Aye, it's like nothing I've ever seen."

"Hard to believe the sun can be so beautiful yet inflict such cruelty," he said, almost to himself, as if he'd read my mind.

I glanced sideways at him, taking in his fine profile, but looked away quickly before he caught me. As always seemed to happen when he stood close to me, I felt a soft tingle ripple through my body.

"Soon you will see the moon rise before the sun sets. Also, like nothing you've ever seen before, Kate."

For some days now he'd been addressing me by my first name when we were alone, as casually as if we'd been lifelong acquaintances. And, indeed, I felt as if I *had* known him forever. For a moment I forgot about my parched throat and itching blisters and stood beside him with a contentment I hadn't felt in years.

With no warning it arrived one evening at suppertime, dropping through the open hatches and bouncing onto our metal plates. Something fell on the back of my neck and when I put up my hand to brush it away, I felt moisture. It couldn't be, could it?

"Feck me, it's raining!" yelled Patsy.

With gleeful shrieks the girls dropped their utensils and raced up the ladders from the hold, spilling onto the deck. They spun in circles, arms out and palms up, faces upturned to the sky, mouths open to taste the first precious drops of rain. Even Phoebe joined us in our communal celebration of baptism.

Several days of rain turned the heat from a blazing sun to a sultry humidity. It was still hot, but at least we were not getting burned. Our spirits began to rise. Laughter and conversation were restored and we welcomed any new distraction.

One morning, I was down on my hands and knees scouring the deck when a giant wave washed over me, and the ship rocked from side to side. From the top deck above I heard loud shouts.

"Whales to starboard!!"

And from the sailors up on the rigging, shouts of "Whales, ahoy!!"

I dropped my brush and, with a crowd of other girls, rushed over to the right side of the ship and leaned over the railing, just in time to see a huge creature jumping out of the ocean and landing on its back as if doing a somersault. I gasped. It was a whale! Doctor Harte had told us earlier that, if we were lucky, we might see one or more as we approached the equator.

"Their breeding season for the humpback whales has passed, and the males have begun to swim north" he'd said, "leaving the females behind to give birth. We are likely to see mothers and their calves."

We had listened to him with interest, but nothing could have prepared us for the actual sight we were witnessing now. The adults had to be forty feet in length, and the smaller ones, we assumed, were the calves.

Mary came to stand beside me, holding her kitten.

"Aren't they grand, Kate?" she said. "I've never seen the likes of them."

"Aye, and them out playing with their babies," put in Sheila, as she watched them, shaking her head in wonder.

I expected Lizzie or Patsy to make a cheeky comment but neither of them did. The magnificence of the whales had awed even the likes of them into silence.

"Now I've seen everything," said Phoebe. "This is my second journey to Australia but last time I never saw flying fish nor whales! You girls are lucky. You're seeing things most people never see in their lifetimes."

I stood looking out to sea, long after the whales had disappeared, thinking about what Phoebe had said. The predictable, familiar life on our farm seemed to me now like a childhood fantasy. And while many of the new and unfamiliar experiences had been uplifting and wonderful to behold, I couldn't help but worry about what else lay ahead.

"Permission to come aboard, Captain?"

The voice came from somewhere above the orlop deck just before eight o'clock the night before we crossed the equator. Our mess group were on our way down to our sleeping quarters but we all stopped in our tracks and turned around.

"Who are you?" came the captain's voice through a speaking trumpet.

"I am Neptune, god of the sea," came the voice again. "My consort, Salacia, and I come to receive tribute from all my subjects who have not yet visited this part of our dominion!"

"Welcome!" replied the captain. "Come aboard!"

We stood transfixed as two figures appeared beside us. One was a man wrapped in what looked like the skin of a porpoise. The creature's grotesque head rose above him from behind, making him look seven feet tall. Holding the man's arm was a woman in a colorful headdress and gown with many petticoats. She wore gold earrings, silver chains around her neck, and the florid face-paint of a gypsy. We gaped at them as they swept past us and up the steps to the top deck. On their heels came a trio of men, their faces blackened with tar, and wearing wigs of seaweed. One was wrapped in a sheep's skin and carried a saw, while the others sported long cattle horns and huge, hairy ears. They swung harpoons with great flourish and leered at us like demons through red-painted lips.

Mary gripped my arm, while the others looked on open-mouthed. Suddenly, Patsy broke away from us and ran up the steps to the top deck. We all followed, ignoring the rules and the stares of the private passengers who had begun to gather. I saw Phoebe among the crowd and I pushed towards her.

"What is happening?" I cried.

Phoebe chuckled. "This is Neptune, and his missus, although

the missus looks more like a mister to me, and the other fellers are his courtiers. They visit every ship that's passing the equator. See the one with the saw"—she pointed to the man in the sheep's skin—"he's the barber. Tomorrow he'll shave every sailor who's here for the first time. 'Virgins' they call 'em, or 'pollywogs.' He'll cover them in tar, shave them, then throw them in a barrel of bilge-water."

"Just the sailors?" I said in alarm. "I mean, we are all of us, 'er . . . virgins."

Patsy cackled. "Don't be so sure, Kate."

"No, don't worry yourself," said Phoebe, "they don't touch the women. And they only shave the male passengers if they don't give 'em no money—tribute they calls it!" She paused. "And if there's a sailor they don't like, they might shave more than his beard!!"

I turned away from Phoebe to look up at the poop deck where "Neptune" was interrogating the captain on various matters, such as the name of the ship, number of crew and our destination. He then signaled his attendants, who fetched a barrel of tar and, setting it alight, tossed it overboard into the waves. Then they bid the captain goodnight and left the ship the way they had come.

We stood watching the flaming barrel skim across the black sea until it was out of sight. Then Phoebe turned to us. "Come on now, down to the hold before Mrs. Buckley catches sight of you. Get a good night's sleep. Tomorrow's going to be a day to behold—mark my words!"

"Aye," said Patsy, "should be great *craic* altogether!"

Before she went to sleep, Mary sat beside me in my berth, stroking her kitten. "Do you think they'll hurt Jamie?" she whispered. "He's the youngest of the crew and the other sailors are always making fun of him."

I pictured the young curly-haired boy with the sweet face. "No, of course not," I said. "I think they're just having a wee bit of fun."

Later, while Mary was breathing softly above me, I was restless. I wondered why Doctor Harte had not explained to us what was going to happen when we reached the equator. In the past he had prepared us for every new experience. It was one of the things I really admired about him. He was always anxious to set our minds at ease. I couldn't help wondering if he'd been avoiding me, since it hurt to think he might be. My feelings lately were so confused when I thought about him. I tried not to dwell on them because I truly didn't understand what was happening to me. It was all so new. How I wished Ma was still here. There was no one else I could talk to, so I kept them to myself. "Get over yourself, Kate," I thought, "don't be acting like an *eejit*."

The next morning the ship was bustling with excitement. Neptune and his courtiers had returned but now many of the other sailors had joined them, dressed up in all manner of garb, their faces painted either black or red, so that you couldn't identify them. These were the experienced sailors who called themselves "shellbacks"—the ones who had crossed the equator many times before. Right after breakfast they filled up barrels and buckets with water and ran about the ship grabbing passengers and other sailors alike and demanding "tribute." Most of the passengers paid them, either with coins or trinkets, although some younger men offered themselves up to be tarred with a brush, shaved with the barber's saw and then pushed backwards into a barrel of bilge water to rinse off, while their wives and friends cheered them on. Women and children laughed and clapped and the atmosphere was festive.

Doctor Harte finally appeared at my side.

"Quite the spectacle, eh?" he said.

I nodded.

"They mean no harm," he continued. "The poor fellows work very hard and they need to let off some steam. The ship captains all understand that. It keeps problems and resentments at bay."

"I see they all get extra rations of rum," I remarked. "It's a bit like Christmas."

"Yes."

I looked around for the other girls in my mess. Patsy and Sheila were openly flirting with sailors, Mary sat in a corner looking anxious and Bridie chatted away in Irish with some of her friends. Lizzie was nowhere to be seen. Suddenly I was aware of something happening behind me. I swung around to see the barber shaving young Jamie's face. But as I watched I noticed something else. Two other sailors were holding him down by the shoulders and one of them was painting Jamie's hair with tar. I felt my stomach drop. Jamie wriggled, moving his head from side to side as the barber brought up his saw and Jamie's curls began to drop to the deck floor. I stiffened. Doctor Harte was still beside me, watching silently. I stole a look at Mary, whose eyes were filled with tears. I prayed it would be over quickly.

But it was not. When Jamie's head was completely bald, the two sailors began to strip him. Soon he was naked, lying spread out on the deck. The men began smearing treacle and tar over his chest and stomach and down his legs. Grinning, the barber adjusted his sheep-skin cloak.

"Time to shear the sheep," he crowed.

A cheer went up from the sailors.

Suddenly Mary jumped up and ran towards them.

"Stop! Please! Please leave him alone!" she cried.

The barber grinned.

"Are you his sweetheart, girlie?" He looked at the others. "Jamie's got hisself a girlfriend. Pretty ain't she?" He turned back to Jamie. "You been a bad boy, Jamie? It's against the rules to have a girlfriend on the ship. We need to punish you some more, don't we, lads!"

Traces of blood bubbled on Jamie's chest, and he screamed as the barber drew the ragged saw across it. A sudden rage welled up in me and I rushed forward.

"Stop this right now!" I shouted. "You heathens! Leave him alone!"

The barber cackled again. "Seems our Jamie's popular with the ladies! Dark horse, this lad!"

He pointed to Jamie's groin. "I wasn't going to shave this—saw's a bit unreliable—but seeing as how he needs punishing . . ."

Without thinking I threw myself at the barber, trying to wrest the saw from his hands. As I lunged, its jagged edge ripped across my arm, but I was in such a fury I ignored it and tightened my grasp on the barber's hand, trying to shake the saw free. Suddenly someone was behind me, pulling me away.

"Kate! Stop, Kate, for God's sake."

It was Doctor Harte. I tried to shake him off.

"Leave me alone!" I shouted.

By then, the captain had been alerted and strode towards us. With one look he took in the scene.

"Get away from this sailor," he commanded, "now!"

The men released their hold on Jamie and the barber dropped the saw. Doctor Harte knelt over him and signaled the first mate.

"Help me carry him to the infirmary!" he said.

He turned to look at me. "Your arm is bleeding, Kate."

I looked down at myself. My sleeve was soaked red.

"It's alright," I said, "I'll go down to the hold and bandage it."

"No!" His voice rose in a shout. "Come with me!"

Before I could answer, Mary rushed towards me, pale faced, her face wet with tears.

"I'm coming too," she said.

After Doctor Harte had bandaged my arm in the infirmary I went down to the hold, where I stayed. What I had seen already had sickened me. The hatch had been left open and from the hold I could hear the shouts and singing of sailors, drunk on rum. Later, voices rose in argument and anger. Many of the other orphans became so fearful they descended the ladder, climbed into their berths and covered their heads with blankets.

"Dear Mother of God don't let them come down here and find us. I remember how my da was when he had the drink in him. He went stone mad altogether!"

I thought about Patsy, Sheila and Lizzie and a few of the other orphans who were still up on deck, presumably having the time of their lives. I prayed for their safety.

Mary shuddered. "Please, Kate, tell Phoebe to close the hatches."

"It won't make any difference," I said wearily. "The sailors could just open them up again if they had a mind to."

I knew I should have reassured Mary, but I had no strength left in me to make the effort. I lay back exhausted.

Sometime in the middle of the night I awoke from a restless dream with the feeling I was suffocating. I had to get some air. I struggled out of my berth and stood up. To my relief, the hatches were still open. I guessed that in all the clamor of the evening, Phoebe had forgotten to signal the sailors to close them—or maybe they had just ignored her. Silently, I thanked God and crept towards the ladder, careful not to wake the others. Mary was asleep above me but there was still no sign of Patsy or Sheila. Lizzie, however, was asleep in her berth. I sighed. At least she'd had the good sense to leave them and seek what safety the sleeping quarters offered. Again, I thought back to what Doctor Harte had said—maybe she was reforming her ways after all.

On deck, all was quiet, except for the snoring of sailors who had fallen asleep on watch, and others who had slumped down in their own vomit. Stepping around them I made my way to the starboard railing and leaned over, gulping in the night air.

I looked up at the stars, searching the sky. As a child, Da had shown me how to find the North Star.

"If you ever get lost, darlin'," he said, "just find that star up there and it will direct you home!"

I'd been too young at the time to understand what he meant, but ever since, whenever I was lonely, or upset, I would go outside and look up at the sky. The North Star was my friend and comfort.

Now, no matter how I strained, I couldn't seem to find it in the night sky. I turned and walked to the other side of the deck. Now that we had passed the equator, I thought, maybe it was visible from the other side of the sky.

But it was not to be found. Tears welled up in me and I sank to the deck in despair. It was then I felt a hand on my shoulder. I stiffened, all my senses on alert, prepared to fight off a drunk sailor.

"Kate?"

Doctor Harte's voice was quiet. "What's wrong?"

Gently he brought me to my feet. I was sobbing beyond control. His arms enveloped me and brought me close to his chest.

"There, there, Kate." he whispered. "What on earth is the matter? Is it your arm? Is it hurting you?"

I managed to shake my head from side to side. "No," I mumbled into his chest. "It's just . . ."

"Just what, dear girl?"

"I don't know," I whispered.

He loosened me from his embrace and put his arm around my shoulders. "Come with me," he said gently.

He led me towards the stern of the upper deck and into his cabin. It was as I'd pictured it, paneled walls and shelves stacked with books, a wooden desk on which a map was spread out and a small bed in one corner. The room had no windows, but was lit by lanterns which cast a soft, golden glow. As I'd pictured, too, it was neat and orderly.

He led me to a faded, green velvet chair.

"Sit here while I fetch you some brandy."

Meekly, I did as he said. In the back of my head a voice was telling me to run but I felt no fear at all. The truth was, I felt as safe as if I was back home in my old cottage kitchen. As I waited, I noticed a daguerreotype of a pretty young woman in a frame on one of the shelves.

"Here you are," he said, handing me a glass. "I don't know if you are used to spirits, so I've diluted it with water."

I took a sip. The liquid burned my throat briefly but left a warm sensation in my stomach. I took another swallow while he pulled up a chair to face me.

"I was looking for the North Star," I said.

"Ah, Kate, we're in the Southern Hemisphere now, and you can't see the North Star from here. I'm sorry!"

I let out a low groan. "You mean I'll never see it again?"

He leaned closer. "I'm afraid not, Kate. Not unless you make a return journey to the Northern Hemisphere."

"So I won't be seeing it in Australia?"

He shook his head.

My lips began to quiver, and I fought to hold back tears. "It's, it's just that my da taught me to look for the North Star whenever I felt lost. Now I'll be lost forever."

He put his hand on my arm and smiled. "That's not true, Kate. I understand how upset you and the other girls must be. Everything around you now is new and unfamiliar. But that does not mean it's all bad. Trust me, in time you will see that."

A sudden fury seized me. I shook my head vigorously. "No!" I cried. "You don't understand. How could you? You are here of your own free will. You can go back home any time you wish." I nodded towards the daguerreotype on the shelf. "Back to herself over there!"

He followed my nod, a confused look on his face. He opened his mouth to speak but stopped. I was afraid I had gone too far.

"Forgive me, Doctor Harte," I whispered.

"Call me Nathaniel, please," he said.

We sat in silence for a moment.

"How is Jamie?" I asked at last, changing the subject.

He drew back, his manner suddenly formal.

"His wounds appear to be healing. I believe he will recover well. Poor boy, I think the pain of the humiliation he suffered is greater than the pain of his injuries."

"Do you think Mary could come and see him in the infirmary?" I asked. "She thinks she is responsible for what happened, although she has done nothing wrong. She is greatly upset and you know how frail she is."

"It's against the rules," he began, "but I'll consider it."

I set down my glass on a nearby table and stood up.

"Thank you, Doctor, er . . . Nathaniel," I said. "I should be going."

He stood as well. "Of course."

I reached for the door latch.

"By the way"—his voice came from behind me—"that young lady in the miniature is my dear sister, Charlotte, and yes, I shall be very happy to see her again!"

Two days after we crossed the equator the *Sabine* came to a halt. I woke up in the middle of the night and realized we were not moving. I had grown used to the familiar rocking, even welcomed it, because it helped lull me to sleep. I sat up in my berth and looked around in the dimness but no one else seemed to be awake. Perhaps I'd been mistaken.

The following morning, I was the first one up the ladder when the hatches were opened. I ran straight to the railing and looked around. I had not been mistaken. The sea was calm and there was not the slightest whisper of a breeze. I had the odd sensation that the entire world had suddenly stood still. I looked up at the masts. Sailors scrambled around the rigging but the sails hung from the yards as lifeless as plucked fowl hanging from a hook. A line from a poem I had learned as a child came unbidden to my mind. "Idle as a painted ship upon a painted ocean." It was from the poem, "Rime of the Ancient Mariner," about a cursed ship that had floundered somewhere near the equator. A cold rope of fear coiled through me.

I ran back down to the hold where my mess group was eating breakfast. They all turned to me at once.

"Why in God's name are we not moving?"

"Did something break on the ship?"

"How long will we be stuck like this?"

"There's no wind," I said flatly. "We can't move without it."

Just then Phoebe and Mrs. Buckley arrived, their faces grim. Mrs. Buckley pursed her thin lips.

"Miss Gilvarry is correct," she began, giving me a sour look, "but I wish she had waited for us to explain the situation more thoroughly, rather than making you unnecessarily anxious!"

I held my tongue and waited for her to finish.

"Our captain has informed us that the ship has entered an area called the Doldrums—a rather unfortunate name, I think—but is known for its unpredictable weather patterns. The trade winds can gust strongly one day and cease altogether the next. So we must be patient and wait until the winds become favorable again before we can proceed."

"And how long are we supposed to be patient for?" asked Patsy.

Mrs. Buckley bristled and glared at Patsy.

"As I have said, it is an unpredictable situation. The captain is optimistic we will be delayed no more than two or three days."

"Optimistic, my arse," shot Sheila. "And what if he's wrong? We could be stuck here for weeks, or months even."

"Don't be ridiculous!" said Mrs. Buckley, her voice rising to a hysterical pitch. "How dare you question our captain's experience? How often have *you* ever commanded a sailing ship on a voyage around the world, miss?" She turned to look at the rest of us. "Now finish your breakfast and get on with your tasks—the deck needs a good scrubbing!"

Sheila attempted to follow her as she marched to the rope ladder, but Lizzie restrained her. "Leave it alone, Sheila," she said.

Later, as I scrubbed the deck, I wondered why Nathaniel had not appeared to explain the situation to us. I thought back to my last encounter with him in his cabin. I had behaved badly, losing my temper and mistaking his sister for his lover. I blushed with embarrassment every time I thought of it. But I also welcomed the glow I felt when he asked me to call him Nathaniel. Since then, I'd whispered his name to myself every night, ignoring the voice that warned me I was making too much of it.

I turned my thoughts back to the present. Regardless of what the captain had predicted, I was afraid of what would happen if he was wrong. How would we react to being trapped in this ocean for days on end? Much as I was anxious about what awaited me in Australia, I wanted to get there as soon as possible. This delay just prolonged the agony.

My anxiety rose the next day when a huge black-and-white bird with a sharp, pink beak, which Phoebe said was an albatross, alighted on the stern of the ship and seemed unwilling to leave. It shocked all of us when it flew near, its wingspan of about ten feet briefly blocking out the sun. I thought back to the poem about the ancient mariner. He had killed an albatross and the crew believed he had brought a curse upon the ship. I hoped no one on board, neither crewman nor passenger, would decide to shoot it.

I finally caught sight of Nathaniel as I was hauling a bucket of dirty water across the deck to empty it. He was coming from the infirmary, his head bowed, his shoulders hunched. My heart lurched at the sight of him. He looked up at me with a weary expression, his eyes heavy-lidded from what appeared to be lack of sleep.

"Kate?" he said.

I smiled without thinking. He was still calling me by my first name.

"Nathaniel?" I said. "You look tired. Have you been in the infirmary all night?"

He nodded but said no more. Then his eyes filled with tears.

I dropped the bucket and put my hand on his arm. "What is it? What's wrong?"

"It's Jamie."

He choked out the words and an ice-cold shudder ran through me. I knew without a doubt what he was about to tell me. Even then, as a torrent of words tumbled out of him, I only heard a few—"wounds," "rusty saw," "fever"—I needed to hear no more.

My first thoughts went to Mary. Who would be the one to tell her? How on earth would she cope with such tragedy? And what about the other orphans? Hadn't they seen enough death during the famine? Well, maybe at least this would be one experience on this voyage which would not be unfamiliar to them. I sighed. Was my heart big enough to hold all the sorrow we were about to endure?

Impulsively, I threw my arms around Nathaniel and pulled him close. I was reminded of the day I had embraced Ma after Da had sunk to his knees and refused to go on to the workhouse. My strong, beautiful mother had for the first time needed *my* comfort and now Nathaniel, our strong reassuring doctor, needed it too.

"It's my fault," he murmured. "I am responsible for every person on this ship. I should have been able to save him."

They buried Jamie at sea. His young body was laid on a plank, wrapped in a shroud, tied with rope, and slid overboard as the captain read from a psalm and raised his hand in a final blessing. A crowd gathered—crew, private passengers and orphans. We stood in silence on the frozen ship, heads bowed. Many women among the private passengers wept, Phoebe blessed herself several times and Bridie began to sing a lament in Irish. Her lovely voice drifted across the sea as if escorting Jamie to his rest. I stood with my right arm around Mary, who stood motionless, cuddling the small kitten to her chest, her pale face wreathed in grief. Nathaniel stood to my left and I was glad of the comfort of his presence. He was as calm now as the sea itself, his earlier turmoil seemingly buried somewhere deep within him.

Throughout the rest of the day, we followed our usual routine of lessons and meals, silent as nuns. It was as if we had become as paralyzed as our ship. No tears were shed, no fears expressed, no questions asked. After supper, no songs were sung, no music played, not even laments. Later we descended in mute procession to our sleeping quarters, each of us seeking the solace of darkness.

We remained imprisoned in the motionless sea. Occasionally a sudden gust of wind sent the crew rushing to the rigging to trim the sails, only for it to die out before the sailors even reached the topmasts. With each glimmer of hope our spirits soared, only to plummet to greater depths than before. Previous impatience turned slowly towards fear.

"What if we're stranded here 'til we die?"

"And what if we run out of food?"

"Or water?"

"Aye, 'water, water everywhere, nor any drop to drink,'" said Lizzie, to my surprise quoting the same "Rime of the Ancient Mariner" which I had recalled earlier.

I gave her a weak smile. "You learned the poem, too?"

She scowled at me. "I'm not a dunce altogether!"

For some time now, Lizzie had not been her usual devil-may-care self—outspoken, disorderly and fond of mischief. Even on the night of the equator revels she had retired to bed early, while Patsy and Sheila stayed up all night. I had grown quite fond of her, but I was still too wary of her prickly nature to ask what was wrong.

"I never took you for a dunce, Lizzie," was all I said.

I finally sought out Nathaniel. One night at curfew, knowing that Phoebe had become very slack about taking a bed-count, I ignored the hold and made my way uninvited to his cabin.

"Kate?" he said in some alarm when he opened the door. "Is something amiss? Is one of the girls ill?"

He turned to reach for his coat hanging on the back of the door.

I was suddenly embarrassed. Why on earth did I come here? What had I been thinking?

"Er, no, nothing like that," I said. "I just—well, I just missed your company."

As I spoke, I imagined Ma shaking her finger at me, and calling me "brazen" and "bold." I turned away quickly. "I shouldn't have come. I'm sorry!"

He reached for my arm. "No, don't go. I've missed your company too."

He led me to an armchair, then poured me a snifter of brandy and one for himself. Without his formal coat, wearing a simple cotton shirt, the sleeves rolled up to his elbows, he looked young, almost like a boy my own age. I began to relax.

"How are the girls coping with this frightful situation?" he asked. "They must be very distressed."

I nodded. "Many of them are."

"And you?"

"Me? I think with everything that's happened I've used up all my fear. I don't believe we'll be stuck here forever. I am impatient, though!"

"The longest account I ever heard was of a ship stuck in the Doldrums for forty days. But the captain assures me it's usually only for three or four days. This didn't even happen on my previous voyage here. Just bad luck, I suppose."

"Aye," I said. "But don't let anyone shoot an albatross."

He laughed aloud. "Ah, you're familiar with the 'Rime of the Ancient Mariner,'" he said. "What a clever girl you are."

"Lizzie knows it too," I said.

We fell into silence. In the stillness of the cabin, I imagined that we were the only two people in the world. I smiled. "I'm sorry I was so impertinent the other night."

He grinned at me. "Ah yes, when you accused me of having a lover."

"I did not," I cried, indignantly.

"Actually, I was rather flattered."

My cheeks blazed, and I bowed my head.

He pulled his chair closer. "It's the truth, Kate. I confess I have some feelings for you that I am at a loss to explain. You—you are not like the other girls." He stared at me, his blue eyes earnest "I know—er, I realize—what I mean is . . ." He took a quick sip of his brandy. "It would be most inappropriate for me to form any relationship with a young woman in my charge. I would be taken for a cad. And . . . although it seems you might not re-buff me, I, as an older, experienced man, have no intention of taking advantage of you and that's what I'd be doing."

He took another gulp of his drink while I sat in silence, my emotions tumbling over one another.

"Were we to have met in another time and place, things would be different. But, Kate, you are so young, and have your whole life in front of you. Who knows what awaits you in Australia? Please forgive me if I have given you wrong signals. It was not my intention. I swear I would never want to hurt you!"

I felt tears welling up and I fought them back. I was so morti-fied, I jumped up from the chair. "Please excuse me, Doctor Harte," I said, "I must leave. It was irresponsible of me to come here alone. I should be getting back before I am missed."

I pushed past his outstretched hand and fled to the door, slam-ming it shut behind me. In the night silence, the thud it made was as loud as a cannon. The hatches were secured when I re-turned to the hold. I tried to wrest them open, but I hadn't enough strength. Instead, I sank wearily down on the deck.

After a while, two shadows fell over me. I looked up at Patsy and Sheila.

"Well, well, what've we here?" asked Sheila, laughing. "If it isn't our handsome doctor's pet orphan! Where do you think she's been, Patsy? I'd say she's been enjoying a jar of his special medicine in his cabin."

"Oh aye," said Patsy, "sure didn't I see them locked tight to-gether the morning wee Jamie died—their arms around each other. 'Twas a lovely sight, so it was!"

"We should tell Mrs. Buckley, so we should," said Sheila.

Patsy grinned. "We should—but we won't, will we? Better to keep it a secret between us. You never know when we might need to use it."

Sheila grinned. "Well then, I'll just go fetch a sailor boy to open the hatch."

The following evening after supper, as I sat on the deck with the other girls, I noticed something strange on the horizon. A veil of low clouds had shrouded the setting sun turning it from orange to a ghostly gray. I watched as the sun disappeared but the clouds remained, dimming the stars with their shadow. I held my breath as darkness, black as soot, closed in on the ship from all sides. No one uttered a sound. I was dimly aware of sailors standing all around us, alert, waiting for what I didn't know. Then, from the deck above I heard the captain's voice shouting orders, and the sailors began to scramble. A sense of anticipation replaced my earlier uneasiness. After the paralysis of the previous days, it seemed as if something was finally about to happen. Thunder maybe, or lightning—anything would have been welcome to break the weary monotony. And then it came, at first a faint tapping on the deck and then a deluge. Suddenly, I was soaked to the skin. The girls around me squealed, and Patsy cursed aloud, but my only instinct was to turn my face up to the rain and laugh.

And at last, I had the sensation of the ship moving forward, and the flutter of the softest breeze, like my mother's fingers caressing my cheeks.

The atmosphere on the ship lightened as we sailed southward out of the Doldrums towards the Cape of Good Hope at the southern tip of Africa. Nathaniel informed us that we would reach it in about three weeks and, once we had rounded it, we would enter the Indian Ocean and sail eastward to Australia.

By my count, we had been aboard the *Sabine* for a full forty-five days. It should have seemed like a lifetime, but the sameness of the days, each a replica of the previous one, had made it seem shorter. I made up my mind to concentrate on one day at a time. After all, we were only about halfway through the journey. If I thought about how far we still had to sail, the journey might become unbearable.

I was already missing Nathaniel's company and the special re-lationship I'd thought we'd shared. Now we were back to formal-ity—Doctor Harte and Miss Gilvarry. I tried to avoid his eyes, which was not difficult since he ignored me altogether. It made me sick at heart. I blamed myself for my foolishness. All these feelings were new to me and I wished fervently that Ma was here to talk to. But she wasn't, and that was that. So I formed a stiff upper lip and went about my days as best I could.

The other girls in the mess were beginning to show signs of strain. Maybe it was the fear that Australia was looming closer and their anxiety was growing, but I noticed that even Bridie had begun to flaunt the rules—slacking on her work and ignoring or-ders—blaming such shortcomings on her difficulty understand-ing what she was being told. I knew this was not the case since she was doing so well in her English lessons with me. Patsy and Sheila flirted openly with sailors and laughed in Phoebe's face so often that she gave up trying to control them.

I worried about Mary, who had not spoken since Jamie's death, although she still went meekly about her duties, the kitten fol-lowing her everywhere. I was concerned about Lizzie too. She spoke only when spoken to, using as few words as possible and spent as much time as she could lying down in her berth, even during the day.

When I noticed that Lizzie was no longer bothering to go to the galley at mealtimes to fetch the food for our mess, leav-ing Mary to struggle alone, I decided I needed to confront her. She was lying sullenly in her berth one afternoon when I ap-proached her.

"Lizzie," I began, as gently as I could. "Are you unwell?"

She turned her back to me. "Mind your own bloody busi-ness!"

My temper rising, I turned her back to face me. "Look at me!" I shouted. "It *is* my business and the business of the rest of our mess. It's not fair of you to put all the responsibility of the mess on young Mary. So I will ask you again, are you unwell, or just being a lazy, selfish bitch?"

I surprised myself with my language. I had never used that word before. Another new milestone, I thought. Lizzie began to sob. I was immediately sorry I had shouted at her.

"Are you sick, Lizzie?" I said more gently. "Do you want me to call Doctor Harte?"

"No!" she said through her sobs. "What can *he* do? Bloody nothin'. So just go away and mind yer own business!"

I was turning away when Patsy and Sheila came down the ladder to the hold. Sheila ran over to Lizzie, while Patsy glared at me.

"What've you been saying to the girl?" she demanded. "Can't you see the state she's in?"

"I was just trying to . . ." I began but gave up.

Sheila came to stand beside Patsy.

"Well, mind yer own business, you nosy bitch," she said. "Patsy and me can look after her."

I shrugged and walked over to the ladder.

"And don't be running to Phoebe or that witch, Buckley," Sheila shouted after me.

"Aye, and don't be telling your fancy-boy doctor, either," added Patsy. "We don't need him down here poking and prodding her like a prize cow! Just keep your mouth shut, Kate."

I raced up the ladder, anxious to get away from them and out into the fresh air. I went straight to the railing and leaned over, looking out to sea, breathing in the cool, fresh air. What on earth was going on? I wondered. I shrugged. Well, whatever it was, they were not going to let me in on their secret. That much they had made clear. I reminded myself again that no matter what my da had told me long ago, I was not responsible for everyone around me. My only duty was to myself!

The *Sabine* resumed her journey south, zigzagging, or "tacking" as the sailors called it, captive to the whims of the wind, which sometimes blew her west towards the coast of South America and sometimes back east towards Africa. After our spell in the Doldrums, I was grateful for the wind whatever direction it hurled us. We were at its mercy. The weather had cooled greatly, another welcome event. I realized that sea captains were not unlike farmers, whose livelihoods were so dependent on the weather. Too little rain, crops would wither. Too much rain, crops would rot. Too little wind, ships would stall. Too much wind, ships would flounder. How simple an equation it seemed, whether humans existed on land or sea.

We eventually passed a group of islands called Tristan da Cunha. Nathaniel gathered us on deck and gave one of his speeches. I stood at the back of the group, my eyes closed, listening to his calm, steady voice.

"These islands are volcanoes," he began. "They lie in the South Atlantic roughly halfway between South America and Africa. He paused and I opened my eyes to catch him looking straight at me. "There is said to be a beautiful, perfectly heart-shaped lake at the center of one of the volcanoes."

I felt myself blush, and I fancied I saw his cheeks redden as well. Silly girl, I thought.

He was talking again. "The islands are a British outpost. Many ships put in here to obtain provisions." He smiled. "If we'd stayed longer in the Doldrums we might have had to do so, as well. As it is, I'm told there is enough food to last the rest of our journey, although sadly we won't be offered much variety."

He was right about that. To think that after starving in Ireland we would have begun to turn up our noses at salted pork and dried cod seemed almost treasonous. The sailors *were* seeking variety, however. They began fishing for sharks, which were numerous in the waters around the ship. We watched with fascination as they speared and gutted them, then roasted them for dinner, which they devoured with great relish. I had to admit the smell of roasted shark was very tempting.

Unlike at previous island sightings, none of the orphans seemed anxious to set foot on land. They listened to Nathaniel politely but asked few questions. Afterwards, as Tristan da Cunha slid out of sight, they returned reluctantly to their lessons and tasks. Even the sight of more whales and dolphins failed to summon up their previous enthusiasm. Only the sighting of loud, lusty, black and white penguins on the rocky shores of Tristan da Cunha sparked some short-lived joy. It seemed to me that the novelty of the voyage had begun to wear off, replaced by tedium.

In the past, I would have mentioned these things to Nathaniel but that was now out of the question. All I could do was keep my own counsel and try not to let myself or the others incur Mrs. Buckley's wrath. I had not forgotten that, as head matron, she would be writing her opinion of each orphan for review by the Australian authorities when we landed. Her opinion of us might count against us in our chances of employment or, worse yet, might prevent us from being allowed to stay in the country at all. Early on, I might have welcomed the chance to be turned back to Ireland, but now—after all I and the others had been through on this journey—that was the last thing I wanted. I believed that after all we'd endured, we had each earned the right to stay in Australia.

As we neared the Cape of Good Hope, the winds grew stronger, stirring up the sea. We were ploughing through the water at a higher than usual speed, propelled forward by strong currents. As always, the crew seemed to anticipate something afoot, shimmying like acrobats up the rigging to tighten some of the sails and hoist others, ones they called "heavy weather" sails. I looked up from my needlework to study them. Were we finally in for a real storm? Nathaniel had mentioned several times over the course of the voyage that we had been very lucky not to encounter a bad one. He'd said the heavy rains and high seas we'd experienced so far did not qualify as a "real storm," although he didn't go into detail as to what a real storm would look like. I suppose he didn't want to alarm us. Now, as I watched the crew go about their work, clearing the decks of any loose objects, securing coiled ropes and checking that locks on the hatches were sound, my stomach began to tighten. I wanted desperately to seek out Nathaniel and to hear his reassuring voice, but that was no longer possible. I hadn't realized how much his comfort meant to me. I shrugged and went back to my sewing.

Phoebe looked up at the sky, then at the masts.

"Looks like we're in for a right battering," she said. "It ain't far off by the looks of it."

It was the following night when the storm finally hit. The wind picked up to gale force and we struggled to reach the hold without falling. All the lantern lights suddenly went out and we held on to each other in the darkness, trying not to stumble on objects that, despite the crew's earlier efforts to secure them, had blown loose in the wind and were rolling around on the deck. There was a loud crash and something heavy and wet wrapped around my legs, threatening to topple me over. I leaned down and felt the wet canvas of a sail that must have been ripped free.

We eventually reached the hatch, which two of the crew had just opened, and one by one we made our way down the ladder and staggered to our berths like drunken sailors. The lanterns down in the sleeping quarters still provided dim light but swayed furiously with the motion of the ship. We climbed into our berths, shivering with fear. No one uttered a word as we lay there listening to the rattling and creaking from the deck above, and the squealing and squawking of the livestock below.

Before the crew could secure the hatch again, a great rush of water came roaring through the still open hatch, soaking ourselves and our bedding. Wave after wave it came, washing the sailors down the deck and rocking us so hard that our heads went down and our feet up in one direction and then the other, like an out-of-control seesaw. Some girls began to retch, others screamed and sobbed, while a few prayed aloud to the Virgin

Mary for mercy. But no mercy came. Throughout the night we lay, our frozen fingers clinging to the sides of our berths, while the waves rocked the ship.

Just before dawn, the wind eased, and the ship grew steadier. Could it be over? I wondered. Gingerly, I eased out of my berth and climbed the ladder to the open hatch. Once on the deck I looked around at the debris strewn everywhere. Sailors were already aloft trying to replace the sails that had been torn from the masts. Incredibly, the masts, yards, and rigging looked intact, and I silently thanked God for it. Other crew were trying to control livestock which had been brought up from below. I ventured up to the top deck. The captain, looking windswept, his clothing soaked, stood on the poop deck shouting orders to the crew in a hoarse voice. I looked around for the other passengers but could see no one. I assumed they must have all been hiding in their cabins. I wondered where Nathaniel was. I was surprised that he hadn't come down to our sleeping quarters to check on us. Had he given up on us just like Phoebe and Mrs. Buckley seemed to have done? I chased the thought away. More likely he was in the infirmary caring for sailors who'd been injured during the storm.

I went back down to the orlop deck and saw that no fire was burning in the galley, nor was there any sign of the cook. It hardly mattered, I thought, since breakfast would not be on the minds of many this morning. I sighed and began to shiver. My damp clothes clung to me and I went back down to the hold to see if I could find some dry garments, but I didn't hold out much hope.

No sooner had I reached my berth than the rain began, charging at the ship in angry squalls. A sudden glare of light flashed across the room, followed by a resounding crack of thunder. Girls shrieked as they awoke from restless dreams. I tried to reassure Mary, who sat straight up, a terrified look on her face.

"It's alright, love," I said, "it's just thunder and lightning, that's all. The ship's not rocking the way it was last night, so it will all be over soon."

Patsy snorted from her berth beside mine. "Some chance," she said. "I don't think the divil is finished with us yet."

Sheila and Bridie stumbled out of their berths and came to sit beside us.

"Some *craic* this is," muttered Sheila, between yawns.

Bridie nodded. "'Tis worse than any storm at home."

"Of course it is, you *eejit*," growled Patsy, "we're out in the middle of the bloody ocean."

The noises on the ship had begun again—rattling and creaking—but a new noise drew my attention. It was groaning, coming from one of the berths. I put out my hand to silence the girls.

"Ssh!" I said. "Do you hear something?"

Patsy was about to retort when she stopped and nodded.

Without thinking she and I jumped up and, on impulse, made for Lizzie's berth. Instinctively we knew the groaning was coming from her.

"Are you alright, Lizzie?" I shouted.

Patsy reached over to touch her, but Lizzie didn't move.

Then another lightning flash lit up the room and we saw it. Lizzie was lying stiff and pale-faced and covered in blood.

"Mother of God," cried Patsy. "Lizzie!"

"Stay with her," I shouted. "I'm going to fetch Doctor Harte."

For once, Patsy put up no argument and simply nodded.

I raced to the ladder and up to the deck. The rain was lashing down now, scudding in blinding sheets across the deck. I clutched the railing of the steps leading to the top deck. Wood splinters pierced my palms and the soles of my bare feet, but I ignored the pain. I was out of breath by the time I reached the deck and stumbled to Nathaniel's cabin, where I pounded on the door. There was no answer so I turned around and retraced my steps, pushing against the wind, down to the lower deck towards the infirmary. As I was crossing the deck, I heard a deafening noise behind me that rose above the claps of thunder, cracks of lightning and the roar of the wind. The noise sounded like it was coming from hell itself. I froze and swung around. In the dimness I watched the main mizzenmast come tumbling down, crashing to the deck. I backed away, staring at the shards of wood and crumpled sails. I made a quick sign of the cross, thanking God for sparing me.

Turning back from the horror, I staggered towards the infirmary, tripping and rising several times, until I reached the door. I didn't even bother knocking. I rushed in and found Nathaniel bending over a sailor, securing a bandage on his leg.

"Nathaniel!" I cried. "Nathaniel, come quickly!"

His head shot up and he looked at me in alarm.

"Kate! What on earth . . ."

"It's Lizzie!" I shouted. "You have to come now!"

He turned to the sailor, pointing to the bandaged leg. "Try not to move it."

Nathaniel reached for an oilskin raincoat hanging on a doorknob and threw it at me. "Put that on," he said, "or you'll catch your death!"

I looked down at myself and realized I was wearing only my soaking cotton shift, and my hands and feet were bare and bleeding. I took the coat and put it on, while he, still in his shirt-sleeves, grabbed his doctor's bag and followed me out into the storm.

"Thank God, you're finally here," Patsy shouted when she saw us. "You took your bloody time, so you did. What kept you?"

I started to protest but even in the dim light I could see the look of desperation on Patsy's face. Sheila and Bridie stood beside her, Sheila as pale as a ghost, Bridie clutching rosary beads and chanting prayers in Irish. The girls parted to let Nathaniel bend over Lizzie. She lay as still and pale as when I left, her hands deathly white against the blood-soaked blanket. It was only then that I noticed a long knitting needle lying limply in her left hand. I gasped. For God's sake, what had she done? I looked at the others, but they avoided my eyes. Nathaniel leaned over her, putting his ear close to her chest.

"She's still breathing," he announced, "but barely." He looked up at us. "Fetch two sailors immediately. I need to take her to the infirmary."

"Yes, Doctor!" Sheila raced out.

"The rest of you, please bring as many dry blankets as you can find. We must keep her warm."

As I turned with Patsy and Bridie, Nathaniel called after me. "Kate! Take this please and put it somewhere safe!"

I stared at the knitting needle in his hand. He had wrapped it in gauze but the sight of it still made me want to retch. I shrank back.

"Please, Kate," he said again.

I looked at his weary face and his rain-soaked shirt, then at poor Lizzie, still as a statue, and I summoned what strength I had left. Reluctantly, I reached out and took the needle, hiding it under my raincoat. I made my way back to my berth and shoved it beneath the mattress. Then I went to help Patsy and Bridie find some blankets.

By the time the sailors arrived, the other girls had begun to wake up and silently took in what was happening. They watched as Nathaniel directed the men how to lift Lizzie out of the berth, urging them to be careful ascending the ladder. The storm had not weakened. High waves still rolled us from side to side and the wind still put up a furious roar, while rain squalls battered the ship.

Mary stared at the scene, her face as pale and waxen as Lizzie's. I was about to go to her when Nathaniel turned to me.

"Come with us, Kate," he said. "The rest of you, stay here and try to get what rest you can."

For once, Sheila and Patsy made no remarks, just nodded meekly.

"Keep an eye on Mary," I said to Patsy, as I followed Nathaniel and the others.

My last glimpse was of Bridie standing beside Lizzie's now empty berth.

"May God spare her," she said.

"That's all I can do for her for now," Nathaniel said as he collapsed into a chair beside the bed where Lizzie lay sleeping.

Without thinking I asked, "Why don't you go back to your cabin and get some rest? You look exhausted. I can stay with her. I'll come and tell you if anything changes."

I hardly had the words out when he shouted, "No! I'm staying here. I have lost one patient already on this voyage and I will not lose another!"

His eyes blazed briefly, exposing something between anger and desperation. Stung by his rejection, I backed away from him and sank down on a chair in the corner of the room.

"I was only trying to help," I said, sulkily.

I was suddenly ashamed of my selfish reaction. I put it down to exhaustion. I took a deep breath. "I'm sorry, Nathaniel."

He shook his head. "No, it is I who should apologize, Kate. You were a great help to me tonight, and it is a comfort to have you here."

We sat in silence. Furious waves no longer rolled the ship, and the wind and rain had ceased. The awful sounds of crashing masts and sails had stopped. The only sound now was the snoring of the sailor with the bandaged leg.

After a while, Nathaniel spoke. "Did you know she was pregnant?"

I nodded. "She never said so, but I guessed she might be. I think maybe Patsy and Sheila knew. They'd become very protective of her."

Nathaniel sighed. "How on earth did she think she was going to hide it?"

I shrugged. "I think at first she wanted to believe she was

wrong. And when she finally realized the truth . . . well, this was how she tried to fix it."

He shook his head. "Foolish girl. She could have killed herself and the baby, too. It could still happen. She has lost a lot of blood. The baby still has a heartbeat but we won't know what other damage she might have caused until the child is born."

"When will that be?" I asked.

"I'm guessing a bit here, but I'd say she's at least four months along. She will start showing very soon. Her condition will certainly be evident by the time we reach Australia."

It was then I fully realized the peril Lizzie was in. When the Australian authorities examined her on arrival, they would no doubt send her back to Ireland on the next ship.

We both lapsed into silence again. Then I said, "I assume Mrs. Buckley will be informed, and Phoebe?"

Nathaniel studied my face before speaking.

"I do not condone what Lizzie tried to do," he began, "but I do understand the desperation that drove her to it. However, as the ship surgeon, and the person responsible for all of you girls, I am expected to give a report about your individual physical and mental readiness to fulfill the requirements of this assisted immigration program, and unless . . ."

He let his words hang in the air while he looked earnestly at me. I understood exactly what he was suggesting. Could her condition be kept a secret from everyone, and from the authorities? I also realized that by hiding the truth, he would possibly be subjecting himself to censure.

I considered his words, running over the arguments in my head. "Well, I don't think the girls will say anything, but you never know. Phoebe might be persuaded to keep quiet, but not Mrs. Buckley, although she seems to have abandoned us already, since many of the girls ignore her orders. However . . ."

"Yes?" Nathaniel stared at me.

"Lizzie committed a mortal sin," I burst out. "She tried to kill her child." I watched as a frown crept across his face. "I'm—I'm sorry, Nathaniel, but I don't know if I can forgive her for that. And I don't know if I can cover it up. Wouldn't that make me just as guilty?"

My stomach was in knots as I tried to coax my words out. My mind was in turmoil. Killing was against the Commandments and surely killing a child was the worst sin of all. Hadn't the priests and nuns always said that? Wouldn't Ma and Da be horrified if I acted as if what Lizzie did was alright?

"Forgive?" Nathaniel was suddenly on his feet. "And who gave you the right to forgive? Isn't that God's job?"

My anger and frustration mounted. "Why did you give me that needle to hide?" I shouted. "Why did you put me in this awful position?"

"Because I believed in your sense of fairness, Kate," he said quietly, "and because I thought I knew you."

"Knew me?" I said, giving way to the tears that stung my eyes. "I don't even know myself anymore. Ever since I set foot on this bloody ship, I have lost a piece of myself every day."

"But you have also found new pieces," he said. "You have discovered strengths you never knew you had—courage, compassion, resilience"—he smiled at me—"and, yes, defiance! No, you're not the same girl who started out on this journey and nor are any of the other orphans. You have all grown in ways you never expected. Even poor Lizzie. I'm doubtful she would have taken such a step if she were back in Belfast among friends and relatives. But here she was faced with a terrible choice—the promise of a better life in a strange land, or the certainty of being sent back to Ireland and a life of poverty for her and her child."

He looked down at Lizzie, who was still sleeping, her breathing shallow and fitful.

"Well, let us wait to see if she and the child recover. For now, I intend to report that she had a rupture of one of her internal organs and will remain in the infirmary until she is fit to return to her lessons and duties."

I nodded. "I will talk to the others and let them know what to say happened to Lizzie. But, of course, it will be up to them what to do."

He smiled then. "They'll do the right thing, Kate," he said, "and so will you!"

I slept little that night. The sea had turned calm but my thoughts rose and fell like angry waves. I imagined the needle beneath my mattress was piercing me like a dagger. Each time I dozed off, an angry Father Burns, the workhouse chaplain, hovered over me, scolding me about losing my faith, and I awoke with a start. My parents appeared too, Ma in tears, and Da with a sad look. In the morning I awoke in a sweat. I got up and dressed, removed the needle from beneath the mattress and held it under my apron as I climbed the ladder out of the hold. I walked to the port side of the ship, threw it as hard as I could over the railing, and watched as it disappeared beneath the waves.

In November, two weeks after passing the Cape of Good Hope, we reached the Indian Ocean. The next day a ship appeared, bearing towards us. From its colors, Nathaniel said, it was from India, and carrying cargo, post, but no passengers. It drew alongside us, and we stood at the railing gawking at its crew. Sheila and Patsy waved vigorously at them and they waved back, grinning. Our captains greeted one another, shouting through cone-shaped trumpets. A boat was lowered so that they could collect the post from Australia which was addressed to some passengers and crew on the *Sabine*. None of us orphans expected any post, but Mrs. Buckley and Phoebe each received letters and Nathaniel was handed a box full of letters and newspapers. He excused himself to go to his cabin to read them. He shrugged as he passed by me. "Business!" he declared. I wondered if maybe he had a lady in Australia whose scented letter was in the box, as well.

Phoebe, as it turned out, had a husband living in Australia, and her plump cheeks turned pink as she ripped the envelope open. We wondered who was writing to Mrs. Buckley. Was there a Mr. Buckley? Somehow, none of us had pictured her with family or friends. But we were obviously wrong. She smiled, something we had seldom seen her do, as she held the letter to her breast and disappeared to her cabin.

Even though none of the girls had expected a letter, a lonely feeling came over us when we walked away empty-handed. None of us knew anyone in Australia, but that just reinforced the fact that we were journeying to a land filled with strangers and where we, too, would be strangers.

I stayed up on the deck that evening, ignoring the eight o'clock curfew. Phoebe and Mrs. Buckley were nowhere to be seen, no doubt in their cabins rereading their letters. I had not seen Nathaniel since he left to read his boxful of papers. I stood at the railing looking out to sea, glad to be alone with my thoughts.

"May I join you, Kate?"

The familiar tingle I always felt in his presence flowed through me and I was glad he couldn't see my burning face in the dim light.

"Alright, Nathaniel," I said quietly.

The sound of his name on my tongue brought on a pleasant new sensation, but as we stood, our bodies close together, it was replaced by a looming anxiety. I felt that something was wrong. Although he had said nothing and though I couldn't see his face in the darkness, I knew in my soul that he was troubled.

"Kate . . ."

"Nathaniel . . ."

We both spoke at once. I stepped back and turned full on towards him. "Yes?"

"Kate, there is something I need to discuss with you—something that I read in the post today."

I waited.

"Em . . . It concerns orphan girls who already arrived from Ireland. It seems . . ."

We were interrupted by the ship's first mate, who rushed up to us and tugged breathlessly at Nathaniel's sleeve.

"Doctor, there is a passenger, Mrs. Herbert, who has gone into labor and is in some distress. Please come at once!"

"Of course!" Nathaniel said.

He turned to me, suddenly formal. "I'm sorry, Miss Gilvarry, my news will have to wait."

I watched him hurry off with the first mate, then I turned back to the railing. A bright moon had risen and I watched in fascination as luminous, bright specks appeared at the side of the ship. As I stood, the waters became more turbulent, sending forth brilliant green sparks and flashes. It was as if the ocean was reflecting the agitation that unsettled my heart.

The Indian Ocean was a huge body of open water and Nathaniel had told us we would not be likely to see much land as we crossed it but that winds called "westerlies" were still strong and would chase us east across the open water towards Australia at a swift pace.

"If all goes according to plan, we should get our first sighting of Australia at Cape Leeuwin in about another two weeks, and—he paused—"we could reach Sydney by Christmas Day."

His words were met by a shrug from most of the orphans. It was not just us, but the paying passengers, too, who appeared to be growing restless. At night, loud, raucous shouting and drunken singing drifted down from the upper deck while young, single men strolled about our deck making lewd remarks. All Mrs. Buckley and Phoebe could do was herd us down below and lock us in the hold. Nathaniel appealed to the captain about the young men, but no action was taken to stop them. I expected Patsy and Sheila to be delighted with the new attention but I was wrong. They both seemed to have lost their earlier brazenness. I put their shift in behavior down to Lizzie's predicament.

Nathaniel had saved both her and her baby, and four weeks after that awful stormy night, she finally returned from the infirmary to the sleeping quarters. Her face was gaunt and drawn but her belly had grown round. She'd gone straight to her berth without a word to any of us. Later that night, Bridie slipped down to the cargo hold to find her travel box. She returned with a cotton dress which she offered to Lizzie. Lizzie threw it back at her.

"What would I be wanting with that oul' thing?" she shouted.

Bridie tossed the rejected dress on Lizzie's bed.

"Since I'm a much bigger size than yourself, this will hide your condition for a while—at least until we get off the ship."

"Aye," put in Sheila, who had come to stand beside Bridie, "hide it from the matrons, and the nosey ould fellers who'll be inspecting us when we dock in Australia."

She didn't mention the other orphans, but she didn't need to. Most of the girls had worked out what had happened, even if they didn't know the details, and they passed no remarks. It was as if they had all formed an invisible, protective circle around Lizzie, even those who disapproved of her vulgar talk and brazen ways. She was one of us and it was us against the world.

Lizzie finally accepted Bridie's dress but her mood did not improve. She directed her anger and frustration towards Nathaniel.

"It's all your fancy boy's fault, so it is," she shouted at me. "He should just have left the child to die and me with it! He had no business interfering with me!"

"He's a doctor, Lizzie," I said as patiently as I could. "It's his job to save lives, not destroy them!"

Lizzie brought her face close to mine, tears welling in her eyes. "And what am I supposed to do now," she cried, "me with a child on the way, and not married? Sure what respectable house is going to take on the likes of me?"

"You can't be sure of that—" I began, but she cut me off.

"Och, you know fine well I'm right, Kate Gilvarry! So don't be telling me lies!"

She moved away from me, her tears flowing freely now. Patsy and Sheila tried to touch her but she pushed them off and went back to her berth. We all looked at each other but said nothing. We knew the truth of what she had said.

*   *   *

The next evening after tea I sought out Nathaniel, who stood, as usual, on the top deck looking out to sea. Like many of the other orphans, I had begun to ignore the rules restricting our movements about the ship, while Mrs. Buckley and Phoebe appeared to have given up trying to enforce them.

"I'm worried about Lizzie," I said.

He swung around, a look of concern on his face.

"Why? Is she ill?"

"No," I said quickly. "But she's in a bad way, just the same. She's convinced there's no future for her now in Australia and she wishes you'd let them both die."

He turned pale. "Do you think she'll try to hurt herself?"

I shrugged. "She might try, but some of the girls and I are taking turns watching her during the night. She curses every one of us but we do it, anyway." I paused and followed his gaze out towards the horizon. "We're determined to get her to Sydney safely but . . . after that?"

He took my elbow. "Come with me," he said, "I have something to show you."

I followed him to his cabin and sat down, while he rummaged through a cardboard box, which sat on the floor. He pulled out some papers and placed them on his desk.

"You need to read these," he said. "I was going to show them to you earlier, but I later decided doing so might needlessly alarm you." He sighed. "Now, though, given Lizzie's situation, it's important you know what to expect."

I looked at him but couldn't read the expression on his face. He turned away from me and went towards the door. "I have to look in on a patient in the infirmary," he said. "I won't be long."

When he'd gone, I pulled a chair over to the desk and adjusted the lamp. What on earth was it I needed to see? I lifted a newspaper from the top of the pile. It was a copy of the *South Australian Register*, published in Adelaide in October of 1848. Nothing on the front page caught my attention but on the second page an article had been outlined in red ink, presumably by Nathaniel, which had the words *"Roman Emperor"* in the bold-typed headline. That was the name of the ship which had left Plymouth a month before ours, carrying orphans to Australia.

Eagerly, I began to read.

This splendid emigrant ship, it began, *has made a passage of less than three months from England . . .*

I let out a sigh of relief and gratitude that it had arrived safely. But as I read on, my mind began to cloud and words and phrases exploded in front of me like gunshots. *"Fraught with the most serious evils;" "fraud upon the colonists;" "they are a rough lot;" "the colony will become a receptacle for unfledged thieves, juvenile bastards and incipient prostitution."* I read and reread the article to make sense of it. Surely it couldn't be referring to orphans like us. But it was, and worse, it was referring specifically to orphans from the Union workhouses of the north of Ireland. I sat back in the chair, breathing hard. My shock eventually turned to anger. How dare the Australian authorities criticize us this way! Then the full thrust of the situation hit me, and my anger turned to fear. If we were so unwelcome, what on earth was to become of us?

"Kate?"

I hadn't even heard Nathaniel return.

"Kate? You look pale. Are you alright?"

I gazed at him. "Why, Nathaniel? Why are they saying these terrible things about us? What have we done to deserve it?"

Nathaniel came and sat beside me. He shook his head.

"I'm sorry, Kate, but there's actually more."

I waited while he picked up a document from the pile on his desk. "This is a letter I received from a colleague of mine who lives in Sydney. He says there has been growing resentment across Australia towards the immigration scheme ever since the first orphans landed in Sydney at the start of October."

"But why?" I cried.

Nathaniel took a deep breath.

"According to my colleague, when the *Earl Grey* ship landed, the ship surgeon, Doctor Henry Douglass, wrote a letter to the governor, criticizing the orphans, particularly those from Belfast. He complained that they used the most abominable language, fought with each other, and refused to follow his orders."

Nathaniel paused and searched through the letter, stopping at a paragraph outlined in red ink. "Here is the part where Douglass really gets going. He describes the orphans as either 'professed public women' or 'barefooted little country beggars.' Then he accuses Lord Earl Grey and Irish authorities of scraping these girls from the streets and into the workhouses so that they could be got rid of to Australia under the immigration scheme. He even singled out fifty-six of the orphans as the worst behaved and insisted that they be sent north to Moreton Bay rather than be allowed to land in Sydney!"

I bent over, trying to slow the tide of nausea that threatened to overwhelm me. "Why?" I whispered again. "Why would he hate us so?"

Nathaniel leaned close and put his hand gently on my shoulder.

"Because he is obviously a hate-filled man, Kate, and he is a disgrace to his profession. But I fear his accusations will fan the flames of prejudices that already exist in some measure in the colony—whether it's religious bias, resentment towards the English government or opposition to using Australian funds to subsidize this immigration scheme. A pebble thrown in a stream can cause ripples wider than we can ever anticipate." He sighed. "Hate spreads faster than love, Kate."

That night I lay in my berth unable to sleep. What was I to do? What *could* I do? Should I tell the others? What purpose would that serve other than to put the fear of God into them? I cursed Nathaniel for telling me. Once again, I'd been put in the position of worrying about everyone else. Was that to be my lot in life? I tried to tell myself that we would not meet that same fate. Nathaniel, I knew, would never complain about us the way

Dr. Douglass had. But the beautiful, bountiful fantasy I had earlier imagined of a golden, welcoming Australia, faded and died within me.

On November 29, 1848, eighty-seven days into our voyage, we had our first sight of Australia. We had reached Cape Leeuwin on the southwestern tip of the continent. There wasn't much to see—just a few small islands and rocks. What was important, Nathaniel informed us, was that we had now entered the Southern Ocean and our route would take us along Australia's southern coast. We would pass Adelaide and Melbourne, and then turn north to Port Jackson and Sydney Harbor. When pressed by the orphans as to how long it would be until our arrival in Sydney, Nathaniel stuck to his earlier prediction of Christmas Day.

"Another fecking month!" sighed Patsy.

"Will ya stop your whinging," shouted Phoebe, "and thank your lucky stars we made it this far in one piece!"

I would have usually offered some words of encouragement to the girls, but I stayed silent. Besides Lizzie, I was probably the only one dreading our arrival in Sydney. Again, I silently cursed Nathaniel for having warned me about the reception we might get. I'd decided not to mention it to any of the others. What if the newspapers and Nathaniel's friend had exaggerated? What if we met no trouble on our arrival, were all let stay in Australia, and all got jobs as promised? So what was the point in worrying everybody?

As the *Sabine* made her way along the southern coast of Australia, each day seemed longer than the last. We entered a stretch of ocean called the "Great Australian Bight," passing giant cliffs and rocky shorelines. I shivered as we sailed south of Adelaide, where the *Roman Emperor* had docked a month earlier and, without thinking, I made a hurried sign of the cross.

A few days after we passed Adelaide, Phoebe announced that our travel boxes were being brought up from the cargo hold so that we could air out our belongings and pick out the clothing we would need for our arrival in Sydney.

"Keep in mind even though it will be around Christmas Day when we get there, it will be summertime in Sydney. You'll have to get used to everything being topsy-turvy from what you've always known." She let out a wicked laugh. "It'll keep you on your toes, I warrant!"

That evening, as each of us knelt, unpacking our boxes, I thought back to the night in the workhouse when we had opened our boxes for the first time. How we'd squealed in delight, admiring the contents, the likes of which we had never seen in our lives. I pictured girls hugging the dresses and twirling with them as if they were lovers. I remembered Matron O'Hare giving up on any sort of control, flopping down on the floor with them and laughing. How innocent we had been then—excited and hopeful and trusting as children on Christmas Eve! I opened my own box and saw the beautiful bonnet with the red velvet ribbons staring out at me. Gently, I picked it up and cradled it to my heart.

As we drew closer to Port Jackson, which would be our first stop before entering Sydney Harbor, activity on board started to speed up. Anticipation filled the air. Sailors scrambled to ready the ship for landing—scraping masts, mending sails, scrubbing decks, painting railings, and airing hammocks. Paying passengers packed their trunks and lined them up outside their cabins for collection. Nathaniel ordered Mrs. Buckley and Phoebe to ensure our quarters were spotless. Our deck was to be scrubbed and holystoned, the floors in our hold swept and mopped, all unnecessary articles either discarded or packed in our travel boxes.

"Doctor wants everything clean and shiny as a new pin," Phoebe crowed. "He's a devil for cleanliness. Never seen the likes of him."

Mrs. Buckley chimed in. "The immigration inspectors will be judging all of us, but mostly Doctor Harte and myself, on the condition of the ship, as well as on the behavior and decorum of you, our charges."

Phoebe rolled her eyes. "What she means is that if everything is not shipshape neither she nor the doc will get paid."

"Nor you, either," Mrs. Buckley retorted, giving Phoebe a pointed stare. "We will be submitting reports on each of you," she went on, "including a recommendation of your suitability to be put forward for employment after you land." She regarded us with a self-satisfied smirk. "And I think most of you know what sort of report you will be getting! Now, get on with your work!"

When Mrs. Buckley left, we gathered around Phoebe.

"Would she really try to stop us from staying in Australia?"

"And after we've come all this way?"

"Oul' bitch," spat Patsy, "'tis us should be judging *her*!"

Phoebe sighed. "It's the rules, girls. And if I don't agree with her, she'll find a way to stop *my* wages. My husband, Charlie, has been over here serving a sentence for stealing," she began, "and he finally got his ticket-of-leave a year ago. I came over then to be wiv' him. But he needed time to get government approval for a bit of land where we hope to do some farming. We agreed I'd go home and come back again this year." She pulled an envelope out of her pocket. "This is the letter I got from him last month," she said, tears beginning to brim in her eyes. "He says we've been granted squatters' rights for a nice bit of land, but he'll be counting on my wages to buy seeds and some livestock." She sighed. "So you see why I can't go against Mrs. Buckley. I'll have to back her up on her report. I'm sorry, girls!"

"Phoebe," I finally spoke up, "do you know who's getting a bad report?"

I held my breath waiting for her answer, even though I already knew.

"You, darlin'," said Phoebe, "she's had it in for you from the start. She turned to the others. "And the rest of you in this mess, exceptin' for Bridie and Mary, and she'll be particularly hard on *her*!"

I winced as she pointed straight at Lizzie.

Afterwards, Mary and Bridie went silently to their berths but the rest of us stayed awake, talking late into the night.

"She knows about the baby then," said Lizzie. "I'm done for now. I won't even be allowed off the ship."

"You can't be sure how much she knows," put in Sheila. "She might just be reporting that fight you had with Bridie months ago."

"If that's true, she'd be reporting Bridie as well," said Patsy. "No, I think she just disliked us from the start, the way she did with Kate here!"

They turned and looked at me and I knew they were hoping I could solve the matter. I took a deep breath and fought against the urge to throw up my hands and let fate take its course. But as I looked at their solemn faces I felt a rush of pity for them, and for myself. We'd been through so much already, so why should whatever chance we might finally have for a decent life be snatched away from us at the last minute? A wave of anger and indignation surged through me.

"I can't promise anything," I said, in answer to their unasked question, "but I will do what I can."

I found Nathaniel the next day and told him about Mrs. Buckley's intended report.

"Does she know about the baby?"

"We're not sure."

He nodded but said nothing.

Over the next few days, we busied ourselves cleaning the ship to Nathaniel's satisfaction, hardly speaking a word to one another. One evening Phoebe came and stood beside me as I was polishing the railings on our deck.

"Mrs. Buckley doesn't know Lizzie's got 'erself in the family way," she whispered. "She suspected it right enough, but I told her there weren't nothing to it. I said, if there was, then Doctor Harte would have reported it."

I looked at Phoebe. "But *you* know?"

Phoebe laughed. "So do half the girls on the ship but they'll say nowt about it. And nor will I."

I smiled. "Thank you, Phoebe."

She put a plump hand on my wrist. "No thanks necessary, my duck. But for the grace of God, it could happen to any one of us."

After she left, I rushed straight to Nathaniel's cabin.

"She doesn't know," I said, bursting in without giving him a chance to speak. "Phoebe knows, but she won't say anything."

"I thought for a minute you'd come to give me a taste of my own medicine," he said, smiling and pointing at the polishing cloth in my hand.

A blush burned my cheeks as I pushed the cloth into my pocket. "I'm sorry, I just couldn't wait to tell you. I believe Phoebe will be good to her word."

He nodded. "Yes, I agree. I will have a talk with Mrs. Buckley tomorrow. I've been thinking and may have come up with a satisfactory plan. Remember when I told you about the girls from the *Roman Emperor* who had been sent up to Moreton Bay because Dr. Douglass insisted on it? Well, I shall ask Mrs. Buckley to recommend which of our girls would be better suited to that location, given that the competition for labor there is much greater than in Sydney and they would stand a better chance of quick employment. And I will let her know that I will accompany them to ensure that they are settled." He grinned at me. "I warrant the good Mrs. Buckley will see my request as a validation of her status as matron."

"But what if she suggests all of us go—Sheila and Patsy—and me?"

He grinned. "Don't worry, Kate. I didn't say I would accept *all* her suggestions!"

"It was the best we could have hoped for," I explained to the others later that night when the hold had been secured. I turned to look at Lizzie, who sat on her bed hugging her knees, her face pale in the lantern light.

"I'm sorry, Lizzie, but at least you'll get to stay in Australia, and Doctor Harte said it will be easier to secure employment up there. He will go with you to see you settled."

"How far is it?" she whispered.

"I don't know, exactly," I said. "Somewhere on the coast north of Sydney. You must travel there by steamer."

Sheila leapt to her feet. "Where Lizzie goes, I go, too," she said. "We started out on this journey together and we're going to stay together. Anyway, she'll need somebody by her side after the doctor leaves!"

Lizzie burst into tears. For a moment she looked very young. "Oh, Sheila, I'd be afeard to go up there alone. I'd as soon drown meself."

"We'll have none of that talk now," said Sheila, sitting down beside Lizzie and hugging her.

Patsy looked from one to the other. "There might just be a crowd of us," she said. "Oul' Buckley would think it a just punishment if the whole lot of us were shipped away to some godforsaken place at the back of beyond!"

I shook my head. "No," I said, "Nathaniel won't let that happen."

As Nathaniel had predicted, we reached Port Jackson on Christmas Day, 1848, and as he'd also predicted, the weather was glorious. The sky was clear blue and the ocean sparkled. That morning we all rushed up to the deck, straining to catch a glimpse of Sydney, but our view was hampered by two steep, sandstone sea cliffs rising out of the water ahead of us to our left and right.

"Those are the Heads," Nathaniel said. "They form the gateway to Sydney Cove."

"Why have we stopped?" shouted one of the girls.

"We can't sail into the harbor," answered Nathaniel, "because there's not enough wind or current. So, we must be towed in by a smaller boat. We must wait for a pilot. The waters around here are unpredictable, and we need an experienced seaman to guide us." He looked around at the disappointed faces. "But," he began cheerily, "it's Christmas Day, so let's enjoy it."

As if on cue, passengers on the upper deck began singing Christmas carols and the rest of us joined in. This was not going to be like any Christmas I remembered, I thought, but then almost everything we'd seen and done in the last months had been new!

Later that morning, we attended a service at which Nathaniel read a Bible verse from the Book of Matthew about the birth of Jesus and concluded with a quote from the Book of John: "This is my commandment. That ye love one another, as I have loved you." He smiled as he read the last words, and I imagined he looked directly at me. Then the captain gave a Christmas blessing, expressed thanks for our safe passage and led us in more carols, his fine voice lifting our hearts and spirits.

After the midday meal, which included a surprise offering of cooked shark, Nathaniel arrived in the hold along with the cook, carrying a tray of mugs filled with punch, which they set down at our mess table with great flourish. We all cheered.

The rest of the day passed pleasantly. Freed from our cleaning duties, we relaxed on the deck in the afternoon sunshine and told stories about Christmases past—some sad, some amusing. Maybe it was the effect of the punch, but no one became melancholy, as I had feared such reminisces might cause. The sense of sadness that finally took hold later that night had more to do with the present than the past. Most of us were strangers when we boarded the *Sabine* that August evening, but something had happened during these last months—a kind of sorcery that had turned us into kindred spirits, even closer than family. Maybe it was the rituals repeated each day that caused it, or simply that we had been crammed together for so long in such a small space with no opportunity for escape, but I believed it was more than those things. We had boarded this ship as equals in poverty, deprivation and hopelessness; together, we had survived dangers we never could have dreamed of and experienced a new and unfamiliar world around us; together, we had faced the fact that even the sky had turned upside down; and together, we had braced ourselves for an uncertain fate in a land at the end of the world. Soon we would disperse in all directions. Our bond would be shattered. None of us wanted to let go. Not yet.

The next morning, the pilot arrived and proceeded to tow the *Sabine* into Sydney Harbor. As we moved along, the paying passengers on the upper deck began singing a rousing version of "God Save the Queen." We orphans, on the other hand, were somber and silent as we watched the shore come slowly into view. I saw the grass first, which hugged the shoreline. It was an odd, dull green, nothing like the emerald green of Ireland; and drab, gray rocks dotted its surface. Out of the grass sprouted strange-looking trees with tall, silvery, thin trunks, their bark peeling, their leaves languishing aloft. All appeared to be bathed in a pale, pink haze. From the shore, the land sloped upwards and stopped at a line of mountains. About halfway down the harbor, a large, white house sat back, atop a slope, looking for all the world like an English manor house.

"That's the governor's mansion," said Phoebe from behind me, "as grand as any you'd see in England or Ireland."

"The rest of the place doesn't look anything like Ireland," I said.

"Well, what did you expect? We're on the other side of the world from the British Isles. You'll get used to it, love. Some of it is really very beautiful."

I shrugged, unconvinced.

At last, we dropped anchor at Garden Island from which we would be ferried to shore. I turned with the other girls to rush down to the hold and collect our belongings, but Phoebe put up her hands. "Stay where you are, girls," she said. "The paying passengers get off first, then they'll unload the cargo, then you'll have to wait for the inspections. It will be several days before you are cleared, and then you'll get in one of them little boats and be rowed over to the wharf. So just be patient."

All afternoon we watched as the paying passengers disembarked. It was funny to watch them as they tried to walk up the wharf. They staggered like drunkards and some fell to their knees. I realized all of us would have to get used to walking on land again after so many months at sea. Over the next few days, after the last of the passengers had disappeared, seamen unloaded cargo. I hadn't realized how much the *Sabine* had been carrying that was destined for delivery in Sydney. Crates of medicines, blankets and household supplies, along with sacks of flour and casks of whiskey, were hauled onto the wharf to porters who wheeled them away to storehouses. Sheep, cattle, and a few goats were swum ashore and handed over to rough-looking, barechested men in canvas overalls. It occurred to me that we orphans were cargo, too, but a much less important cargo since we would be the last to leave the ship. Each night, we watched the moon come up before the sun went down and reluctantly descended into our hold to wait for the next morning, hoping it would be the day we could leave. By now we were all anxious for the ordeal to be over.

On the morning of New Year's Day, we woke to the sound of shouts and heavy footsteps thudding on the top deck. Phoebe came bustling down the ladder to the hold.

"Up with ye, now," she called. "The authorities are here."

We dressed and stood silently beside our berths. I stole a look at Lizzie. She stood pale-faced and trembling, wearing one of Bridie's frocks. Mary stood beside me, looking almost as nervous as Lizzie. She had still not spoken a word since the day Jamie died, except when Nathaniel had to coax the kitten away from her, explaining that it was against the rules to take it ashore. But even though he told her he'd found a very nice sailor who would take good care of it Mary still screamed aloud in protest. Now I reached out and squeezed her hand. Her skin was cold to the touch.

Nathaniel descended the ladder, followed by Mrs. Buckley and two uniformed men. He nodded at us.

"These are our orphan girls," he said to the men. "And these are their sleeping and eating quarters. My . . . er, the girls have worked hard to keep everything clean. I think you'll find all in order, gentlemen."

The older of the two men nodded. "If it's like the rest of the ship, Doctor Harte," he said in a strong English accent, "I expect we'll have no complaints."

We stood motionless, watching while the men proceeded to examine the hold, tipping out mattresses and blankets and shaking them, bending to inspect the floor, rubbing their hands across the tables and chairs looking for dust or lingering crumbs.

The older man spoke again. "As I expected, Doctor. Clean and neat as a pin. Nearly impossible to believe after four months at sea. I'll be giving you and your staff the highest recommendation."

Mrs. Buckley flushed and thrust out her chest. "Thank you, sirs, we worked extremely hard to maintain it in this condition."

I looked around at Patsy, who was glaring at Mrs. Buckley. I knew she was dying to say a few choice words and I gave her a warning look. She swallowed them down.

"All of our girls worked hard as well," said Nathaniel to the departing men, "and I hope you will reflect that in your report."

When they had gone, Phoebe clapped her hands. "Alright girls, time for your immigration inspections. Have your papers ready and answer any questions loud and clear. No need to be nervous!"

One by one, we climbed the ladder out of the hold for the last time. A warm sun greeted us, but a rainstorm or thunder would have been more fitting, given that we were about to face the men who would determine our fates. Would we be sent back to Ireland? Or banished to Moreton Bay—or worse—Van Dieman's Land? And if we were allowed to stay in Sydney, would we be welcomed? Memories of the ugly reports I had read in Nathaniel's cabin that day floated back to me.

I was glad to see Nathaniel standing by the table where an immigration agent and health officer sat. I watched as, one by one, girls passed through their inspections. Then it was our turn. Our mess had stayed in line together. Bridie went first, her expression calm as she spoke her name loudly in English. She was passed through quickly and so was Mary, although she merely mumbled her name. Next it was Lizzie's turn. Sheila, Patsy and I held our breath. Nathaniel edged closer to Lizzie. The health officer looked her up and down and said something to Nathaniel, which I couldn't hear.

Nathaniel smiled at him and said, "Yes, some of our girls have recovered very well from the famine. Lizzie here proved to have a fine appetite once she got her sea legs."

The officer peered at Lizzie again. "Aye, well, I've heard many of these Irish girls are stout and thick-waisted and this one is no exception."

The immigration agent looked down at a paper in front of him. "Looks like she's a bit of a troublemaker from what your matron says. Certainly not a suitable one for work in Sydney."

"No, she is on the list for Moreton Bay," said Nathaniel. "I will be accompanying her and others there myself to see that they get settled."

The agent raised an eyebrow. "No need for that, Doctor."

"I insist," replied Nathaniel. "They are my charges. I am responsible for every one of them."

The agent shrugged. "Next!"

We watched as Sheila passed through quickly. The agent was clearly satisfied to send her to Moreton Bay along with Lizzie.

Then it was Patsy's turn.

"Why not Moreton Bay for this one, as well?" the agent asked.

Nathaniel chimed in again. "Yes, Miss Riley here had a defiant streak when she joined us, but she was able to curb it as the voyage wore on, and instead took the initiative to learn to bake and"—he grinned—"she succeeded very well. Miss Riley's baking talents would be a fine addition to any worthy household in Sydney."

Thank God Patsy had the good sense not to interrupt.

The agent shook his head and sighed. "You have already earned superior reports from the ship's inspectors and the captain of the *Sabine*, himself, Doctor Harte, so I shall take you at your word on this." He turned to Patsy. "And you, Miss Riley, can show your gratitude to the good doctor here by working hard and applying yourself." He stamped her papers.

Then it was my turn. The health officer, clearly bored with the process by now, gave me a hasty look and stamped my health papers. I tried to control my trembling as I approached the immigration agent who was studying Mrs. Buckley's report. I waited, not daring to look at Nathaniel. When he'd finished reading, the agent eyed me up and down, then turned to Nathaniel.

"Your matron says this one has trouble following rules! Bit too big for her britches, I'd warrant."

"Indeed, Miss Gilvarry has been known to take the initiative at times," said Nathaniel calmly, "but only when she believed one of the girls in her mess was in some danger. This young lady has natural leadership skills—the other girls look up to her and respect her judgment."

The agent grunted and was about to interrupt but Nathaniel put up his hand.

"What Mrs. Buckley's assessment does not reflect is that Miss Gilvarry has a refined manner and an excellent command of the English language. I believe she would be an asset to any well-bred Sydney family." He paused and smiled. "It would be rather a shame to send her to an outpost like Moreton Bay where such skills would likely be underappreciated."

The agent studied Nathaniel for a moment, then turned to me.

"You appear to have a champion in your corner, Miss Gilvarry.

I hope you're grateful. I shall follow Doctor Harte's advice for reasons I have already stated." He wagged his finger at me. "But mind my words, miss, you need to climb down off your high horse. Remember, you are here to be a domestic servant, not the mistress of the manor!"

He stamped my papers and thrust them at me. "Welcome to Sydney!"

Part Four

Sydney
1849

After we passed through the immigration inspections, Phoebe and Mrs. Buckley tried to hurry us towards the sailors who were waiting to lower us from the *Sabine* into small boats and row us to shore. Bridie, Patsy, Mary, and I ignored their orders and rushed instead towards Lizzie and Sheila to hug them goodbye, assuring them that we would all meet up again soon, although none of us believed it. I was in tears as I turned to face Nathaniel. Everything in me wanted to move closer, to find comfort in his warm embrace, but I was aware of the many pairs of eyes watching us. Instead, I stood where I was.

"Thank you, Doctor Harte," I mumbled, "for everything you have done for us."

The others nodded in agreement.

Nathaniel cleared his throat. "It was my pleasure, girls," he said. "I will be visiting you at Hyde Park when I return from Moreton Bay. I want to make sure you are happy with your work assignments before I sail back to England."

The others turned and shuffled towards Phoebe who, by now, was shouting at us, but I couldn't bring myself to move. Instead, I stared into his face and he into mine. Before I could speak, Mrs. Buckley grabbed me roughly by the arm and pulled me away. I looked back at him. He hadn't moved.

"Goodbye, Nathaniel," I mouthed silently.

"Goodbye, Kate," he said aloud, "God bless!"

When we reached shore, Mrs. Buckley and Phoebe hurried out of the boat without so much as a goodbye. Phoebe flung herself into the outstretched arms of a short, balding man. Some of us smiled wistfully as we watched their reunion. I looked around for Mrs. Buckley, just in time to see her walking away in the company of a tall, well-dressed woman, engrossed in conversation. Shrugging, I climbed out of the boat and staggered unsteadily onto the wharf, just as the paying passengers had done a few days earlier. It was a strange sensation walking on a solid surface as opposed to a constantly moving ship deck.

Passersby turned to stare at us as we walked by, two by two, remarking on our crumpled dresses and colorful bonnets. I tried to ignore them, keeping my eyes on my feet lest I should fall. I held on tightly to my bag, in which I had stuffed the items I now thought of as mine—the plate, mug, and utensils I had been given when I first boarded the *Sabine*, soap and a washcloth, and a small piece of linen on which I had embroidered a horse, a mountain, and green grass to remind me of home. Bridie walked ahead, sweating in a woolen dress. It was the only choice she had left since she had given away her one cotton dress to Lizzie. Patsy walked beside her, looking left and right, exclaiming loudly about everything she saw, while Mary clung to me in silence. Birds flew overhead, making startling and unfamiliar sounds, while untamed animals scurried past our feet. Smells filled the air, some sweet, some stale, and some so pungent they burned my throat.

Patsy stopped abruptly, causing Mary and me to slam into her.

"Jesus, Mary and Joseph," she shouted, "did you ever see the likes of that? What class of a creature is it at all?"

She pointed to an animal hopping along beside us on its back legs. It was as tall as us, with brown fur, a pointy face, and large ears. I had to look at it twice because sticking out of a pouch in its belly was a miniature of itself.

Patsy laughed aloud. "D'ya see the wee baby looking at us?

Fair play to the mother. Why didn't women ever think of carrying our babies like that?"

"Move along now, girls," called a young matron escorting our procession, and we obeyed, straining our necks to look back at the strange animal.

As we climbed a hill called Macquarie Street towards the Hyde Park Barracks, where we were to stay until assigned to a position with a local family, it occurred to me that I was in yet another procession, not so different from the one from my family farm to the workhouse almost one year ago. Again, we were fleeing the known for the unknown, from freedom to confinement. I prayed I would not be lodged here for long.

The barracks, I learned later, had been built to house English and Irish convicts, until "transportation" had ended nine years earlier. I shivered as we walked up to an imposing three-story, red sandstone building, with a triangular-shaped roof topped by a clock tower. The entrance was flanked by two tall stone pillars and two huts that might have once been guardhouses. Inside the graveled courtyard were several smaller buildings located near the main barracks, and the entire complex was enclosed by high, stone walls.

Another matron came out of the barracks to greet us and led us through a big arched door with a fanlight above it into what she called "the dormitory block," and upstairs to the second floor. After nearly four months sleeping in the narrow, dark confines of the ship's hold, I was pleasantly surprised to find a huge, bright, airy room, newly plastered, painted and lined with sturdy iron-framed single beds covered in crisp, clean linens. We were each assigned a bed and shown where to stow our belongings, before being led down to a dining room where we were served hot soup and fresh bread.

As we'd entered the barracks grounds earlier, I had noticed several girls about my age sitting in the sun. I was uncomfortable with the sullen looks they gave us, even though they said nothing. Now in the dining hall I spied them sitting by themselves at a corner table.

"I'm going to see what them ones are up to," said Patsy, suddenly getting up.

"Why?" asked Bridie.

Patsy shrugged. "I heard the Irish accents. Be the look of them, I'd say they're orphans like us. If so, they've been here a while."

I watched nervously as Patsy walked over and sat down beside them nice as you like, as if she belonged there. It was something I'd always admired about Patsy—no matter what fear she had, she almost never showed it. The girls scowled at her when she approached but she ignored them. Eventually they fell into conversation.

When Patsy returned, she was red in the face. "Yez won't believe what they're after telling me," she said. "They're all orphans from the *Earl Grey*, the first ship to dock in Sydney. Two of them were placed in positions so awful they up and ran away. The police caught them and brought them back here. As for the others—they've been here for three months and not a job in sight!"

"Why?" I asked.

Patsy shrugged. "All I know is every one of them's from Belfast, and all but one are Catholics."

I swallowed hard, remembering what I'd read that day in Nathaniel's cabin. The rising resentment towards the Irish orphans was worse against Catholics, and against girls from Belfast! I tamped down the anger that welled up in me.

"Well, there's two sides to every story," I said.

Bridie and Mary nodded in agreement.

"Happy New Year!" snapped Patsy as she walked away.

Later that night, as I lay in the comfort of a real bed for the first time since we'd left our farm, I knew I should be grateful. But all I could summon up was fear for what lay ahead.

* * *

The day after we arrived at Hyde Park Barracks, the Sisters of Charity came to greet us. Finding that everyone in our mess was Catholic, they were delighted to talk to us.

"We can assure you that your Catholic faith will be respected here," one young, pale nun began. "We will ensure your employers agree to give you adequate time off to attend Mass on Sundays. There's a lovely church nearby in Charlotte Place called St. Patrick's. We'll also ensure that you will not be required to eat meat on Fridays or other feast days."

I nodded and tried to look pleased. Bridie shifted impatiently in her chair, while Patsy took a fit of choking as she tried to suppress a laugh. Only Mary showed genuine interest. She raised her hand.

"Is your convent nearby?" she whispered.

The young nun smiled. "Yes, it is. And if you'd like to visit us while you are here at Hyde Park, I'll be happy to escort you over there."

Mary gave a huge smile—the first I'd seen from her in months. "Yes, please, Sister," she said. "I'd like that."

Later that evening, the head matron assembled the newcomers in the dining hall.

"I called you together," she said, "to lay out for you what to expect in the coming days. As you know you are all to be presented to prospective employers soon. We have already posted notice of your arrival in the *Sydney Morning Herald* and are taking applications. We are most careful in our evaluations—we want only the best and most reliable class of people involved. As you can imagine, this process will take time . . ."

"How long?" someone shouted.

I twisted around hoping it wasn't Patsy, but it was a girl I hardly knew. Patsy glared at me. She'd known what I was thinking.

The matron continued, ignoring the interruption. "As I was saying, the process will take time. In this case, I would expect up to two weeks—hopefully sooner! You will be told the day before so that you can make yourselves ready to present the best appearance." She turned to leave. "While you are waiting, you can pass the time as you wish, but you may not leave the barracks grounds without permission."

With that she disappeared through the door.

The only consolation I took from her words was that two weeks would give Nathaniel time, if he'd meant what he said, to come back from Moreton Bay and visit us. I deliberately pushed to the back of my mind what he had also said—that after he saw us, he would be sailing back to England.

For the next two weeks we waited in the hope that we would soon be moving on. Fortunately, the weather continued to be fine and we spent most of our days outside, sitting on the grass beneath a tree the head matron called a "weeping lillypilly." We all giggled when she said it and began calling it the "sillypilly." It was, however, a beautiful tree that reminded me of the weeping willow trees back home. It reached about thirty feet into the sky, with a canopy of green and pale pink leaves, and was covered in wispy white flowers. There were two of them, one on each side of the dormitory block. The one on the west side had been claimed by the "*Earl Grey* girls," as we had begun to call those who'd been there a while, so we claimed the one on the east. We gathered underneath it each morning after breakfast and stayed until lunchtime, talking, or sewing, or silently dwelling on our private thoughts, grateful for its shelter from the sun.

As the days wore on, I felt myself falling into a deep melancholy, something I had never experienced, even at the height of the famine. I was sure it had to do with my loneliness for Nathaniel and maybe the fact that we now had nothing with which to occupy ourselves but our thoughts. But, as I look back on it, I believe it was a loss of hope. Up until this moment, I'd fought fear, anger, and uncertainty, but there always remained a tiny but persistent pinprick of hope that shone through the dim veil of my anxiety. Now, I felt that light ebbing away. As I curled up in bed each night, I prayed that the morning would bring the light's return.

As opposed to my downward slide, Mary's spirits appeared to soar. The young nun, good to her word, had come to the barracks several times to collect Mary and ask permission to take her to visit the convent. Mary had begun to talk excitedly over the evening meal about her day.

"It's such a peaceful, wee place," she said, "it's as if they've shut out the world and all its noise and cruelty."

Bridie and I nodded, while Patsy rolled her eyes. I was happy for Mary. She was such a fragile little thing; I was glad she had found a sanctuary and I prayed whoever she was indentured to would be kind to her.

We were sitting in our usual place under the lillypilly tree one morning when Matron came marching towards us.

"Your attention, girls, please!" she began.

We sat up straight.

"I have just been informed that our first set of prospective employers will be here tomorrow at nine o'clock sharp. After your midday meal today, you will go immediately to your dormitory and prepare yourselves to meet them. You will ensure you have a clean, well-pressed dress to wear, and your best shoes are polished. You will also bathe, wash and brush your hair and, of course, you will wear your bonnets. It is important to make a good first impression. I will come and inspect you tomorrow after breakfast and escort you downstairs to the hiring room."

I hardly slept that night, wondering what the next day would bring. Would I be hired? And, if so, would it be by someone I would respect and trust and who would treat me well? That was asking a lot, I knew. From what the *Earl Grey* girls had said, all the authorities wanted to do was get rid of us as fast as possible, and they were likely to palm us off on anybody who showed an interest, respectable or not.

The next morning Matron lined us up and inspected us, one

by one, examining our hands and fingernails for cleanliness, tucking unruly hair beneath our bonnets, and pinching our cheeks to give them color.

"I suppose you will do," she sniffed. "Now, divide yourselves into groups of six!"

We all shuffled around. Mary, Bridie, Patsy, and I were joined by two of the *Earl Grey* girls whom Patsy had befriended. We were the first group to go downstairs.

"Follow me," Matron said. "Remember, speak only when you are spoken to, and answer all questions clearly but briefly. And for goodness' sake, stand up straight!"

The hiring room was light and airy as the morning sun streamed in the windows. Matron led us over to one side of the room and told us to wait. She then opened wide a set of double doors, allowing the crowd of people waiting in the hallway to flood in. We stared at them in awe. Women in fashionable dresses and large hats came close to inspect us, looking us up and down as if picking out the best cut of meat. There were other women, more plainly dressed, with sour, pinched faces. I took them to be housekeepers sent on behalf of their mistresses. I bowed my head, as if to hide from them.

"Look at me, not at your feet," one of them said as she roughly lifted my chin up with bony fingers.

I did as she said, holding down my temper. She had an Irish brogue. Was this any way to treat your countrymen? I thought.

Greatly outnumbered by women, most of the men looked prosperous, with high-collared shirts, colorful cravats, fine, silk frock coats, and top hats. Some had pocket watches on chains hanging from their waistcoats, and some carried gold-knobbed canes. I thought maybe we should be flattered that they'd chosen to wear such finery to visit us. But there were also other, rougher looking men, dressed in loose cotton trousers and wide-brimmed, slouching hats. The men examined us as closely as the women had. Some asked us to turn around, their eyes lingering on certain parts of our bodies. There was something in their manner, a hint of entitled ownership, that made me shiver.

Matron and her assistant waited attentively to identify any girl in whom a patron had shown interest. Mary was summoned first. I suspected it was because she looked so fair and innocent and, I thought, with her blond curls and pink cheeks, more British than the rest of us. I couldn't hear what she was saying, but I saw her shake her head defiantly as she was being questioned by several men and women. It was only when a stout woman in a nun's habit approached her that she began to smile and nod.

Soon Bridie was called. She moved forward calmly, as was her way. I edged closer so I could hear what was being said. A carelessly dressed, burly man with a red face pointed at her.

"A big, strapping girl like her would be a fine asset on my farm," he told Matron. "I'll take her."

Bridie answered him in Irish. I didn't understand what she said but he glowered at her. "Never mind," he told Matron. "This one has too much of a mouth on her. I'll wait for the next lot!"

Several of the women turned to each other. "Another one without a word of English," they grumbled.

I wanted to shout at them that Bridie was a refined girl who knew more than all of them put together about how to run a genteel household. Were we to be hired or dismissed merely on the way we looked? I thought again of the articles I had read about resentment towards Irish-speaking Catholic girls.

One of the fashionably dressed women moved close to Bridie. "Bridie O'Sullivan?" she inquired.

She was a tall, handsome, middle-aged woman, erect and with thick, glossy black hair swept up beneath her elegant bonnet. She wore a long-sleeved, rose-colored day dress with a high neckline, and a narrowly-cut skirt which showed off her shapely figure. She studied Bridie with calculating, dark eyes, then looked down at a pamphlet she held. "I see here you have experience working for the English gentry in an Irish manor house?"

Matron jumped to attention. "Mrs. Pitt, may I point out that Bridie has extensive experience working in a manor house in Ireland, called Muckross House, owned by a well-respected member of the British Parliament, Mr. Henry Arthur Herbert. I'm told the house has sixty-five rooms and entertains the best society in Europe." She giggled nervously. "I imagine it's the sort of house dear Queen Victoria herself might one day visit. I think Bridie would be a great asset to your fine house. She would require very little training."

"Except for the fact that she doesn't speak English," said Mrs. Pitt doubtfully.

Bridie looked at Matron and then pointed towards me. "She's teaching me," she said in English.

Mrs. Pitt's rouged lips fell open. "So you *do* speak it!"

"Yes, but only a little bit," said Bridie.

At first, I was confused. Bridie certainly knew more than a "little bit" of English. Why was she pretending otherwise? Perhaps she had taken a dislike to Mrs. Pitt. And then it dawned on me—she was doing it for my sake!

Mrs. Pitt pointed at me, and Matron called me forward. She took a deep breath and looked down at the papers in her hand. "This is Kathleen Gilvarry, from the North of Ireland," she began.

Mrs. Pitt perked up. "A Protestant, then?" she said hopefully.

"My mother was," I replied.

I could have lied and said I was Protestant, too, but I wasn't about to deny who and what I was.

Matron spoke again. "She reads and writes in English as well as speaking it," she said, "and has taught a number of girls both in the workhouse and on the ship to do so."

"Age? Experience?"

"Sixteen," I said before Matron could reply. "And no, I have not been trained as a domestic servant. I am educated, however, and was hoping to train as a teacher before the famine came. I am a quick learner, however, and—"

Mrs. Pitt waved her hand at me impatiently. "Yes, yes!" she said.

She studied me some more while Bridie stood by silently.

"I like this one." She pointed to Bridie. "I do a great deal of entertaining. I am, in fact, a prominent hostess in Sydney. My husband, Major Pitt, is, as everyone knows, a relative of William Pitt, who was prime minister of Great Britain, and after whom Pitt Street in the city was named." She paused and sighed. "So, you can understand that I am held to a very high standard by Sydney society—a standard that is as high as any to be found in our dear Mother England!"

When she had finished speaking, no one moved. She cleared her throat. "Well, then, to get back to business. I had not planned to hire two girls. Major Pitt and I had agreed that one would be enough to show our support for our Governor FitzRoy in his immigration endeavors. But"—she looked at Bridie—"I will not get the best out of this girl if she doesn't understand what I'm saying." She turned to me. "I suppose I'll have to take *you* as well. Mind you, you will not just be an interpreter, you will be expected to pull your weight at any tasks our housekeeper demands." She sniffed. "At least your mother was a Protestant, which suggests you were brought up with proper standards!"

Bridie and I looked at each other and then at Matron. It was clear to me that we were not being given much of a choice in the matter.

"Prepare the details," Mrs. Pitt said to Matron. "I will arrange transportation for them both, tomorrow morning at nine sharp."

And, without another word, she swept out.

Matron looked around the room, then clapped her hands and pointed to our group. "You girls may go now. Please send down the next group."

Neither Patsy nor the two *Earl Grey* girls had been hired. They rushed ahead of us up the stairs to the dormitory.

"Did you hear that oul' feller ask me if I was a virgin? The bloody cheek of him!" said Patsy. "I told him where to go, so I did!"

"I'll not be putting meself through that again," said one of the *Earl Grey* girls. "I've had me fill of oul' lechers pawing at me. I'd rather make me own way beyond on the streets!"

She brushed away tears with a rough gesture and threw herself face down on her bed.

I wanted to reassure Patsy that this was just the first round—that there'd be plenty more chances to be hired, but the angry look on her face silenced me.

We were finishing the evening meal when I heard a familiar voice in the corridor outside the dining room. My heart leaped. It was Nathaniel. Thank God he had arrived before Bridie and I left. Just then the door opened, and Matron called my name. I almost knocked over my chair in my haste to answer. She gave me a suspicious look.

"Doctor Harte wants to speak with you. Please do not dawdle."

I rushed out the door and stopped in alarm at the sight of Nathaniel standing in the dimly lit hallway. He looked weary and unkempt. Dark circles curved under his eyes and a rough stubble covered his usually clean-shaven chin. He looked as if he hadn't slept in days. He must have registered my alarm, for he smiled then and came towards me.

"Ah, Kate," he said. "It is good to see you." He turned to the matron. "May I have a private word with Miss Gilvarry, Matron?"

"As long as it does not take long, Doctor," she said stiffly. "Lights-out is in less than an hour." She pointed to a door. "You may use my office."

I settled myself on a sofa in the small room, while Nathaniel sat down opposite me, his legs stretched out, ankles crossed. I yearned suddenly for the comfort and the privacy of his cabin on the *Sabine*.

"I hear you and Bridie have been hired by Mrs. Pitt," he said. "Well done!"

I smiled. "It was Bridie's doing. She pretended she needed my help with English even though we both knew better."

He laughed. "Then you are greatly in her debt."

"I'll only know that after we get to Mrs. Pitt's house," I retorted. "She may have tricked me into hell for all I know."

Nathaniel shook his head. "From what I understand, Mrs. Pitt is rather obsessed with appearances. I think if you and Bridie keep that in mind, you will fare well. Besides, the Pitts are not only wealthy, but well regarded in Sydney. And while it may not be heaven, the Pitt House will not be hell!"

He smiled again. "I understand Mary has been indentured to the Sisters of Charity as a domestic servant?"

I nodded. "I think it's perfect for her."

"And Patsy?"

I shook my head. "No luck today, but there's always tomorrow."

He nodded but said nothing.

"So, tell me how it went in Moreton Bay," I said, changing the subject. "Have you found places for Sheila and Lizzie?"

"Yes. I was able to place all the girls whom I escorted up there. Moreton Bay was just as I thought, a barren, unwelcoming place. But the settlers there seem to be good, solid people, and they are in urgent need of help." He grinned. "And much less picky than the good people of Sydney."

I waited for him to go on.

"Sheila was easy enough to place. A young couple, an English prisoner who has earned his ticket-of-leave, and his wife, have opened a shop selling drapery goods. Sheila, as you remember, is an excellent seamstress, and from her work in the mill is well versed in handling fabrics."

"And Lizzie?"

"Yes, well that was more of a challenge. Just as I was losing hope, I met a Methodist minister and his wife, recently moved there. They are a very dignified couple who are unable to have children."

A shrill alarm rang through me. I feared what might be coming.

"I was open with them about her condition and I spoke honestly with Lizzie. The couple agreed to take her in as a maid, and . . . well, they proposed that when the child was born Lizzie would allow them to adopt it and stay on as a maid if she so desired.

I shot up straight in my chair. "Surely Lizzie couldn't have agreed to that!" I shouted. "She wouldn't have agreed to give up her child!"

Nathaniel took a deep breath. "I didn't force her," he said, "you must believe me. I admit she fought me on it at first but, in the end, she realized it was the best for her child's future."

"What if she changes her mind?" I whispered, knowing of course what the answer was.

"That would be regrettable," Nathaniel said, looking earnestly into my eyes, "but it would be her decision. She would have to be prepared to fend for herself and the child in a very lonely outpost. I hope she would think long and hard about it."

"Sounds to me like you sold her out at the first opportunity. How could you, Nathaniel?"

He bowed his head and sighed. "I did the best I could, Kate!"

We sat in silence for a time. The bell rang for lights-out. He stood up and moved towards me, and I stood also. We were only inches apart. I could see the fatigue in his eyes, and something else, maybe longing. The annoyance I had felt with him over Lizzie faded away, and all I wanted was to throw my arms around him and beg him not to go, not to leave me alone in this place.

"Nathaniel, I—" I began.

"Shh, Kate," he whispered as he leaned forward and put his lips on mine.

He pulled away again quickly. "I'm sorry I must go, Kate. I must leave you to find your own way now. I took on an obligation to see you and the other girls safely across the sea to Australia and see you settled." His eyes filled with tears. "I cannot stay with you, Kate. It wouldn't be proper for me to do so. You are young and have yet to fully experience the world."

He reached into his pocket and took out a slip of paper. "Here is my address in England," he said. "Please write to me sometime.

Let me know how you are faring." Just as he was about to say more, there was a sharp knock on the office door and Matron's voice called his name.

"Doctor Harte, it is time for Miss Gilvarry to retire."

"Of course," he called back.

He looked at me then. "Goodbye, Kate," he whispered. "God speed!"

I could get no words out. I merely nodded as I watched him leave. When he had gone, I pushed past Matron and hurried upstairs to the dormitory.

The sun beat down mercilessly on Bridie and me as we sat in the cart Mrs. Pitt had sent for us. The conveyance was called a "dray" and was pulled by two bullocks. A tall, broad-shouldered, silent man, wearing loose cotton trousers and jacket and a battered, slouched straw hat, pointed at us to climb into the back of the cart and sit with our travel boxes wedged at our feet. I was reminded of the journey from the Newry Workhouse to Dublin all those months ago, except *that* cart had been much more comfortable. It struck me that drays were more suited to carrying cargo than people. But then, after all, cargo is what we were.

Leaving Hyde Park Barracks that morning had been bittersweet. Bridie and I hugged Mary and wished her well. I was nervous that she might react badly to being separated from me for the first time since our journey began. But she smiled through her tears and I could see that she was genuinely happy with the future before her.

Patsy was another case altogether. She resisted hugs, pushing us away with curses.

"I don't want to be hearing your oul' palaver," she said roughly. "Yez know as well as I do what's ahead of us." She looked at the two *Earl Grey* girls. "These girls and meself will have to look after ourselves as best we can. Sure amn't I well used to it after my years on the streets of Newry? To think I traveled all this way only to take up living the same life as before!"

"It doesn't have to be this way," I began. "I told you that Sheila and Lizzie found places up in Moreton Bay . . ."

She brought her face close to mine. "Aye, so they did! But at what price? Sheila will be slaving away in the back of beyond and poor Lizzie will have to give up her child! Quite a bargain your fancy doctor struck!"

I sighed. There was nothing more to say. Patsy's cruel honesty pierced my heart. Now, as we moved across the courtyard in the dray, I looked back and saw Patsy's pale face pressed against the dormitory window, her untamable red curls sprouting out defiantly around her head.

Sydney's streets were clogged with vehicles, from heavy, slow drays like ours, transporting goods of all kinds, to light, open carriages pulled by well-groomed horses, conveying well-dressed passengers out for a morning ride. Bridie and I twisted our necks staring at everything and everyone. We made our way down Macquarie Street, towards the harbor, past Hyde Park and its open lawns where a group of boys were playing cricket. On King Street we pointed in awe at the orderly, terraced buildings that lined each side of the street, housing both private residences and shops, along with hotels, warehouses, churches, and public houses. We exclaimed at such sights, and while the elegant buildings were indeed a pleasant shock, there were still some crude huts here and there, which gave us an idea of what the town had been like even a few years before. We giggled when we turned to Pitt Street, recalling how Mrs. Pitt's chest had expanded when she told us that Pitt Street was named after her husband's family. We passed over Bridge Street and I spotted Charlotte Place where the young nun from the Sisters of Charity had told us there was a Catholic church called St. Patrick's. I made a mental note of it, hoping Bridie and I might go there on the following Sunday.

The driver stopped the dray at Queen's Wharf and signaled us to wait. Just two weeks before, we had stumbled out of the boat here on our sea legs and made our way in procession up the hill to the barracks. I hadn't dared even lift my head. Now, I looked all around me, greedy to see everything. I'd already seen the strange trees and the kangaroos, but I wasn't prepared for the variety of animals scurrying around us, or the strange colorful birds. I had no names for any of them. Bridie pointed to a stout, furry creature clinging to the trunk of a nearby tree. He had a large head with fluffy ears and a black, round nose. His face reminded me of a baby, and I laughed aloud. As I was laughing, I was startled by a white-chested bird with brown and black markings flying in circles above me. I could have sworn he was imitating my laugh. As I listened to him, I laughed even more.

Just then Bridie gripped my arm and pointed towards the harbor. I followed her gaze. A small boat was pulling up to the wharf. I had to squint in the sunlight to make out what I was seeing and, when I found focus, I held my breath. Bridie's eyes had grown large. Neither of us said a word as we watched a small group of men and boys climb out of the boat, carrying fishing nets and a basket of gleaming fish. The small boys were completely naked, and the men wore either scanty cloths tied about their waists, or loose trousers but no shirts. It wasn't the lack of clothing so much that startled me, but the color of their skin. It was darker than any I had ever witnessed on a human before, and it glinted in the sun. These must be the people Nathaniel had once told us about, I thought, the people who had been in Australia for thousands of years before white men discovered it. "Aboriginals," I remembered he called them. I wished he was here now so I could share this experience with him.

I looked at Bridie, who was sitting open-mouthed, then turned back towards the fishermen. I noticed that people, particularly women with small children, moved away from the party, tugging their children by the hands. The group didn't seem to pay much attention. They were probably used to it, I thought. I felt no alarm when I looked at them, but rather pity for yet another indigenous people. I didn't know much about their situation, but I couldn't help thinking that my own people had been chased off their land by invaders and I felt an unexpected kinship with them.

My thoughts were interrupted by the return of our driver. He carried a wooden box on his shoulder and swung it down on the floor of the dray beside our travel chests. He made no eye contact, nor said a word as he slid onto the driver seat and urged the bullocks forward.

It was about noon, and the heat was becoming unbearable. I yearned for the shade of the "sillypilly" tree up at the barracks. Sweat trickled down the back of my neck and my throat was parched. I tapped on the driver's shoulder, and he swung around, his blue eyes boring into mine. Startled, I leaned backwards.

"I was wondering if we could find some water to drink?" I said, shrinking under his stare.

He shrugged, acting as if he didn't understand me. Bridie asked him the same thing in Irish. He gave her a broad grin and a nod.

"I can take ye to a pub, but I don't think Mrs. Pitt would approve," he said in English, with an Irish brogue. " 'Tis not far to the house now."

With that he urged the bullocks forward.

Curious, I looked down into the crate he had set in front of us and was surprised to see it filled with young plants and cuttings in pots. I had not taken our driver for a gardener but, there again, I was now in a land where surprises were around every corner.

My first impression of the Pitt House was its lightness. I had expected a gray, granite building, solemn and daunting, like many of the manor houses I had seen in Ireland growing up. They'd been more like castles than houses. But this house, built of earth-toned sandstone blocks, seemed to float above the ground. It was elegant in its design—a central main structure, balanced by two identical wings—just three stories high, and with tall, sashed windows spaced evenly along the front. A portico, supported by four columns, led my eye to the entrance and from there, I looked up past iron balconies and attic windows to a slate roof.

Once I caught sight of the house I forgot about our driver's earlier rebuff and tapped him on the shoulder.

"Is this the Pitt House?" I called, although I was somehow certain that it was.

He nodded silently.

"Then, can you stop here please so that we can get a good look at it?"

He did so and Bridie and I climbed out of the dray and stood admiring the house, shielding our eyes from the sun with our hands. I forgot the heat for the moment as I stood there, Bridie beside me.

"Did you ever see the likes of it, Bridie?" I asked.

She shook her head. "I thought 'twould be bigger," she said. "Muckross House was ten times the size of this!"

"But it's beautiful," I whispered.

I let my eyes travel one more time over the house on the hill with the mountain range behind it, and down the slope of the front garden, which was lush with foliage and flowers in dazzling colors. I didn't recognize many of the plants, but I did see hydrangeas and roses, and felt a small rush of pleasure.

"We'd better be moving on," called the driver.

When I turned back towards him, I gasped at the view below me. I could see all the way down over distant rooftops to the ships anchored in Sydney Harbor. I silently thanked God for sending me to this heaven.

The driver turned the dray into an entrance on the far side of the house, and we rumbled up a gravel pathway past the house itself, stopping outside a coach house in which two elegant carriages stood.

"Follow me," he said. "I'll be carrying your boxes in after yez."

He slid down from his seat and hoisted our travel boxes, one on each shoulder. I couldn't wait to get a glimpse inside this beautiful house. But, instead, the driver led us past sheds and stables, towards another sandstone building in the rear of the main house. It was laid out just like the main house, but much smaller, and without columns, balconies, or other decoration.

The driver walked to the building and halted at a door.

"This is where the servants sleep," he announced. "The kitchens are here, too, along with the bakery ovens, wine cellar, and storage larders, and over there is the farm garden where they keep the animals."

I glanced in the direction he was nodding, and saw a pig, a cow, and several chickens in a fenced-in pen, like the one we'd kept the livestock in at our own wee farm in Ireland. I looked at Bridie, confused, while a wave of disappointment began to flow through me.

Bridie shrugged. "Well, this is more like it," she said matter-of-factly, pushing open the door. "We'd best be going in. I'm scorched with the heat!"

The driver put up his hand. "Wait," he said to Bridie. "Mrs. Pitt wants yourself sleeping in the big house." He turned to me, and as he did, I thought I saw pity in his eyes. "You're to sleep here, miss."

"No," shouted Bridie, "we're to stay together."

"It's all right, Bridie," I whispered as I pushed past her.

Then, inhaling a deep breath, I willed myself to follow as the driver led me into the outbuilding and dropped my travel box at my feet. I stood in the large kitchen, staring around, unsure what to do. A woman was turning a slab of meat on a spit above a fire while another was sliding rounds of dough into an oven built into a brick wall. They each looked at me briefly before turning back to their tasks. I began to cough from the smoke and my clothes clamped around me, damp with sweat. I thought I might faint.

"I suppose you're the Irish girl they've sent me to replace the wench who ran off yesterday?" A huge woman in a long white apron over a gray dress, her red face encased in a white bonnet, came bustling down a narrow staircase. "I saw the two of you get out of the dray. I was hoping I'd get the big girl. She'd have been more of a help to me than a puny thing like you!" She let out a sigh and shrugged. "Oh, well, s'pose I'll have to make the best of it." She drew closer and stared into my face. "Do you have any cooking experience?"

I shook my head no.

The woman grasped my hands and inspected them, turning them over and back. "Doesn't look you've done much hard work at all," she sniffed, dropping them. "I don't know what Mistress Pitt expects me to do with you. I shall have to have a word with her. In the meantime, let's get you a uniform. Follow me!"

I fought back tears as I followed her up the narrow staircase and into a tiny room.

"This is where you'll be sleeping," the woman announced. "You'll find a dress, apron, and bonnet in the cupboard." She examined me closely. "Those clothes of yours have seen better days, especially that bonnet. Get changed and come downstairs." She turned to leave the room, then looked back. "My name is Mrs. Melrose. I'm the head cook and the kitchen is my domain. You'll be taking all your orders from me. Oh, and what's *your* name, miss?"

"Kate," I stuttered. But she was already gone!

I looked around the room. It held only a bed, a wardrobe, and a dresser on which stood a delft washbasin and water pitcher. The walls were bare and painted a dull mustard color. The only thing I welcomed was a small window, which I rushed over to open. I stood before it, filling my lungs with the humid air. Then I sank down on the bed, wondering how I was going to survive this ordeal. I had already signed the indenture agreement that bound me to Mrs. Pitt's employment until I reached the age of nineteen, over two years from now! There was a clause that said I could leave before that time if I got my employer's permission to marry. Otherwise, if I just ran away, the police would take me back to Hyde Park Barracks where, as a runaway, I would be unlikely to be rehired by another employer. And if I was, could I be sure I wouldn't end up in an even worse situation? Under the agreement I was to be paid nine pounds a year, going up to ten pounds when I turned seventeen. I thought of my wee brother, Christy, back at the workhouse and my promise to come back for him. How else was I going to get enough money to fulfill that promise?

I swallowed hard and stood up. Reluctantly, I changed into a gray dress and white apron I found in the wardrobe. I took off my bonnet, smoothed its crumpled, crimson ribbons, and placed it in the top drawer of the dresser. I picked up the plain white bonnet, tied it under my chin, took a deep breath, and went downstairs.

The rest of the day seemed like an eternity. I kept hoping Bridie would come and take me over to the main house, but there was no sign of her. Mrs. Melrose found tasks for me to do—sweeping the floors, taking out rubbish, and washing the dirty dishes the maids brought back from the midday meal, which had been served at the main house. When they sat down for their own midday dinner, I was directed to a chair at the end of the long table. Several male staff joined the women. I gathered from their conversation that the younger ones were grooms and a footman. An older, grim-faced man wearing a dark suit came in. He turned out to be the butler, and everyone shuffled to their feet in respect, chairs scraping on the brick floor. Then the door opened again, and I was surprised to see the dray driver. He stooped as he entered the doorway, pulled off his hat, and nodded at the others.

"Good day, Luke," said the butler. "I saw you planting new shrubs this morning."

Luke nodded. "Aye, wanted to get them in the ground before the rains come."

So, the dray driver was named Luke and was also the gardener! I remembered the crate full of plants he had collected that morning at the dock. Mrs. Melrose hadn't bothered to introduce me to the others, so I kept my head down, even though I was aware of the curious looks from the young grooms and the footman. I felt myself blush as I picked at the food on my plate.

It was late that night, after I'd washed the dishes from the evening meal, when Mrs. Melrose ordered me to bed.

"Six o'clock in the morning, sharp!" she announced. "I'll be needing you to collect the eggs. I'll rap on your door!"

I practically fled up the stairs to my room, anxious to be alone. I climbed on the bed and lay there, my heart pounding. I wanted to close my eyes and pray to God that I would be able to survive the next two years in this place, but God had let me down before. Over and over, He had given me glimmers of hope, only to douse them just as quickly. Even Nathaniel had deserted me. I realized that once again I was going to have to rely on myself alone. At least I was no longer responsible for anyone else, and that was something to be thankful for.

One morning, a few days after I'd arrived at Pitt House, Bridie peered through the doorway of the kitchen, wearing a white uniform and the bonnet from her travel box. I clapped my hand over my mouth. Bridie laughed.

"Ye look like you've seen a ghost. Sure 'tis only meself that's in it."

"Oh, Bridie, I know it's you. You're a sight for sore eyes."

Bridie waved her hand at me impatiently. "Come on," she said, "Luke is waiting to take us to Mass."

"Mass?" I said. "What day is it?"

"It's Sunday! Now get dressed. I'll meet you at the coach house."

I'd lost track of the days of the week, so it took me a few minutes to let Bridie's appearance sink in. Even if I had thought about Sunday, I would never have dared ask Mrs. Melrose about attending Mass. I rushed up the stairs, changed into a dress and retrieved my bonnet from the wardrobe.

"And where do you think you're going, miss?" Mrs. Melrose looked up at me as I came down the stairs.

"Bridie and I are going to Mass," I said timidly.

"Mass, is it? On whose say-so?"

"Mrs. Pitt," I lied. "She sent Bridie here to fetch me. She's outside waiting."

Mrs. Melrose stared at me, her face like stone. "Well, off with you," she said finally, "you'll hardly be missed for all the good you do around here! But don't be dawdling. I'll expect you back in an hour and this will count against your afternoon off!"

She turned her back and I rushed out the door before she could change her mind. I ran past the big house, expecting to see the dray waiting, but, instead, Bridie sat nice as you like up in an open carriage, one of the two I'd seen in the coach house when we'd arrived.

"You took your time," she said.

"Aye, well, the cook wasn't too happy about it."

Luke stood beside the carriage, dressed in a black suit and a top hat. In a fleeting moment I noticed how handsome he looked. He bowed and climbed up into the driver's seat, urged the small black horse on, and we rumbled down the gravel pathway and out onto the road. As soon as we passed Pitt House, Bridie and I collapsed in giggles in the back seat.

For the rest of the journey, we both talked at once. I described my days mopping floors, washing dishes, and collecting eggs. "And all this while nobody's said a word to me, except give me orders," I said.

"I'm sorry, Kate," she said, "I didn't know. Anyway, I've been in my own kind of hell. Mrs. Pitt's got my head annoyed with questions morning, noon, and night. She's got catalogues full of photos of china, furniture, rugs, and all the rest, and keeps asking me which ones I think would have been admired at Muckross House. She's mad to have the latest style in everything." Bridie paused and giggled. "I got so sick of it I picked out a china pattern I told her was all the rage with the rich, but I didn't tell her it was the rage with rich Irish Catholics, not Anglo-Irish Protestants!"

I fancied I heard Luke laughing in the front seat.

We lapsed into comfortable silence. It felt so good to have my friend beside me. I hadn't realized how much I'd missed her. What I *had* noticed was that her English was much better than I recalled. I wondered if maybe she'd been able to speak it all along—long before she boarded the *Sabine*. I smiled to myself—there was far more to Bridie than I'd ever given her credit for.

"Here we are," Luke announced as he brought the carriage to a halt in front of St. Patrick's Church in Charlotte Place.

Bridie and I climbed down and joined a crowd of people flowing through the wide, arched front door. The church was a long, narrow building, made of stone, with a beautiful stained-glass window above the front door, and two pointed stone pillars on either side. A cross topped the triangular roof. An organ was playing as we entered and made our way down the narrow aisle towards the altar. More stained-glass windows lined the walls on either side. I breathed in the smell of incense and let the music wash over me. As I knelt beside Bridie in a pew, I closed my eyes and was back in our wee chapel in Killeavy with my family and neighbors all around me.

I didn't take communion, because I hadn't fasted the night before, nor had I been to confession. I sat in the pew instead, and watched people going up to receive the host, and to my surprise, I recognized quite a few girls from the *Sabine*. I hoped I might see Patsy or Mary, but there was no sign of either. I turned back to look at the altar just in time to see Luke leaving the communion rail, his head bowed.

When the service was over, we spilled out onto the pavement and into the sunshine. I realized now that this had been the first taste of normalcy I'd experienced in many months. Bridie and I climbed back into the carriage, smiling at one another. We said little as we drove up past Hyde Park Barracks. I knew we were both thinking about Patsy. I was dying to go in and inquire about her, but it was not my place. Luke turned the carriage on to William Street and out towards Pitt House. As we drove, I saw, scattered amongst the "big houses," small, circular huts, crudely constructed of bark and tree saplings, with grass roofs. I hadn't noticed them before, and I wondered who lived in them until I saw a group of dark-skinned children playing outside one of the huts. Of course, I thought, these are the homes of Australia's native people, just like the fishermen we had seen at the harbor. Another reminder that the rich-poor divide was the same here in Australia as back in Ireland.

When we arrived back at Pitt House, Bridie leaned close to me.

"Keep your chin up," she said. "I'll be getting you out of that kitchen."

I smiled at her but I didn't believe her. Mrs. Melrose wouldn't let me go despite how much she criticized my work. She'd keep me there out of spite. I climbed down from the carriage and waved goodbye to Bridie, then trudged on heavy limbs towards the kitchen.

Three weeks went by before I was finally summoned to the main house. A maid came to tell Mrs. Melrose that the mistress wished to see me. I listened without looking up as Mrs. Melrose fumed and grumbled while the maid repeated her request. I finished washing a pot in the sink and wiped it dry. I had no idea why Mrs. Pitt wanted me. My hopes of moving into the main house had faded, even though each Sunday Bridie begged me to be patient. Now I feared I was about to be dismissed altogether. My hands began to tremble and I folded them under my apron. The maid led me out of the kitchen, Mrs. Melrose's voice echoing in my ears.

"Mind you don't dawdle. You've work to do!"

I followed the maid through the rear door and down a hallway towards the front of the house and into a large room.

"Wait here in the salon," she said.

I drew in a deep breath as I looked around me. Sunlight poured in through a glass-domed ceiling three stories high and shone down on a beautiful, curved staircase made of stone and wood. I felt as if I was standing in a great cathedral. Marble busts on pillars stood on either side of the front entrance while floor-to-ceiling sashed windows ran along one wall. I moved closer to a window and was captivated by the view of the harbor in the distance; I could even see the north and south "Heads" the *Sabine* had passed through on its way to docking at the wharf. I was so engrossed I forgot where I was and was startled by a voice from behind me.

"Miss Gilvarry?"

I swung around. Mrs. Pitt stood in the middle of the room. She looked so regal in a long blue gown, her black hair pinned up with sapphire ornaments, that I almost curtsied.

"Yes," I stuttered. "You sent for me, ma'am?"

She drifted towards a small, curved sofa of crimson velvet and sat down.

"Come closer!"

I did as she said and stood while she examined me from head to toe, my heart beating furiously.

"Well, you are much more presentable than your friend Miss O'Sullivan," she said. "I have been hesitant to allow her in the dining room when guests are present because of her some-what uncouth appearance."

I didn't dare answer her.

"You, on the other hand, look much more refined." She sighed. "Miss O'Sullivan has asked several times that you be moved out of the kitchens so that you can help her with her English. That was my original intention, but I decided to give you to Mrs. Melrose instead after her kitchen maid left without warning. I'd hoped I might get along without your help, but the girl lapses into Irish at the most inopportune times." She sighed daintily. "Anyway, I am giving a garden party, well, a picnic really, two Saturdays from now. Governor FitzRoy will be in attendance and I need everything to be perfect. While I am an experienced and, need I say, expert hostess, it has been difficult to keep up with the latest trends in England. I've decided that because of the im-portance of this event you should work with Miss O'Sullivan advising me on every detail. And I will expect you to be on hand as a serving maid when the party begins. If all goes well, then I shall make this arrangement permanent." She stood. "That will be all. I will send the maid to show you to your room, and a footman to bring your belongings from the kitchen house."

She swept out without another word. I stood, trying to assess what had just happened. I was to help plan a picnic with Bridie, which was to be a test. If Mrs. Pitt was satisfied, I would not have to return to the kitchen. If not . . . well, I didn't want to think about that. I also didn't want to think about the awful things Mrs. Pitt had said about Bridie. Deep down I felt I had let her down. I should have spoken up and defended her.

The following fortnight was a frenzy of activity at Pitt House. Mrs. Pitt had planned the menu, which we presented to Mrs. Melrose, who grumbled loudly as she read it.

"Cold roast chicken and beef, salted ham and corned beef, oysters and prawns, meat pies? Sounds to me like enough food to feed the entire British Navy!" She shook her head. "Bloody extravagance!"

Bridie and I were to look the drink menu over and make suggestions, in accordance with Mrs. Pitt's ongoing desire to outdo the best of English hostesses. She never mentioned a cost limit of any sort. Bridie suggested champagne, which I understood was imported from France at a very high cost. She had me explain to Mrs. Pitt that for her affair to stand out above others, that champagne was a must. Bridie also, surprisingly, turned out to have an excellent grasp of wines, and I crossed out many on Mrs. Pitt's list, substituting others that Bridie said were far superior, even though more expensive.

I became a little anxious. "Bridie, are you sure these are better? You're not playing another trick on Mrs. Pitt, are you? Because if you are, I'll be sent back to the kitchen, and you'll probably be sent back to the barracks."

She looked offended. "I know better than that," she snapped. "And I know what I'm doing. I was very friendly with the wine steward at Muckross House and he taught me a lot about wines. We're not all ignorant *culchies* down in Kerry!"

I didn't bring the subject up again.

Mrs. Melrose insisted on going to the markets herself to pick out the meats, fish and cheeses, but left it to Bridie and me to select the condiments—preserves, relishes, and chutneys—and table linens. We spent an afternoon exploring some of the finer shops in Sydney to make our selections. I felt as if I were in a dream. Never, even before the famine, had I seen such an array of condiments in colorful jars adorned with ribbons, decorative tins full of chocolates and delectable pastries on gleaming, silver stands. I marveled at how such a variety of goods could have been transported all the way from England and the European continent in ships like the *Sabine*. For once I agreed with Mrs. Melrose that it all seemed very excessive.

The day of this excursion, we were driven by a groomsman and I wondered where Luke was. When we returned, I saw him directing a group of rough-looking men on the front lawn grooming the landscape. So, he was not just a gardener, I thought, he was in charge. Bridie saw me staring at him. "Aye, himself is the head gardener," she said. She nodded towards the men. "Them's prisoners sent to help out for the big event."

I shrank back in alarm.

"Luke used to be one of them," Bridie continued, "but he got awarded his ticket-of-leave by Major Pitt a couple of years ago on the condition he stay on and take care of the gardens."

"How do you know so much?" I asked.

"Sure aren't all the maids up at the house in love with Mr. Luke Kinsella?" She laughed. "They watch everything he does. But he pays them no heed."

"What did he do to get transported?" I asked.

She shrugged. "I don't know. Could have been anything from

stealing bread to murder. Some of the maids say he was involved in an insurrection against the English but I think they're just making it up! Makes him seem more romantic. Stupid *eejits!*"

I gazed at Luke with interest. He was handsome enough, I supposed, tall and broad shouldered, with a full head of black hair, and dark blue eyes. I guessed him to be in his late twenties—about the same age as Nathaniel. My stomach dropped a little as a sudden image of Nathaniel floated in front of me. I shrugged and, with effort, drove the image away. There was no point pining for him now. He had gone back to England and that was that!

"Come on," I said to Bridie. "We'll be late for supper."

The morning of the picnic dawned as hot as every morning before it since landing in Sydney, and I could now safely predict a scorching afternoon. I smiled to myself, realizing that after all the surprises of the months before, there were now things I could count on. But, in the current circumstances, the realization brought little comfort. I sighed, thinking of the day ahead, picturing myself serving endless refreshments to picnic guests while a relentless sun beat down on me. For once, I envied Bridie, who'd been told by Mrs. Pitt that she must stay inside, out of view of the guests. I wanted to hide away too.

An army of additional servants had been hired for the event. Groomsmen and footmen, waiters and maids, began arriving early in the morning. From the attic window of my room, I saw Luke driving a dray filled with prisoners up the gravel path. Bridie had told me that prisoners were very useful as free labor for the rich people of Sydney. I assumed that Luke had handpicked this group, knowing which men would behave in a way that wouldn't alarm the genteel guests. I wondered if some of the extra maids might be female convicts. Well, at least Bridie and I were being paid, I thought.

The picnic was to be held on the terraced front lawns of Pitt House. Guests would be free to wander along brick pathways, through fruit orchards and stands of fig trees, to ornamental gardens featuring native and exotic plants. Besides the sweeping view of the harbor, the biggest attraction, I thought, would be the delightful stone grotto which stood nestled in the center of the garden, a cave-like structure almost hidden among ferns, ivy, and mosses. I saw it for the first time when I explored the front lawns with Bridie. It reminded both of us of the grottos dedicated to the Virgin Mary that dot the roadsides of Ireland. Benches faced a small pond and I had imagined myself sitting there for hours, lost in memories.

Now, I had no time for daydreaming. I dressed quickly and rushed downstairs. The Pitt House bustled with all the activity of a carnival. Footmen rushed in and out, carrying rugs that they spread on the front lawn, on which they placed cushions, folding chairs, wicker tables, and fabric sunshades. Maids followed to spread linen tablecloths and napkins on the tables, and set them with porcelain plates, teacups and saucers, as well as crystal wineglasses, and silver cutlery. A red-faced Mrs. Melrose, followed by a procession of kitchen maids, arrived carrying platters of beef, chicken and salted meats, to be kept in the coolness of the Pitt House until carved and served on crystal trays when guests arrived.

Bridie and I filled colored glass bowls with jams, chutneys, and fresh fruits, displayed pastries and cold pies on trays, and sliced Stilton and cheddar cheeses, which would be served with fresh-baked bread. When the wine and champagne were brought in, Bridie asked that one bottle of each vintage be opened so that she could taste it. The suppliers ignored her until Mrs. Pitt wafted into the room and ordered them to do as Bridie asked, then disappeared. I watched fascinated as Bridie held each sample up to the light, twirled the glass, sniffed the wine, sipped it, and spat it out into an empty bowl. The suppliers watched her in awe, anxious now for her decision. When she nodded approval, they smiled and went off to the cellar to unload their wares. The Pitt House butler stood by, watching Bridie with suspicion, but she ignored him. At length, grumbling under his breath, he left to oversee the deliveries of beer and spirits.

By noon, the garden had been set up and Mrs. Pitt walked about, inspecting each table, straightening a chair here, or a sunshade there, and returned to the main house without a word. When she appeared later in the main salon, she was wearing an elegant, white, lace-trimmed gown, white kid shoes, and a large white hat adorned with blue and pink flowers. Carrying a matching fan, she walked regally down the beautiful, curved staircase, and sat down on the red velvet curved sofa. Major Pitt, whom I had only caught glimpses of now and then, stood erect beside her, stern and stiff in his military uniform. Just then, a trio of violinists began to play, and the first guests arrived.

As the afternoon wore on, more and more guests arrived and I lost count after the first fifty. They arrived in all types of transport, from hansom cabs to open carriages, which they abandoned on the streets around Pitt House, leaving the prisoners to tend to the horses. They were elegantly dressed, and I wondered how they could stay out in the heat so long and still look crisp and fresh. With every hour that passed, I envied Bridie's reprieve from mingling with the guests outside. Perspiration clung to my body, my stockings stuck to my legs, and my hair, which I had piled up under my white bonnet, began to straggle down each side of my face and my forehead. Every time I entered the house to fetch another jug of lemonade or punch, I swallowed a glass of it, and after a while I didn't care who saw me.

Mrs. Pitt finally retreated with a small group of ladies to the indoor salon, where they sipped champagne and gossiped. She smiled, obviously enjoying the compliments she was receiving— the champagne, and the wine, had been a great success and I hoped that there was nothing left to go wrong.

I had taken refuge from the heat in the empty dining room of the Pitt House when four men entered and sat down at the table. Major Pitt spotted me and clicked his fingers.

"Whiskey," he commanded, "and a platter of cold chicken."

I nodded. "Right away, sir."

I recognized the governor immediately. There'd been images of him hanging on the wall at Hyde Park Barracks and his portrait took pride of place above the mantel in the dining room of Pitt House itself. Governor FitzRoy was a tall, handsome man of about fifty. He had dark wavy hair, lush graying whiskers, and dark eyebrows. He was dressed in military uniform, dark blue with a red collar, his chest glittering with medals. When he walked in beside Major Pitt, I noticed he had a slight limp. When he first arrived, he was alone, and I'd wondered about his wife. Bridie whispered that she'd died in a coach accident a few years earlier and he'd been driving. That explained, I thought, the fact that since his arrival he'd been surrounded by elegant young women—and some not so young. The third man was white haired and wore a black coat with a white linen clergy collar. His wife was one of the ladies sitting with Mrs. Pitt in the salon. The fourth man was stockily built and fashionably dressed. He had red, well-fed cheeks, and an air of self-assurance even in the company of such important men.

I brought their food and drinks as quickly as I could, so as not to keep them waiting. They were already engrossed in conversation when I returned, puffing on their cigars between words. I set the platter of chicken in the middle of the table, along with four glasses and a decanter of whiskey. They paid no attention to me, whatsoever. I might as well have been invisible as they kept on talking.

"This business of the Irish girls is beginning to be a problem," said the governor. "I wish I hadn't allowed Earl Grey to talk me into it."

"It wasn't just your decision, Charles," said Major Pitt, "the English Parliament and our own authorities had to accept it."

"Well, that was all well and good until they found out the sort of girls they were getting from Ireland," said the clergyman. "A far cry from fresh-faced Protestant English and Scottish girls. No, they've sent us the dregs of the workhouses, and mark my words if they are let stay, and marry local men, their Papist ways will poison our population."

I fought to stop my hand from trembling as I was pouring out the whiskey. I felt as if I had been violently slapped. They were talking about us—the orphans—about me! I had the same sick feeling I'd had when I read the newspaper article in Nathaniel's cabin on the ship—and the same tears began to erupt.

"I think, Reverend Lang, that your fear of Papism is somewhat exaggerated, but we have definite evidence of how ill-suited these girls are. Look at the crowd that arrived on the *Earl Grey* and the *Roman Emperor*. Not a well-trained servant among them," said the stocky man.

The clergyman gave a dismissive laugh. "Exaggerated or not, Mr. Martin, even *you* published an article in the *Herald* calling them a fraud upon the colonists and likely to badly affect our community's social and moral interests."

I froze where I stood. Those very words were imprinted on my brain—and the person who wrote them, this Mr. Martin, was sitting within yards of me. My whole body started to shake. I knew I should run, but I could not bring my legs to move. I stood there in silence for a while longer.

"The problem is that it is our colony's funds that are subsidizing this scheme," the governor said.

"Indeed," Major Pitt spoke up, "and what are we getting for it? Certainly not the good domestic help we'd been promised. We were sold a pig in a poke!"

I could stand it no more. I hurried out of the room into the hallway. But I could go no further. There was no one about, so I loitered there, even though part of me didn't want to hear another word. The men had all begun to speak at once. Only snatches of the conversation registered with me.

"Competent domestic help—bah. Their knowledge of household duties barely reaches to distinguishing the inside from the outside of a potato!"

This remark was met with laughter.

"And their only intellectual exercise has been trotting across a bog to fetch back a runaway pig!"

The laughter grew louder.

"Well, let's hope those who are here begin marrying our prisoners right away. After all, bringing them here as domestic servants was only part of the plan—our real plan, as you know, was to civilize those brutes of prisoners so that the colony can get on with building settlements."

"Just so," someone murmured, "just so!"

I was about to rush back into the room, when the stocky man, Mr. Martin from the *Herald*, came bursting out.

"Which way to the privy?" he demanded.

Startled, I pointed it out. Then without even thinking, I followed him outside into the darkness, and waited, my heart thumping. When he emerged, I stepped in front of him, blocking his path.

"How dare you?" I shouted. "How could you say such things? You don't know anything about us—about me! We don't deserve it. We didn't ask to come here, but it was you who invited us and promised us the moon! And when we arrive here after months on a ship, locked up every night in a filthy hold, this is how we're greeted? Criticized, insulted, ridiculed, and . . . and then we're to be thrown to the convicts, like Christians to the lions!"

He stared at me, his mouth open in disbelief. "You had a choice, young lady," he said, as he tried to push past me.

I blocked his way again. "Yes, we had a choice," I shot back, my voice rising, "the choice to stay in Ireland and starve!"

Martin came closer. "I'll have you know I was born in Ireland, miss. I have not been unsympathetic to those suffering in the famine."

"Then you're an even bigger hypocrite than I thought!"

I was aware of people gathering around us but I was beyond caring. My throat ached from the effort of shouting and my shoulders heaved as I fought for breath. Martin pushed roughly past me. But I was not finished.

"Yes, I used to be able to tell the inside of a potato from the outside," I called after him. "We were all well acquainted with it since it was the only crop we were ever allowed to eat, the crop that kept us alive." I took a deep breath. "My name is Kate Gilvarry, and I dare you to print what I've said!"

But Martin had already disappeared inside the main house.

As I stood trembling in the dusk, I felt a hand on my arm. I turned and saw Luke.

"Come away, now, Kate," he said.

Despite the sultry heat of the evening, I began to shiver as I sat beside Luke on the small bench beside the grotto. He took off his jacket and placed it around my shoulders. We'd walked away from the Pitt House in silence, down the now empty brick terraces, and into the center of the garden where the grotto stood. I was aware of stares from those who'd witnessed the scene with Mr. Martin—maids, footmen, and a handful of guests—but I kept my head down. By the time we reached the grotto, the last guests had gone, leaving servants to clear away the remnants of the day's festivities.

By now, shame had replaced my anger. What had I done? How had I dared to confront the reporter from the *Sydney Morning Herald* in such a manner—shouting at him like a fishwife in front of everyone in sight? Surely I had taken leave of my senses. I had gone mad! I didn't even remember exactly what I had said, just the blazing anger I had felt upon hearing what those men were saying about me—about us! But beyond their words, it was their laughter that had ignited an uncontrollable rage that I could not contain. It had spilled out of me, erupting in all directions, blinding me to reason or consequences.

Reality finally crept into my mind. I would, at best, be sent back to Hyde Park Barracks. At worst, I might be dragged before a magistrate for disorderly conduct. I would forfeit my pay. I would be unlikely to find another indenture. And what if Mr. Martin decided to publish the incident in his newspaper along with my name for everyone to read? I began to sweat. What if Nathaniel were to read it? What if all the girls from the *Sabine* were told of it? What if word even got back to Matron O'Hare in Ireland who I'd promised that I'd be a credit to the Newry Workhouse? I put my head in my hands and began to sob.

I felt Luke's arm around my shoulders, but his presence brought me little comfort. When I finally sat up straight, I looked at him in the moonlight.

"Thank you," I said.

He nodded.

Just then, Bridie arrived. "I thought I'd find you here," she said. "I'm after hearing from the maids all about what you did."

"What shall I do, Bridie?" I said, my voice hoarse. "Where will I go?"

Bridie was calm as always. She reached over to pull me to my feet. "Well, I can't answer where you're going to end up," she said, "but for now you're coming with me up to the house."

I stiffened. "No! I can't go back there. Mrs. Pitt . . ."

"Herself is fast asleep in her bed and so is everybody else. Come on now, Kate."

She nodded to Luke, and taking me by the arm steered me up to the main house. As Bridie had said, there was no one about. She led me up the back stairs to the attic and saw me into my room. "Go on with you now," she said, "get a good night's sleep."

In a daze I closed the door and stood for a moment. Then I removed my uniform and bonnet and put them in the wardrobe. I pulled out my Sunday dress and lifted my old bonnet with the crimson ribbons out of the dresser and set them on the bed. I picked up my other belongings and put them in the travel box and closed the lid. Then I sat down on the bed and waited for the morning.

Mrs. Pitt sat in her usual place on the red velvet curved sofa in the salon. She stared at me in silence while I stood trembling before her.

"From your lack of uniform, I see you have anticipated that you will be leaving your indenture at Pitt House," she said finally.

"Yes, ma'am," I murmured, smoothing my old dress.

"You recognize, then, that your disgraceful actions of last evening warrant your being dismissed from my service? In fact, your abominable behavior deserves more than dismissal. It deserves that you be charged with the crime of disorderly conduct."

"Yes, ma'am," I said, again.

She lapsed back into silence but held me in her cold stare. I wished she would just dismiss me and get matters over with. I was almost relieved when she began to speak again, this time directing a torrent of anger towards me.

"How dare you accost Mr. Martin, editor of Sydney's most prominent newspaper, in such a manner? Do you have no idea of how inferior your place is in our society? Do you have so little regard for Major Pitt and me, who have extended our generosity to you and Miss O'Sullivan, that you disgrace us by acting like a guttersnipe?"

I wanted to say that Bridie had nothing to do with my behavior, but I didn't dare interrupt her.

"As a girl with a Protestant mother, I had expected more from you. But you have turned out to be just as ill-bred as all the rest!" She sighed heavily. "I value my reputation above all else and you, Miss Gilvarry, almost destroyed it. Mr. Martin would have been justified in reporting the entire incident in the *Herald*, which would have caused my husband and me to be the object of gossip all over Sydney! As it is, dear Mr. Martin has been gracious enough to spare us such humiliation by agreeing to withhold any mention of the incident."

"I'm sorry, Mrs. Pitt. I didn't mean to—"

She waved her hand at me impatiently. "I do not wish to hear what you have to say, girl. I have talked the matter over with Major Pitt and we have decided not to send you back to Hyde Park Barracks. Doing so would require a hearing before the immigration authorities, and such proceedings would be required to be published in the newspapers for all of Sydney to read. Your scandalous behavior could well be seen by others as a weakness in our judgment. And, as I cannot bear to see my dear husband humiliated in such a way, I have agreed to keep you here at Pitt House! But . . ."

She paused, and my heart began to thump in my chest.

"But you will return to the kitchen under Mrs. Melrose's strict supervision. You will be permitted to leave the grounds of this house only on Sunday mornings for worship when you will be in Miss O'Sullivan's charge. You will never set foot in Pitt House again, nor will you talk to any of the Pitt House staff whom you may encounter in the kitchen or on our grounds." She rose abruptly. "Now get out of my house, I never want to lay eyes on you again!"

She rose and walked out of the room. I held back tears as I watched her go. I had made my bed, I thought, and now I must lie in it. Mrs. Pitt, no matter her reasons, had handed me a reprieve. Swallowing hard, I turned and left the beautiful house where I no longer belonged.

As I crossed towards the kitchen outbuilding, Bridie strode towards me.

"Well?" she said. "Are you staying or going?"

I choked the words out. "I'm staying, but back in the kitchen with Mrs. Melrose. And I'm only allowed out to go to Mass. And I'm not to talk to you or any of the other staff. And I'm never to set foot inside the main house again."

"Come on, then," said Bridie, grinning. "Luke's waiting to take us to Mass. You can pray to God to forgive your sins and thank Him for saving your arse!"

Mrs. Melrose took great pleasure in gloating over my downfall.

"I should have seen it coming. The quiet ones are always the worst, so they say—still waters run deep! If I were Mrs. Pitt, I'd have dragged you before a magistrate and insisted you be sent back to Ireland. Mark my words, from what I hear, there's plenty of them orphans out there just like you who don't know their place! I'm not happy she's pawned you off on me, but I suppose I'll have to make the best of it. I intend to make you serve the penance you deserve, miss."

Good to her word, she gave me the dirtiest jobs she could think of—cleaning out the pig pens, emptying chamber pots, including those of the other kitchen maids, and cleaning out the ashes from the kitchen ovens. In addition, I attended to my "day duties." I scrubbed and swept the floors; washed the dishes, pots and pans; scraped the leftovers from all the meals into a bucket, and took them out to feed the animals. I rose each day before dawn and fell into bed at midnight. I went about it all in a daze, numb to the smells and filth that surrounded me. It was my penance, as Mrs. Melrose had said, and I accepted it.

The only people who spoke to me in those months were Bridie and Luke. Bridie came every Sunday to collect me and we rode with Luke in the carriage down to St. Patrick's Church and back. Luke had been instructed by Mrs. Pitt to take no detours of any kind. Nevertheless, I spent each day of the week yearning for Sunday, longing for the outing, no matter how brief, that allowed me to keep my sanity. Bridie kept the conversation lively, sharing gossip from the main house, and reporting on Mrs. Pitt's continued efforts to impress the good people of Sydney. She never mentioned the incident with Mr. Martin, and for that I was grateful. One Sunday, however, not long after the picnic, I was leaving the church after Mass when I was surrounded by a group of girls, all of whom I recognized from the *Sabine*.

"We heard what you did, Kate," whispered one.

"I wish I'd had the nerve to do what you did," said another.

Bridie stepped in front of me. "How did yez hear about that?" she demanded.

"Was it in the newspaper?" I said, anxiety filling me.

"No," said the first girl. "One of our girls heard her employer, who was at the picnic, talking about it, and she told me, and I told others, and so the word got around. You're a real hero standing up for us like that!"

"Aye, particularly since hardly a day goes by down here in the city when we're not cursed at by every class of people, some of them very respectable looking," said another. "Every time another ship comes in with orphans the aggravation gets worse, so it does."

I didn't know what to say to them. All I had felt was guilt and shame over my outburst, but now—well, now I allowed the tiniest sense of pride to lodge in my heart.

March and April came and went. Everyone around the dinner table in the kitchen began talking about the scarcity of rain. Apparently, 1849 was turning out to be an unusually dry year and Luke appeared quite concerned about it.

"If we don't get good rains in May and June, we're in for a terrible drought," he said one day at dinner. "I'm afraid we'll lose a lot of our plants and, for the farmers in the Outback, there'll be no water for the crops or for cattle or sheep to drink, and feed will be scarce."

Everyone nodded. The younger ones seemed less concerned, but the elderly butler agreed with Luke.

"I remember the last drought twenty years ago, which dried up Lake George and caused the Darling River to stop flowing," he said. "We lost so many crops and livestock we were afraid we were all going to starve."

I said nothing, as usual, but my mind shot back to Ireland and to the famine, and a sudden melancholy filled me. Then another thought came. Perhaps the people in this strange country would finally realize how the Irish had suffered. Perhaps that might ease the resentment towards us.

My seventeenth birthday came and went unnoticed. I thought back to my last birthday at the workhouse when Mary and the others had brought me a special card and sung to me. Was that only one year ago? It seemed like a lifetime. The one good thing it meant was that my wages would increase from nine to ten pounds a year. I had spent almost no money since my arrival at the Pitt House. I was saving it all towards my passage back to Ireland when my indenture ended in two years. I had promised Christy I would come back for him, and nothing that I'd experienced so far in Australia had changed my mind. I had written twice to Matron O'Hare, asking how Christy was, but had received no reply. Still, I buried any doubts I had about his well-being. Every now and then my thoughts turned to Nathaniel. I'd had no word from him since he left, and although he had asked me to write to him, I hadn't done so. What would be the use?

In June the heavy rains finally came, and everyone's spirits rose, including my own. I welcomed the cool, humid air after the scorching months of summer and the dry autumn. It started as a trickle—a few showers here and there, but one Sunday afternoon after returning from Mass, I was sitting on the bench near the grotto when the heavens opened and rain poured down in wave after wave, flooding the ground and soaking my clothes. I jumped up and ran towards the kitchen building, my head down, before colliding with Luke, who was running towards me.

"Come with me," he shouted, water teeming down his face. "You'll catch your death out here."

He took my arm and pulled me forward. I didn't have time to think about where he was taking me until I found myself inside the gardener's hut. "You can wait here until it slackens," he said. "I'll make some tea."

It took me a while to catch my breath.

"I'm not supposed to be here," I said at last. "I'm not even allowed to talk to you, much less be in your hut."

He turned around from filling a kettle and laughed aloud. "Well, it's your choice, Kate. Follow the rules and risk falling face down in the mud and drowning before you even reach the kitchen, or break them by staying here with me. And I assure you that you have no reason to be afraid of me."

I felt my cheeks redden. "I didn't mean it that way," I said.

I watched him as he made the tea, almost smiling when I saw the way he warmed the teapot before adding the tea leaves, the way Ma used to do. It was as if he read my mind. "My ma taught me to do it this way," he said.

He brought me a cup of steaming tea and we sat down at a wee table opposite each other. I noticed traces of soil under his fingernails, which reminded me of Da's when he'd been out planting crops. I warmed my hands on the cup and looked around the small room. Besides a sofa and table, there were two chairs, a dresser, and in the far corner a small cot. A wooden shelf ran along one wall that held an assortment of books, and below it stood a desk, with a pot of ink, a pen, and a leather-bound notebook. An archway at one end of the room led into a glassed-in shed where I could see a row of garden pots with plants at various stages of growth. An earthy, musty smell filled the room, laced with the smell of soil and the faint fragrance of blooming plants. It was not an unpleasant odor, but, rather, an oddly comforting one, as the wind whistled outside. A large window at the other end of the room looked out onto a grove of trees and, in the distance, the grotto. I blushed thinking he must have seen me sitting at the grotto when the rain started and had come out to rescue me.

"I saw you from my window," he said, confirming my thoughts. "In fact, I see you there often after we've been to Mass on Sundays."

"It's my favorite place," I said. "Mrs. Melrose lets me have an hour to myself on Sunday and it's where I always come."

"You're supposed to have an entire afternoon off once a week," he said.

I nodded. "Well, Mrs. Melrose is still punishing me on account of my behavior at the picnic. She counts my Sunday mornings at Mass against my time off and then grants me the extra hour out of what she calls 'the goodness of her heart.'"

He smiled. "I didn't think she had a heart!"

I shrugged. "I don't mind. I'm lucky to still be employed here and earning wages. I could have been dismissed altogether, or worse, arrested by the magistrates."

"Still, it must be hard for you," he said, "a young girl like you confined to this place, forbidden to talk to anybody."

I didn't answer. Instead, I looked up at the shelf. "You have a lot of books," I said, changing the subject.

"I've always been a reader."

"And a writer too, I see," I said, nodding towards the journal on the desk.

"Well, I'm hardly a writer now," he said, looking down at the soil behind his nails, "but I was at one time."

I waited for him to say more, but he sipped his tea in silence. The rain had increased to the point where I could no longer see through the window. What had been a sunny morning had turned gray and ominous. Soon, Mrs. Melrose would become aware of my absence. Would she send someone to look for me? I stood up suddenly.

"I have to go!" I said. "Mrs. Melrose will be looking for me."

Luke didn't rise from the table. "Sit down, Kate," he said calmly, "you're not going anywhere until this rain has stopped. When it does, I shall escort you up to the kitchen and explain to her that I found you lying face down in the mud beside the pond."

"She won't believe you!" I said.

"Maybe not, but how much more can she punish you than she's already doing?"

I sat down again. "Alright, I'll stay," I said, "but first you have to tell me what crime you committed."

He looked startled but laughed aloud. "Well, you're not trapped in the company of a murderer! I was arrested for inciting rebellion by writing an anti-British article in a pamphlet that found its way into the wrong hands. I was found guilty of treason and transported on the last ship to Sydney in 1840." He paused. "At least I wasn't sent to Tasmania, where most of the rebels were sent. I was assigned to a convict group working for Major Pitt while he was having this house built. He's a keen botanist—did you know that? Anyway, my gift for gardening impressed him and he offered me a ticket-of-leave—a release from my sentence—if I would come to work for him and give him ten years of service. I agreed, of course."

I listened with fascination. There was so much I had not guessed about him. An Irish rebel? No wonder the maids at Pitt House were so taken with him.

"So you will be free to leave next year," I said, "but then what will you do? Go back to Ireland?"

He gave a wan smile. "I love Ireland, and I have missed it a great deal, but"—he paused—"Australia is my home now, and my future. I have already approached Major Pitt about securing a plot of land—"

"A squatter?" I interrupted. "Our sub-matron on the ship, Phoebe, told us her husband had been granted squatter's rights on some land and they plan to run a farm."

He smiled. "Yes, a squatter! I want to grow crops, and maybe raise a few cattle, and, of course, I'll plant some flowers."

He looked like a boy, excited and hopeful.

I couldn't help but smile too. "It sounds wonderful," I said. "I wish you luck."

I had been so caught up in his story that I hadn't noticed the rain had stopped. I stood up. "Well, I suppose I'd better go and face Mrs. Melrose," I said.

He stood, bowed, and offered his arm. "May I escort you, my lady?" He laughed.

"You may," I said.

The June rains reduced to a trickle by the end of the month, bringing renewed fears of a drought. Mrs. Melrose had grudgingly accepted Luke's explanation for my absence but muttered that she would be keeping a closer eye on me. I didn't dare acknowledge him during mealtimes in the kitchen and, as if understanding, he never spoke to me. He did, however, begin to join more readily in the conversation with Bridie and me on Sundays on our way to and from Mass. He turned out to have an excellent sense of humor—an eye for the comical in everyday events—which added greatly to my enjoyment of those weekly excursions.

Each Sunday I was warmly welcomed outside the church by the girls from the *Sabine*, who hadn't forgotten the account of the tongue-lashing I had given Mr. Martin from the *Herald*. In fact, the story seemed to have taken on a life of its own—exaggerated far beyond reality. One Sunday, however, I noticed a new girl in their midst—one of the *Earl Grey* girls I had met at Hyde Park Barracks. I rushed towards her, anxious to hear how she and her friend were doing. She had finally been matched for indenture as a nanny, she told me, looking after several children while the mother went out to work.

"The missus has her own business making dresses and hats over on Pitt Street," the girl said, smiling. "She took on my friend, as well, to help her with the business. She's a lovely woman, so she is."

I was happy to hear her good news, but I worried that she hadn't mentioned Patsy.

"And what about Patsy?" I finally asked.

The girl's smile disappeared. "She wasn't as lucky as us," she began.

I waited, my heart beginning to thump.

"She's living beyond on Pitt Street," she said finally. "I came across her one day when I was taking the children over to visit their ma's shop. I recognized her by her wild red hair."

"And?" I said.

"Well, she never got an indenture and she finally ran away from Hyde Park. She's living at a place down near the corner of Pitt Street and King Street." The girl looked down at the ground. "She's living at what they call a 'brothel.' She crossed the street when she saw me. She didn't want to talk to me. I can't blame her, I suppose."

Before I could ask her for more details, she hurried inside the church. Bridie, who had stood by in silence during the conversation, and I looked at each other and it was clear we had reached a mutual understanding. After Mass, we were going to tell Luke to take us to the corner of Pitt and King Streets. We were going to find Patsy.

Luke didn't put up any protest when we announced our intention. It was a cool, dry August morning and the traffic on Pitt Street was relatively light. I sat gazing out at the rows of shops of all kinds—greengrocers, coffeehouses, drapers, milliners, paperhangers, florists, as well as a variety of pubs and hotels. But all the time my heart was beating loudly. As we approached the corner of King Street, Luke pulled the carriage over to the side and stopped.

"You should get out here," he said. "I would start over there if I were you," he went on, pointing to a house squeezed between two taverns. As Bridie and I climbed down I wondered how he'd known which building to visit. All we had told him was that we were going to find our friend Patsy, and he obviously had put two and two together. It occurred to me then that as a single man he may well be acquainted with this part of town.

Bridie and I looked at each other. "Well, no point standing here like two *eejits*," she announced, approaching the house and banging the brass knocker on the front door. There was no answer. Bridie banged the knocker again, this time more loudly. We waited and were almost ready to turn away when we heard bolts being pulled back and the door creaked open a few inches. A red-faced older woman wearing a crumpled bonnet poked her head around the door and peered at us.

"What do you want?" she rasped. "If youse are collecting for charity you came to the wrong place!"

Her Belfast accent was unmistakable.

"We're looking for Patricia Riley," I said.

"Nobody here by that name!" she snapped and began to close the door.

"Wait," I shouted, "she might go by Patsy Toner."

"She's asleep. Come back another time!"

I was about to plead with the woman, when Bridie stepped forward and held out some coins. "We can make it worth your while to wake her up!" she said.

The old woman sniffed, then snatched the money out of Bridie's hand. "Come in," she said. "Wait here!"

We followed her into the house and shut the door behind us. Stale smells of beer and cigar smoke filled the air. We stood in the hallway and watched the woman as she awkwardly climbed the creaking stairs, holding on to the paint-chipped banister. Gilt-framed pictures of scantily clad women lining the staircase wall rose with her as she ascended. The gaudy red wall-coverings had peeled in places, exposing strips of old yellowed brick beneath.

I tried to take a deep breath but began to cough instead from the dust that seemed to cover every surface. All I wanted to do was turn and run outside, away from this dreadful place. But I forced myself to stand my ground.

We heard the woman knocking on a door up on the landing, and muffled sounds from inside the room. The woman began to thump on the door and shout.

"Come down now, you hear me? There's two women here looking for you. They're after asking for you by name."

The door opened and Patsy's familiar voice drifted down the stairs.

"Get out of my sight, you oul' witch! Can a body not get some rest on a Sunday morning? And me after being up the whole night diddling with every class of toe rag who wandered in off the street!"

"You'll go down and see them, Patsy Toner, and that's an order!"

Patsy said something I couldn't make out, then suddenly appeared, leaning over the landing banister. Bridie and I stared up at her. She wore an old shift, like the ones we'd all been given in our travel boxes, and her red hair had grown long and even wilder than before. Her face was thinner than I remembered and her skin was the same yellowish color as the exposed brick on the walls. But as she came down the stairs and stood in front of us, hands on her hips, it was her green eyes that alarmed me the most. Even though now they blazed with anger, I could still see a haunted look behind them.

"Well, if it isn't the two busybodies come to gloat," she said. "Well, you've seen me now so you can go back and report that I'm living like a queen in a palace at the minute."

"No, Patsy," I began, "we didn't come to gloat. We came to . . ."

"To save me, is it?"

"We just wanted to see if you were alright," said Bridie, her normally calm voice shaky.

"Well, you've seen me now, alive and kicking. So be on your way."

She turned and began climbing the stairs but stopped about halfway up and looked back. "I hear you gave that newspaper feller a thorough tongue-lashing," she said. "I didn't think you, the wee doctor's pet, had it in you." She laughed aloud. "But keep up that sort of thing and you'll find yourself living in this palace with the likes of me!"

"How did you hear?" I asked, startled.

"Sure you'd be surprised at how many things my customers tell me when they're lying beside me all contented. There's plenty of them comes over from Pitt House. Isn't that right, Sadie?" she called to the old woman who was leaning over the banister taking in every word.

"That's right," called Sadie, "footmen, butlers, gardeners!"

I felt as if I was going to vomit. I backed up towards the door. "I'll be going now, Patsy," I called up to her, "but I promise I'll be back."

Patsy didn't answer. Her door slammed shut. I grabbed Bridie's arm and rushed her out of the house and up the street to where Luke was waiting. He said nothing as we climbed into the carriage. Bridie and I were silent, too, as we drove back to Pitt House, each of us lost in our own thoughts.

After my visit to Patsy, I could hardly get her out of my mind. How could she bear to live in that awful place? How could she bear to lower herself to satisfy the whims of all those men? Each time I thought about it I became physically ill. I knew that Patsy had lived a hard life back in Newry but, much as she joked and exaggerated about how wild she was, it never occurred to me that she was involved in prostitution. I might have believed it of Sheila and Lizzie—they always seemed rougher and bolder—but Patsy? Maybe I'd just been too naïve back then. No matter, now I preferred to believe only what I saw with my own eyes. And I'd seen how Patsy was living. And I knew the truth was that her unlucky start in the world had followed her all the way to Australia.

I found myself wondering if my life as a scullery maid was all that *I* deserved. It took everything in me not to let that belief take hold. It would be so easy for it to happen to someone like me, or the other orphans, in this strange, unwelcoming place. Mrs. Melrose was fond of drilling into me that I should be grateful for everything I had—a roof over my head, food in my belly, and a steady wage. And I was indeed grateful for those physical comforts, but it wasn't my body that was grieving—it was my spirit.

As the weeks went by, I went back to spending my free hour on Sundays sitting at the grotto. I had found my dog-eared diary at the bottom of my travel box and begun to write in it again—not the dates and days of the week as I had done aboard the *Sabine*—but rambling, uneasy thoughts about the future. Nathaniel was still on my mind and visited me in dreams from which I always woke filled with sadness. My earlier homesickness returned. I missed Ireland and my family, especially Ma. I realized, too, that Christy's and Paddy's faces were slipping out of my memory, becoming fuzzy and unformed, and that frightened me.

I knew I needed the hope of a happy future to maintain my sanity, and so I set my imagination free and wrote down my girlish fantasies about Nathaniel, my brothers, and Ireland, and clung to them all as truth.

Every now and then Luke would come and sit with me at the grotto. He smiled when he saw me writing in my diary but he never inquired about it. He obviously respected my privacy and I admired him for that. I realized that I had begun to see him differently after our visit to Patsy. I became more convinced that he was familiar with that brothel, Sadie, and, who knows, maybe with Patsy, too. I saw him as more than a gardener, a coach driver, or a convict—I saw him as a man. Yes, a kind and reliable man, but also a mature man with needs and desires that I couldn't begin to guess at. It made me curious.

"Tell me about your childhood," I asked him one day.

He looked surprised that I had asked the question. In truth I had surprised myself.

"Not much to tell," he said. "It was happy." He hesitated, but realized I was looking for more. "My father was a barrister and my mother a teacher. I had no brothers or sisters and I grew up in the Wicklow Mountains, near Dublin. I was encouraged to follow my father into the law but even as a child my passion was the land." He smiled as if remembering. "I had my own wee patch at the bottom of our property and I grew plants and flowers of all sorts."

"But you also wrote pamphlets about rebellion," I said.

He sighed. "Yes. My parents were both active in movements for Irish independence. Writing the pamphlets is what landed me here in this penal colony." He paused, then smiled. "But as I told you, I already have my ticket-of-leave and my contract with Major Pitt expires next year. Then I'll be free."

"Yes," I said. "I remember."

We sat in silence, and another question, bolder than the last, slipped out of me totally against my will.

"Were you ever in love?"

I had truly startled him. His mouth flew open in surprise.

"I'm sorry," I said hurriedly, "I had no right to ask you that."

"No, you didn't, but I shall answer it anyway." He drew a deep breath. "Yes, I fell in love with a young lady named Maeve."

"Oh, that was my wee sister's name," I said. "What happened to her?"

"I married her," he said.

His words hit me like a blow to my chest. A thousand thoughts swam through my mind. "So, is she still in Ireland? Will she come here like Phoebe did?" I finally blurted out.

He bowed his head and said nothing. I waited in silence. "I don't rightly know what happened to her. She was supposed to join me here over a year ago but she never arrived. I waited for her ship to dock, but she was nowhere to be found. She was listed as a passenger but no one could tell me if she ever made the journey. Major Pitt made inquiries here and in England but to no avail. In the end the authorities concluded that she was lost at sea."

"Drowned?" I breathed. "How can you be sure?"

"It wasn't unusual for passengers to die on the long voyages from England to Australia. There were many diseases aboard the ships, including the one I sailed on. But I also heard that the ship captains and ship surgeons often lied about the number of deaths recorded on the journey by insisting the passenger never sailed, or by striking the passenger's name from the ship's log altogether. You see, their pay was lowered based on the number of deaths. I've also talked to other men—er, convicts—whose families never arrived."

He turned away from me. "Or maybe she just changed her mind about coming to Australia," he said.

He stood up then and gazed out towards the pond in the distance. It was clear the conversation was over. Should I just slip silently away, I wondered? Instead, I walked closer to him and whispered, "I'm sorry for your loss, Luke."

There was nothing more to say. I left him there and trudged up the hill to the kitchen, slipped past Mrs. Melrose and went up to my room.

God bless Bridie. It was her calmness and good humor that got me through those days. I'd begun to think of her as a sister—part of our family of orphans who had sailed on the *Sabine*. On Sundays, she kept me laughing with accounts of the goings-on at Pitt House—which maid and footman had been caught carrying on in the back corridor; the fit Mrs. Pitt had thrown when a pig escaped into the house, standing up on the red velvet sofa with her skirts pulled up to her knees, while Bridie chased the animal out; and the nonstop talk of privies.

"Privies?" I said, "but why?"

"Oh, haven't you heard," she said, "there's a plan by the water department to stop burying the—er—waste in holes in the ground like they do now, and sending it instead through pipes down into the harbor! It's the talk of the town, so it is. They've called for a vote on it. Major Pitt is against it because he thinks it will cost too much money—he's tightfisted, you know—I swear with him every penny's a prisoner!"

"Except when it comes to his wife's social events," I said, remembering the extravagant picnic earlier in the year.

"And when it comes to him buying exotic trees and plants from all over the world," put in Luke.

"Aye, that's been true," agreed Bridie, "but he's after the missus now to pull in her horns and she's mad as a wet rooster about it."

"Are they running out of money?" I asked.

Bridie shrugged. "Don't know," she said, "and I don't care as long as I get me wages every month."

We lapsed into silence for the rest of the journey.

Our Sunday outings had become predictable. We rode to Mass with Luke, chatted with the orphans we knew and, every few weeks, returned to the brothel at Pitt and King Streets looking for Patsy, to give her a little money. But time after time she refused to see us and we grew tired of bribing Sadie to force her out of her room, nor could we trust her to give Patsy the money we brought for her. It was clear Patsy no longer wanted us in her life and so, with sad hearts, we ended our visits.

One Sunday, when we returned from Mass, I saw a hansom cab waiting on the street outside the Pitt House. A burly, well-dressed man with a top hat climbed out of the carriage as we pulled into the gravel drive, and waved at us.

"You can stop here, Luke," said Bridie, waving back.

Luke did as she said, and she climbed down and walked towards the man. "I'll see yez next Sunday," she called over her shoulder.

Luke and I both turned to watch her. The man smiled and bowed as he removed his hat, took Bridie's hand and kissed it, then led her to the cab. He was shorter than Bridie by a foot, and even from this distance I could see that he was much older.

"Who's that?" I said to Luke.

He shook his head. "I've no idea. But I'd say our Bridie's a dark horse!"

I was so consumed with curiosity I didn't think I would get through the week. Every time I tried to put the incident out of my mind another thought burst into my head. Was that man a relation of Bridie's that she hadn't mentioned to us? Maybe he had just arrived out of the blue and surprised her. He was obviously well-to-do, based on his clothes and his refined manners. Then my thoughts grew more suspicious. Had he kidnapped Bridie? I hadn't seen her all week. But no, she had gone to him willingly and let him kiss her hand. I tried to think back to hiring day at Hyde Park—had he been there and tracked Bridie down because he wanted to hire her away from Pitt House? I chased that thought out of my head immediately. I couldn't bear to think that I might be left here without her.

I was so distracted that Mrs. Melrose lost her temper with me several times, threatening to send me back to Hyde Park despite what it would do to Mrs. Pitt's reputation.

"I've had many misgivings about you, miss, particularly since you're one of them Irish orphans I've read about," she said, "but I never took you for a scatterbrain, forgetting this and forgetting that! You'd better straighten up right now or I'm going to Mrs. Pitt. Now, get on with your work!"

At last, Sunday arrived. Before I could open my mouth, Bridie put up her hand.

"I know you're mad to know all about last Sunday. I'll tell you only what I want you to know, and I'll be answering none of your questions! Understood?"

"Yes," I said, taken aback by her sudden firmness.

Luke chucked the horse's reins and the carriage moved out onto the street.

Bridie straightened her back and sat upright in the carriage. "His name is Mr. Terrence O'Leary," she began, "and he owns and runs the Emerald Isle Hotel and Tavern on George Street. He emigrated from Ireland twenty years ago, and not as a convict as you might be thinking, but to make his fortune." She paused and looked towards Luke. "No offense to convicts, Luke," she said, "yez are as good as anybody else."

Luke made no reply.

"Mr. O'Leary is a well-off man and often comes to Mrs. Pitt's parties. As a result, he knows two things about me—that I know all there's to know about wines and that I can sing. Mrs. Pitt boasted to him about the wines I'd ordered for the picnic and he heard me singing in the empty dining room one night when I thought nobody was about." She paused. "You recall that Mrs. Pitt doesn't want me to be heard or seen by her guests. So, since Mr. O'Leary runs a hotel and a popular tavern, you can see why he's interested in me. I can help him with ordering the stock and I can sing for me supper in the tavern."

My stomach fell. "Oh, Bridie, you're not leaving us, are you?" I cried.

Bridie laughed. "I said no questions, but I'll answer that. I'll only leave if I'm thrown out on me arse," she said.

"Then what does he want?"

"He wants to marry me."

I was too stunned to say anything. Even Luke turned around to stare at Bridie.

She laughed aloud. "What? You two don't believe any man would be interested enough to marry me?"

I shook my head furiously. "No, that's not true!"

"Come on, Kate, be honest. Everybody knows I'm no oil painting. But looks aren't everything. Mr. O'Leary's attracted to what I can do to help his business more than my looks." She laughed again. "Anyway, he's no prize either when it comes to looks!"

Something in Bridie's protests didn't ring true. I realized that she must have been hurt more than I ever thought by Mrs. Pitt's attitude towards her. Even though the thought of her leaving Pitt House terrified me, I was genuinely happy for her. I reached over and took her arm.

"I wish you all the best, Bridie. You deserve it."

She shook her arm free of my touch. "Will you whish't, Kate. You think I'm going to jump at marriage in case it's the only chance I'll ever get? I'm not that daft. And besides, I'm not nineteen yet and so Major Pitt and herself would have to give me permission to marry and I can tell you now that Mrs. Pitt isn't about to agree to it." She smiled. "So you're stuck with me for a while longer, whether you want me or not."

I threw my arms around her. "Oh, Bridie," I said, "of course I want you to stay. You're the only one keeping me sane in this place."

The year 1850 dawned hot and humid, accompanied by a foul smell that rose out of Sydney Harbor and clung to everything in its path, wrapping itself around blades of grass and leaves of trees, crawling over rocks, brushing the pavements and streets with its vile stench. Like a snake, it coiled through door crevices and window sashes, invading grand houses and tar-papered huts alike. People covered their faces with handkerchiefs as they rushed through the town, disgusted with the smell of their own clothing. At first, the town leaders were at a loss. Rumors circulated blaming the invasion on everything from spoiled cargos brought in by foreign ships to an unknown species of insect or animal, or a pox sent by God to punish Sydney's sinners!

As it turned out, the people of Sydney were indeed the sinners at fault. The smell was finally traced to the pipes that had been installed to bring Sydney's sewage down to the harbor, instead of burying it in pits as had been the custom. One outfall pipe had deposited raw sewage into the area of Fort Macquarie. Once the mystery was solved, the town fathers set about forming committees and summoning water specialists to find a solution. In the meantime, Sydney's citizens continued to hold their noses.

At the time, I couldn't help thinking the harbor smell was, for all of us—myself, the orphans, Luke, and the Pitts—an omen of bad things to come. Growing up in Ireland, I was well used to superstitions. The old people claimed almost everything was a sign—whether it was the "banshee" or fairy-woman crying out in the night predicting death, crows perched left to right on a tree branch predicting bad luck, or the sight of a white horse in the morning predicting good luck. I used to laugh at such stories, but their predictions came true often enough that I never discounted them altogether.

Early in the year, I began to sense that all was not as it should be around Pitt House. Two of the kitchen maids left and Mrs. Melrose's mood grew more contrary as a result. Although orphan girls were still arriving from Ireland under the Earl Grey scheme, Major and Mrs. Pitt were dead set against hiring any of them as replacements, even though, like Bridie and me, they would be paid a lower rate than non-indentured staff. Then, the butler retired, though he was tight-lipped about his reasons. When the head housekeeper followed him out the door, I asked Bridie what she thought was going on.

"Herself has been in the worst of form," she said as Luke drove us to Mass one Sunday, "finding fault with everyone and everything."

I shook my head. "Yes, and she doesn't seem to be entertaining as much lately. Am I right?"

Bridie nodded. "That's true," she said, frowning. "She's cut down on the food and drink orders lately. As you know, she used to throw money around like there was no tomorrow, but now she's counting every penny." She hesitated as if deciding whether to say more. "And, last week," she went on, lowering her voice so that Luke couldn't hear her, "she sold that red velvet sofa in the salon. She cried when they came and took it away. It was a favorite of hers."

"How's the Major behaving?" I said.

"Aw, sure he's going around with a face on him as long as your arm and growling at everybody in sight. His brother was here yesterday and I heard them shouting. Something about money and a bank."

But the trouble was not just in the Pitt House. Mr. Martin from the *Sydney Morning Herald* had begun publishing more articles criticizing the Earl Grey scheme and the orphans now "pouring" into the colony. Apparently, my defense of myself and the other orphans had not softened his attitude towards us. The *Herald* was publishing not only its own stories, but reprinting accounts from other newspapers such as the *South Australian Register* in Adelaide, the *Melbourne Morning Herald*, and the *Melbourne Argus*. In all cases the accounts railed against the "Irish Orphans" using much the same language that I had heard from the men in the Pitt House the night of the picnic. They accused the Irish authorities of taking "professed public women and barefooted little country beggars" and putting them into the workhouses so they could qualify under the Earl Grey scheme and, as a result, rid themselves of undesirables. The *Goulburn Herald* expanded the argument by accusing England of "shifting from her

shoulders the entire bulk of both her convict and pauper population and depositing them upon the shores of New South Wales."

As I read those accounts, I was sickened to learn that anti-
orphan sentiment was not confined to Sydney but was growing in
Melbourne, Adelaide, Moreton Bay and elsewhere. The drum-
beat against us was growing louder. Citizens became wary of hiring orphans, a wariness fueled by employers' accusations of their
insolence, idleness, and bad language. At the beginning of 1850,
the *Herald* reported that there were now four hundred women in
Hyde Park Barracks, some of whom had been there for over two
months, and warned another two hundred were due to land from
the *Thomas Arbuthnot* ship in February.

I knew I should be grateful that I arrived when I did. I could
easily have been one of the girls now stranded without prospects
at the barracks. But my anger overshadowed my gratitude. I was
angry at everyone involved—the Irish workhouse guardians and
the English government—who had promised us a better life; the
Australian authorities who had welcomed the scheme, in the
hope that we would civilize the hordes of single male convicts in
the colony as well as ease the labor shortage, and who'd agreed to
pay our way; the employers who believed the scathing rumors
about us; and the newspaper editors and politicians and clerics
who had whipped up this fervent hate. Most of all I was angry at
the famine that had robbed me of my family and my future.

As the weeks went by, I felt a growing unsteadiness. Nothing
seemed solid anymore. The ground under my feet felt as unsteady as when I was aboard the *Sabine*. I found myself longing to
be back on the voyage, where the world was contained within the
physical confines of the ship, where the daily routines were predictable, and where Nathaniel was close by to reassure me when
fears overwhelmed me. Perhaps it was memories of Nathaniel
that caused me to seek out Luke and the reliability of his stable
presence. After all, the emotional undercurrents that laced every
encounter with Nathaniel were not there with Luke. I felt free to
be myself.

Our meetings at the grotto became more frequent. From the beginning I sensed that he, too, was having concerns about the state of things at Pitt House. Finally, one day, I asked him the question that I had been avoiding.

"Staff are leaving every week," I began. "Will you be going soon? Did you get your land grant yet?"

He shook his head. "Not yet. The Major's preoccupied with other things. I've reminded him a couple of times, but . . ."

"Oh," I said, trying to hide my relief that he would be staying for a while longer. "You must be getting impatient."

He sighed. "I am. I've a piece of land picked out near Bathurst on the other side of the Blue Mountains. As I told you, Major Pitt helped me with the grant application. He's promised me he'll follow up on it soon with the government land office. I can't wait to get started. There's crops need to be in the ground soon, and livestock to be bought, and a dwelling built. I want to call it 'Tara' after the ancient hill back in Ireland were the High Kings were crowned."

I laughed. "Of course," I said, "my da used to talk about it. He said that they stood on Lia Fáil, the Stone of Destiny, and if they were the rightful king the stone let out a mighty roar."

But he wasn't listening. Instead he was looking out towards the pond. "Major Pitt has assured me that because he is sponsoring my application it will be accepted without any bother. Of course if the drought gets worse, it might be as well to wait."

I stood up. "I need to be getting back. Mrs. Melrose is watching me like a hawk."

"What do you think of my plan?" he asked unexpectedly.

I was taken aback. "I'd need to think about it," I began, reluctant to say that my only concern was keeping him here, "and besides, I can't picture what it's like out there in the Outback. Wouldn't it be lonely?"

His eyes clouded. "My plan was to bring Maeve with me, but now . . ."

"How do you know she would have liked it?"

"Oh, I think she would have settled into it well enough. Maeve was not a pampered city girl. She grew up on a farm and loved being outdoors. In fact, you put me in mind of her."

For the first time, I blushed in his presence. I looked away quickly, aware that he was staring at me. "I have to go," I said.

I was out of breath by the time I reached the kitchen. Confused thoughts tumbled over one another. He had seemed as shocked as I was at his words, as if a truth had slipped out without his permission. I tried to calm down. So what if I reminded him of her? It meant nothing, but I had to admit that his words had made me want to run, just like my early encounters with Nathaniel. The difference was that I had been in love with Nathaniel. I was not in love with Mr. Luke Kinsella, nor, I was sure, was he in love with me. I had clearly read too much into what he said.

"You've lost the run of yourself altogether, Kate," I scolded myself.

My eighteenth birthday came and went, as unremarked as the last. Under my indenture, Mrs. Pitt was to now start paying me eleven pounds a year, a one-pound increase. It was the one thing I was looking forward to, but when I asked Mrs. Melrose where the extra money was, she shrugged.

"I can't tell you when you'll see it, miss."

"But it's in the indenture contract, on my birthday I'm supposed to—"

"You should be grateful for what you're getting, miss," she said, cutting me off. "There's better workers than you here waiting for a rise in their pay for months now."

She had stalked away before I could ask any more questions.

When I saw Bridie the following Sunday, I asked her about it.

"I got me rise on me birthday in January," she said, "but a few of the maids are complaining about Mrs. Pitt's broken promises. You could go to the emigration authorities, but I don't think you'd get far, knowing the attitudes of them oul' buggers towards us!"

I sighed. Bridie was right of course.

Most of the orphans I saw at Mass said they had no problems with their employers about their wages. They were sorry for me, they said, but given the growing furor against the orphan immigration scheme, there wouldn't be much I could do about it.

"I know you spoke up for us once, Kate, but what good did it do? And now, well, given the times that's in it, I'd count my blessings that I have a job and not stuck waiting beyond in Hyde Park Barracks like a prisoner."

I let the issue drop. Some nights in my room I would pull out an envelope from my travel box and count what money I had saved since arriving at Pitt House. I had to admit it didn't amount to much—certainly not enough to pay my way back to Ireland, even in steerage, to find Christy and Paddy. Slowly and surely, my early dream of returning to Ireland to reunite with my brothers began to crumble.

The year lingered on. Temperatures dropped as summer turned into autumn, but the much longed-for rains were sparse. It was as if the whole world around me was holding its breath waiting for something to break the torpid spell. I was reminded of our days in the Doldrums when the *Sabine* sat unmoving on a lifeless ocean. Back then, every wisp of wind sent the crew running to open the sails, only to have hopes dashed when the wind dropped again.

Word came that the Earl Grey scheme was over. The pressure of opposition from the colony had been too much for England. The last ship, the *Maria*, had docked in Sydney in August. There would be no more. I wondered what would happen to the girls now languishing at Hyde Park.

I found myself clutching at even the smallest hint of normalcy as an omen of better things to come. What I didn't realize was that it was the hints of normalcy that were covering up the upheaval that was about to burst upon us. The eruption came on an ordinary day in September 1850. The staff of Pitt House were going about their daily routines when we were all summoned to the main salon, where Major and Mrs. Pitt were waiting. I had a fleeting thought of how sad it was that Mrs. Pitt could no longer sit on her red velvet sofa. Instead she stood a few feet apart from her husband, her dark eyes blazing with anger. He stood erect and in full dress uniform. The gathered servants shuffled a little, then stilled. An air of expectation filled the room.

"We have called you here," Major Pitt began, as if he was addressing a battalion of soldiers, "to tell you that some major changes are imminent." His gaze was directed not at the people before him but on the front window, which framed the view of Sydney Harbor. "You must be prepared in due course—"

"Pitt House has been sold!" Mrs. Pitt's voice was high-pitched as she glared at her husband. "There is no point in beating around the bush. The new owners have their own staff and will be moving in here in one month. Between now and then the Major and I will require the services of only a few of you who will be notified separately of our decision; the rest of you must make immediate plans to secure employment elsewhere. You must vacate this house within a fortnight. That is all!"

For a moment, no one spoke, then came the outbursts.

"What about the wages we're owed?" one of the footmen called.

"We'll need references!" cried a parlor maid. "We'll not get jobs without them."

"Are we supposed to keep working here in the meantime?"

Everyone began to speak at once, but Mrs. Pitt turned on her heel and strode towards the door, waving her arm in the air. "Speak to Major Pitt about those matters!" she called over her shoulder.

Everyone looked at the Major, who bowed his head. "I regret the inconvenience," he began. "You may bring your concerns to my solicitors, Messrs. Waggoner and Clark, if you wish. My wife and I shall be leaving Pitt House forthwith and will not be available. That will be all."

With that he brought his feet together and raised his arm. I had the ridiculous notion that he was about to salute. But he dropped his arm again and marched out of the room.

We watched them go. Some of the maids began to weep, other staff to grumble and shout, while others stood open-mouthed. I made my way through the crowd to where Bridie stood at the back of the room. My heart was beating fast but I had not yet taken in what had happened.

"Bad cess to them!" she said, her face red. "It's not as if we didn't see it coming," she went on. "Sure we had plenty of signs over the last few months. But I can't believe they'd put people out on the street with only a fortnight's notice, and them behind on all their wages."

"Will you be kept on for the month, Bridie?" I asked.

She nodded. "Aye, herself's after notifying me this morning."

"And what about afterwards?"

Bridie shrugged. "I'll be making Mr. Terrence O'Leary a happy man, so I will."

"You're going to marry him?" I burst out in surprise.

"No! What did I tell you before? But I'll be moving into the Emerald Isle Hotel and going to work for him!"

Luke came up beside us. "Well, that's that, then," he said.

I found my voice. "But why?" I said. "What happened?"

"The Major told me the bank he owned with his brother failed. He blames the brother for it. I almost feel sorry for him. This place was his pride and joy. Now he'll have to walk away from these beautiful gardens and all the special trees and plants he shipped here from around the world! I suppose he wanted the land here to look like his native England."

"Sorry, my arse!" said Bridie. "Foolish *amadans*, the two of them—himself spending money hand over fist so he could have the best gardens in Sydney and her wasting money trying to impress the wealthy of Sydney with her parties. Now it's the likes of us will be paying the price. And not a bother on them for the hardship they've inflicted on everybody here!"

One by one, the staff, including Bridie, returned to their quarters. I couldn't bear to go into the kitchen just yet, so I walked down to the grotto. I was surprised to find Luke there.

"So this is it," I said, as I sat down beside him, brushing away the tears that threatened to escape. "I suppose tomorrow I'll be going back to Hyde Park, that is if they're still taking us in now the Earl Grey scheme is over."

"Is that what you want?"

I swung around, angry now. "Of course it's not. But what choice do I have?"

"There's always a choice," he said.

"Like what?"

He turned around to look straight into my eyes.

"You could come with me, Kate."

My mouth fell open. "Come with you?" I repeated. "Where, to the Outback?"

"Yes," he said, not taking his eyes off me. "I've been thinking about it for a while. We could build a good life together, Kate. And we'd be independent. Our future wouldn't be tied to the whims of others like the Pitts." He reached over and took my hand. "Think about it, Kate, please?"

I was so startled I could hardly catch the thoughts that raced through me. I wanted to run but my body wouldn't move, so I sat frozen in place. Luke's blue eyes bored into mine as if trying to read my mind. I stared back at him, as if seeing him for the first time, and I realized how little I knew about him—Irish rebel, convict, gardener, would-be farmer. Was that enough to make such a commitment? Granted, I had begun to enjoy his company and his friendship—but . . . My thoughts turned to Nathaniel. I would have readily gone anywhere in the world with him if he'd asked me and, in truth, I didn't know much more about him than I knew about Luke. The difference was that I'd fancied myself in love with Nathaniel. But what had I known of love at the age of sixteen? Now, two years later, I realized deep down that there was a lot more to love than blushing and trembling in a man's presence.

I let out a deep sigh. Then another thought occurred to me. Luke hadn't mentioned marriage. What if he was just suggesting that I move to the Outback and live with him in the house he intended to build? My anger rose.

I snatched my hand out of his and stood up. "How dare you?" I shouted. "You think I'm the kind of girl who'll jump at the chance to live with a man at the drop of a hat? Think again, Mr. Kinsella. I'd starve before I'd ever stoop to that! What you're asking me to do hardly ranks above what poor Patsy's been forced to do beyond in that brothel." I turned to go. "But don't worry, I'm sure there's plenty of girls right here would oblige you. After all, I hear that all the maids are in love with you!"

I didn't know what I expected him to do or say, nor did I care, but when he laughed out loud, I could hardly contain my fury, or my tears. I was about to unload another tirade on him when he put up his hand.

"Kate, oh my darlin' Kate," he said, smiling, "you have it all wrong! I am not asking you to come and live with me in sin. I am asking you to marry me!"

I sank back down on the bench. "Marry you? But I don't love you, Luke," I blurted out.

"Sure I know that, Kate," he said. "But I believe in time you will grow to love me, and I am willing to wait."

"But," I began, taking a deep breath, "you don't love me either."

His smile faded. "It's true I don't love you the way I loved Maeve," he said, "but I do have feelings for you, Kate, and I'm certain they'll continue to grow. All we need is to give it time. In the meantime, as my wife you will have my protection, and a position of respectability."

I respected his honesty. Luke was a good man, I knew I could do worse, and I was confident he would treat me well.

He stood up then and took both my hands in his. "I don't expect an answer from you now. It's a big decision, and I will understand if you say no. All I ask is that you consider it. Now, go to bed, Kate. It's been a long day for all of us."

That night I finally wrote a letter to Nathaniel. I took out the crumpled paper bearing his address, which I'd kept inside the back pages of my diary and smoothed it out. *Devon, England*, it said—the other side of the world. I wrote quickly on the blank pages, tracing everything that had happened since I'd last seen him at Hyde Park Barracks. I told him about the Pitts and their parties, about Bridie's surprising skills and her friendship, about my outburst at Mr. Martin of the *Sydney Herald*, about my banishment to the kitchens and Mrs. Melrose, about Mary going to the convent and Patsy to the brothel and, finally, about the Pitts abandoning Pitt House, and all the staff with it. I stopped then, my pen hovering above the paper as my thoughts whirled. Slowly I began to move the pen again, laying down the words as if they were being dictated by a power over which I had no control. I told him about Luke and about his proposal. I set forth my arguments both for and against accepting it, reasoning in the way I supposed an impartial judge might do, and thus I reached the only logical conclusion—that I would accept it.

When I'd finished, I tore out the pages from my journal and stuffed them quickly into an envelope before my tears could fall on them. As I sealed it, I tried not to think of what a cold, lifeless message it contained. Yes, it was an accurate account of my two years in Sydney and a clear explanation of how I came to the decision to marry Luke, all of it true as far as it went but, out of shyness, shame, or lack of courage, I had failed to admit the most important truth of all—that I was, and always would be, in love with Nathaniel Harte.

The following Sunday the priest at St. Patrick's read out the banns announcing our marriage intentions. The *Sabine* girls and other orphans, along with some maids who'd worked at Pitt House, stood up and applauded, afterwards gathering around me to wish me well. Luke wasn't there, though. He'd gone to inspect his land near Bathurst—assuring me he would be back in time for the wedding. The orphans all knew him, of course, since he'd attended Mass with Bridie and me every Sunday, and the maids knew him even better.

"Aren't you the lucky girl," exclaimed one of the maids, "and him so handsome!"

"Isn't it well for you, Kate," said another, "and him with a farm already leased and ready for you to move into."

"And, given the times that's in it, you won't even need the Pitts' permission to get married."

I smiled, masking the nervousness which gripped me at times when I thought about what I was doing. "Aye, I'm lucky," was all I said.

We had set the wedding date for the day we were all to leave the Pitt House. Bridie insisted on helping me plan the details and I was grateful for her help. The ceremony would be at St. Patrick's. We would invite some of the Pitt House staff but certainly not the Pitts nor Mrs. Melrose, and we would invite as many orphans as we knew, including Mary and Patsy. The reception would be at the Emerald Isle Hotel and Tavern, which Mr. O'Leary had already agreed to. He had also agreed to be our best man. Bridie was delighted to be my maid of honor and she'd insisted on making the dresses for both of us.

The next two weeks were such a whirl of activity that I had little time to worry about my decision. When I'd finally told Luke I would marry him, his eyes lit up and he broke into a broad grin. He lifted me off my feet and twirled me around until I was dizzy.

"You'll not regret it, Kate!" he said. "It will be a grand adventure, so it will. I'll leave all the arrangements to you and Bridie. I want to go ahead and see the state of the land over there before you come. I've hired on some ex-convicts—men I know well—to help clear the land for planting, put up fencing, and dig irrigation ditches, and—"

"But what about a house, have they built it yet?" I interrupted as a sudden panic took hold of me.

He hesitated. "Er, no, not yet," he began and, seeing my alarm, went on. "But we'll have one up soon. In the meantime we'll be bunking down in tents . . ."

"Tents?" I said, fighting to control my astonishment.

"Aye, Kate, tents! It's coming summer now and, unless we have a downpour, it should be very comfortable. That's how most of the squatters start off. It's a pleasant way to sleep really, in a tent or outside under the stars, not cooped up in some hot wee room the way you are here. It'll all be part of the adventure."

I took a few deep breaths, trying to tamp down the bile that was rising in my throat. This was all so new, and I had no idea what to expect. There again, I'd had no idea what to expect since the morning I'd left the Newry Workhouse.

"I'm sorry," I said at last. "I know I sound like a spoiled child."

He nodded. "No bother, Kate. I understand."

The next morning I stood at my bedroom window and watched him leave. As if sensing me there, he looked up and waved. I waved back, then sat down trying to fight off the fear that threatened to overwhelm me. I prayed that he would make the journey safely and be back in time for the wedding. After all, I depended on this man. For better or worse, I had harnessed my future to his.

Good to his word, he returned the day before the wedding, looking exhausted from the journey. I ran out and hugged him, unable to disguise my relief.

"Did you not think I'd come back for you?" he asked.

I put on a brave face. "I knew you'd be back," I said. "Come here to me 'til I tell you all the arrangements we've made . . . er, well, that Bridie's made."

He laughed as I linked my arm through his and led him into the Pitt House.

The next evening, I walked down the aisle of St. Patrick's Church wearing a simple white cotton dress that Bridie had made, trimmed with lace and tiny pearl buttons, and carrying a bouquet of summer flowers Luke had picked out for me. Instead of a veil, I wore a floral wreath, my hair unpinned and floating around my shoulders. Bridie walked ahead of me wearing a blue dress of similar style and carrying a posey of white carnations. As we walked, the church was filled with the sounds of a harpist and violinist playing a graceful, haunting tune by the famous blind Irish harpist Turlough O'Carolan, called "Planxty Irwin." Visions of home drifted before me as I listened to the beautiful, ancient melody. I fought back tears thinking of Ma and Da and my brothers. How much I wished they could see me. Nathaniel's face appeared unbidden before me and I shook my head slightly and closed my eyes to erase the image. When I opened my eyes again I focused on Luke, who stood beside Mr. O'Leary at the foot of the altar. He was so handsome in a dark suit and white shirt that my heart swelled. He looked at me, a faint smile on his lips, as he reached for my hand.

I was barely aware of the priest's voice as Luke and I knelt and exchanged our vows. I felt as if I was in a dream. When we stood and faced the congregation, I began to tremble. I was afraid I might faint, but Luke took my elbow and steered me firmly towards the front door while the musicians played the lively "O'Carolan's Concerto" with great gusto.

Outside, the bells of St. Patrick's were ringing and we were surrounded by well-wishers, including as many of the orphans as could get the time off. I breathed in the cool, early evening air. We rode over to George Street and the Emerald Isle Hotel in a hansom cab festooned with white ribbons. The guests followed us in separate conveyances. Along the street, people waved. Bridie and Mr. O'Leary, who had arrived before us, greeted us as we entered the hotel. In the large dining room, tables had been set with food, and a group of musicians were already playing an array of Irish tunes. I held tightly to Luke's hand as we sat down at a long table facing the guests.

I hardly recognized young Mary when she approached us. She

was sixteen now, and as lovely as ever. She wore a long black dress and a simple white veil, indicating that she was intending to become a nun but had not yet taken her vows. Something about her radiated peace. I moved to hug her but pulled back, unsure if such intimacy was allowed. I needn't have worried because she threw her arms around me and pulled me into a fierce hug, tears filling her huge blue eyes.

"Oh, Kate," she said, "it's grand to see you. You look beautiful. Congratulations on your marriage. I've thought about you so often in the last two years."

"And I you," I began, "and I'm sorry I never had a chance to visit you, but I was sure you were happy at the convent. I saw the joy in your face from the moment you met the Sisters of Charity at Hyde Park. And now look at you—you're radiant!"

She smiled. "You're right, Kate, I'm very content there."

Her young face clouded slightly. "I see Bridie here, looking well. But what of Lizzie and Sheila, and Patsy?"

"Lizzie and Sheila found positions in Moreton Bay," I said.

She smiled. "Ah, sure Doctor Harte would have made sure of that! And Patsy . . . ?"

I swallowed. "Well, Patsy didn't get an indenture," I began. "Bridie and I saw her once or twice. She's making her way as best she can."

I was glad when Bridie came over and interrupted us.

"Wonders will never cease," she said. "Come and see the lovely cake your woman, Mrs. Melrose, is after bringing in. You'd better come and thank her."

"But—but we didn't invite her!" I said.

Bridie waved her hand impatiently. "Och, well, when I heard from a kitchen maid she was making a cake for you, I changed my mind."

As the evening wore on, more musicians arrived. It seemed Mr. O'Leary knew all of them. Some of the orphans had brought their own instruments and joined in. Bridie stopped supervising everything long enough to sing a few songs in Irish. Everyone in the place was soon up dancing jigs and reels. Luke, it turned out, was a fine dancer. He pulled me up on the floor and didn't let me sit down until the music finally stopped and the guests started to drift out. As I stood at the door thanking everyone for coming, I thought I saw a fleeting shadow in the hallway. Instinctively, I knew who it was.

"Patsy?" I called. "Patsy, is that you? Come on in."

Slowly, she approached me. She wore a faded yellow dress, which made her skin look sallow in the lantern-lit hallway. She was thin as a rake and her face was gaunt. Even her red hair, which lay limply on her shoulders, seemed to have lost its defiance.

"Patsy!" I breathed. "I'm so glad you could come. It means a lot to me."

I moved to embrace her, but she pushed me away.

"Och now, stop your oul' palaver," she said, "aren't we all a bit past that carry on?"

"We're never past friendship, Patsy," I said. "We'll always be friends. Come on in, there's plenty of food and drinks left."

She stood her ground. "I just came to wish you luck. You and himself. I never thought you'd ever get over your fancy doctor boyo, but it looks like you finally got some sense."

Just then Luke came up beside me. He and Patsy looked at each other.

"Thanks for coming, Patsy," he said. "Kate was hoping you would."

Patsy said nothing.

"Do you two know each other?" I said, thinking back to my suspicion that Luke might well have been one of Patsy's customers.

"No, but you described her often enough," Luke said.

Patsy forced a grin. "Aye, sure I'm one of a kind."

She backed away towards the door. "Tell the Bridie one I was here. And ask wee Sister Mary to keep me in mind when she's praying for sinners! Goodnight now!"

Before I could say more she was gone. I made to go after her but Luke took my arm and steered me back into the hallway.

"Leave her be, Kate," he said. "It's late, and we have an early start in the morning!"

My heart was beating fast as he led me upstairs to the room where we were to spend the night. All evening I had chased out of my mind the moment when I would be expected to perform my marital duty. I didn't even know what that meant, and there was no one to ask. I swallowed hard when I saw the big four-poster bed, laden with pillows and cushions. Bridie had arranged for us to stay in the "bridal suite," and I appreciated her good intentions. After all, she had no idea of how things really were between Luke and myself!

I stood, not knowing what to say or do.

As if reading my mind, Luke put his arm around me. "It's alright, Kate," he whispered, "don't be frightened. I know this is all new to you. I was hoping there'd be two beds, as I'm sure you were. No matter, I'll turn my back until you get undressed and into bed. Then I'll turn down the lamps, and sleep on the sofa." He smiled at me. "And don't be worrying your head about the journey to Bathurst. Even though we'll only have one tent, I've two mattresses packed on the dray and on fine nights I'll be sleeping out under the stars, and on bad ones I'll sleep underneath the dray. I promised I'd take care of you, Kate, and I will!"

His final words flowed gently through my mind as I drifted off into sleep.

Part Five

The Outback
1850

During my time at Pitt House, I had often gazed out at the Blue Mountains, which rose in the distance behind Sydney as if guarding the town, and wondered what lay beyond them. I heard stories of escaped convicts who had attempted to cross them, believing the path would lead them to China and freedom. None of them had ever returned and the citizens of Sydney continued to watch and wait for the mountains to whisper their secrets. I'd read that it was not until 1813 that a group of European explorers finally breached the vast sandstone barricade and returned with tales of lush valleys and streams that lay beyond. A road was built across the range in 1818, which followed the explorers' trail, and then descended the inland slopes following a trail originally marked by the Aboriginal people. The mountains' secrets revealed at last, would-be settlers began to venture into the "promised land" beyond.

And now it was our turn. At dawn on a clear October day in 1850, Luke and I—as Mr. and Mrs. Kinsella—set out from the Emerald Isle Hotel with two drays, four bullocks, a packhorse and two dray drivers, known as "bullockies," in the direction of Emu Plains and the Blue Mountains pass. All our worldly possessions were stored in the drays, along with new mattresses, blankets and a folded tent, our food for the journey and eating utensils secured on the packhorse. I had dressed in a long cotton skirt and long-sleeved blouse, my cloak pulled around me, and new leather boots. I had taken my bonnet with the red velvet ribbons from my travel box that morning and put it on, knowing it was hardly practical or appropriate. Luke had stared at it but said nothing.

Bridie and Mr. O'Leary came outside to wish us Godspeed. I cried as I hugged Bridie.

"Goodbye, Bridie," I whispered. "Thank you for everything."

Her voice was hoarse as she spoke. "Sure, you've nothing to thank me for, Kate. Wouldn't you have done the same for meself."

"I'll miss you," I said.

"Sure you'd think you were away to the moon itself," she said. "You'll only be a hundred miles from Sydney. You can come and see us any time. And you can write. Thanks to you I'll be able to read what you wrote!" She pushed me away. "Now go! Don't keep your new husband waiting!"

"Look in on Patsy once in a while," I said, as I mounted the dray.

She nodded.

As our little procession began to move, I was reminded of another procession of carts long ago in a faraway country, filled with young orphans in colorful bonnets, riding out to meet their fate. I sat beside Luke in the first dray, lost in memories. Just like then, I felt neither sadness nor hope but anticipation tinged with anxiety. And, like back then, I could conjure up no picture in my mind of what lay ahead. Again, I was moving forward on faith—faith in Luke, faith in myself, and faith in God.

As we moved slowly west on the Parramatta Road, the base of the mountains seemed to move farther away. Luke had warned me it could take several days to cover the forty or so miles to the foot of the pass, depending on the weather. A few times I looked behind me to see the outline of Sydney recede along with the hustle and bustle and noise of the metropolis. I thought about the day I first saw the harbor as the *Sabine* was towed to the wharf; the walk up the hill to Hyde Park Barracks; my first sight of a kangaroo and the first time I caught my breath at the beauty of Pitt House. I sighed. Everything that had become familiar in this new land was now confined to memory—another chapter of my life closed shut.

At sunset the first night, we made camp on a grassy verge near a stream bordered by mangroves and river oaks. I watched as Luke relieved the packhorse of its burden, watered it and tethered it to a nearby tree for the night. Next, he went about making a fire. He laid a circle of stones on the ground, piled twigs, branches and leaves into the center, and lit them with matches he had managed to find in Sydney. He put a kettle filled with water from the stream on the fire to heat and then set about mixing flour, water and salt, kneading the mixture into a round loaf, which he then put in a pot and set on a rock above the flames. The loaf was called "damper" and I'd eaten some on the *Sabine*, although at that time it had been sweetened with raisins. While he was busy cooking, the two bullockies unharnessed the bullocks, led them to drink at the nearby stream before setting them free to graze on the grassy verge. Later, they tied a rope loosely around the legs of each of the animals thus hobbling them in order to prevent them from straying. That done, the bullockies began erecting the canvas tent, sinking the pegs into the ground and securing them with stones. They dragged in a mattress and blankets and set a candle in a tin saucer on a log beside the bed.

When we had all finished the meal of tea, damper and salted pork, Luke pointed towards the tent. "There," he said, "that should do you nicely."

"But—what about you?"

"'Tis a fine night," he said. "Sure I'll be sleeping under the stars. And the bullockies will sleep under the drays. Don't worry, these lads sleep with one eye open, and their muskets in their arms. Neither man nor beast will get past them. So you can rest easy."

I wanted to protest, but a greater part of me wanted to appear brave. "Very well, goodnight then," I said, and went into the tent.

I took off my cloak, bonnet and new boots, lay down on the mattress on the hard, grassy ground and covered myself with a blanket. I lay stiffly, afraid to blow out the candle. Eventually, it burned down and I had no choice but to snuff it out. I lay, alert to every noise, my muscles coiled and ready to spring at any hint of danger. Most of the birds had grown silent, but there were other noises—rustling, scratching, and scraping—coming from outside. Trees stirred in the wind and frogs croaked in the nearby stream. But when a loud barking began, I jumped up, grabbed the mattress and blanket, and dragged them outside the tent to where Luke was lying, snoring gently in his sleep. If he woke and heard me, he said nothing. I laid down my mattress alongside his, wrapped myself in the blanket from head to toe, and tried not to move.

The next morning, after a breakfast of tea and damper, we packed up our belongings, snuffed out the fire, and proceeded on our journey west. I was stiff from the previous night and every muscle ached but I said nothing in complaint. I'd made this decision freely and must live with the consequences. After finding my way to the stream to rinse my face and hands, I returned and asked Luke to show me how to build a fire outdoors since back in Ireland we'd always relied on turf fires in our cottage fireplace for cooking and warmth. I wanted to make myself useful and I was beginning to realize how much I would need these skills as the journey continued.

The sun rose high in the sky and by noon the heat was almost unbearable. I had long ago shed my cloak. I yearned for rain but I knew that would slow our journey by turning the roads into puddles of mud. Now sweat trickled down the back of my neck and my clothes clung to me. We moved slowly, the bullocks straining under the loaded drays. Every now and then I cast a sideways glance at Luke, who sat silently beside me, looking straight ahead. He wore the same cotton shirt, trousers, and battered, slouched hat as when I first saw him waiting for Bridie and me outside Hyde Park Barracks. How could I have even guessed then that within two years I would be married to him and leaving Sydney for an unknown future beyond the mountains? I was grateful for his silence, which gave me time to take stock of my situation. I let my thoughts wander freely—trying to imagine what Luke's piece of land would look like. I had been brought up on a farm, so surely this could not be that different, I reassured myself. But no matter what rosy pictures I painted in my imagination, a tiny coil of dread settled in my stomach that could not be shifted.

As we drew closer to Emu Plains, the road became more crowded. We passed groups of people on foot, some leading pack-horses, some pulling wheeled carts full of their belongings, like the carts filled with cargo I had seen sailors wheeling at Sydney Harbor, and some carrying their bundles on their backs. Men, women, and children trudged along in the grueling heat, all in search of a better future, just like Luke and I were. In turn, we were passed by single men on horseback, and families in covered horse-drawn carriages. These were people with more means than us but, like us, in search of greater prosperity than they had in Sydney. Adventurers, all, I thought.

Emu Plains turned out to be a busy settlement, smaller and cruder by far than Sydney but, by virtue of its location at the foot of the Blue Mountains, was a natural stopping place for travelers preparing to ascend the mountain range. As we drove down the main street I saw feed stores, blacksmiths' huts, and stables to accommodate horses, as well as provision stores and cafés and, in the center of town, an inn. Luke signaled the driver of our dray to pull over, then he stepped down and told me to wait while he went inside. A few minutes later he emerged smiling.

"Get your things, Kate," he said, "we have a room for the night."

Any nervousness I might have had left me, so relieved was I that I would be spending the night indoors and not out in the wilderness.

"'Tis the last night for a while we'll have a comfortable bed," he was saying as he escorted me to the door. "And a hot meal besides. No damper for us tonight."

I followed him through the crowded building, up a flight of stairs and into a room at the end of the hall. The room lacked the elegance of the bridal suite at the Emerald Isle Hotel but, rustic as it was, to me at that moment it was a palace. I dropped my bag on the floor and turned to the dresser where a jug of water sat in a large bowl. I poured a little of the water into the bowl and plunged a cloth into its cool depths. I mopped my face and neck, sighing with relief.

When I turned around Luke was watching me, smiling.

I smiled back. "This is lovely," I said.

He held out his hand. "Come on now, Mrs. Kinsella, let us descend and dine like royalty in this fine establishment."

Afterwards, he stood with his back to me while I undressed and crawled into the large bed, moaning at the comfort of the thick mattress. I pretended to close my eyes as he began to undress but couldn't stop myself from stealing a few glances at the outline of his strong shoulders, narrow hips and long, muscled legs. When he slid in beside me I lay unmoving, inhaling the earthy scent of his naked skin, and listening to his soft, steady breathing, while letting myself drift into a contented cocoon of sleep.

The next morning we joined the crowd of travelers gathered at the foot of the Victoria Pass waiting our turn to ascend the Blue Mountains range. The pass had been completed twenty years before, Luke said, and provided a faster alternative to the older, Great Western Road pass.

"I've been back and forth on it a few times in recent years," he said, "and I've come to no harm. You've nothing to fear from it, Kate."

But his reassurance did little to calm my nerves as I stared up at the steep rock formations in front of me that seemed to touch the sky. How in God's name would we ever get up there? Everything in me wanted to jump out of the dray and run back to Sydney. I must have turned pale because Luke reached over and squeezed my hand.

"Don't be looking up at it, Kate," he said, "just keep your eyes on the ground in front of you. After all, I'd warrant you survived far worse on the ship's journey from England and lived to tell about it."

I knew he was trying hard to keep me calm, but bringing up the memories of raging storms aboard the *Sabine* was not helping. I closed my eyes and nodded, praying that the ordeal would soon be behind us.

Our drivers finally steered the drays onto the pass and we began a slow, gradual ascent up the mountain. The pass itself was no more than twelve feet wide, enough for only two carts to pass at a time, going in opposite directions. As it was, we met very few people traveling back down the mountain—the great majority were clearly would-be settlers on their way to claim a piece of far-away earth as their own. I looked from side to side at the vegetation that lined the pass. Tall eucalyptus trees rose out of thickets of bushes and vines, crowding together to form a thick, dense forest on both sides of the road. The trees reached towards each other, forming an arch overhead, which shaded us from the merciless sun. I remembered that Luke had once told me there were hundreds of varieties of eucalyptus trees and that it was their oil wafting across the mountain terrain and mixing with light and water vapor that created the blue haze which gave the Blue Mountains their name. At the time I hadn't paid him much attention but now, as I looked around me, I saw exactly what he had meant. I smiled as I registered this new piece of knowledge in my mind.

I shifted my gaze to the line of carts ahead of us—drays, carriages, packhorses, and people on foot—a slow procession like ants moving along the hot road. I shook my head. Yet another procession. How many had I endured since that first day when I had walked down a faraway mountain road with my neighbors, leaving everything I knew behind? Was this my fate, I thought, to wander the earth like a lost pilgrim, joining procession after procession in search of home?

Ahead of us, the line of carts stopped. Word came down the line that a bullock had lost its footing and slipped into a ditch, damaging the wheel of a dray. Our driver let out a curse—something about bullock drivers who didn't know what they were doing—and climbed out of the cart. Luke followed him, handing the reins to me.

"Stay here!" he said, as he joined a group of men hurrying to the damaged dray.

I was too astonished to speak. I grabbed the reins and held them stiffly in my hands, afraid to make any movement. But the bullocks seemed content to stand still and rest. When Luke and the driver returned, I smiled at them, pleased that I had kept the bullocks in check.

"Were you able to help?"

"Aye," said Luke, as the line began to move again. "We pulled the animal and the cart out of the ditch and fixed the wheel for now. Hopefully it will do them until we get down the other side. The bullock wasn't injured but we had to lighten the load it was carrying by dividing it up among some other carts. But they're on their way now, please God."

"What if you couldn't have fixed it?" I asked.

Luke shrugged. "Aye, well, we'd have had to push it off the road altogether, so everybody else could pass."

"What, leave them there alone?" I said.

"Aye."

I said nothing more. The reality of our situation began to sink in. So many things could go wrong on this journey—weather, accidents, illness, robbery. We were at the mercy of fortune! I realized, too, that perhaps this place was no different than anywhere else. Hadn't we been at the mercy of fortune back in Ireland when the famine struck? I suddenly felt very small in a large and dangerous world.

As the day wore on, the road ahead became steeper and our pace slowed. The higher we climbed, the more difficult it was to breathe. I wanted to ask Luke why this was happening, but he sat so stiffly, focused on the road ahead, that I felt I would be disturbing him. I realized he would never be as approachable as Nathaniel had been. I turned my attention back to the roadside where the scenery around us had changed. The tall eucalyptus trees thinned out and shrubs of various sizes and colors covered the forest floor. It reminded me of the woodlands back in Ireland, and I expected to see a rabbit or red fox shoot out onto the road at any minute. The road eventually leveled out and the forest and woodlands retreated, leaving only low, scrubby shrubs and sharp-edged spinifex grasses that reached in all directions across a flat expanse of land. We were so high up on the ridge I felt as if I could touch the clouds. But a glance at sheer, sandstone cliffs in the distance told me our ascent was not yet over.

As sunset approached, some of the travelers began to pull off the road to make camp for the night. Luke leaned forward to talk to our driver. From what I could hear, they were discussing whether we should do so too. Every part of my body yearned to lie down. We had taken few breaks during the day, mostly staying in the moving dray to drink water and eat some cold leftover damper and salted pork. I had joined with a few women in relieving ourselves at the side of the road, the group huddled together to shield each one of us in turn from prying eyes, and for that I was grateful.

By the time we pulled off the road, most of the other travelers had already made camp and the last rays of the sun were burnishing the cliffs ahead of us. The bullockies positioned the drays on a flat piece of ground and, along with Luke, began hacking at some shrubs to clear the ground for the mattresses and the tent. Again, Luke collected stones for a fire circle and, tired as I was, I set about finding what twigs, sticks and loose tree bark I could gather for fuel. There was no stream nearby, so we used water from the barrel we had filled that morning to make tea and water the animals. I was so tired I didn't care if we had damper or not, but I realized the men needed to be fed so I took out flour, mixed it with water, and shaped it into a loaf as I had seen Luke doing earlier. When the dough was ready I put it in a pot over the lighted fire. I sat back on my heels and looked at it with satisfaction. Luke smiled at me and nodded.

"Far cry from the Pitt House kitchen," he said.

"Aye."

As we had done the night before, we finished our meal of damper and salt pork, and Luke set up the mattress for me inside the tent, while he lay out in the open. I was still wary of sounds—unknown creatures lurking around us—but I tried to calm my fears. After all, I would be sleeping in a tent for many more nights to come. I may as well get used to it. So, I lay down, pulled the blanket over my head, and fell into an exhausted sleep.

I awoke the next morning just before sunrise and went in search of twigs and leaves to start a fire. As I ventured farther away from the tent towards the distant forest, I fancied I saw smoke rising through the trees. At first I thought it was other travelers starting their own morning fires, although I wondered why they would have set up camp so far away from the road. As I stood watching the smoke curl silently above the tree branches, I felt goose bumps rise on my arms, and had the unmistakable feeling that I was being watched. It was the sort of feeling Ma used to say meant someone was walking on your grave. Irish superstition, I thought, as I shrugged and hurried back to the camp site.

I said nothing to Luke about what I'd seen. He would only have put it down to my rich imagination—a thing he did quite often. Instead, I took my place quietly beside him in the dray and held tightly to the bench as we climbed ever steeper towards the west. There was no longer a canopy of trees to shade us from the naked sun. I thought back to the day of the picnic at the Pitt House when I had complained about the heat. How little did I know at the time what punishment this land could mete out to humans and animals, and I wondered how anyone had managed to survive it.

At last, we reached the highest ridge and I urged Luke to stop the cart. I stood up and strained my neck to finally see what lay beyond the mountain range. Many other carts halted, too, and people stood up in them, squinting into the bright sun at a valley spread out below. We stared down through parched eyes at green, lush grass and glittering streams, and I was reminded of my first glimpse of the green grass of Madeira from the *Sabine*. Without thinking, I grabbed Luke's arm.

"Oh, Luke, it's beautiful," I said. "You never said it would look like that."

He smiled at me. "'Tis the promised land alright, Kate."

At last the procession moved on. The road ahead of us began a steep descent, bending and curving so close to naked cliff edges that I was sure we would tumble over. My heart was in my mouth as I closed my eyes, gripped the seat, and tried not to cry out. Every now and then, though, the path would flatten out as we passed through a sheltered gully close to the cliff face where waterfalls danced on tropical trees, lush ferns and green vines, and the temperature cooled.

And so we traveled on for three more days, all the while descending on the treacherous, rocky terrain, winding a path through every type of vegetation I could have imagined. And around every bend, as I beheld the beautiful valley laid out before us, I thanked the magnificent Blue Mountains for finally revealing their secrets.

After making camp for the last time on the mountain, we arrived in the small settlement of Hartley, which lay near the foot of the Victoria Pass. It was a welcome sight for travelers, where we could water the animals, pick up supplies, and enjoy some fresh food. I would have been delighted to spend the night and rest again on a thick, clean mattress as we had done back at Emu Plains at the beginning of our journey. But Luke was anxious to keep going.

"I'm paying the bullockies by the day," he said, "and, besides, I want to see how the men have been getting on since I left them on the property last week. They're generally reliable lads, but you've heard the saying 'when the cat is away, the mice will play.'"

I didn't argue with him. I realized I had little idea of the responsibilities that came with securing a claim on such unsettled land. The burden of making sure that everything was in order had apparently been weighing on him during the journey—even in that short time I had noticed how preoccupied he was. He talked little and smiled less. I was not about to add to his concerns.

Hartley, with its dirt roads and crude huts, and a few government buildings, let me imagine how Sydney must have looked in years past. We stopped there briefly and stocked up on supplies and water. After we left the town center, we passed scattered farms and homesteads. I might have thought I was back in Ireland except for the thick forests of the bush, and the sheer sandstone cliffs in the far distance. Eventually, we turned northwest, following the Fish River towards Bathurst, the nearest town to Luke's land.

The air had cooled, although the sun was still bright. I leaned back in the dray and inhaled the fresh breeze that whistled through the flowering river oaks and the distorted trunks of river red gums that lined the Fish River. Eventually, we reached the crossing point—a narrow, wooden bridge that would take us into the Bathurst plains, and I was a little alarmed at the sight of it. Would it hold all the traffic that was crowding on to it? Why was it not made of more sturdy material, like stone? I concentrated on looking down into the water, which glinted in the sun, and through which silver fish streaked in abundance, and cranes and ducks called from swamps and lagoons. I smiled when I realized how fresh the water smelled—unlike the unfortunate odor that still haunted Sydney Harbor. Birds flew out of the tree branches, calling as they circled the river in elegant flocks—white parrots, black-billed kingfishers and laughing kookaburras—while long-legged herons delicately picked their way along the muddy sands of the riverbanks.

It was near sunset when we arrived at Luke's "settlement." In his determination to get there before darkness, he decided to forego a visit to Bathurst to check on his settler claim and go directly to his land. He swapped places with one of drivers and took the reins, turning the dray eastward and continuing to follow the river. As we progressed, the path became rockier and narrower and most of the earlier traffic faded away. I was struck by the sudden silence of the land. The only sounds were the waterfowl, which continued to call from across the river, and the rustling of the wind through the trees. Soon Luke turned off the path and drove across a flat expanse of land along a creek. The land was covered in tufts of coarse grass, pebbles and rocks, and occasional small puddles. We moved through a stand of trees and came out, at last, into a clearing which sloped upwards towards a cliff topped by thick forest. Luke stopped the dray and stood up to look around, shading his eyes against the setting sun.

I didn't know what to think. Surely this couldn't be the farm, this "Tara" as he'd once described it to me. Where were the outbuildings? Where was the fencing that marked the boundaries of the property? All I could see in the distance in every direction were stands of trees as thick as the forests on the mountains. As I sat, I saw two figures running towards us and I gripped Luke's arm. He turned as if surprised to see me there.

"It's alright, it's only my workers."

He waved back at them. "Explain yourselves, you lazy buggers," he shouted. "You were under orders to plant a patch of corn, but I see no sign of it. All I see is a tent you put up for your own comfort. What in God's name is going on?"

The men stopped short. The bigger of the two took off his hat.

"Ah sure, Mr. Kinsella, we had the corn in the ground alright, but last night some animals or birds came and scattered the lot of it."

"Aye," shouted Luke, "while the two of you were cozy in your tent with a bottle of whiskey. Did I not tell you to take turns on watch during the night?"

The smaller man piped up. "I do not drink whiskey, Mr. Kinsella, as you well know. I prefer to drink rum."

The bigger man bowed his head and said nothing. Luke shook the reins and the bullocks moved forward, causing both men to jump out of the way.

"*Feckin' eejits*," Luke muttered under his breath.

I watched as both drays were unloaded and the bullocks unharnessed and watered and allowed to graze. Later, when our belongings had been unloaded from the drays and the packhorse, Luke paid the bullockies, who then harnessed the animals back onto one of the drays and headed back the way we had come. Luke's two men scurried about, watering and tethering the packhorse alongside another horse in a small, fenced paddock, then hurriedly raising the tent we had brought with us, pounding the pegs into the hard ground with rocks. I passed no remarks as I looked up at the lopsided structure. I looked around to see what I could do to distract myself from the alarm I was feeling. The men had already built a fire, so I set about filling the kettle from a rain barrel outside their tent and hauling out the pot to make damper. As the fire was low, I decided to go in search of twigs and leaves for fuel. But the bigger of the two men laid his hand on my arm in warning.

"'Tis best I go for that, ma'am," he said, and I recognized his Irish brogue. "You'll have to be going into the forest beyond for fuel and, well, 'tis safer if I go meself."

"Thank you," I whispered.

That night I lay on the straw mattress inside the tent, swatting away flies and trying not to notice that the ground underneath me moved and shifted with burrowing insects. As before, Luke chose to sleep outside. I wanted to cry, but no tears would come. So this was to be my new home? Of all the images I'd had, this barren, unfriendly place was not among them. I wanted to scream at Luke—to demand why he had not been honest with me about what lay ahead. Clearly he didn't see this place the way I did. To him, this was his opportunity to become a free man beholden to no one—not the English government, nor Mr. Pitt, nor at the whim of those who could have reversed his ticket-of-leave. He had chosen this piece of land, and it was his, and no one would take it away. I had no doubt he would work hard to make a go of it. I remembered how my da labored on his wee patch of land, and his pride in what he could coax it to produce. I understood. I did! But none of that understanding could ease my dread of the consequences of what I had done. I was married to this man and I'd made a pledge before God to stay with him for better or worse. My anxiety about wild animals and predators that had plagued me on the journey from Sydney to this place faded in face of the new reality that while Luke was now a free man, it was I who had become the prisoner. And it had been my own doing!

I awoke late the next morning to find Luke and the men had already been at work, digging trenches in the dirt into which they scattered corn seeds we had brought with us from Sydney. The trenches formed a large square, marked by saplings around which they tied rags that flapped in the breeze. I assumed the rags were an attempt to keep the birds away, but it turned out they had another purpose.

"The way a stranger knows that a patch of land is spoken for is when they see a square of it already planted," Luke said as he sat down beside me while I was heating the kettle on the fire they had set earlier. "They don't go in for fences much in these parts."

I nodded. "I was wondering about that last night," I said.

He looked at me then, his expression solemn. "I know it must have been a shock for you, love, last night when you saw this place. I should have explained things in a bit more detail before we set out. I'm sorry."

I nodded again. I could have shouted at him that the shock had kept me awake most of the night and that if he'd explained the reality of this place I never would have agreed to come with him. But I'd made up my mind to say nothing. What would be the use? Instead I said, "It's going to need a lot of hard work to make it right but I'll try to help you as much as I can . . ."

Luke reached over and squeezed my hand. "Thank you, Kate," he whispered.

"Well, that's the corn in, now," the bigger of the two workers called as he approached the fire, the second worker close behind him. He grinned, exposing misshapen teeth through his graying beard, and dropped his axe and shovel beside him. "Any chance of tea, ma'am?"

I poured a mug and handed it to him. "Ah, that's lovely, ma'am," he said, taking off his hat, sinking down on a nearby log and rubbing his big hands together. "Me name is Malachy, ma'am, Malachy McGrath, from the mighty kingdom of Kerry, in the Emerald Isle itself."

I couldn't help but smile at his booming voice and lively blue eyes.

"Lovely to meet you, Malachy," I said.

The second man spoke up then. "Your leave to present myself, madam," he said, removing his hat and bowing. "I am Phineas Dobbs, late of the Duchy of Cornwall in dear Mother England, at your service."

Malachy and Luke both rolled their eyes as Phineas spoke. His voice was high and thin, compared with Malachy's growl, and his accent and manners those of an aristocratic English gentleman. I swallowed a giggle as I stared up at him. He wore the same cotton trousers and shirt I had seen on many convicts and laborers around Sydney, but his clothing looked clean and well laundered even though he'd been digging dirt trenches. Around his neck was a snowy white kerchief, and in his hatband a jaunty, colorful bird feather. I poured a mug of tea for Phineas, which he declined, rising abruptly and walking to his tent. Curious, I waited. He returned carrying a delicate china cup and saucer with a floral design. "I prefer the comfort of my own bone china, madam," he said, pouring the mug's contents into his cup.

At length Luke stood up. "Time to get back to work, lads! We need to start clearing the land for planting the barley."

I watched them go, still shaking my head at Malachy and Phineas. Just meeting them had improved my mood. If nothing else, I might be greatly entertained, I thought.

By sunset, Luke, Malachy, and Phineas packed up their tools, rinsed their faces and hands in a nearby water barrel, and made for the fire, which I had already set. Malachy had piled twigs and branches near his tent so that I didn't have to venture into the forest for them. They were in good form that night, filled with a sense of accomplishment.

"Tomorrow we'll get started on the house for you," Luke said. "You'll need something more substantial than a canvas tent."

I smiled, hiding my concern that he had said the house was for me and not for us. I decided I was being too sensitive and, anyway, I was going to be grateful for a house no matter what it looked like. Hopefully, I would no longer have to lie on a mattress on the ground shifting with ants and God knows what else.

After Malachy and Phineas retreated to their tent, Luke stayed on. He poured us each some rum in an enamel mug called a "pannikin," which I sipped silently. The men's voices drifted from their tent, Malachy's hearty brogue and Phineas's high-pitched patter stirring the night air.

"They're quite the pair, aren't they?" said Luke, smiling.

"Different as chalk and cheese," I said.

"Aye, but you'll never find two more loyal friends. They bicker all the time, but they'd give their lives for each other, and that's the truth."

"How do you know them?" I asked.

"We all sailed here on the same convict boat."

"What were their crimes?"

Luke grinned. "Well, I think we'll never know for sure but Malachy was accused of petty thievery and Phineas of forgery! They've hung men in England for less, so they counted themselves lucky to be transported. Malachy saved Phineas's skin more than once from other prisoners who didn't like his way of talking. When I became gardener at the Pitt House I had them assigned there as often as I could. And—when I finally had this chance, I brought them out here to Tara. I'd trust them with my life, and yours too, Kate."

"Are they still prisoners?" I said, a little uncertainly.

"No. They both earned their tickets-of-leave."

"But I heard that many of the settlers could get convict labor for free—" I began, but Luke interrupted me.

"That's true," he said, "but I've no notion of ever employing men without paying them a living wage. I know myself what it was like to be treated as a slave, and I would never treat others like that." He paused and took a sip of his rum, looking out at the blackness that lay beyond the firelight. "If the only way I could make a go of this place was on the backs of other men, then I wouldn't try it at all."

He stood up and took my hand, pulling me up beside him. "Come on, now, Kate, we've a busy day in front of us tomorrow. We must build you a house."

Whether it was the rum, or Luke's reassuring words, I went to sleep that night with a warm feeling in my heart that I hadn't felt in a long time.

"House," it turned out, was far too grand a name for the structure that began to take shape the next day. The first task was to find the best place to build it. After much exploration and discussion, the men finally agreed on a flat piece of rock, less sizeable than they had hoped, but a good starting point. Other smaller stones, they reasoned, could be used to extend the foundation. Next, saplings had to be felled from the forest, dragged to the rock, and inserted into deep holes in the ground to form the walls of the structure while others were laid across the top of them for a roof. The men groaned as they dug through the stony ground, inserting the saplings, and securing them in the sandy soil with larger rocks. Time and again a sapling stood crookedly or collapsed altogether and had to be replaced.

Phineas and Malachy argued loudly over the shape of the saplings.

"They're crooked, sir! They will not suit at all," pronounced Phineas.

"Arrah, sure they were straight enough when we felled them," shouted Malachy.

"The point remains—" began Phineas.

"Point or no point," shouted Malachy, "I'm after working my arse off to chop these trees down and they'll have to do. I'm not going back for more! And besides, if you stand where I am, the building looks straight enough, so it does."

Phineas lifted his chin, pursed his lips and stalked away.

Luke spoke up. "Leave it be. Let's eat our dinner, then we'll start stripping the bark from the gum trees. We'll need big sheets of it for the walls and roof."

I had already started the fire for the midday meal, and I hurriedly heated water, made the damper, and set the salted pork in a pot to which I added some carrots and onions we had brought with us, and poured water to make a stew. I wanted the men to enjoy a little variety for a change—they were working so hard, they deserved it.

The work went on for several more days as the dwelling began to take shape. Sheets of bark were stretched over the skeleton of saplings to make a roof and walls, secured in place with dried mud and tied with narrow strings of bark. Openings were cut for windows on either side of the front, and in the roof for a chimney through which smoke could escape. Luke inspected the bottom of the structure, making sure that no gaps were left through which a creature, a snake or a lizard for instance, could slither inside. I trembled when I thought about that possibility.

By the end of the week, the dwelling was complete. It was divided into a living room and a kitchen. Luke talked of adding an extra room onto the back of it where Malachy and Phineas could sleep, but they both insisted they would rather stay in their tent. Luke and the others moved our mattresses inside, along with two chairs, a table, two oil lamps, and a patterned jug and water bowl. Luke had insisted we bring a rug from Pitt House, like those they'd used for outdoor picnics, and I was grateful for the warmth and sense of comfort it added. The rug was the only item of which Phineas approved. I carefully placed my travel box in a corner. It was scratched and stained in places, but my name was still clearly visible on its lid and I ran my hand gently over it. It had been with me now for almost three years, like an old, familiar friend and good-luck charm.

After we finished supper that night, and Malachy and Phineas had returned to their tent, Luke and I sat for a while around the dying fire. At last he stood and took my hand. "May I accompany you to your palace, madam," he said.

I laughed. "You sound like Phineas," I said.

He pushed open the flap of bark which served as a door and led me inside. The oil lamps cast a golden glow around the room, burnishing the simple, wooden furniture, illuminating the faded blue and rose patterns of the rug, and painting a halo of light around my travel box. I sat down on one of the chairs and looked around, as Luke stood watching me. I noticed how quiet it had become now that the constant buzzing of nocturnal creatures outside had been muted. The bark sheets that Luke had hung over the window openings swayed gently, fanning the night air. For the first time since we'd arrived at the settlement, I felt protected from the outside elements, safe inside this primitive cocoon. As before, Luke turned away as I undressed and lay down on my mattress. Then he doused the lamps and undressed in the dark. Soon I heard his breathing as he drifted into sleep and it gave me comfort.

Within a few weeks the corn we had planted began to emerge through the soil, sending up tender green shoots. It was odd, I thought, that such a simple thing could bring such joy, but it did. Back in Ireland, my da took pride in what he grew, but here it was as if we were witnessing a miracle. Malachy danced around them, while Phineas permitted himself a smile. Luke's chest swelled with pride.

"Do you see them, Kate?" he said, his face alight. "There's our future right there. They'll soon be ready for harvest. And God willing so will the barley we've planted. In March we'll sow wheat, and before long we'll have a nice rotation of crops."

I smiled and nodded. I had done my part, I thought, since my job had been to water the seeds, twice daily. It was hard work, carrying buckets back and forth from the nearby creek, and spilling the water on the thirsty ground. Luke had plans to divert water from the creek to create a pond, which would serve as a reservoir from which water could flow along trenches to the crops themselves without the need for hand-watering. But that improvement was at least a year away.

It was December now, almost high summer, and by midday the heat was almost unbearable, but I kept busy. Besides a sense of satisfaction that I was doing my share to make a go of the farm, it kept me from brooding about my loneliness. Besides Malachy, Phineas, and Luke, I had not spoken to another human being in almost two months. I missed Bridie and our Sunday outings to Mass where we chatted with the other orphans. I even missed the midday meals in the Pitt House kitchen when the staff would gather and exchange gossip, complaints, and stories, even though they seldom spoke directly to me.

I had asked Luke if we had any neighbors and he'd shrugged.

"I've had no time for visiting," he said, "but I'm sure there must be some within a few miles. I heard tell there's a widow woman lives not far from here, but I've never met her."

When I asked him about the nearest town, he laughed. "Depends on what you call a 'town,'" he said. "There's a few places that might have a public house, and a few stables, but that would be it. There'd be no shops or churches. The nearest proper town is Bathurst. It's not Sydney, but growing. That's where I intend to go to sell the corn and barley when it's harvested. I'll take you with me if you like."

"Yes, I'd like that," I said, trying not to show my disappointment at his answers. He truly seemed to have no idea how isolated I felt in this wilderness.

"Does Bathurst have a post office?" I asked.

"It does, why?"

"I'd like to write to Bridie and tell her how well I'm getting on," I said.

I went back to my daily routine and asked no more questions. Besides cooking the meals and watering the seeds, I spent time keeping things as orderly as I could. I swept out the hut daily, using an upside-down branch as a broom. I also swept a small clearing in front of the hut that I liked to think of as a front garden, imagining that one day we might have pots of flowers growing around the front door. Once a week I brought the rug outside and hung it on a rope line Malachy had strung up for me, so that I could beat the dust out of it. I also did a load of washing every other day, hanging the laundry on the same line. I had offered to do the two workers' laundry as well, but Phineas insisted he would do it himself since, according to Malachy, Phineas felt no one else could do such things as well as he could! I thought at times that my days spent washing and scrubbing on the *Sabine* had paid off well and that Nathaniel's eagerness for hygiene had stuck with me. Each time I had that thought, I beat Nathaniel's image out of my mind as I beat the dust out of the rug on the line.

At last, in mid-December when the first harvest of corn and barley had been picked and loaded onto the dray in canvas sacks, Luke pulled me up to sit beside him, and we set out for Bathurst. I dressed carefully in a cotton day dress and my bonnet with the crimson ribbons. I don't know exactly what I was thinking, but I didn't want to arrive in this new town wearing my ragged farm clothes. I smiled to myself. Perhaps I'd spent too much time around Mrs. Pitt and her constant desire to impress. The weather was hot, but I prayed that no rain would come that would turn the narrow, unpaved roads into rivers of mud and delay our journey from Tara. As it was, our bullocks were not capable of moving at more than a few miles an hour—rain might have halted them altogether.

I could hardly contain my excitement about getting away from Tara and being with people again. I prattled away to Luke even though I knew he was paying little attention.

"Do you think there'll be a Catholic church there? I'd love to go to Mass. It's been so long. And shops? I need to buy some new dishes, and maybe some preserves like they sell in Sydney—just for a treat now and then. And maybe I could find some medical supplies—we have nothing at the hut—bandages and salves and the like in case someone gets hurt or comes down with a fever. And I'd love to find some needle and thread and maybe a few yards of material so I can make curtains for the windows . . ."

I knew I sounded like a child, but I didn't care. Luke only grunted in reply, but I could no more have stopped my outpouring of words than I could have stopped a river from flowing. Finally, he turned to me.

"I'm glad you're excited, Kate, but keep in mind our main purpose in Bathurst will be business. I intend to get as much money for the crops as I can and use some of it to buy more seeds and perhaps some livestock—maybe chickens or a pig. I do not intend to spend it on unnecessary items. I also must go to the colonial secretary's office to secure my land grant. Major Pitt assured me he would submit the papers but I won't rest until I have the deed to Tara in my hands."

I felt as if Luke had thrown a jug of cold water on me, drowning my enthusiasm. He was right, of course. We were running a business and we needed to make a profit. A thought occurred to me then. Was this farm a joint venture, or was I merely a bystander and unpaid laborer? Why had I never even thought about this before? At least at Pitt House I'd been earning a wage—until the Pitts fell onto hard times. I had money that was mine to spend or save as I saw fit, and I had spent very little of it, all the while hoping to save enough for my return trip to Ireland to find my brothers. As Luke's wife, surely I should be entitled to half the profits from this farm, but I knew that was unlikely to ever be the case. Luke was, and always would be, in charge. Whatever I spent, I would only do so with his permission. And, for the next few years at least, I would be spending very little.

I hung my head and bit my lip as this new reality took hold. All I could do now was be an obedient wife and pray for the success of Tara. It was not the life that I would have chosen, yet in retrospect it was exactly the life the Earl Grey scheme had contemplated for me and the other orphans—serve your indenture, marry an older man, preferably an ex-convict, become his helpmate in a life of domesticity, and bear him many children. There was never anything, spoken or unspoken, about orphans becoming independent, free women! I shrugged. Was there anywhere in the world where such a presumed role for women would ever be anything different?

I hardly spoke for the rest of the journey. It had hardly rained at all in the last months, which meant that the roads, or tracks, were in good condition, and riverbeds were so dry that we forded them with ease. However, we had to stop often to find water for the animals, which slowed our progress. By the time we reached Bathurst, my excitement towards the outing had cooled considerably. When Luke suggested that I walk around the central square and look at the shops, while he went to the granary warehouse to sell the crops, I did so with little enthusiasm. He hadn't seemed to notice my change in mood and I had said nothing to convey my disappointment. Keeping such feelings inside was not a good thing, I knew, but, in truth, there was very little to say.

Bathurst was not as large as Sydney but was nonetheless a bustling town with handsome public buildings, churches, schools, and even a hospital. There were general stores, blacksmiths, carpenters, tailors and other tradespeople, and several hotels, inns, and taverns. Like Emu Plains and Hartley, the town also catered to farmers. There were agricultural supply stores and warehouses where farm produce could be traded.

People crowded the main square, their numbers swelled by those who were traveling by stagecoach and were connecting here mid-journey. Many were well-dressed but, as in Sydney, just as many were ordinary farmers like ourselves, in town to trade their produce and buy supplies. I found the post office and, on a sudden whim, arranged to rent a box for six months for the name "Kathleen Gilvarry Kinsella," where I could receive any post. I quickly scribbled the box number and *Bathurst Post Office* on two envelopes as a return address and dropped my letter for Bridie into the outgoing mailbox, along with a letter for my brothers addressed to Matron O'Hare at Newry Workhouse. I had sent a similar letter to the workhouse every couple of months since I had been in Sydney—but I never received a reply. With each letter I said a little prayer. Maybe one of these days it would be answered.

Bored now, since I had no prospect of buying anything, I made my way back towards the granary and found Luke coming out the door, smiling.

He took me by the elbow. "Sold the lot of it for more than I expected," he said.

I smiled weakly. "That's wonderful."

"Aye. Come with me now to the colonial office, and if my luck holds, I'll be walking out of there with the deed to Tara."

It was hard to ignore his excitement, and I gave him a genuine smile.

The colonial secretary's office was in a nearby sandstone brick building. As we climbed the steps people hurried past us, most clutching papers or envelopes. Some wore military uniforms, others fine coats and cravats, while others were dressed like Luke, in cotton shirts, trousers, and slouched hats. I stood beside him as he approached a sallow-faced clerk at a desk, gave his name and explained his business.

"I take it you want to apply for a grant," the clerk said, eyeing Luke with gray, almost colorless eyes.

"No. I made application eight years ago, after I received my ticket-of-leave," Luke began.

The clerk sat upright. "So you are a convict!"

"No. I completed my sentence while working for Major Pitt in Sydney," Luke said, and I could see he was trying to hold his temper. "Major Pitt is the one who arranged my ticket-of-leave, and he is the one who made the application for a grant on my behalf."

The clerk leaned back in his chair. "Do you have a copy of it?"

Luke hesitated. "No. That is what Major Pitt told me. And, as recently as two months ago, he told me he would be in touch with your office to get a copy of it. It would have his signature on it, and would include a recommendation of my suitability . . ."

He didn't finish his sentence, as the clerk stood up abruptly.

" 'Pitt,' did you say? I shall have to check the records. Do you have a map showing where this supposed grant is located, and a copy of your ticket-of-leave?"

Luke pulled an envelope out of his pocket and held it out. The clerk took it.

"Wait here!" he commanded.

There was nowhere to sit down, so Luke and I stood looking everywhere but at each other. I didn't need to look at him to know the anxiety he was feeling. There was nothing I could say to calm him and any words of optimism would have sounded insincere to both of us. After what seemed like an eternity, the clerk returned, a smile I took for smugness on his face. My heart sank.

"Well, well, Mr., er, Kinsella is it?" he said as he sat down, handed Luke back his envelope, and spread some papers out on his desk. He looked up, pursing his lips before speaking.

"First of all, there is no record of Major Pitt ever having made application on your behalf, let alone signed such application, or vouched for your character. The parcel of land on the map you have and which you have named 'Tara'—rather whimsical, I'd say— anyway, there is no application from a Mr. Kinsella for a grant on it." He took a deep breath. "Several months ago, however, a grant application from one 'Captain Sparks' was approved by this office, based in part on his military service and, coincidentally, on a strong recommendation from Major Pitt!"

Luke's face drained of color. "What? That can't be right! Show it to me."

The clerk laid a slim hand on the document in front of him. "I can't do that, Mr. Kinsella. Such records are confidential. I have given you the grantee's name and that is all I am permitted to disclose to you."

"Well, this 'Sparks,' whoever the feck he is, hasn't shown himself to claim this land. I'm the one who's after plowing it, sowing crops on it, and building a house on it."

"So you're squatting on it," said the clerk with a sneer.

"No!" Luke yelled, as bystanders turned to watch. "I'm a settler! A free man. And I've every intention of living there for as long as I please. I'm entitled to the bloody rights to it."

"Not according to the law, Mr. Kinsella," said the clerk. "Even if Captain Sparks has not yet taken up possession of the land, the fact that he has made application, which has been granted, means he is entitled to take possession at whatever time he chooses. All I can advise you to do is to complete an application now so that it is on record, and then do what you can to find Captain Sparks and discover his intentions."

Luke put out his hand. "Then give me a copy of his application so I can find him."

The clerk stood up. "I'm afraid I cannot do that. As I said, applications are confidential. But I have a blank application form here, Mr. Kinsella."

He held the paper out to Luke, who backed away and spat on the floor.

"Give it to me," I said. "I am his wife." Then I turned to Luke. "Come on, Luke, let's go now."

I trembled under the stares of the bystanders as I led Luke from the office and out onto the street. Our earlier joy at the success of his crop trading had shriveled like a wind-dried leaf.

It was a long, silent journey back to Tara. When we arrived, Malachy and Phineas came running, excited to hear our news. But Luke ignored them, signaling them instead to take the sacks of new seeds, and other food supplies we had bought in Bathurst, out of the dray and store them. Then he walked away, towards the forest, his head bent. The men looked at me in confusion.

"I'm sorry," I said, "but we had some unsettling news. It appears someone else has been granted the rights to Tara!"

Malachy spoke up. "How can that be? Sure didn't Major Pitt himself promise the land to Luke?"

"Apparently he changed his mind," I said.

"The craven blackguard!" roared Malachy. "And after how hard Luke worked for him on his feckin' gardens all these years! He kept up his end of the bargain, so he did." He paused and took a deep breath, his face growing red. "I've a good mind to set out for Sydney this very night and wring that bastard's scrawny neck until he squeals!"

Phineas rolled his eyes. "Hardly the best way to deal with this situation, Mr. McGrath," he said. "Brawn seldom beats brains!"

Malachy sputtered. "And what would you suggest, fly boy?"

Phineas stuck out his chin. "Something much more subtle," he began. "Could it not be arranged for Mr. Kinsella's original application, approved and signed by Major Pitt, to suddenly surface?"

"You mean forge it?" I said in alarm.

"It would not be the first time such a *coincidence* has happened, madam, and it won't be the last. I have been known to accomplish *coincidences* of much greater importance than a trivial piece of paper."

"No," I shouted. "Luke would never permit such a thing."

Phineas huffed. "As you wish, madam. But my offer stands."

The next morning, when I emerged from the hut, Luke was saddling up one of his horses.

"I'm going to Sydney," he said. "I need to find Pitt and force him to face me. He needs to explain what's going on. Either that boyo at the colonial office was lying, or if not, I need to find this Sparks feller and force him to give up his rights!"

A raft of arguments ran through my head, but I realized there was nothing I could do to stop Luke. He had to work this out for himself. I was fearful for him, though. I had never seen him in such a temper.

"Won't you take Malachy with you?" I said.

Luke frowned. "I can look after myself. Besides, I'm not leaving you out here in the wilderness with just Phineas to protect you."

He leaned over and kissed me on the cheek. "I'll be back as soon as I can."

With that he mounted the horse, chucked the reins, and rode away. I watched him go, a cloud of dust rising from the horse's heels as he galloped towards the river.

I awoke the following day, feeling a strange sense of relief. The tension I had felt on the way to Bathurst when I realized what my future here on Tara would be like—beholden to Luke for every penny—had only increased when we received the bad news about the land grant. I had never seen the dark side of Luke before. He switched between silent brooding and angry outbursts, and I didn't blame him. The entire foundation on which he had imagined his future had been destroyed in seconds by what Phineas had referred to as a "trivial piece of paper." I imagined the emotions flooding through him—anger, disappointment, powerlessness, shame—the same things I would have felt myself. I had no personal fear of him, as I was convinced he would do me no physical harm. Still, I'd been terrified of saying something unwittingly that would cause his anger to explode.

He would be gone for at least a fortnight, I reasoned, as I set about laying a fire and making breakfast for Malachy and Phineas. It hadn't yet sunk in that I was now in charge of the farm, and the men might be looking to me for their orders. But Malachy laid the question out directly in front of me.

"What would you have us be doing now, ma'am?" he asked. "We can't sow the wheat until March, and the corn and barley are finished for the season."

I almost panicked at the suddenness of the question, but I took a deep breath and tried to think back to what Da might have done in between the rotation of crops.

"Well, I'd start by cleaning out the seed beds from the corn and oats," I said carefully, thinking ahead as I went along. "The ground will need to be turned over and leveled, ready for the wheat planting. And it will need to be watered." Then I had a sudden idea. "And then you can start work on the water collection and storage system Luke had planned. As I understand it, we need some way to store the water and a way to direct the flow to the crops."

I stopped, hoping what I was saying made sense.

Malachy nodded. "Aye, he talked about it surely. I think he had in mind a small pond to hold the water from the creeks or maybe the river itself. We'd need to dig a good-sized hole and line it with rocks, and then dig ditches to divert the water into it."

I brightened up. "Yes, and then dig furrows between the lines of crops and direct the water so it can get to the roots."

"'Tis a mighty undertaking, ma'am," said Malachy, "but with

the scarcity of rain these many months, we may well be needing another way to water the crops, or we'll lose them entirely."

He pushed his hat back from his forehead and scratched his scalp, lost in thought.

"At the risk of sounding contrarian," Phineas piped up, while Malachy let out a loud moan, "in consideration of the uncertainty of the future ownership of this property, I would venture to point out that building a dam and irrigation channels would require considerable labor on our part which might well inure not to the benefit of Mr. Kinsella, but to some unknown interloper named Sparks! I vote that we wait until Mr. Kinsella returns to assess the situation."

Obviously pleased with himself, Phineas leaned back and sipped primly from his china teacup. Malachy gaped at him open-mouthed and then at me. I realized then that I had made a mistake telling them about the new land grant. I should have waited for Luke to return from Sydney. But what was done, was done! Now, I took a deep breath, stood up and rested my hands on my hips.

"I will remind you, sir," I said, glaring at Phineas, "that in the absence of Mr. Kinsella you are obliged to take your orders from me. You are not being paid for your opinion, no matter how well-reasoned you believe it to be. You are being paid for your labor. I have set forth what I want done and I expect you to comply without question. That will be all!"

I stalked into the hut and closed the bark flap behind me, my heart beating fast. Looking back on it, I was reminded of the night of my outburst at the *Sydney Herald* editor at the Pitt House picnic. A torrent of words had poured out of me then, and I had been as surprised as the onlookers. Like then, this outburst was fueled by anger and determination. I knew that if I didn't establish order there and then, I would never get it back. And I was angered that Phineas was about to give up so easily. Surely, Luke deserved optimism and support from his workers, and from me.

And, if there was anything life in this new country was teaching me, it was that persistence and risk-taking were what paid off. This was no place for the faint of heart.

Two weeks came and went with no sign of Luke. I had taken to marking off the days on my calendar, just as I had on the *Sabine*. Today, I realized, was Christmas Day and nostalgia for home threatened to overwhelm me. Memories of the holiday back in Ireland—a holly wreath hanging on our front door, our kitchen ripe with smells of soda bread and fresh apple pie, the caroling of young village lads outside our cottage, and cold treks home from midnight Mass, anxious to see what presents awaited. I tried to push the memories away, but I realized they were a gift that would be with me my whole life and so I invited them in and relived them for a while.

I was sorry I hadn't something special to give to Malachy and Phineas to mark the holiday—a special treat of some kind. I wished now I had bought something in Bathurst. To their credit, they passed no remarks. A simple greeting of "Happy Christmas" and a day off from their labors seemed to suffice. Phineas's attitude towards me, which had cooled after our conversation about who was in charge, had become about as friendly as a man like him was capable of being.

I was sitting outside the hut in the midday sun, embroidering a Christmas scene on a scrap of cloth I had found at the bottom of my travel box, when something made me look up. I saw a movement on the horizon and I shaded my eyes to get a better look. It was someone on horseback and they were riding straight towards my hut. I first thought it was Luke and my heart lifted. I would be so glad to see him alive and well. But the more I stared, the more I was sure it was not Luke. My body tensed, the hair on my head prickled and I looked hurriedly around for Malachy and Phineas. Malachy had seen the figure, too, and stood outside his tent cradling a musket in his arms. My logical mind told me I should be glad to greet our first visitor—wasn't this, after all, what I had been yearning for? But logic was no match for the dread that consumed me—a naked helplessness of a kind I had never experienced before.

"Get in the hut, ma'am," Malachy said, his voice even but firm.

I retreated quickly, dropping my needlework on the ground. Once inside I stood, trembling, and carefully lifted the corner of the bark flap that covered the window. Malachy had moved to stand in front of the hut door, his gun still in his arms. The rider drew closer, stopped, and dismounted to face Malachy. I could see a gun strapped across the back of the saddle. The rider was tall and sinewy, wearing the canvas trousers and shirt of a farmer, with a straw hat pulled down over their eyes.

"State your business," called Malachy.

The rider laughed, a throaty, warm sound, then removed their hat.

I watched in astonishment as long, silver hair tumbled down the rider's back, and framed a lean, sunburned face.

"I'm Lucy Foster, come to make your acquaintance and wish you a happy Christmas Day. I'm your neighbor to the west."

She moved closer to Malachy, her hand outstretched. Malachy, somewhat taken aback, spat on his right hand and rubbed it on his trouser leg, before taking hers.

"You'll have to forgive us, ma'am," he said. "We're wary of strangers in these parts."

"Not at all!" she said. "I understand how it is. I've been running a farm on my own for three years now since my husband died, and with three young'uns and all."

I could hide myself no longer. I felt foolish for having been so frightened. I smoothed my skirt, took a deep breath, and opened the flap of the hut.

"Hello, Mrs. Foster," I said, "how kind of you to come. Please come and sit down and I'll make tea. In the meantime, can I offer you some water?"

I led her to the fire circle and gestured for her to sit down on an upturned log.

"Oh, I'm sorry," I said, still nervous, "I'm Kate Kinsella. My husband, Luke Kinsella, has the grant for this property, but he is in Sydney just at the minute. He'll be sorry to have missed you."

I ignored Phineas's arched eyebrow when I mentioned Luke's ownership. Instead I gave him a sharp look, which I hoped he understood meant that he was not to contradict me.

Up close, Lucy Foster was what the Irish would have called a handsome woman. It was hard to guess her age—I would have said in her early forties—though she moved like someone much younger. She sat now on the log, sipping a mug of water, her long legs stretched casually out in front of her. Her hands bore the scars of hard labor, however, and her face was wrinkled from too much sun, but her dark eyes were lively and full of humor.

"How old are your children?" I asked.

She smiled and her face softened. "Two lads, fourteen and sixteen," she said, "and my daughter is ten. She was born after we came to the farm."

I wanted to ask where they were. Had she left them alone?

"Don't worry," she said, as if reading my mind, "they're with Maria. Although my lads are big enough to take care of themselves, Maria's been caring for my daughter since she was born."

I smiled. "Oh, a maid then. Did she come with you to the farm?"

Lucy looked straight into my eyes. "Maria? No. She wandered onto our farm out of the bush shortly after we arrived. Her family had been butchered by a group of soldiers, probably renegades. Anyway, she barely survived. She was hardly more than a child herself at the time so we took her in. She's devoted to our children."

I looked around at Malachy and Phineas. Malachy was staring at her, taking in what she had said. While she did not say it directly, it was clear that Maria was one of the native people. I had been in Australia long enough to know that taking an Aboriginal person into your house would have been greatly frowned upon, seemingly at all levels of society.

"And d'you have any men working for yez?" Malachy asked. "I mean you can't be running a farm by yourself."

Lucy smiled. "Ah now, you'd be surprised what you can do if you put your mind to it. But yes, we still have the workers that my husband hired in the beginning." She took the tea I handed her and a piece of damper. I was embarrassed not to have anything better to offer. Again, as if reading my mind, she signaled to Phineas. "Would you mind bringing over that saddle bag?" she said, pointing to where her horse was grazing.

Phineas, surprised at being pressed into service, jumped up and did as she said. He brought the bag to her and bowed with great flourish.

"I brought some raisin cake just baked this morning. I thought you might enjoy having it on Christmas Day. It's not the sort you'd have had in England, but it's the best we can do out here in the wilderness."

"Did you bake it yourself, madam?" Phineas asked, and I knew what he was getting at. So did Lucy Foster.

"It was Maria who baked it. I taught her the recipe years ago." She paused. "But don't feel you have to eat it," she said, looking directly at Phineas. "One of my two laborers won't touch anything from her hands either," she said evenly.

Phineas looked at Malachy, who was glaring at him. "Oh, I should love some," he said, taking a slice and nibbling at it slowly.

"It's delicious," I said. "Please thank Maria."

Lucy Foster nodded. When she brushed away the crumbs of her cake she cleared her throat and looked solemnly at each of us.

"I'm afraid this is not just a social visit, although it is a pleasure to finally meet you."

I waited, my muscles tensing. Phineas held his teacup in the air, while Malachy stared at her.

"I had a visit at the farm last week from a 'Captain Sparks.'"

Ignoring my look of astonishment, she hurried on. "I don't know if you are aware of it or not, or even if it's true, but he insisted that he had the grant to your land, Mrs. Kinsella. He told me he had not yet taken up settlement here, but he'd had a surveyor explore the area, and thought both your property and mine would be well-suited to grazing. He—"

"Grazing?" I cried. "But we're farmers!"

"He said he believes there is little future in farming," she went on, ignoring my interruption, "and that much more money can be made from grazing cattle or sheep, and my sons agree with him. They tell me that people like this Captain Sparks call themselves 'pastoralists' and are acquiring farms at an alarming pace—some farther north than anyone could have imagined."

She paused, but the rest of us remained silent.

"And are ye thinking of selling out to him, ma'am?" asked Malachy at last.

"Yes," she replied. "As I've said, it's just me and our two workers running the farm now, along with my two boys, but, to be honest with you, I'm exhausted, and without my husband . . ." She let her words trail off.

"Why do you think this Mr. Sparks has not yet paid Mr. Kinsella a visit as well?" asked Phineas.

"Oh, he plans on it," she said, "but he has heard that Mr. Kinsella is in Sydney and intends to wait until he returns."

"A well-informed boyo then, I'd say," murmured Malachy.

Mrs. Foster rose. "I'd best be going before sunset," she said. "My path will take me into the bush and I'd rather not travel through it in the darkness. From what I understand from Maria, the Aboriginal tribes do not like to have their camps disturbed by the white man and, in return, they do not generally disturb us on our farms. A sort of unspoken peace treaty if you like. Obviously there are always exceptions, like the renegade soldiers who killed Maria's family."

She smiled as she mounted her horse. "Thank you for your

hospitality," she said. "I'm sorry to have brought such unwelcome news on Christmas Day. But I thought it best that you were warned, rather than be caught by surprise. I hope we shall meet again soon." She looked at me. "Perhaps your husband can bring you to stay with me for a few days soon. This can be a very lonely place for a woman!"

"Thank you," I murmured. "I would like that."

Malachy, Phineas and I sat unmoving around the fire, none of us saying a word. It would take some time before we were able to digest what Lucy Foster had said. All we could do was stare after her in silence as she rode away in the direction she had come, eventually disappearing into the bush.

That night I tossed and turned, my mind racing with thoughts of what dangers this Captain Sparks might bring. Up until now my idea of danger had been limited to wild animals and reptiles, or dingoes, the wild dogs that roamed the land at will and attacked livestock. I also worried about "bushrangers," the Australian version of highwaymen about whom I'd heard stories in Sydney. They roamed the Outback robbing farmers, molesting women, and stealing livestock. The stories were no doubt exaggerated, but there were enough accounts in the newspapers to make me believe in the threat. Now it was Captain Sparks whose image loomed large in my imagination. I had no idea, of course, what the man looked like—but it didn't matter—he was a fiend nonetheless, determined to chase us off our land. By morning, I had made up my mind to ask Malachy to show me how to shoot a gun. If Mr. Sparks, or anyone else, tried to threaten us, I wanted to be as able as anyone else to defend myself and my property.

"Sure that's hardly necessary, ma'am," Malachy said when I asked him. "A young slip of a girl like yourself. Sure you're safe enough with the two of us, and with Mr. Kinsella himself when he's around."

"Well he's not, Malachy," I said firmly, "and this is not a request, it's an order."

He tried to hide a smile as he nodded. "If your mind's made up then, sure we can start today. Won't your husband himself be proud of you when he sees what you've been doing."

After breakfast that morning he led me to an area past the creek on the outskirts of the forest. He carried a musket, along with an assortment of other things like flint, wadding, powder cartridges, a ramrod, and the metal shot for ammunition, and laid them on the ground. I looked down at them, puzzled. I hadn't realized that firing a gun involved so much beyond simply holding it to your shoulder, aiming and pulling the trigger. Several minutes of preparation were needed before each shot—more if you didn't know what you were doing. Added to that, if you were under attack you'd have to keep a cool head on your shoulders, otherwise the one shot might be all you'd get.

Malachy called the process "loading and priming" and patiently explained the purpose and placement of each item. "You push the wadding down with the rod only so far," he said, "otherwise you're likely to spill the powder."

I watched intently as he went through the steps. When the gun was ready he handed it to me. Tentatively, I took it in my two hands. It was much heavier than I expected and I almost dropped it. Malachy was beside me in seconds.

"Hold it up to your shoulder, ma'am, like this. Steady, now."

My hands and arms were trembling as I raised the weapon and pointed it towards a tree that stood apart from the others.

"That's the girl, now," he said, "pretend that tree is the blackguard Sparks. Hold her steady, train your eye along her barrel, ease back the trigger and fire."

A flash of powder exploded in my face and the gun jumped backwards against my shoulder, knocking me off balance. The ball flew high and wide past the tree and fell harmlessly to the ground. To Malachy's credit he didn't laugh at my feeble attempt, although Phineas, who had come up behind me, let out a whoop.

"Not your strong suit, madam," he crowed. "Perhaps you should stick to sewing!"

I wanted to burst into tears of shame, but I held them back.

"Leave her alone, Phineas," Malachy shouted. "Sure 'tis her very first try. And wasn't she the brave wee lass to even think of trying." He turned back to me. "You should see the cut of himself with a musket. Couldn't hit a wall if it was right in front of him."

I held the gun out to Malachy. "I think that's enough for to-day," I said. "Maybe we can try again tomorrow."

Later I thought about the gun. The weapon frightened me, it was so violent. But out here in the Outback, life was different than in the city, and the only way to protect ourselves was with guns. I sat beside the fire and gazed towards the bush into which Lucy Foster had disappeared the day before. I fancied I saw smoke rising through the treetops, just as I had one morning when crossing the Blue Mountains. Her story about Maria had caused me to remember that people lived there—people just like us who also needed to protect themselves from intruders—although we, the Europeans, were the intruders. This was their land and they were protecting it in the same way Luke and I were trying to protect Tara. But their weapon of choice was a spear—a weapon that required a great deal of skill but was so much more accurate and cleaner when it arced towards its prey, as opposed to our hot metal balls flying haphazardly through the air.

January 1851 dawned, but there was still no sign of Luke. I became increasingly anxious about his safety. I occupied myself with my daily chores and my shooting lessons. I would never be a great marksman but, as my confidence grew, I was satisfied that I could hit a target, man or dingo, some of the time. I also had begun riding the other horse that Luke owned. Perhaps it was watching Lucy Foster ride away on Christmas Day and the sense of freedom and independence she conveyed that inspired me. I had ridden horses back in Ireland and, although I was a little rusty at first, I was soon enjoying morning rides around Tara.

The dawn of a new year caused me to reflect upon my life. It was two years since I had disembarked from the *Sabine* and marched with the other orphans to Hyde Park Barracks. I felt as if I had lived a lifetime since then, weighed down by so many new experiences in such a short time. Would it always be so? I wondered. Would there ever come a time when my life would be familiar and predictable?

It was the middle of January on a sunburned day when I saw a rider approaching on horseback. I jumped up and ran inside the hut for my musket, which was primed and ready to shoot. When I emerged again, Malachy was approaching at a run, his musket in his arms. This time, he did not order me back into the hut. Instead, we stood together, our weapons held taut against our shoulders and aimed squarely at the rider.

"Don't shoot! What the feck's wrong with the two of yez?"

It was Luke. I dropped the musket and ran towards him.

"Oh Luke, you're back," I cried. "I was so worried about you!"

"Worried enough to shoot me?" he asked. "Do you even know how to use that thing?"

He dismounted and I threw my arms around him in a tight hug, then stood back to inspect him. He looked weary. His chin was covered with a scraggly beard, and his normally clear blue eyes were dimmed by dark circles. He was thinner than before and looked older by several years. I put my arm through his.

"Come on," I said. "Let's get you some water and food, and then you can tell me all about what happened in Sydney." I turned and waved at Malachy. "Take his horse, Malachy, and give him some water, and unload the saddlebags."

"Yes, ma'am," said Malachy as he came running.

Luke raised an eyebrow. "I see you've learned how to give orders!" he said.

He smiled as he spoke but I sensed something more serious beneath it.

"Sure someone had to take charge with the man of the house away," I said airily.

I didn't press Luke for information. Instead I waited until he had eaten and walked around with Malachy to see what progress they'd made in his absence, while I followed at a distance. He nodded approvingly when he saw the newly tilled land where the wheat would be sowed in March, and even more so when he saw the irrigation ditches that had been dug, awaiting water. He stopped short when he saw the large hole lined with stones where water from the creek would be collected to be used for future crops.

"Who told you to do this?" he asked.

"Why, Mrs. Kinsella!" said Malachy. "Clever lassie you have for a wife."

Luke turned to me, astonished.

"Well, Kate, it seems you have been managing quite well without me. Maybe I should have stayed away longer!"

I had expected, if not praise, at least a thank-you for my efforts, but I felt that Luke was scolding me. I tried to see things from his point of view. Was he feeling useless since the farm seemed to be running well without him? Should I have left everything alone and allowed Malachy and Phineas to do only what they thought necessary? Or did Luke have the same opinion as Phineas—if the land was no longer his, what was the point of all that effort? I bit my lip to hide my disappointment.

Later that evening, Luke went for a swim in the river, changed his clothes, and came to sit by the fire. Malachy almost had to drag Phineas away to their tent.

"Let's leave this man and his wife to themselves," he said. "I'm thinking they have a lot to talk about."

Malachy was right. I began by telling Luke about Lucy Foster's visit and what Captain Sparks had told her. "We've been waiting for him here since Christmas Day," I said, "but hoping you'd be back before his visit. That's why I asked Malachy to teach me to shoot."

Luke stared into the fire. "Aye," he said at last, "it all matches up with what I found out in Sydney. I finally tracked down your man Major Pitt—slobbering over his ale at the Emerald Isle Tavern. He's taken to the drink since the wife threw him out! He finally admitted he'd never filed my application. Instead, he offered to recommend this feller Sparks for the grant on Tara in exchange for canceling a debt he owed him. So he was lying to me all this time. Seems Sparks jumped at the chance, but he never did forgive Pitt's debt." He laughed. "Honor among thieves! Anyway, Pitt was crying after me when I left, begging my forgiveness. Useless, backstabbing bugger!"

I let some silence hang between us before I spoke again.

"And so, did you go and find Sparks? According to Mrs. Foster, he knew you were in Sydney."

"No, I tried, but I gave up looking for him. It was a waste of time. Turns out he's got a finger in many pies. A bad article, so I heard. I went to the land commissioner's office in Sydney, but they told me even less than the boyo in Bathurst." He sighed. "I suppose, once a convict, always a convict, that's what the ones in charge think. And the military officers protect one another. I talked to a lot of people who knew this Sparks, and they all agreed that he's a money-grubbing, ignorant, good-for-nothing. Mrs. Foster was right. He's hell bound on taking as much land as he can, by hook or by crook, and grazing sheep on it. There's a lot more money to be made in wool than in farming. He obviously picked Tara because there's water close by and the land is good for grazing."

He stopped talking and we sank into another uneasy silence.

"So what are we to do?" I ventured at last.

He looked up suddenly, as if startled to find me there. "Feck all," he growled.

Later that night, before Luke settled down to sleep on his mattress, he thrust an envelope at me. "Bridie sent you this," he said, "probably full of useless gossip!"

I stared at the envelope for a while, but I held myself back from opening it. I wasn't ready for any more news tonight, good or bad, I just needed to sleep.

* * *

For the next few days, Luke paced around Tara with a face like thunder. Malachy, Phineas, and I gave him a wide berth as we quietly went about our daily routines. One morning, however, when I went out of the hut to light the fire for breakfast, he was waiting for me, his horse saddled, his saddlebags packed.

"Where are you going?" I asked, surprised.

"I was offered a job at a sheep station in the Northern Territory," he said. "A feller I knew in Sydney told me about it. He's going up there himself. Seems shearing the wool off the sheep at certain times of the year can earn you good money."

"But . . . but, you know nothing about sheep!"

"The feller says it's easy enough to learn and he promised to show me the ropes."

I hardly knew what to say. "How long will you be gone?"

"About a month, maybe longer. And before you say anything else, I need the money, Kate." He walked closer to me and put his hand on my arm, but I pulled it away and tried to beat back the tears that were itching my eyes. His expression softened. "Look, I know it's going to be hard on you, Kate, but it can't be helped."

"But we'll be planting the wheat soon," I said, "and won't you earn a fair amount from that crop?"

He sighed. "Unlikely," he said. "I believe we're in for a terrible drought this year. We've had hardly any rain in the last months, and the creeks are beginning to dry up and the rivers are running low. I saw signs of it everywhere on my way back here."

"What about the irrigation channels, and the dam we're building?"

"They're only going to work if we have water to divert." He shook his head. "It's no good, Kate, it's likely the wheat will not survive. I only hope I'm wrong. I've told the men to go ahead and plant it anyway in early March."

My anger began to rise. "How am I supposed to manage with you gone that long?" I said desperately.

He smiled. "That's my least concern, Kate. From what I see, you've managed quite well without me for over a month as it is. Malachy even tells me you're a fair shot for a woman."

If he thought he was reassuring me, he was wrong. It wasn't a matter of whether I could "manage" or not. We were supposed to be facing this farming challenge together—that's what he had promised, and that's what I'd believed. I never bargained for him to be gone for a month or more at a time, and me here on my own at the mercy of anybody or anything that came along.

I turned to walk away. "You should have just gone up north straight from Sydney," I shouted. "I gather you had your mind already made up!"

"Ah, Kate—" he began.

I let my anger escape, knowing I couldn't contain it. "Don't 'ah, Kate' me. You're a selfish bugger, so you are! You never cared about me at all. All that palaver about falling in love, and making a future together—you never meant a word of it, did you? I still don't know why you wanted to marry me—it certainly wasn't for the comfort of it—you've never once reached out to touch me! So all I can surmise is that you were using me. Well, maybe I was a fool when I agreed to marry you, but I'm a fool no more, Luke Kinsella. So go on, off with you now. But don't count on my being here when you come back—*if* you come back!"

My outburst left me breathless. Malachy and Phineas had come out of their tent and stood watching me, open-mouthed. Most likely they'd heard everything I'd said, but at that moment I didn't care. I didn't care if I'd embarrassed Luke which, by the crimson that rose on his cheeks, I had. It was the truth. I couldn't look at him any longer. I was wrung dry. I ran inside the hut and pulled the bark flap closed behind me.

I didn't venture out the rest of the day even though the hot, clawing air inside the hut threatened to suffocate me. Malachy and Phineas took turns tiptoeing to the hut and silently placing mugs of tea, water, and plates of damper just inside the bark flap. Even Phineas didn't utter a word. Every time I looked around the hut, particularly at Luke's empty mattress, more thoughts raced through my head, most of them angry. How dare he treat me this way? What had I done except try my best to help keep up my end of the bargain? But it hadn't been a fair bargain. I went over in my head what I had said to Luke, what accusations I had flung at him. Were they justified? The more I thought about what I'd said, the more embarrassed I became. I knew I needed to forgive myself for the outburst. How could I have done otherwise? After all, I was only expressing the frustrations that had welled up in me over the past few months—the disappointments, the fear of the future and, yes, the growing thought that I must be undesirable to men, given that Luke had never touched me and appeared to have no interest in doing so. By the time night fell, I had no energy to even wonder what I was supposed to do now. I'd threatened to leave, but how? Where would I go? And what about my marriage vows? For the moment I had no answers.

When I lay down on to my mattress to go to sleep, I found the envelope from Bridie under the blanket. I sat up and lit the lamp again. I needed to hear Bridie's calming voice and so I tore the envelope open and began to read. Little did I know it was the worst thing I could have done at that moment.

> *Dear Kate,*
>
> *I've missed you. I hope you're doing well out in that Godforsaken land beyond the mountains. Luke was very tight-lipped about how things were with yez, but he never was much of a one for talk, was he? He looked well, though—handsome as ever.*
>
> *I'm still at the Emerald Isle. Mr. O'Leary's business has grown greatly since I've been here. I remind him of this fact every chance I get. More and more people are coming to hear me sing. The Governor was here last week. And guess what? The director of the Royal Theater was just here and he's invited me to do*

*a concert at Christmas time at the Royal itself. The
wine business is going over well and bringing more
money into the place. Mr. O'Leary keeps pestering me
to marry him. But why should I? Amn't I better off
keeping my part of the profits to meself. If I was his
wife I'd have to be giving it all to him!*

*Mrs. Pitt barely shows her face in town anymore. I
hear she's living beyond the city in what she'd call
'greatly reduced circumstances.' As for the Major, he
drags his arse into the Emerald Isle every night. In
fact that's how I knew Luke was in town—the Major
was slobbering over him, crying almost. Luke was disgusted. The high and mighty have taken a mighty fall,
just like Humpty Dumpty! (Wasn't that the feller fell
off the wall?) I still go to Mass at St. Patrick's on a
Sunday and enjoy the craic with the other orphans.*

*And Patsy Toner came to tell me she was leaving
town. She said she's going to Bathurst. Maybe she's
joining the Gold Rush! Have you heard about the
Gold Rush? There's rumors everywhere that
somebody's after finding gold up near you in Bathurst,
and every man and his brother are on their way out
there hoping to make a fortune. There'll be more of
them arriving in Sydney Harbor every day, and in
Melbourne, too, once the rumors are made official.
Can you imagine—Sydney full of Chinamen with pig-
tails, and men of every class and color?*

*Anyway, back to Patsy. She's either out to find gold
or find her fortune catering to all of them men that's
crowding up there. God forgive me for saying it. Good
enough, though, that she thought to come in here and
tell me she'd be leaving soon. She said she'd been in
touch with Sheila and Lizzie up in Moreton Bay, and
they told her they were both escaping to the goldfields,*

as well. They plan to open a business near Bathurst.
If they're to be believed, there's a fortune to be made
not just from gold but from charging people an arm
and a leg for every item under the sun that they'd need
to set up camp. More power to them all, I'd say. Patsy
said she'd stop back in before she left.
     Well, I think that's all for now. Oh, and wee Sister
Mary beyond at the convent is praying for us every
night! Write soon.
     Bridie
     P.S. I'm enclosing a letter that came for you from
Doctor Harte. It was sent from the Pitt House to Hyde
Park Barracks, and one of the matrons brought it into
the Emerald Isle to me, thinking I'd know how to find
you. Who needs a post office when the likes of us Irish
Orphans can find each other no matter where we are?

I read Bridie's letter twice, trying to ignore the burning desire
I had to tear Nathaniel's letter open and devour it. Anticipation
held me back, but so did fear. At last I could hold off no longer. I
pulled the lamp closer to the bed and slit the envelope open with
my fingers.

     My dearest Kate—
     I hope this letter finds its way to you. I've
addressed it to Pitt House, since that's where I know
you've been indentured along with Bridie. Since you
are required to stay at least until you are nineteen, I
assume you are still there (unless you've married of
course!).

I winced when I read the last part. I looked at the date of his
letter and realized he'd been writing to me at almost the same

time I was writing to him on the night before my wedding. Our letters had crossed in the post. I took a deep breath and picked his letter up again, my hands trembling.

> *I suppose I can understand why you did not write to me to let me know how you were getting on, but I confess I was very disappointed not to hear from you. I can only hope that you have been getting along splendidly and enjoying your new life. For myself, I found it very difficult to settle down once I returned to England. People around me said it was because I was still finding my "land-legs" but the truth is that I was missing you, dear Kate, so much more than I ever thought possible. I cannot tell you how many times I had to stop myself from jumping on the next ship to Sydney. There were times I was so desperate I would have signed on as a sailor just to be able to see you again. As it was, I told myself over and over that I must not interfere with your life and, instead, I threw myself into practicing medicine with my father.*
>
> *My early instincts that such a role was not for me turned out to be well-founded. I stayed less than a year on Harley Street attending to the ills of well-to-do ladies. For a while afterwards, I threw myself into the study of the role of cleanliness in medicine. I know many on the Sabine laughed at my obsession with hygiene, but it is becoming a growing field of study among my more progressive colleagues. Oh, Kate, you have no idea how much more useful I could be treating immigrant and indigenous groups in Australia than the London aristocracy.*
>
> *And now, Kate, I must get to the most important news I have to impart. It is as difficult for me to write as I know it will be for you to hear. Some months ago, I made a journey to the Newry Workhouse. I knew*

how much you needed to hear word of your brothers.
In fact, I had written several letters of inquiry there in
care of Matron O'Hare but had received no reply. At
length I decided to take matters into my own hands
and go there in person. I discovered that Matron
O'Hare had retired, but the new matron assured me
they had no boy named Christy Gilvarry in their pop-
ulation. Nor had she any information on Patrick
Gilvarry. I prevailed upon her to tell me where Ma-
tron O'Hare could be found and eventually she did.

Matron O'Hare is in frail health but her memory is
sound. She recognized your name immediately, Kate.
In fact she lit up upon hearing it. However, she told
me that your little brother Christy had run away from
the workhouse a few months after you left. It was in
the dead of winter, and when they found him, he was
frozen and hardly able to breathe. Fortunately, Ma-
tron O'Hare was still at the workhouse when they
brought him in. She knew immediately who he was.
She arranged for Father Burns to give him the Last
Rites, and . . . I'm so sorry about this, Kate . . . they
buried him next to your mother in the paupers' grave-
yard.

I dropped the letter. A guttural scream rose from somewhere deep inside me, escaping through the window openings into the hot black night, carrying across the forests and mountains and oceans, and coming to rest in the snow covered, desolate graveyard where my brother now lay.

I didn't finish reading the rest of Nathaniel's letter. For several days afterwards I was frozen with grief. My mind flooded with memories of wee Christy in good times and in bad. I tried to focus on the happy times when he played tricks on us, when his face glowed with impish pleasure. He had changed, of course, after the famine came. Some of the spirit had gone out of him and he seemed more nervous and younger than his years. He clung to Ma in a way he hadn't done since he was a baby, as if afraid that she might leave him. And then when she did leave I remembered clearly his stoic little face as he stood beside her, unwilling to kiss her goodbye. The loneliness I saw there now pierced me anew and I cursed the famine. I stopped short of cursing God, knowing it would do me no good.

February came and went. The heat remained relentless, and there was still no sign of rain. Malachy and Phineas went about their work as usual, and I did the best I could to keep busy. Rations were beginning to run low. The beef Luke had purchased in Bathurst back in December was almost gone, and what was left was hardly fit to eat given the amount of salt I had to rub into it to preserve it. There was still corn left over from our first crop and I spent hours grinding it into meal with a small hand mill so that I could use it for baking instead of flour, which was rapidly dwindling. I cried with frustration as I picked the weevils and flies out of it. We still had salted pork and Phineas went off in search of fish, but the creeks were almost dry, the rivers running low, and he usually returned empty-handed. I began to believe that I was living in hell. Several times I almost asked Malachy to take me to visit Lucy Foster. I was desperate for another woman to talk to but I didn't want to leave Phineas alone at Tara. What if Captain Sparks came while we were gone? The man's specter hovered like a ghost, causing us to flinch at every unfamiliar sound.

Near dusk one evening all three of us raced outside, muskets cocked, at the sound of riders approaching. My heart was pounding but I was ready for Sparks. Before we could do anything, Lucy Foster's voice cut through the blackness.

"Don't shoot, please. It's me, Lucy. I'm sorry about the lateness of the evening, but Maria and I have something for you."

We waited as they became visible in the firelight. Lucy was accompanied by a small woman—on a second horse, wearing a cotton shirt, long skirt, and boots—who slipped daintily down off the horse and reached for a bundle tied up in canvas. I watched as she carried the bundle to the fireplace and set it down. Then she returned and retrieved a long stick that had lain across the saddle in front of her. I gasped when I looked more closely. It was not simply a stick. It was a spear, milled to a sharp point on one end and taller than she was.

"Maria killed two kangaroos yesterday, and we decided to bring one to you. I'll bet your rations are running low just like ours. Maria has already skinned it and prepared it for cooking. She insisted on coming with me to show you how to roast it, Kate." She approached and took me by the arm. "Come on," she said. "My daughter, Poppy, is staying with a friend of mine in Bathurst, so we took this opportunity to visit. By the way, is Luke back yet?"

"No," I said, trying to hold down the bile that threatened to erupt. I knew people ate kangaroos here, but I'd never seen them do so. And I never expected that I would need to cook one.

Malachy rushed forward. "That's mighty good of you, Mrs. Foster," he cried, "sure we've been eating like we're doing penance, our stores are that low."

I brought out watered rum in pannikins and handed them around to Malachy and Phineas and to Lucy. Maria waved me away. Up close in the firelight, I could see her shining, intelligent eyes. She was not much older than myself. I recalled Lucy telling me about her on her last visit. Poor girl, I thought. She's an orphan just like me. I tried not to watch as she pulled the canvas wrapper off the animal, and taking a knife from her belt began to cut through the carcass. The carcass was surprisingly clean and intact. I realized then that if the animal had been killed by a musket ball, it would have been shredded to pieces. As it was, the spear had left only a small incision. Maria concentrated on her work without looking up, rubbing spices into the flesh. Phineas rushed to bring more twigs and branches for the fire, as she cut a large piece of meat into smaller pieces and pierced an iron stick through them. She held the stick over the fire, turning it from time to time. I thought back to the *Sabine* and how I had learned to enjoy roast shark and other fish the sailors caught and cooked. I took a deep breath. Here's to another new experience, I thought.

"Maria showed me how to cook kangaroo," said Lucy. "It's apparently how her ancestors always cooked it, not like the Europeans, who cook it in a pot the way they cook any other meat. This way is much tastier."

The smell of the meat was appetizing and, in spite of my earlier repulsion, I found myself looking forward to it. It tasted gamey, as I'd expected, but while it was pungent, it was also slightly sweet. I suspected Maria's spices, as well as her cooking method, had done much to improve the meat's flavor. Phineas too, despite his earlier reluctance to eat Maria's raisin cake, appeared to be relishing the meal. After we had eaten our fill, Maria wrapped up the rest of the animal and handed it to Malachy to store. Then she took out a small pipe, lit it, and walked a distance away from the fire, puffing on it. I looked inquiringly at Lucy.

"Pay no attention to Maria." She laughed. "She likes her privacy, and her pipe!"

I poured more drinks and we sat together enjoying an easy conversation about the weather, drought prospects, and upcoming planting season. In answer to Lucy's question about Luke, I told her he had gone to a sheep station to earn some extra money because he was concerned about drought ruining the crops. I gave no hint of my anger with him for leaving. Lucy nodded.

"Can't say I blame him, Kate," she said. "We'd be facing the same problem if we hadn't agreed to sell to Captain Sparks. Has he been here yet?"

"No," I said. "He hasn't. I'm hoping Luke will be here when he comes."

"Sure and what do we need Luke for," declared Malachy, his bluster fueled by the rum. "Sure we're fit for that blackguard any day of the week."

"Be careful just the same, Malachy," said Lucy. "My two sons and our workers were present when he came to see me but I still had a terrible feeling about the man. There's a monster in him. Maria sensed it. She grabbed her spear and crouched in the corner watching him the entire time. He cursed at her, but she held her ground."

That night I invited Lucy to sleep in our hut on Luke's mattress. Maria chose to sleep outside on a blanket. The girl seemed to have no fear. Lucy and I talked quietly well into the early hours. I finally found myself telling her about my anger at Luke.

"I'm not surprised, Kate," she said gently. "You are too young to be left out here on your own. This wilderness is hard enough on any woman, but for a young girl like yourself who's new to this country—it's especially hard." She sighed. "I was about your age when I came from England. I was trained as a nurse and looking for a bit of excitement. I was only a year in Sydney when I met my husband. He was much older than me and had emigrated as a free man. He was a builder by trade and for a while I thought Sydney would always be our home. But, like so many other men, he got the urge to own land. After all, the government was giving it away. Neither of us knew a thing about farming, but neither did most of the settlers. Your Luke was a gardener, I hear, so at least knew about growing things." She paused again. "I'm sure some of the orphan girls who sailed here with you would have adapted to this life alright—but I can see you're more refined than most. I'd have taken you for a teacher, maybe."

I blushed. "It's what I always wanted," I said. "But I've no excuse, my da was a farmer."

She laughed. "I'd say being a settler out in the wilderness of Australia is a far cry from being a tenant farmer in Ireland. Besides the roughness of it, the blasted insects and the heat, it's the bloody isolation that's the worst. Men see it differently, I suppose. But women, we need each other for support and sociability. It's hard to come by out here. Don't blame yourself, Kate, for feeling the way you do."

I drifted off to sleep, letting her words play in my head. And the next morning, I shed a tear as I watched her and Maria ride back into the bush.

March arrived and still no rain, and no Luke. The men and I set about sowing the wheat. None of us had much enthusiasm for the labor but hoped for a miracle all the same. Every now and then, thunder exploded overhead, followed by the crack of lightning like a volley of gunfire. Each time we heard it we looked to the sky with our tongues out, eager to taste the first drops of rain. But no rain came. I recalled our days on the *Sabine* when we were stuck in the Doldrums and the heavens teased us time and again with the promise of wind. The nights were the hardest. Lucy Foster's sympathy and understanding had eased my spirit for a while but hadn't erased my profound loneliness. I had come to believe that this limbo would last forever.

Around mid-March we had the crops in the ground. There seemed little else to do now but wait. I set about cleaning out the hut as best I could—scrubbing, sweeping, dusting—deliberately ignoring the fact that things would be just as dirty the next day. I washed laundry and pressed Luke's clothes and mine with a hot stone. I took out the rug from Pitt House and beat it mercilessly. Malachy took to riding around the boundaries of Tara each day and night on the lookout for intruders, both animal and human. He shot a couple of dingoes, but that was all. That's why I think he was delighted when I ran out one night screaming at him that there was a snake in the hut. He raced in to see it—a red-bellied black reptile—slithering across the floor. But before he could fetch his musket, I picked up a stout stick and ran back into the hut. Without any conscious thought, I brought the stick down squarely on the creature's back, screaming words I wouldn't even remember later. Malachy stood open-mouthed as I repeated the motion over and over, long after it was dead. Finally he pulled me out of the hut.

"You're alright, girlie," he said. "It can't hurt you now. Go and sit by the fire and I'll clean up in here."

I did as he said. Phineas, who'd been sitting on a tree stump, poured me a pannikin of rum, which I swallowed eagerly. It was then I began trembling. Phineas took a blanket and draped it around my shoulders. He watched me with a look of alarm but said nothing. When Malachy returned after disposing of the snake, he dragged my mattress out near the fire and nodded at Phineas. Without a word, Phineas went to their tent and returned with both their mattresses.

" 'Tis a grand night for sleeping under the stars," said Malachy, as he placed a mattress on either side of mine.

The month wore on. If we'd had rain, the men would have been busy redirecting water from the creeks into the irrigation ditches they had dug earlier. But as it was, the creeks were almost dry and even the nearby river was low. But each day all three of us walked back and forth to it for water to soak the newly planted wheat. The soil was so thirsty it was dry again within the hour. The whole endeavor reminded me of a story I'd heard somewhere as a child about a man who spent every day pushing a rock up a hill, only for it to roll down again. I'd wondered at the time why he kept doing it. Now I thought I understood. The man was human, and humans have something deep down inside them—call it perseverance or stubbornness—that causes them to keep going in the face of adversity. Maybe that thing is hope.

I was beginning to seriously worry about Luke. He'd been gone twice as long as he'd promised. I regretted that I'd sent him off with angry words. So when Malachy came racing up to the hut shouting, "Your husband is back, ma'am, I just saw him in the distance!" I almost jumped for joy. I quickly changed into clean clothes, ran outside the hut, and saddled the horse. I shouted for Phineas to light the fire in preparation for the evening meal. Then Malachy and I rode towards the river in the direction Luke would be coming. Sure enough a rider appeared and I started to raise my hand to wave. But as I did, something held me back. The rider was still too far away to see clearly, but a feeling came from somewhere deep down inside my body that this was not Luke. I shouted a warning to Malachy, but he was too far ahead to hear me. I picked up my pace and followed.

The rider slowly came into focus. He was much bigger than Luke and dressed in a red and black army uniform. As he drew closer, I saw his heavy jowls and thick, white hands. He wore no hat, and his gray hair was painted in strands across his head. I swallowed hard.

Malachy stopped his horse as the man raised his arm in greeting. I could only imagine the alarm Malachy must have been feeling. He glanced over his shoulder at me, and I nodded, indicating I had recognized the stranger. Slowly, I rode towards Malachy and halted my horse alongside his.

"I am Captain Sparks," the man was saying, his voice deep and clipped. "I am here to see Luke Kinsella. I have business with him."

"He's not here at the minute," said Malachy evenly.

The man uttered a guttural laugh. "I intend to see for myself," he said. "I hope Mr. Kinsella is not cowardly enough to hide behind his laborer or"—he paused and looked directly at me—"behind his lady's skirts."

I found my voice. "I assure you he is not here, sir!"

"Assure me all you wish, miss. It will do you no good."

With that he urged his horse directly towards us so that we had to scatter aside at the last minute. Ugly brute, I thought.

Malachy and I turned and followed Sparks. He was riding at a gallop now, his fat rump rising and falling in the saddle. He stopped only when he reached the hut.

"Hardly a mansion, is it?" he snarled, as he dismounted and strode into the dwelling.

I ignored Malachy's attempt to stop me and followed Sparks into the hut. I was desperately trying to control my temper. This fellow was worse than I'd imagined. How dare he barge his way onto our property and into our home without so much as a by-your-leave?

"You will not find him here," I said sharply.

He turned and looked at me, his eyes greedy as they examined me from head to toe. I was reminded of the men in the hiring room back at Hyde Park Barracks and how they'd looked the orphans over with an air of ownership.

"Where is he?" he asked sharply.

"He's at a sheep station north of here somewhere," I said, shrugging. "I don't know exactly."

"And he left you here unprotected?" he said. "Not much of a gentleman, I'd say."

"I have laborers here," I said, "and I'm quite capable of taking care of myself."

He smiled. His teeth were yellow and sharp-edged, reminding me of a shark.

"That feller who met me is an ex-convict if ever I saw one. And I'd warrant the other one is, too. You see, I called on your neighbor, Mrs. Foster, and she told me the setup here at—what is it you call it—oh, yes, 'Tara.' That's comical."

I said nothing.

"What she didn't tell me is how pretty a mistress this Mr. Kinsella is keeping."

"I am his wife," I said indignantly.

"Even better," he said slyly. "As for Mrs. Foster, she's handsome enough, but too old for me. And, besides, she has that native slut living in her house. Can't imagine what's wrong with you people out here."

I made to speak, but he moved closer. "You, now, are a different kettle of fish altogether. Are you Irish? I hear you Irish girls are wild. And very experienced, if you know what I mean."

I stalked out of the hut. I couldn't bear to look at the man's leering face any longer. My heart was beating fast but I quelled the fear. I would not let this thug scare me. I walked to where Phineas was sitting near the fire, seemingly unperturbed, while Malachy stood nervously, eyeing his musket.

"So what do we have for supper?" Sparks said as he emerged, his big frame filling the doorway of the hut. "Mrs. Foster was most hospitable, although I wouldn't eat anything that savage of hers put in front of me. But she had plenty of good rum, so we passed the time pleasantly. As you've likely heard, she has sold me her farm and is moving on. And I suppose you know by now, Mrs. Kinsella, I have the grant on this property." He paused and looked around. "Too bad you wasted your time planting crops. I just want this land for grazing. It's a good location and has plenty of water."

"Not now, it doesn't," muttered Malachy. "And it won't. The drought's already started."

"Don't bother me," said Sparks, settling his bulk on an up-turned tree stump, and loosening the brass buttons of his jacket. He looked at Phineas. "A pannikin of your best rum, my man! Chop, chop!"

I prayed Phineas would not chance a clever remark. Thankfully, he just did as Sparks ordered. In the meantime I put some salt pork in a pot on the flames with a few vegetables and brought out some left-over damper. I was not going to try to be polite to this boorish man, no matter who he was.

"And when will his lordship Kinsella be back?" said Sparks.

"We don't know. Not for a while, I should think," I said.

"Doesn't matter. I've no reason to wait for him. I want all of you off my property by the end of the month. I want that excuse for a house torn down, and these ditches put back in order. My livestock won't need irrigation ditches."

Sparks ate slowly, in between pannikins of rum, criticizing the food and the damper and generally insulting all of us. I decided to try to ease the situation.

"I understand Major Pitt recommended you for the grant," I said.

He turned towards me, his face crimson, and spat on the ground. "That's what you understand, is it? Well, let me tell you something, miss. I didn't need his damned recommendation. He's nothing but a drunk, and a failure. Spent all his money on foreign trees and shrubs, as if what grew in Australia wasn't good enough for him. And that wife of his was the biggest snob in Sydney. Well, they had their comeuppance."

"I was told you promised to forgive his debt to you, in return," I said, at the risk of provoking him.

He slammed down his pannikin on a rock beside him. "You were told, were you, you cheap little gossip? Well, for your information, he owed me a great deal of money, and I still intend to make him pay, one way or another."

I realized I had said too much. I stood up. "Well, I shall leave you to rest for the night, Captain Sparks," I said as evenly as I could. "I assume you brought your bedroll with you—a soldier like you is never without one, I'd wager. And I expect that you are comfortable sleeping in the open. But if you'd like, we have an extra tent that we can erect for you. Once you have unpacked your horse, I will take it for water, and settle it for the night."

He glared at me and stood up. He was unsteady on his feet. I didn't care, the more rum the better. The more he'd sleep. And the sooner we'd be rid of him.

Later, when everyone was settled, I lay on my mattress. I knew I wouldn't sleep that night. I hadn't even undressed. I lay, wary of every sound. Malachy and Phineas had elected to sleep outside the hut. I smiled. It was good of them to think of it but I doubted they'd hear anything amiss. They were heavy sleepers, particularly when rum was involved.

I must have dozed off, for when I woke I had the sensation that I couldn't breathe. Something was obstructing my mouth. Dimly, I realized it was a large hand, Captain Sparks's hand. Instinctively, I bit down on it. He gasped and slapped my face, cursing me.

"Keep your mouth shut, Irish slut," he growled. "I'm going to take you outside. I can't have you waking those two fools up. If you know what's good for you, don't make a sound."

He lifted me up and stumbled outside the hut. Malachy and Phineas were fast asleep. I wanted to scream, but fear made me think better of it. He threw me roughly face down over his saddle and climbed up on his horse. Soon he was riding at a fast pace away from the hut. My face was close to the ground as the horse's hooves thundered, and I felt Sparks's heavy hand on my back as he rode, but I could see nothing.

It was the smell of the trees and the sound of night birds that told me we were near the forest. Eventually he pulled in the horse's reins and stopped. He dismounted and pulled me to the ground. I lay there trembling in the blackness. Then he was on top of me, crushing me against the hard earth. He fumbled with my clothes, baring my breasts. He clutched one in his hand, brought down his mouth and began slobbering over it, his teeth sharp. I cried out, but no sound came. It was as if my throat was locked shut. He shoved my clothes up to my waist, and pulled my legs apart, scratching and pinching my inner thighs. He lowered his trousers and I could feel his flesh clammy against mine. My mind was in turmoil. Noise was exploding throughout my body, but I knew no sound was escaping. His weight was so leaden on top of me that I could hardly move. Finally, I managed to free my arms and began to scratch—his face, his eyes, his ears, his scalp—anywhere I could reach his flesh, and all the while he kept thrusting at me. Then all my senses shut down.

When I awoke, I was aware of a weight on top of me. My mind raced to memory. It was still happening. How could this be? Then I realized he was not moving. Could he be asleep? As the sun's rays penetrated the blackness, I was aware of his face buried in my shoulder. I peered over him and saw a long stick protruding from his back. Panicked, I turned my head from right to left. Maybe I imagined it, but I fancied I saw Maria sitting cross-legged on the grass, watching me. I opened my mouth to speak but could form no words. When I looked again she was gone!

The cool, wet cloth on my forehead was soothing. I tried to open my eyes but I was blinded by the sun. I heard voices around me, distant and unrecognizable. I closed my eyes again and surrendered to the dream. Later, when I woke again, someone was holding a mug between my lips.

"Drink now, love, it will do you good."

The voice sounded familiar. It was a woman. I sipped the water but coughed as I tried to swallow.

"Easy now, just a little at a time."

I tried again, this time feeling the cool water trickle down my throat.

"Thank you," I murmured.

"That's the girl, Kate," she said.

I opened my eyes then. The glare of the overhead sun had gone, and I was able to peer at the woman.

"Lucy!" I said. "Lucy. What are you doing? Where am I?"

She smiled. "You've had a bad time," she said, "but you'll be alright. Can you sit up now—it will make it easier to drink."

She put her hand on my back and helped me pull myself up. I was sitting by the fire. Malachy and Phineas sat across from me, leaning forward, somber looks on their faces. Maria was on her knees, tending some pots.

Then memory assaulted me like a violent wave, and I screamed. "Help me!" I shouted, looking frantically around. "Stop him. Don't let him near me!"

Lucy tightened her hold on me. "It's alright, Kate. He's gone."

"But what if he comes back?"

"He won't be back," whispered Malachy. "He can't hurt you anymore."

I closed my eyes, trying to blot out the terrifying, fractured images that assaulted my memory. A sharp pain pounded my head and my ears buzzed with the sound of a thousand flies. I tried to speak, but the words stuck in my throat. I lay back limply against Lucy.

When I came to, again, my panic had eased. I shifted myself out of Lucy's grip and looked from one to the other, examining each of their faces.

"Tell me what happened, please," I said. "I must know. Did he . . . was I . . . ?"

I could hardly get the words out. Malachy and Phineas winced and nodded towards Lucy. I looked hard into her face as she began to speak.

"He tried to, Kate, but from what I can see he didn't succeed. Someone killed him before he could."

"The spear," I breathed. "That was what I saw in his back."

Lucy nodded. "Obviously one of the natives. You were close to the bush after all. Whoever it was must have seen him or heard you screaming." She paused. "Then after they killed him they would have disappeared into the bush. That is their way."

I looked over to where Maria knelt by the fire and our eyes locked. "I know," I said. "Please, if you can, let them know I am very grateful."

It took a few days for the swelling on my face to subside, longer for the bruises and scratches elsewhere on my body to heal, but there would be no healing the memory. It would always be a part of me. And so I folded it away somewhere deep behind my heart.

Lucy stayed with me for two more days, then left, insisting I come to stay with her as soon as I was well enough. Malachy and Phineas tiptoed around me at first, but I finally had to ask them to stop behaving as if I was some hothouse plant. That loosened their tongues.

"May he rot in hell," shouted Malachy. "Bloody bastard!"

"The proper punishment would have been to be boiled in oil," said Phineas, "but, given this lawless land in which we find ourselves, all I can hope is that the dingoes feast themselves upon his blubbery flesh."

Malachy then filled in the rest of the puzzle. "When we awoke that morning, we saw that Sparks's horse was gone and we were relieved. But when you didn't come out of the hut, and we searched and found it empty, it finally dawned on us . . ."

"Dawned on *you*, sir," interrupted Phineas. "I spoke of my alarm upon wakening but you chose to ignore my superior intuition!"

Neither of them admitted that, in fact, Sparks had dragged me right past them and they didn't wake from their rum-soaked sleep. But—what was done was done. I didn't want to imagine Luke's reaction when he found out, though.

"We saddled up and rode off looking for you," said Malachy. "It took a while, but we found yez near the edge of the forest, and himself lying there with a spear the length of me two arms buried in his back. It took the two of us to lift him off you and I brought you back to the hut, while Phineas rode over to get Mrs. Foster."

"And the good lady didn't hesitate," said Phineas. "She fetched her medicine box, and her, er, maid, gathered some bottles. Potions of some kind, I assumed. And followed me forthwith."

I looked at Malachy. "And what did you do with his body? Should we call the police? After all he was murdered. Someone is bound to miss him."

He shook his big head. "I'd say there's more people toasting his end than are missing him," he said. "The spear proves it was the natives done it and the police won't be accusing any of us, or them! And anyway, when the dingoes have had their feast there won't be much left of him to identify." He paused. "We *did* think to take his belongings and burn them, though!" He finished speaking with a look of pride.

"*We?*" Phineas said.

Another thought occurred to me. "Was there anything in his pockets? Identification? Or money?"

They both shook their heads. "Nothing at all, ma'am," mumbled Malachy, "and if there had been we'd have burned it and brought the money to you, wouldn't we, Phineas?"

"Indeed," said Phineas in a tone that lacked his usual certainty.

Later I said, "What happens now? Mrs. Foster was counting on selling him the land. And what about Tara?"

"Luckily, Mrs. Foster already has her money from the blackguard and I don't expect she'll be wanting to give it back to any of his survivors." Malachy chuckled. "And as for Tara—I'd say it's Luke's."

"If he even wants it," I said.

After our conversation, I thought about how Phineas had described this land as "lawless." The Outback certainly didn't operate under the same system as Sydney, or probably Melbourne, or Adelaide, either. But I didn't agree with him that it was entirely lawless. Instead of an organized legal system, there was nonetheless a kind of rough justice that, though unspoken, everyone seemed to understand. Every man and woman who ventured out here to settle land faced the same equally unforgiving perils without fear or favor, and it followed that a similar give-and-take kind of justice had taken hold. This new land still had much to teach me.

At last, Luke returned. Malachy spied him in the distance and rode out to meet him and tell him the news. When he arrived at the hut he was trembling.

"Kate!" he shouted as he rushed in. "My God, Kate, are you alright?"

I had no answer for him. Instead I burst into tears. He moved closer, threw his arms around me, and held me while I sobbed. He was covered in dust, his beard ragged, and he reeked of animal dung, but I clung to him just the same. He was the sanctuary I had been seeking ever since the day Sparks had come. We stood together for a long time, until he gently untangled me from him and led me to a chair. He pulled up a stool and sat, his eyes searching my face. As I stared back at him, I saw an expression I had never seen from him before. Where I had expected rage, instead I saw anguish.

"I'm so sorry, Kate! How can you ever forgive me for leaving you alone here with that monster on the loose?" He was weeping openly now. Again, I had no answer for him. How was he to know I didn't blame him? It was myself I blamed. I had driven him away with my harsh words and complaints.

"It's not your fault, Luke," I whispered at last. "Please don't blame yourself."

My words brought him no comfort. He began to rock back and forth on the stool, sobs wracking his body, like the keeners at an Irish funeral. I stood up, took his arm and guided him towards his mattress.

"Lie down, now, Luke," I said. "You're exhausted. Rest, now, we can talk again in the morning."

He didn't try to fight me. He was drunk with sorrow. Like a child, he let me lower him onto the mattress, remove his filthy shirt and trousers, pull off his boots, and gently lay a blanket over him. He was asleep in minutes. I tiptoed out of the hut and over to where Malachy and Phineas sat in silence. Phineas poured some watered rum into a pannikin and handed it to me.

"He's in a bad way," said Malachy at last. "He blames himself."

I nodded. "He does. But he's exhausted, too. A night's sleep will do him good."

Malachy nodded. "I think he had a rough time at that sheep station. Did you catch the stink of him from being around them dirty oul' sheep? I was tempted to throw him in the river to wash it off before bringing him to you. But once I told him about Sparks, nothing could stop him from galloping straight here!"

"I'm glad you told him, Malachy. I wouldn't have had the heart to do it."

"A fine sentiment, madam," put in Phineas, "to want to spare your husband's feelings, but it is you who needs comforting, not . . ." Malachy's glare stopped him from saying more.

I stood up. "Goodnight," I said. "I'll see you in the morning."

Over the following days, Luke seldom left my side. He had Malachy bring a barrel of water into the hut to wash, which he did unashamedly, scrubbing his chest and limbs roughly, and shaving off his beard.

"I must have smelled like a manure pit," he said. "How could you have stood being near me? I could hardly stand myself."

"I admit it was pretty foul," I said.

"Malachy said Mrs. Foster came and took good care of you," he said. "I must visit her personally and thank her."

I nodded. "Her maid, Maria, was a great help as well. You must thank her too."

Every now and then, Luke would explode with a string of curses, berating Malachy and Phineas for their failure to stop Sparks, and then berating himself. It was his way of letting his anger out.

"I'm just glad he's dead," I said at last. "Please don't mention his name anymore."

Luke nodded. "Killed by a spear, so Malachy said."

"Yes," I said.

One day, about a week later, I decided it was time for a real talk with Luke. I persuaded him to ride with me beyond earshot of the men. It was a cool, early May day, a reminder that it would soon be winter in Australia. I was careful to avoid the area where I guessed Sparks had brought me, although I found myself examining the ground and ditches for any sign of human bones. We reached the place where Malachy had first taught me to shoot, a level, grassy place shaded by several trees. We dismounted and I spread out a blanket on the ground. I had brought some cold pork and damper for our midday meal.

"Not exactly up to Mrs. Pitt's picnic standards," I joked.

Luke laughed. It was nice to see his smile again. He was beginning to look like his old self. When we had eaten, I took a deep breath.

"Luke," I began, "we need to talk about the future."

He nodded. "And the past, too," he said.

I was reminded of the long talks we used to have in the gardens of the Pitt House at the grotto, near the pond. How long ago that seemed. What a different person I was back then. Luke leaned back on his elbow and waited for me to start. I swallowed hard, and then the words flooded out.

"Luke, I know I made a pledge to marry you 'for better or worse' and I've tried my hardest to live up to that, but the truth is . . . the truth is I can't do it anymore."

He opened his mouth to speak, but I put up my hand.

"And no, this has nothing to do with what Sparks did, although it might have made my decision more urgent. I knew what I was doing when I agreed to marry you. I no longer had employment, little prospect of new employment, and I had very little money— certainly not enough to sail back to Ireland. And you were, and are, a trustworthy man, and you had been good to me. No, I was not in love with you, as I told you, but I believed in time that would change. And, I admit, part of me was excited about a new adventure. When I saw the Hartley Valley as we came down the Blue Mountains, with its green pastures, cottages, and flower gardens, I truly thought I would be entering paradise."

I paused to fight back tears. "But that's not what Tara turned out to be. Oh, Luke, I tried to make the best of it—to put up with the flies, the mosquitoes, and the animals prowling in the night. I tried to make myself useful, to cook, clean and help with the planting. With every day that passed, I let my dreams fade, and accepted the reality that was in front of me. Even after we went to Bathurst and you scolded me for wanting to spend money, and I realized I had lost much of my independence, I accepted it. And when it seemed we had lost Tara, I was ready to help you fight to get it back. I was determined to stay true to my marriage vows. And God help me, Luke, I still am." My tears began to flow freely. "But above all, it's the isolation, Luke. I know I'll never get used to it!"

He sat up then. "Stop it, Kate!" he shouted. "Stop it, right now!"

The shock of his anger dried my tears. I stared at him open-mouthed.

"You have it all wrong," he said, his voice calm. "I am not as trustworthy as you think."

I waited.

"We are not married, Kate! There, that's the truth!"

I clenched my arms to my stomach as if to defend myself from more body blows. What on earth did he mean?

"Maeve isn't dead," he said, his eyes boring into me and his lips trembling, "even though she was declared so. I knew better. She'd returned the ticket I'd sent her for her passage, saying she was in love with another man and was staying in Ireland."

"But—" I began, but he held up his hand to halt my questions.

"I know. Under Australian law, I'm a free man, but under the Church's law, I'm not. Maeve said she was petitioning for an annulment, which would render our marriage null and void—her family was very influential with the Church, so I'm sure she got it approved, even though our marriage had been consummated. There's no divorce in Ireland, as you know, but she and her new lover will live together regardless of the law." He paused and took a deep breath.

"Then, why—"

He put up his hand again. "Let me get it all out, Kate, before I lose my nerve. I lied to you, and I'll never forgive myself for that. I gave in to weakness and loneliness. I'd been telling the lie about Maeve's death for so long, I suppose I almost believed it. Besides, I convinced myself I could make you happy. Why I thought that I don't know, I clearly had failed to make Maeve happy. I never stopped to think what would be best for you— that you deserved someone who honored and admired the strong, independent girl you are, not a broken failure like myself."

He paused for a moment then went on, his voice faltering and hoarse. "The things you said to me the night I left for the sheep station were all true, Kate, and I deserved your anger. Except you were wrong about why I never consummated our marriage. I wanted to desperately. It took everything I had to hold myself back. You are beautiful, Kate. But my conscience had started eating away at me. I could see how unhappy you were, and how hard you tried to make the best of this marriage. Deep down I knew you'd never leave me of your own accord because we were still married in the eyes of the Church. It was the notion of the Church annulment that made me finally realize that reasonable grounds for it—that is, forcing myself not to make love to you—was the one gift I could give you, not to make up for the lie, but to ease the guilt I knew you'd carry your whole life if you left me. And maybe I thought it might ease my own guilt just a bit for what I'd done to you."

He stood then, turned his back to me, and walked some distance away. I stared after him, dazed, while a pair of kookaburras in a nearby tree circled above us, their mocking laughter filling the sky.

I hurried to my horse, leaving Luke standing with his back to me, and rode towards the hut. I was so full of emotion I felt as if I might explode, yet I knew I would be unable to say one more word to him. A storm of thoughts spun in my head so fiercely I had to grip the reins to keep my balance. I bit down hard on my lower lip to keep from screaming. When I reached the hut, I almost tumbled from the saddle in my haste to get inside. I didn't even stop to tie up the horse's reins. I pushed through the bark flap, closed it firmly behind me, and stood in the dim light breathing heavily. Bile rose in my throat and I was afraid I might vomit. I stood there for some time trying to gain control of myself. At last all thought and emotion drained out of me, leaving me feeble as the drought-starved wheat crop outside. Weakly, I lay down on the mattress and closed my eyes.

Before dawn, two days after Luke's confession, I put my few belongings in my travel box and handed it to Malachy, who waited to drive me to Lucy Foster's place. Lucy had agreed to drive me to Bathurst. When Malachy left to put my box in the dray I turned to Luke. We stood a few feet apart.

"What will you do with Tara?" I said.

"I want nothing to do with it," he said, his voice flat. "The place is cursed. Whoever wants it is welcome to it."

"And what will *you* do?"

He shrugged. "I'll be leaving for the sheep station in the Northern Territory. The owner offered me a job as stockman while I was there, and I'll be taking him up on it. I've asked Malachy and Phineas to go with me." He paused. "And what about yourself?"

"Me, well, I'll go as far as Bathurst and stay a while. Bridie said Lizzie and Sheila might be going there. It would be nice to see them. After that—well, I don't know."

It struck me then that we were like two strangers having a polite but strained conversation. I turned to go.

"Wait," said Luke, moving closer, "I need to give you this." He reached into his pocket and pulled out an envelope. "This is half the profits from the sale of the corn and barley, and half of my wages from the sheep station."

"No," I said, ready to protest as he handed me the envelope.

"It's your share, Kate," he said. "We were partners, after all."

At that moment, all pretense of strangers fell apart. I threw my arms around him and he stepped into my embrace.

After climbing up into the cart beside Malachy I gazed around at Tara for what I knew would be the last time—at the frail-looking wheat crop, the irrigation ditches where no water flowed, and at the lopsided hut that had been my home for almost a year—all of it a symbol of broken dreams, both Luke's and mine.

Neither Malachy nor I spoke until we were within sight of the Foster farm when he leaned over and patted my knee.

"Phineas and me, we're going to miss you, love," he said, his eyes moist. "You're a grand *girleen*, so you are. You're a credit to Ireland. And I wish you every bit of luck in the future. May God bless you!"

It was a short speech, but he'd said everything there was to say. I smiled as he helped me down from the dray, carried my travel box to Lucy's dwelling, then bowed and returned to the dray. He turned the bullock around and chucked the reins, and drove away in the direction we had come, without looking back.

I was glad that Lucy was there. I wouldn't be left alone to think about what had happened. She brought me tea and a slice of Maria's raisin cake but asked no questions. It was clear she understood and was sensitive enough not to probe too much.

"Luke asked me to drive you to the Bathurst Inn. It is a much shorter drive from our farm than from Tara, so if we leave soon we should be there before dark."

"I appreciate it . . ." I began.

"It's no bother," she said, waving her hand. "I have to fetch Poppy—my daughter—from my friend's house over there, so we can kill two birds with one stone."

"Have you decided where you are going after this?" I asked.

She nodded. "Well, my sons have already gone to Melbourne to buy some sheep to start their grazing business." She smiled. "Ah, the enthusiasm of the young! As for me, I intend to move back to Sydney with Poppy and Maria. I still have friends there, and nurses are always in demand."

"When you settle in, you must go to the Emerald Isle Hotel and find my friend Bridie O'Sullivan and let her know your address. I would love to visit you and Maria if I'm back there."

It was early evening when we reached Bathurst and I was shocked to see the activity. The population appeared to have exploded since my previous visit. Weary-looking men trudged through the streets carrying what looked like everything they owned in bags which hung from their shoulders by a leather strap. Hanging off the sides of their bags were iron kettles, teapots, and pannikins; and from their belts, knives, or tomahawks protruded.

"What on earth . . ." I began.

Lucy shook her head. "Gold!" she declared. "Rumors have been spreading for months of a gold find near here, and these fools dropped everything and raced here to be the first in line!"

I recalled now that Bridie had mentioned such rumors in her letter but I hadn't paid much attention to it.

"Is it true?" I asked. "Is there really gold hereabouts?"

Lucy frowned. "Like I said, it's just rumor now. The government hasn't confirmed it yet, but I imagine Bathurst and every town near it will be overrun once they do!"

She halted in front of the Bathurst Inn and I climbed down and lifted my travel box out of the back of the dray. I was sad to leave Lucy, not just because she had been a good friend, but I was also nervous about being left alone.

"Thank you, Lucy," I said, "for everything . . ."

She waved her hand at me. "No thanks necessary. Go on now and start your new life. I wish you well, Kate."

With that she urged the bullock forward and was soon swallowed up in the traffic that choked the main street. I stood until she was completely out of sight, then I picked up my box and walked slowly towards the front door of the inn.

Inside, the inn was just as crowded as the streets had been. Men and women of every "class and color," as Bridie had described in her letter, pushed past me, shoving me this way and that as I made my way to the clerk to get my room key. The din was deafening—shrill, harsh voices warring with each other as I struggled down the hallway. At last I pushed open the door of my room and slammed it shut behind me. I dropped my travel box and stood with my back leaning against the door until my ragged breathing calmed down. Despite my hunger and thirst, I had no intention of venturing back out until morning.

Part Six

Freedom
1851

Sheila and Lizzie were not hard to find. A few inquiries with local shop owners in Bathurst were all that was needed.

"Those two Belfast ones, you say, sure everyone knows them. A brazen pair they are, too, but they'd make you laugh despite yourself. And good businesswomen. They know how to find a bargain and to sell it on for twice the price. Sure everybody's doing the same since the gold diggers flooded into Bathurst."

I waited a few days before venturing out to find them. I needed time to compose myself after leaving Luke. I had to decide what, and how much, I was prepared to tell them. They most surely had heard from Patsy about my marriage, so I decided to simply say that Luke was up in the Northern Territory. I'd say I'd heard from Bridie they were here in Bathurst, and I wanted to see them again. At last, confident that I had my story straight, I put on a clean day dress and my bonnet with the red velvet ribbons and set out.

I'd been told that their shop was on the corner of William Street but I didn't know the name of it, so I began at one corner and worked my way down with no success. I crossed the street and was preparing to work my way up the other side when I saw a large, oblong tent sitting a few yards away from the row of shops. Hanging above the entrance was a crude wooden sign on which the words "Emporyum, S and L Proprietrusses" were scrawled in black letters. I smiled at the misspellings. A young woman dressed as a leprechaun in a green coat, buckled shoes, and top hat and carrying a bronze pot full of what looked like fake gold nuggets, stood outside calling out to passersby.

"Best prices between 'ere and the diggins," she cried in a strong English accent. "We buys, we sells, we takes gold or cash. We got everything you'll want for finding gold. All you 'ave to do is make a wish on this lucky leprechaun and you'll be finding your own pot o' gold."

I looked up and down the street but saw no one else hawking their wares outside their shops. I had to admit she was effective based on the crowds she attracted. I was in no doubt that I had found Sheila and Lizzie's place of business.

I pushed my way through the entrance and was overwhelmed by the scene before me. Goods of all kinds were heaped together in no apparent order or category. Bags of sugar and flour and barrels of pickles kept company with ankle boots, picks and shovels, saddles, and serge trousers. Bread, ale, cheese, and butter shared shelves with hats, rope, washing pans, and candles. I was almost deafened by the noise of customers shrieking and swearing, and the cloying odors of the merchandise in the hot tent made me feel a little faint. The aisles between the shelves were so narrow I had to turn sideways.

I finally made my way to the counter where two women stood, one of them totting up sales, and the other examining goods brought in by people hoping to sell them off.

"I'll give you no more than thruppence for this piece of shite," one said, examining a round metal pan a man had given her.

"But it's hardly been used," he said. "We were only at the diggings a week when the wife wanted to give up and go back to Sydney. I paid ten times that for it new."

"Maybe you can keep it as a souvenir then." The woman shrugged. "Take it or leave it."

The man took the money and shuffled off.

I moved forward and took his place.

"What is it you're wanting?" the woman said, without looking up. "You're holding up the queue."

She was stouter than I remembered, and her once ruddy cheeks paler, but I knew at once who she was.

"Sheila?" I said. "It's me, Kate. From the *Sabine*."

She lifted her head and stared at me. "Who?"

"Do you not remember me, Sheila?" I touched my bonnet. "Do you not remember these?"

Her eyes widened with recognition. "Och, Jesus, Mary and Joseph, 'tis yourself, Kate Gilvarry! What in the name of God are you doing here?" She turned to the other woman. "Lizzie!" she shouted. "Lizzie, do you see who's here? 'Tis the doctor's wee pet from the boat, Kate Gilvarry!"

Lizzie looked up from the bill of sale she was writing and her mouth fell open in surprise. She stared at me but offered no greeting. I wasn't sure what to make of their response. I hadn't expected that they would throw their arms around me, but I had hoped for a warmer welcome.

"I heard you got married. Was it to the doctor?" Sheila asked.

"No," I said. "My husband's name is Luke Kinsella. I met him in Sydney. We have a farm not too far from here. He's away up north at the minute. Bridie wrote and told me you two might be in Bathurst, so I thought it would be nice to pay you a visit."

I tried to control my nerves, as I prattled on while they both continued to stare at me in silence.

"I—I can see you're busy," I said. "Maybe we can meet at a more convenient time. I'm staying over at the Bathurst Inn. Perhaps you could join me for dinner this Sunday?"

They looked at each other.

"Aye, why not?" said Sheila. "It might be good *craic*."

"Wonderful," I said uncertainly. "Well, goodbye then."

I made my way back down the narrow aisles and out onto the street as fast as I could, all the while feeling them staring at my back. I went straight to the inn, took off my bonnet, sat down on the bed, and tried to push away the self-pity that crept over me. Did I have any friends left in this godforsaken land? I wondered.

I passed the next few days quietly. I went out to the post office to check for any letters in the box I had rented. There was nothing of any interest. I went to the nearby Catholic church and arranged for a Mass to be said for wee Christy and Ma. I had only one living relative now, my brother Paddy, and who knew where in the world he might be. I'd hoped there might be a letter from Nathaniel—he would have received my letter by now telling him I was a married woman. Should I write to him and tell him it had all been a mistake? I could make no decisions in my present state, so I decided to wait.

On Sunday evening, I sat in the dining room at the Bathurst Inn and waited for Sheila and Lizzie. As I sat, I wondered if they would even come. The inn was more crowded than it had been when I'd first arrived and I amused myself watching the various groups of people present. I was suddenly aware of a child—a wee girl about two years old, with black, curly hair, deep dimples in her cheeks, and clear blue eyes—standing beside my chair and pulling at my dress. I looked down at her.

"Hello," I said, thinking she had escaped from one of the groups of prospectors, "what's *your* name?"

"Sabine," she said in a loud, clear voice.

I gaped at her, unsure what to say. Just then Lizzie came running over and scooped her up in her arms.

"Sabine!" she cried. "Don't be so bold. I told you to wait for me." She looked at me. "I'm sorry if she annoyed you, Kate. She's got a mind of her own."

"She—she's gorgeous. Congratulations, Lizzie."

She sat down, taking Sabine on her lap. I couldn't take my eyes off the child.

"Sabine?" I said.

Lizzie's pale face reddened. "Aye—I decided to call her after the ship that brought us here, and where your Doctor Harte saved the child's life, and mine too!"

I looked at Lizzie now. Unlike Sheila, she appeared much thinner and paler than I remembered, and older. Her open defiance seemed to have disappeared, replaced by an air of patience. Was the change due to motherhood or exhaustion, or both? I wondered.

Sheila arrived with all the bluster I remembered. That part of her had not changed. She wore a gaudy red dress, her throat and arms adorned with baubles. She looked around.

"So this is how you rich people live?" she said. "A far cry from the grandeur we had in Moreton Bay, eh, Lizzie?"

I ignored her remark. After we'd ordered and the server had brought us drinks, I said, "So tell me about Moreton Bay, and what brought you here."

"Not much to tell," said Sheila. "That place is at the arse end of Australia. It's ugly as hell, cold and damp in the winter, hot and humid in summer, and surrounded by water. There's nothing to do and nowhere to go, the boredom would drive you innocent so it would. There used to be a prison there, but it's closed now. Too bad—at least the prisoners might have been good for some *craic*. Right Lizzie?"

Lizzie nodded and gave Sabine a drink of water.

"How were your placements?" I asked. "Nathaniel, I mean Doctor Harte, came to Sydney after he left you and told me a little about your circumstances."

"Aye," put in Sheila, "and did he tell you Lizzie here had to promise to give up her baby to that couple?"

I nodded. "He did." I turned to Lizzie. "But obviously you didn't."

Sabine let out a squeal and pounced on a plate of beef the server brought.

"I'll tell you what happened," said Sheila after ordering her second round of rum. "My indenture wasn't that bad. I worked in a drapery shop for an English couple. They weren't bad people, but the wages were low, the hours long, and I was bored out of my skull."

"Aye, your employers were saints compared to mine, even though the man of the house was a clergyman," said Lizzie, warming to the conversation. "They had me down on my knees scrubbing floors day and night, washing and ironing and cooking. The wife never lifted a finger. They said I deserved penance for my sins. And what could I do? I had nowhere else to go." She paused and leaned back, smoothing Sabine's hair. "The thought of giving them my baby to raise terrified me. But I signed the papers the day after she was born just the same, may God forgive me."

"It was another year before we decided to make a run for it," said Sheila. "I'd heard people in the shop talking about the rumors of gold being found up here. People were leaving Moreton Bay in droves. So I dressed up as a man, and Lizzie and I posed as a married couple with a child, on our way to the diggings. The hardest part was getting on and off the schooner we had to take to Sydney without being fingered. If there hadn't been such a crowd of people we would have been caught and sent back. Then we joined the procession of people going over the Blue Mountains. We had to go on foot."

"I can't imagine," I said. "It was bad enough when Luke and I made the journey by dray." I looked at them and smiled. "Congratulations on getting through it."

We were silent for a few minutes, all of us lost in memory. I thought about Lizzie escaping with her child and I hoped the authorities would never find her. But I said nothing to her.

"And now you have this emporium," I said. "And it looks like you're doing well."

"It took us a wee while to get going," said Lizzie. "We hadn't much money to buy stock. But once we realized the prospectors who were walking away empty-handed from the diggings were offering their equipment for next to nothing and we could sell it on to the fellers just arriving, for far more money, we decided to jump in."

"Ah, sure it's easy done," said Sheila. "Most of the customers are so anxious to make a killing in gold, they'll pay almost anything for supplies. You just need to know how to charge. Some of the other shopkeepers don't like it but that's their worry. There's nobody stopping them from charging more."

"And nobody else has a leprechaun hawking their wares out in the street," I said.

Lizzie giggled. "Aye, that was Sheila's idea!"

"But wouldn't it be easy for burglars to break into your tent at night and rob you?" I asked, posing a question that had been bothering me.

"Well, we sleep behind the counter," said Lizzie, "and we pay two fellers to keep watch at night. They have dogs, too, so God help any boyo tries to rob us—there's more than one has left with part of his arse missing."

I spluttered as I tried to swallow my tea. I'd forgotten how direct the two of them were in their talk. It was like old times on the *Sabine*. I thought of Patsy.

"I heard from Bridie that Patsy's coming here to join you?"

"Aye," said Sheila, "she should be here any day. We're going to set up a wee coffee tent next to our place with an oven, coffeepots, and the rest, and Patsy can run it. Sure she can make damper with the best of them after what she learned on the ship."

"And more than that—bread, cakes, and the like," said Lizzie.

I said nothing about what I knew of Patsy's circumstances in Sydney.

Sheila ordered another rum and sat back staring at me as if she was sizing me up. "You've changed, you know," she began. "You seem less, well, less bossy than you used to be."

"Bossy?" I said.

Lizzie piped up. "Well, you weren't *bossy*, exactly, more like you were better than the rest of us. Always talking down to us, like you were our teacher."

I swallowed hard. Was that how they'd seen me?

"I don't believe I'm better than anyone else. Far from it.

Maybe I came across that way on the ship, but I can tell you it's not true now. After being a skivvy in Sydney for almost three years, and months in the Outback fighting off flies and snakes, and"—I hesitated, trying to rid myself of the image of Captain Sparks—"and other things, I'm not the naïve girl I was on the *Sabine*. I even learned to fire a musket!"

Sheila and Lizzie stared at me as I spoke.

"Good on ya, Kate," Sheila said at last.

Just then, a man stood up and shouted for silence. He waved a newspaper in his hand.

"This is the *Sydney Morning Herald*, dated May 15th, 1851." He paused to clear his throat. "It says that the Government of New South Wales just declared that gold found at the Macquarie River near Bathhurst has been examined and is found to be genuine and Surveyors believe there is a good chance that more will be found in that area." He paused to draw a quick breath before continuing. "And, furthermore that the discoverer of this gold, Mr. Edward Hargraves, is bringing nine working miners to an area near Bathurst, called Ophir, to begin new diggings . . ."

He had barely finished when a great cheer erupted around the room, including from our table. Even Sabine clapped her small hands with excitement. Then I remembered something.

"May fifteenth," I exclaimed, "that was my birthday. I'd forgotten all about it."

The girls clapped. "That's a lucky sign if ever I saw one," said Sheila. "It means gold is where you'll find your fortune, Kate. So you'd better get your arse out to the goldfields and start digging!"

If I'd thought Bathurst was crowded when I'd first arrived a week or so before, now it was bursting at the seams. The *Herald* article was picked up by newspapers the length and breadth of the colony—from Brisbane to Moreton Bay, from Sydney to Melbourne and Adelaide, and towns in between, and no doubt would soon appear in foreign newspapers, as well. The *Bathurst Free Press* reported shortly afterwards that . . . *A complete mental mad-*

ness appears to have seized almost every member of the community. There has been a universal rush to the diggings. And they'll be rushing out to the diggings not just from Bathurst, I thought, but in the next months people will be flocking to the colony from all corners of the world.

I'd dismissed Sheila's suggestion that I go to the diggings to try my luck. I'd put it down to her three glasses of rum. I thought of all the reasons why it was ridiculous. First, it was a job for men, and while I saw some women in the Bathurst crowds, I assumed they were either wives who'd accompanied their husbands to take care of domestic duties, or prostitutes who saw a ripe opportunity, given the number of single men here. Next, I wondered if a woman on her own could even get a license to dig, which I understood was required. And as a practical matter how would one woman on her own, without transportation, carry all the equipment necessary for prospecting—picks, shovels, pans to wash gravel and sediment away and separate any gold, rockers or cradles to separate heavier nuggets of gold for those lucky enough to have found them? I'd pieced together all this information about the digging process from conversations in the Bathurst Inn and out on the street. It was all anyone could talk about.

Such obstacles seemed overwhelming, particularly since there was no evidence that any of the newcomers had yet found significant amounts of gold. But when word started to drift in from the diggings of early successes, a distant voice in my head nagged at me to make up my mind. So I decided to take a small, first step by presenting myself at the licensing commissioner's office in Bathurst and procuring a digging license for the month of June.

"I assume you are applying in the name of your husband," the clerk said, eyeing me suspiciously.

I put my shoulders back and looked him straight in the eye.

"No, sir, I am applying in my own name, Kathleen Gilvarry. I am not aware of any law against issuing a license to a woman."

"D'you have the money?" he said sharply. "It's a pound fee, renewable each month."

I pulled a pound note out of my pocket and presented it to him. He scowled and shoved the form towards me. "Sign here," he said sternly, "or make your mark if you can't write!"

I held back a retort, signed the form, waited for him to stamp it, and left.

I was smiling when I left the office. It had been a small victory, but I was proud of myself for doing it. It had been a long time since I had felt even a sliver of confidence. I walked on towards the inn, feeling a sense of kinship with the crowds around me. I decided to visit Sheila and Lizzie and tell them what I had done, but just as I was turning the corner onto William Street, I thought I heard someone calling my name. I swung around and peered through the throng of pedestrians. Then the shout came again, and I recognized the voice immediately.

"Malachy!" I cried. "What on earth are you doing here? Is Luke alright?"

Malachy drew up beside me in the dray. He was grinning from ear to ear.

"No cause to be annoying your head about him, ma'am," he said, removing his crumpled hat. "As far as I know Luke Kinsella is safe and sound and up to his arse in sheep shite in the Northern Territory. 'Tis just that Phineas and meself decided not to go with him. We heard about the gold, and we thought we'd try our luck. Besides, we're a bit long in the tooth for shearing sheep. And Phineas said he wouldn't be able to take the stink of them. He's away to get a license at the minute. Climb in, ma'am, and we'll go back around and wait for him."

On our drive back to the licensing office, Malachy prattled away. Luke had taken their news well, he said. "Sure he was only thinking of our welfare. But he wished us well and told us to take the dray and the bullocks, and anything else we wanted from Tara. So we have tents, picks and shovels, axes, mattresses and provisions—everything a man could want, and once we have the license we'll be on our way. Is this a grand country or what?"

I pulled the form out of my pocket. "I just got a license, as well!"

Malachy's mouth dropped open and he almost let the bullocks collide with a cart. "Fair play to ye, ma'am," he began, "but I didn't think . . ."

"What? That they don't give licenses to women? Well they do, and I decided to get one. It's for the month of June, to be renewed every month, so all I must do now is go to Ophir and stake my claim."

The two of us looked at each other and burst out laughing.

"Sure we can go and do it together. Wait 'til Phineas hears this! You're full of surprises, *girleen*. 'Tis fate brought us all here!"

"Or maybe some lucky leprechaun," I laughed, thinking of the young woman hawking outside the emporium.

That night I thought about what Malachy had said about fate bringing us all here together. Was it a sign of good luck? If I'd still been in Ireland I wouldn't have had any doubts at all. Back there we all believed in signs. But now? After the letdowns of my high expectations for working at the Pitt House, or cultivating a farm with Luke in the Outback, I was reluctant to get my hopes up again. But what did I have if I didn't have hope? I made up my mind there and then to trust once again in fate.

The next day I woke up with a lighter heart than I had known in months and I couldn't wait to let Sheila and Lizzie know the latest news. A queue of their customers stretched from the corner of William Street all the way to the entrance of the emporium. I stepped out into the middle of the street, and made my way past them, ignoring the frequent shouts of "Hey, wait your turn," and "Who d'you think you are," until I was in sight of the leprechaun at the entrance. I slipped around her and squeezed into the middle of the throng inside.

The scene was worse than any country fair in Ireland in the old days. Men fought over the last picks or shovels, trying to tug them from each other's hands while their wives jumped in to assist. A woman opened a sack of flour and tossed its contents over another woman who'd reached for the same sack. Children, freed from their mothers' control, raced around the store knocking over jars and bottles, dousing themselves in perfume, donning hats and gloves and, in one case, a boy shrieking with delight strapped a woman's corset over his shirt.

At last, I reached the counter where Lizzie and Sheila were trying to cope with the situation.

"You there in the red coat, get back here and pay for your goods, or I'll set the dogs on you, you thieving bastard!" Sheila shouted at a man trying to escape under the back of the tent.

A man with a growling dog approached the culprit and he sidled back to the counter. "I—I didn't see you here," he said sheepishly, "sure I wasn't trying to steal anything."

Sheila thrust the bill of sale at him and held out her hand. "You'll pay what you owe me and more on top of that for trying to steal from us, you oul' toe rag," she announced.

The man grumbled under his breath but paid what she asked.

I realized this was no place for a conversation, so I yelled at Sheila. "I've news, Sheila. You and Lizzie come over to the inn tonight if you can."

"Aye," said Sheila, "and you can take Patsy with you. She arrived last night and I know she has no notion of sleeping behind the counter with us again tonight." She turned around and yelled towards the back of the tent. "Patsy Toner, get your arse out here. Kate's taking you with her to the inn. We'll see yez tonight."

Patsy emerged, her face pale and haggard and her eyes huge.

"Hello, Patsy," I called, "you're a sight for sore eyes. Come on with me now."

I took her arm and lifted a flap at the back of the tent where the man in the red coat had tried to escape. Patsy froze as we passed the man with the dog.

"It's alright," I said. "The man works for Sheila. He and the dog only go after robbers."

I pushed her out of the tent in front of me. Back out on William Street, I took Patsy's arm and led her towards the inn. I kept a firm hold on her all the way there, afraid she might break away and run. She was hardly the brash, fearless Patsy I'd known. But then again none of us were the same after our time in this country.

When we reached my room at the inn, I told her to sit on the bed while I gave her a mug of water, which she gulped down. I sat in a chair across from her.

"Welcome to Bathurst, Patsy," I said, smiling, "and to your first glimpse of gold fever!"

Later that night, Patsy and I went to the dining room to wait for Sheila and Lizzie. Patsy had slept most of the day and by evening I began to see glimpses of her old self. After she'd washed, combed her hair, and put on one of my dresses, she was revived enough to start asking me cheeky questions.

"What brought *you* here?" she asked. "I know you got married to that gardener feller from the Pitt House. So where is he?"

I repeated what I'd told Sheila and Lizzie. "He's up working at a sheep farm in the Northern Territory to make some extra money. It's been a bad year for crops."

She regarded me with her keen green eyes that told me she was not inclined to believe me. But I ignored her.

In the dining room I ordered rum for her and a watered rum for myself. Patsy continued to stare at me as if trying to make up her mind whether to say something. Her stare made me nervous and I found myself drinking faster than usual. Finally, I could stand it no longer.

"Is there something you want to tell me, Patsy?"

"Aye, there is," she said, "but I don't know how you'll take it."

"Then out with it," I said, exasperated.

Patsy took a deep breath. "Your man, the doctor, is in Sydney. He went looking for you and found Bridie. He knows you're married, by the way."

Her words had all the force of a rock colliding into my chest.

Nathaniel was back in Australia! My immediate thought was to race there to see him. I took deep breaths, trying to steady myself. At last I nodded at Patsy.

"Yes, I wrote to him just before the wedding," I said, as calmly as I could manage. "I heard from him around last Christmas but at that point he was in Ireland and obviously hadn't received my letter yet. I assume he got it when he returned to England."

"But he never returned home. After he discovered your wee brother, Christy, was dead, God rest his soul"—she made a quick sign of the cross—"he decided to go to Liverpool to see if he could track down your other brother, Paddy. He said he wrote to you about it."

I sat upright in my chair. "What? But I never got a . . ." Then it occurred to me that, after I read Nathaniel's news about Christy in that first letter, I had never read the rest of it.

"Aye, it took a while," Patsy went on, "but it seems he found him. And, to top it off, your brother was thinking of sailing to Australia, so your doctor decided to sail with him. They've been in Sydney since last month."

I wanted to shout at her not to keep referring to Nathaniel as *my* doctor, but there were too many other thoughts crowding my head.

"Paddy? My brother Paddy's in Sydney?"

"Aye, and a handsome feller he is. I met him at the Emerald Isle Tavern before I left. Bridie gave him a job there."

"Then how did Nathaniel know I was married? If he never went home he wouldn't have received my letter."

Patsy gave an impatient sigh, then spoke slowly as if explaining to a child. "Bridie told him all about Luke and yourself getting married and going off to the Outback to start a farm. She had no notion it was supposed to be a secret."

I must have turned pale, for Patsy put her hand on my arm.

"Are you feeling alright, Kate?"

I took a sip of my drink and nodded.

"Have you told all this to Sheila and Lizzie?"

"Aye. Sure they were wanting all the gossip out of me. And this was big news. Lizzie said it was a shame you married Luke and didn't wait for Nathaniel to come back. It was clear as day to all of us you and himself were in love with each other."

"How was I supposed to know he'd come back?" I shouted. "I never heard a word from him the whole time I was at Pitt House!"

Patsy merely shrugged. "That's life, Kate. Just when you think you're doing alright, something comes along and bites you in the arse."

I was desperate to change the subject. "So you're going to open a coffee tent next to Sheila and Lizzie's place, I hear."

Patsy slammed down her drink on the table, startling me.

"That was the plan. But now I see what a fecking circus their place and the whole of this town have turned out to be, I've no notion of it." She paused. "What about yourself?"

"I'm going to the diggings to try my luck," I said. "Two of our farm workers turned up yesterday, and the three of us agreed to go out there together. Do you want to join us?"

The invitation was out of my mouth before I could stop it. Patsy's face lit up with a wide grin.

"Are you codding me?" she said. "Sure I'd love to join yez. It should be some *craic*. Better than serving coffee and cakes to them crazy *amadans* I saw today in the emporium."

She raised her glass, and I raised mine. "*Sláinte!*"

Sheila and Lizzie were delighted when I told them about my plans with Malachy and Phineas. They seemed relieved that Patsy was coming with us. I think her reaction to the chaos at their emporium had made them realize she wouldn't have lasted long there. The next day they sent a dray over to the inn, filled with clothing for Patsy and me, including serge trousers and shirts, hats, boots, two gauze masks to keep the dust out of our hair and face, blankets, mattresses, metal pans, and some small digging tools, as well as provisions including flour, sugar, dried fruits, meat and preserves. The dray driver said he'd been instructed not to take any money from us.

All the preparation activity took my mind off the shocking news that my brother Paddy and Nathaniel were in Sydney. At first all I wanted was to drop everything and rush back over the Blue Mountains to find them. But something told me I needed to try my luck at the diggings first. After all, what did I have to offer Paddy? My stay at the inn and the license fee had left me with very little money. And how would Nathaniel receive me? Maybe he'd even left Sydney for England again. When I left Luke, I knew I had to make my own way, and find my own freedom. My time in the Outback had taught me that. If I was ever to return to Sydney I wanted it to be as a free, independent woman. The diggings might give me that chance—and if I had no luck there, at least I would know I had tried!

On the morning of the first day of June, Malachy, Phineas, Patsy, and I loaded the dray, crammed ourselves into it, and began the journey to Ophir, where the first gold had been found, our licenses in our pockets. We were all in good spirits and we had easily agreed that any gold we found was to be split evenly four ways.

Before leaving Bathurst I made two stops. The first one was at the post office, where I sent the letter I had written the night before to Bridie. I told her that Lizzie and Sheila were making a great success of their store, about wee Sabine, in case she didn't know, and about how the four of us were now on our way to try our luck at the diggings. I also asked her to take good care of Paddy and, finally, asked her to extend my good wishes to Nathaniel. I assured her that I would be back in Sydney very soon. I desperately wanted to ask her to convince him to stay until I arrived, but pride wouldn't let me. Afterwards, I wished I had said just that!

My second stop was at the colonial secretary's office where Luke and I had first discovered that he had no title to Tara. I still had the grant application I had taken that unlucky day. My heart dropped when I saw the same sallow-faced clerk at the desk, but I hoped he wouldn't recognize me.

"Ah, Mrs. Kinsella is it, back again?"

I took the application out of my pocket. "Yes," I said firmly, "I want to enter this application for a land grant on Tara in the name of my brother, Patrick Gilvarry, a free immigrant recently arrived from England and living in Sydney."

He smirked. "As you wish, madam," he said, "but you realize this piece of property is still under grant to Captain Sparks."

I looked him straight in the eye. "Sadly, Captain Sparks is deceased," I said, "apparently at the hands of a bushman into whose camp he accidentally wandered. I'm sure if you check with the military authorities you will find a record of the incident."

The clerk's smirk disappeared, but I carried on quickly before he could throw up any other barriers. "Mr. Kinsella has decided to give up farming and is now employed on a sheep station in the Northern Territory. He will not be submitting any further application for this property and he is aware that I am submitting this one on behalf of my brother. Once I return to Sydney, I shall encourage my brother to have his grant application approved by a person, or persons, held in high regard by the military—maybe even Major Pitt himself."

I fought back blushes at the lies I was telling, and silently asked God for forgiveness. Then I smiled as sweetly as I could. The clerk stared at me for a moment longer, then noisily stamped my application on all three pages, giving me back the last page for my records, all without saying a word.

I gave him a small curtsy, swept out of the office, down the steps and climbed back into the dray.

"You look very pleased with yourself, ma'am." Malachy laughed.

"Yes, Malachy, I am!" I said.

Eventually we left Bathurst behind and turned north towards Ophir. Paved roads gave way to rough tracks as we rumbled through small villages, past derelict farmhouses, and now and then, past a coffee tent, carelessly erected from canvas, or even blankets. Trees lined the route on either side and the occasional kangaroo or wallaby burst out from them and hopped across the path in front of us, momentarily startling the bullocks. I smiled, thinking how excited Patsy and I had been that first day in Sydney after we landed and saw these strange animals for the first time. Now, we passed no remarks at all.

June marked the beginning of winter in Australia and the morning we set out was cool with a light fog. I hoped the journey would be more comfortable than my trek over the Blue Mountains in the scorching heat of last summer. But at the same time I dreaded the possibility of freezing nights. We would be spending at least two nights on the road before we reached the diggings. I put the thought out of my mind, and occupied myself watching the crowds who'd joined us on the journey.

Because of my two stops in Bathurst, we were delayed in starting our expedition. When we'd finally set off, it was to join a procession of prospectors already on the road. Since the official confirmation of gold finds had appeared in the newspapers, the number of people flocking to Bathurst had swelled by at least tenfold. It seemed as if every man and many women in the colony had walked away from their jobs—clerks and carpenters, churchmen and lawmen, masters and servants, pickpockets and prostitutes, and more—all now traveling along beside us. Most rode in drays, like ours, while others walked leading packhorses, and more walked with their belongings on their backs. My ears were assaulted by a jarring chorus of shouts in English and Irish and many languages I'd never heard before. There were people of all colors, but I saw no Aboriginal people among them. They had obviously not succumbed to the gold fever. Perhaps finding gold was of no interest to them. Perhaps they had more wisdom than the rest of us, I thought.

The atmosphere among the throngs was light, almost festive, as if they were on their way to a fair or a circus, and it was contagious. Suddenly Patsy started singing an Irish folk song at the top of her voice.

> *"I've been a wild rover for many a year,*
> *And I spent all me money on whiskey and beer,*
> *But now I'm returning with gold in great store,*
> *And I never will play the wild rover no more.*
> *And it's no, nay, never, no nay never no more,*
> *Will I play the wild rover, no never no more!"*

By the time she reached the chorus, we had all joined in, clapping our hands to the beat of the tune. The crowds around us joined in, too, clapping and singing, even though they didn't know the words. I was reminded of the procession on that hot day in August 1848, when cartloads of young, orphaned girls had sung their hearts out on their way from the Newry Workhouse to Dublin pier, and I brushed back a tear.

As evening descended we pulled off the track into a clearing and prepared to camp for the night. Patsy stood and watched me as I fetched a tent from the dray and began pounding the pegs into the ground with a hammer. I had it up in no time.

"Where'd you learn to do that?" she said.

"The Outback teaches you a lot of lessons," I said. "Didn't you have to sleep in a tent when you crossed the Blue Mountains?"

"Aye, but nobody expected me to put the bloody thing up."

I smiled at her. "Come on, I'll teach you how to build a fire."

I led her towards a stand of trees and showed her how to collect twigs and sticks and leaves for fuel. Malachy set about collecting stones to form a circle for the fire, while Phineas laid out the rug Luke had brought from Pitt House and set out utensils, plates, pannikins, and his own wee set of china.

Patsy gaped at him. "What in the name of God," she began.

"One must keep up one's standards, young lady," pronounced Phineas, "no matter what circumstances one finds oneself in."

For once Patsy was at a loss for words.

I showed her how to boil the kettle for tea, how to heat the salted pork, how set the damper, which from her time on the ship she already knew how to make, and to set it on the fire ashes to bake.

"You'll have to know how to do this when we get to the diggings," I said. "We'll be living in tents while we're there. And everybody will have to do their part."

Patsy opened her mouth to protest but thought better of it.

The next morning we joined the procession, continuing north. The route took us along paths beside the Macquarie River. The government report of the first gold find confirmed that it had happened where Lewis Ponds Creek and Summer Hill Creek, tributaries of the Macquarie River, met. The closer we came to that spot the more prospectors we saw kneeling in the water, washing gravel and soil in tin pans, hoping to separate any gold particles that might be present.

Our progress had slowed considerably, mostly due to the muddy tracks near the river. The bullocks labored to pull our heavy dray, struggling to keep their footing in the mud. Malachy steered them patiently, unlike some others who were whipping their animals to make them go faster. The earlier goodwill seemed to evaporate as prospectors became impatient. Supply wagons challenged drays for right-of-way, and those on foot were often bumped off the track by stray cows or sheep. Tempers grew short, and fights broke out amidst a great deal of cursing and arguing. But so far no one had brandished a pistol or musket. We were saved from that possibility by a sudden downpour of rain that sent people running for shelter under trees or drays.

By the time the downpour ended we were up to our ankles in mud and the dray's wheels were sunk down into it. Darkness would soon fall and Malachy suggested that we stay where we were and dig ourselves out in the morning. So we unyoked the bullocks but didn't bother tethering them, and all four of us spent the night in the dray, shivering under a canvas covering. All we had to eat was cold damper and pork, and the dried fruit Sheila and Lizzie had sent us. But Malachy had ensured we had rum and water readily available and each of us enjoyed a pannikin of the stuff before calling it a night.

It was well past sunrise the next day when we finally righted the dray and set off. As we drew closer to Ophir, the landscape grew more remote and rugged. Small villages gave way to steep hills, dense bushland, and creeks filled with rocks. At one point we had to ford the river Macquarie, which was swollen from the previous day's rain. Malachy pulled off the path and stood up in the dray, surveying the river's length in search of the shallowest crossing point. He turned out to be an excellent scout since we made it across without incident, unlike many of our fellow travelers who had plunged in at the first opportunity and then found their belongings, and sometimes themselves, floating helplessly downriver.

The diggings soon came into focus. Patsy and I stood up in the dray, anxious for our first sight of it before the sun went down. I noticed right away that most of the trees had been chopped down, leaving only stumps jutting out of acres of dug-up earth. Besides the people we had seen panning for gold in the creeks, countless square gravel pits dotted the vast plain and climbed up the sides of surrounding hills. Men's heads bobbed in and out of the holes, creating the impression of so many insects crawling across the brown earth. Each hole, pit, or portion of a creek was marked in some way, either by posts in the ground, a flag, or both. The air echoed with the sound of picks and shovels hitting rock, and the crunch of gravel being shaken through rocking cradles. The entire scene spread out before me was like a picture from a book of fairy tales.

As we drew closer, I saw makeshift camps set up around the edge of the diggings, stretching from the hilltops all the way to the creeks. There were tents, rough shelters, and huts like the one we had built at Tara. The shelters were made from a variety of materials like canvas, bark, and wood, the latter explaining the mass felling of the trees. Scattered amid the dwellings were larger tents, which I guessed were supply stores, like the emporium. There were other tents, no doubt housing government offices and offering other services. I was amazed at how quickly this settlement had grown up.

"Let's find a nice quiet spot near here to spend the night," said Malachy. "By the looks of that place yonder it might be the last quiet night we'll get. Tomorrow we'll decide where to make our claims."

Deciding where to make a claim was easier said than done. Some prospectors had decided to work in the creeks and pan for what they called "alluvial" gold, which had been washed from rocks and deposited in the form of dust or flakes. Prospectors, I heard, were less likely to find any giant nuggets in the creeks, but enough gold dust and flakes could add up to a tidy sum in value. Other prospectors decided to dig into the earth or hillsides, hoping to find a rich vein of quartz which might contain gold. This approach required more physical effort, such as digging through the soil until reaching solid rock, using pickaxes, knives and other tools to crack the rock and excavate, then collecting gravel, and cradling it using a rocker to trap any gold.

We drove slowly around the area, observing the activity up close. Malachy questioned various diggers about their finds. Some answered honestly, others ignored him, and some out and out lied. We had heard from others along the road that some diggers tried to transfer a doubtful claim to an eager new prospector, by claiming great success, but it was time to move on. Some apparently even scattered gold dust on the surface of the pit to support their lie. Often it was more useful to ask people about other people's claims. While Malachy used his easy charm to coax women into telling the truth, Patsy took it upon herself to question the men, which she did with a mixture of flattery, flirtation, and who knew what promises. At one point I saw her giggling with a man wearing a Scottish kilt.

In the end we decided on two claims, one along a creek and the other on the plain near the foothills. Patsy and I were to work the claim along the creek, while Malachy, and a reluctant Phineas, would work the other. I took our licenses to the local office in a nearby tent to register both of our claims, making sure that we followed the size rules and other regulations to avoid fines.

Our claims secured and registered, we decided to pitch our tents together halfway between our two claims, empty the dray, and settle in for the night. The weather had been dry, so we were able to light a fire and enjoy hot tea and roasted mutton along with the ever-present damper. Regulations required tents to be pitched at least twenty feet away from their neighbors, but even that made for little privacy. All evening long, people trudged past us on their way to their own tents or to visit neighbors and friends. The scene was pleasant enough, words and nods being exchanged between strangers and, as darkness grew, the stream of passersby eased and we began to prepare for a peaceful night's sleep.

But our hopes were dashed when a disheveled-looking woman in the neighboring tent emerged, pannikin of spirits in hand, and began cursing her husband in a voice so grating, and so evil sounding, I thought we had tumbled into hell. She circled her tent, growing louder with each revolution, her threats to him rising from bodily harm to death by the most gruesome means. We were amused at first as we doused our fire and stored away our food. But by the time we were ready to sleep, we realized to our horror that she was not going to quiet down anytime soon. Tomorrow, we would have to break camp yet again and set up somewhere out of earshot.

Three days into our digging, Patsy and I knelt by the creek washing silt and dirt in round tin pans. It was monotonous work, requiring pounding the dirt with a stick to soften it, then adding more water and stirring it until some bright specks appeared, which we picked out and set aside. If none was seen, we emptied the pan and began again with more dirt. While tedious, it also required thoroughness, because the gold dust sometimes stuck to the sides of the pan and went unnoticed. To make sure this didn't happen we had to rub the sides hard with our thumbs, creating calluses.

"This is enough to drive a body feckin' innocent," said Patsy for what seemed like the hundredth time. "I can't imagine anything more boring!"

I sighed. "Will you stop complaining, Patsy," I said. "Yes, it's boring, but the reward will be well worth it."

"And what if there's no reward and all we're left with are hands rougher than a washerwoman's, and sore knees!"

I stood up. "That's a chance everyone here is taking. And this work is easy compared with the digging and pounding Malachy and Phineas are doing!"

I snatched the pan out of Patsy's hand just as she was ready to empty it out. I rubbed my thumb around the inner sides of it and loosened some gold flakes.

"Look at this!" I said. "You were about to throw this out. These flakes are worth at least two or three shillings."

Patsy stood up to face me, tearing off her gauze mask and throwing it on the ground. "I don't give a shite," she said, pressing her face close to mine. "I can earn more than that in five minutes diddling some oul' boy, and it's far easier on my hands and knees!"

With that she flounced away. "Catch yourself on, Patsy," I yelled after her. "D'you want to go back to the life you had in Sydney? Do you want to be whoring for the rest of your life?"

I realized it was futile, and mean, so I turned back to panning.

Phineas arrived with a load of dirty gravel that he and Malachy had dug out of the pit for me to wash and inspect.

"Our lady friend appears to have quite a bee in her bonnet," he said, staring after Patsy.

I shrugged. "She's bored with the work!"

"Is she indeed? I would have thought her previous line of work was also rather boring. I mean, there are only so many variations to be had on the theme of human anatomy!"

"There's just no talking to her, Phineas. She seems bound and determined to go back to her old ways. It's all she knows, after all."

By the end of the week we had made modest progress. It was the same all around the diggings. A few had cheered and whooped at a lucky strike but most, like us, had only a few gold flakes or a small nugget to show for a week's labor. I had a new respect for all the diggers' persistence, and a new respect for the gift of hope in the face of such bleakness.

On Saturday night, all frustrations were let loose. No digging was allowed on Sundays, so the diggers and their companions indulged in what "grog" they could find and, as the night went on, began to sing and dance, some even falling into open holes or gravel pits in the darkness. I smiled at the joyous sounds as we sat around our fire. I stopped smiling, though, when I heard shots and a musket ball scudded past our tent. I had a sudden memory of the night on the *Sabine* when we crossed the equator and the sailors, steeped in rum, lost all control. Like then, I made for our tent and lay down, covering myself head to toe with a blanket.

Patsy followed me in and sat down on her mattress. I lowered the blanket and looked over at her. She sat with her head buried in her hands, sobbing quietly. I sat up.

"I'm sorry for the things I said the other day, Patsy," I said. "I had no right."

She looked at me, her eyes red-rimmed. "Och, sure you had every right, Kate. The truth is, the last thing I want to do is go back to the way I was living in Sydney, and beyond in Newry, for that matter. But I don't see how I'm ever going to be fit for anything else."

I got up and went to sit beside her. "I understand, Patsy, and there's no guarantee that any of us will get rich from this. But don't you think it's worth a try? It's the best chance we have of changing our lives for the better." I paused and pushed her wild red hair back from her face. "And we won't be here forever. Promise me you'll try, Patsy. That's all I ask."

She nodded. "Aye, I promise."

On the following Monday, the rains came, flooding the camp and filling gravel pits so quickly that diggers found themselves waist-deep in water. Most scrambled to climb out, while others stubbornly kept digging. Patsy and I gathered our pans and made for our tent, slipping and sliding on the mud-covered ground. There was no sign of Malachy or Phineas. We waited for a while, shivering in our damp clothes, then looked at each other.

"We have to go and see if they're alright," I said, and Patsy nodded.

We put on boots and oilskins and ventured outside, holding on to each other as we plodded through the mud. We met a procession of diggers, drenched and glum, returning from their claims, carrying their spades over their shoulders. When we finally reached our claim, the rain had eased off, but we saw no sign of Malachy or Phineas. Then I heard grunting noises and I bent over the hole to look. Malachy was holding Phineas under the armpits trying to pull him up out of the water.

I grabbed Patsy's arm. "We need to find help!" I shouted.

Within a few minutes four diggers had managed to pull Phineas out and lay him down on the muddy ground. Malachy scrambled out behind them. I couldn't see if Phineas was injured—he was breathing but not moving.

"Can you carry him back to the tent?" I asked the diggers. "It's not far."

Without a word they lifted him up and followed us.

"What happened?" I said to Malachy after we had all arrived at the tent.

"It all came on so fast," he said through chattering teeth. "I told Phineas to get out before we drowned, but he refused.

He'd come across a quartz vein in the corner of the pit and was scraping away at it with his knife. And you know how stubborn he can be."

I nodded and threw a blanket around Malachy's shoulders.

"He was determined to stay," he went on. "But the water was rising so fast, and you know he's a foot shorter than meself, and the next thing I knew he lost his balance and fell, and the water rose over his head." He looked up at me, fear haunting his eyes. "If it wasn't for you two, he'd have surely drowned. I couldn't have held on to him for much longer."

I knew in my heart that Malachy would never have left Phineas to drown alone. He would have stayed in that pit with him until the end. I shivered at the thought.

"We need a doctor," said Patsy, who was kneeling beside Phineas, trying to keep a blanket over him although he kept throwing it off. "This man is burning up with fever."

"I'll go!" I said.

The nearest doctor's tent was pitched on a hilltop some distance away. I'd heard stories that he grossly overcharged for his services and refused to see patients in their tents, so everyone had to go to him. Before I left our tent, I gathered up what gold dust we had and the small nugget, in the hopes of persuading him to come and see Phineas. How I wished Nathaniel was here—I would never have had to beg or bribe him for his services.

The man turned out to be as unpleasant as his reputation. He spat on the ground and laughed when I showed him the gold I had brought.

"You'd to be needing more brass than that, lassie," he said in a Scottish accent, "to coax me out in this *dreich* weather! And can you not see I have a queue of people here waiting for me to tend to their injuries—people that are willing to pay a fair fee?"

"Well, can you at least give me something for the man's fever?"

"Who is this you're talking about?"

"Phineas," I said. "My partner in the diggings."

"Och, thon feller," he said, spitting again on the floor, "I know him rightly. An insult to God, so he is!"

His beady blue eyes squinted behind his spectacles as he peered at me.

"You're a bonny wee lass, I'll say that for you. Now if you'd consider offering me something besides money, I might be able to overlook who the patient is and see what I can do. We might—"

I didn't let him finish. "You're a vile man," I shouted, "and a disgrace to the medical profession! May you burn in hell!"

I hurried out of his tent and past the queue of patients, my breathing heavy. I knew my temper had once more got the better of me. Now what was I going to do? Surely this awful man couldn't be the only doctor at the camp, but I had no way of finding another. As I made my way back to our tent, I racked my brain to think what medicines I might have brought that could help. But there was nothing that could bring down Phineas's fever. We would just have to pray.

When I returned Malachy and Patsy looked at me expectantly. I shook my head. "He won't come, no matter how much I offered him."

Patsy shook her head but said nothing as I told Malachy my conversation with the doctor. She soaked a clean cloth in a bucket of water and applied it to Phineas's forehead. Then she stood up.

"Take over for me, Kate, and try to keep him warm. I'll be going out for a wee minute."

"It's dreadful outside," I said. "Where do you have to go?"

"Jaysus, can a body not go out and do her business in peace without having to report to the likes of you!" she shouted.

I sat down beside Phineas. Malachy had fallen asleep. Poor man was exhausted. I tried to coax Phineas to drink some water but he refused. After a while he began muttering as if delirious, his words making no sense. I bent my head and asked God to help him.

I fell asleep, too, and woke to find Patsy had not returned. I rose and opened the tent flap to look out. It was already dark, and a cold wind blew through the camp. I went back and sat down on my mattress. I was beginning to panic when I heard voices outside and through the canvas wall of the tent saw the shadow of a light swaying. The flap opened and Patsy stepped in with the doctor behind her.

He looked at me in surprise. Obviously he hadn't connected Patsy with me, or with Phineas. He tried to back away but Patsy grabbed his arm and pulled him forward.

"You'll keep to our bargain, laddie," she said. "I'm sure your good wife would be upset to hear you went back on your word, particularly on a promise made to a lady!"

She pulled him towards Phineas, and he knelt beside him.

"I'll expect you to do all you can for him, like we agreed," she said sweetly. "You can see the poor man's in a bad way. Kate here knows a wee bit about nursing. She assisted the surgeon on the ship from England, so she'll be here to help you if you need her."

Grumbling under his breath, the doctor opened his medical bag and proceeded to treat Phineas. When he'd finished, he pushed a bottle of medicine at me. "Give him this three times a day and keep the cool bandages on his head. He's not to go back to the diggings for at least a week."

He stood, closed his bag, and looked at Patsy and myself.

"Youse two are a *quare* pair," he said, trying to disguise a smile. "There's not many as canny as yourselves. Good luck to you!"

"He's right there," said Malachy, who, I realized, had witnessed the entire scene.

It was two more days before the rain stopped and another day before the water had receded in the holes and pits, before anyone could venture back to their claims. I left Patsy to look after Phineas and went with Malachy to the pit. There was still water in it, but it reached only to our knees. Malachy began to bail out the water while I went to the corner where Phineas had been working before the flood came. I had brought his knife with me, a tool with a serrated edge and a pointed tip that many of the diggers carried called a "fossicking knife." When the water level dropped I could see where the dirt and gravel had been worn away and exposed what looked like a rock formation of milky white quartz. I had heard prospectors back at the Bathurst Inn saying that finding quartz was a very good sign that gold might be nearby. I dropped the knife and used my hands to brush away dirt from the rock. More quartz emerged, its thick white veins running through the darker rock.

"Malachy," I called, "bring the lamp over here and hold it steady."

He drew closer to me and peered at the area where I pointed.

"Mother of God!" he exclaimed.

"Is this what I think it is?" I whispered.

Malachy brushed away more dirt to expose even more rock. As he did so, we saw bright yellow specks appear throughout the quartz. They glowed like metal reflecting the light. There was no mistaking that this was gold. The more quartz we exposed the more specks appeared. Malachy stopped brushing the dirt away and we stood together in silence, not even daring to breathe, lest the specks disappear.

"Kate," said Malachy in a loud whisper, "stay here while I fetch two buckets of water so we can start cleaning this. While I'm gone, take a hammer to the quartz and knock it as hard as you can until it cracks. Under no circumstances are you to talk to anybody, not even Patsy if she comes here. Nobody can know what we've found."

I nodded. This was one of the longest string of words I'd ever heard from Malachy, but I knew he was right. Word of a find like this getting out could cause a riot at best and attract thieves and bushrangers at worst.

Malachy climbed out of the pit. "I'll be as quick as I can!"

I picked up the hammer and swung it with all my might.

Malachy and I worked the rest of the week, hammering the

quartz to powder, and then panning it so that the gold, which was denser than the powder, would sink to the bottom of the pan while the lighter crushed powder was washed away. Any visible gold nuggets, and there were a few, we dug out of cavities in the rock with the fossicking knife. Every night we buried our finds in our clothes as we returned to the tent I shared with Patsy, then hid them in my travel box under my other belongings. Patsy spent all her time in the other tent nursing Phineas, so neither of them was aware of what Malachy and I were doing.

By the following week, Phineas had greatly improved, and insisted on going back to the pit with Malachy, while Patsy was eager to get out to our claim at the creek. There was still extraction work to be done in the pit, which would require all of us working together. The night before everyone was to return to digging, Malachy and I shared our information with Patsy and Phineas. We played down the amount of our finds so far, saying we had found some gold but were unsure yet of its worth. They were delighted, if a little annoyed that we hadn't told them sooner.

"The fewer people know of this," I said, "the better. So say nothing to anybody about it until we've pulled out all the gold from our pit, brought it to the gold commissioner's office for registration, and it's been sent to Bathurst under guard by the escort service."

"But when will we see it? When will we know what it's worth?" said Patsy, her eyes wide with excitement.

"It'll be kept in a bank in Bathurst in all of our names," said Malachy. "When we get back there we will have it assessed. Once we know its worth, we can each decide whether we want the cash or credit, or whether we want to lodge it in the bank or take it with us elsewhere."

"Sure and why would we not want to sell it?" said Patsy. "Much good it would do us locked away in an oul' bank."

The next morning all four of us set out for the pit. Phineas made a big show of placing his shovel on his shoulder like a rifle and marching out of the tent.

"Once more unto the breach, dear friends," he exclaimed, "once more!"

In the pit, Patsy peered at the remaining gold flecks in the quartz.

"Aren't they lovely?" she breathed. "Can we not sell a wee bit of it now just to have with us? I'd feel like a queen walking around with that in me pockets."

Phineas puffed out his chest. "So lovely, dear lady, that I was willing to drown for it."

"Aye, and you would have, too, if I hadn't saved your arse!" put in Malachy.

We were nearing July 1, when we would need to renew our licenses for our two claims. Patsy and I agreed there was no point holding on to our claim at the creek since it had yielded very little. Malachy thought it would be best to renew the pit claim to avoid any suspicion. The amount of gold we were finding was diminishing each day and likely to run out soon, but we wanted to be sure we had recovered as much as possible. So on July 1, Malachy and I joined the queue at the licensing office and paid the new price of thirty shillings to renew our lease for one more month.

We worked tirelessly for the next week but pulled out less than one-tenth of what we had already found. Phineas was becoming weak again and Patsy was becoming impatient. One night I talked to Malachy and we agreed it was time to leave. Early the next morning, while Patsy and Phineas were still asleep, we emptied my travel box and loaded the gold into an old flour sack, dusted the outside of the sack with flour to better disguise it, and walked to the gold commissioner's office.

Fortunately, there were no other diggers in line, for when the commissioner took one look at what we emptied out on his desk he let out a shout that could have wakened the dead.

"Where did you find this?" he demanded. "Have you been stealing?"

Malachy shook his head. "No, sir," he said, ignoring the insult, "we dug it fair and square out of our pit. When all the rain came it loosened the dirt in our hole and we uncovered quartz rock. This was buried inside. 'Twas hard work to get it out."

The commissioner eyed Malachy. "Is that all of it?"

"Aye, I think so, sir. We still have a license for the rest of the month, but we're ready to go, and—"

"I'll buy it from you!" the commissioner interrupted.

"It will cost you two hundred pounds," I said, as Malachy looked at me aghast.

The commissioner's face turned red. I worried he was about to arrest me for some violation but then he grinned.

"A hundred pounds, then. My final offer!"

Malachy spat on his hand and slapped the table, reminding me of the way horse traders used to, back in Ireland, when a price was settled.

"Agreed!"

Malachy handed over the license, while the commissioner called in a clerk, a small man wearing thick spectacles, and asked him to examine our find. If the man was shocked at the size of it, he didn't show it but set about examining and weighing the gold and filling out a certificate confirming the weight of twenty-seven troy pounds of high-quality gold. From there, for a fee, the armed escort service would transport the gold to the main bank in Bathurst. Malachy insisted that each of our names appear on the certificate and in the bank's records, and that we be given four individual copies of it.

We almost skipped as we made our way back to our tent carrying the empty flour sack.

"Pack up," called Malachy, "we're leaving Ophir!"

I took out the bills the commissioner had given me for the license, and counted out twenty-five each to Malachy, Phineas, Patsy and myself.

Patsy turned pale. "So you cashed in the gold?"

I laughed. "No, Patsy, that's just for Malachy's license. If we'd cashed in the gold it would have easily been worth ten times that."

Her mouth dropped open. I had never seen her at such a loss for words. She let out a whoop and ran around the tent. "Jesus, Mary and Joseph," she cried, "sure isn't this a grand country!"

"Aye," said Malachy, "so it is!"

Our spirits were high on our return trip to Bathurst, which made the journey seem shorter than the first one, but the more likely reasons were that there were no sudden downpours that caused us to get stuck in the mud, and we had sold off most of our possessions, including one of our two bullocks, before we left the diggings, leaving the dray lighter to pull. The sea of prospectors had not ebbed one bit and an unending ribbon of humanity flowed towards us. We waved and greeted them as we passed, wishing them good luck.

Phineas and I had switched places in the dray so that I sat up front with Malachy, and Phineas and Patsy sat together in the rear. They seemed to have struck up a close friendship. Phineas credited her, and not Malachy, with saving his life and with nursing him through his fever.

"A veritable angel of mercy," he said, whenever he looked at her.

Malachy was clear that neither he nor Phineas would be going back to Sydney.

"Bathurst is a nice town," he said. "Our roving days are over. We just want a bit of peace and quiet. I'd say we'll have enough money now to build a simple, wee house. No more living in tents for us!"

"And does Phineas agree?"

Malachy chuckled. "Well, I suppose he will, if Patsy is staying there too. I've never seen him take to anybody the way he has to that *girleen*. Of course, 'tis early days yet! A month from now he could be firing his china at her head!"

"Let's hope not," I said. "Patsy is really enjoying the positive attention. She's not had much of that in her life."

The afternoon we arrived in Bathurst we went straight to the bank. I suppose we were a sight to behold as we entered the cavernous marble-floored hall, because patrons and staff gaped at us, some of them backing away holding handkerchiefs to their noses. We'd become so used to our ragged, mud-covered clothing we thought nothing of it, since everyone else at the diggings looked the same, or worse. We probably smelled, too, and our skin was rough and calloused. Our boots were dirty and torn. Malachy and I both stopped in our tracks, but Phineas took Patsy's arm and marched straight up to the head clerk and loudly announced our names.

"We have come directly from the goldfields at Ophir," he said, "to have our finds valued." He took out his copy of the certificate from the gold commissioner's office and handed it with a flourish to the open-mouthed clerk.

"If you would be so good, my dear man, as to see to it promptly. As you can see, we have arrived in a state of *deshabille* and are anxious to get to our lodgings to rectify this regrettable lapse in decorum."

Onlookers stood watching the exchange, some smiling, some laughing aloud. The rest of us presented our certificates to the clerk, who scurried away to the back room. He returned with a portly man in tow who greeted us with exaggerated politeness, explaining that he was the manager. All of us asked that our gold be sold and the cash received be deposited equally into accounts for each of us. I instructed him to transfer my account to their branch in Sydney. Patsy had to be persuaded to leave her money with the bank.

"It will be much safer, my angel, than under your mattress," said Phineas. "After all, you never know what ruffian might steal it while visiting in the dark of night." He gave her a wink and she grinned back at him.

The clerk returned with a piece of paper which he showed to the manager, both of whom stared at it in obvious disbelief.

"Is that the assayer's estimate of the value?" I asked politely.

The manager gulped. "Yes, madam," he said, "based on the English government's gold standard, it seems your find weighs in at the amazing total of twenty-seven troy pounds, resulting in a value of thirteen hundred and seventy-seven pounds sterling—that's three hundred and forty-four pounds and five shillings each, minus bank fees, of course!"

"Will you look at the style of youse!" exclaimed Sheila as she and Lizzie joined Malachy, Phineas, Patsy and myself for dinner at the Bathurst Inn the day after our return. "Sure I'd think I was dining with kings and queens!"

"How kind of you to say so, madam," said Phineas, dusting his velvet jacket and adjusting his silk neckerchief. "I assure you this is merely modest attire while I wait for my tailor to order my new wardrobe from London."

Malachy shifted uncomfortably in his chair, poking his finger beneath his stiff shirt collar.

"Give me a loose cotton shirt and serge trousers any day of the week," he said. "This getup has me strangled."

Phineas had dragged a reluctant Malachy with him to the barber and the men's clothing store that afternoon, insisting that now they were rich "gentlemen" they must look the part. In turn, Patsy insisted she and I visit a hairdresser, a milliner, a dress shop, a jeweler and a perfumery. I was as reluctant as Malachy, but Patsy was so excited I didn't want to disappoint her. At the rate she was going, I thought, it wouldn't be long before she'd exhausted the twenty-five pounds she'd been given from the sale of the lease on the pit in Ophir.

Patsy sat now, radiant in a green satin dress, an emerald necklace, and a stylish black hat adorned with green feathers. Her red hair had been tamed into a twisted braid at the back of her neck while a few ringlets were allowed to escape and frame her face.

Many guests stared at her as she entered the dining room on Phineas's arm. I had never imagined she could look so beautiful. Despite Patsy's urging that I "go mad" shopping, I had chosen a modest blue cotton dress edged with lace and a matching hat.

Sheila and Lizzie couldn't wait to hear our stories about the diggings. Phineas was in his element, giving forth to such an attentive audience. The rest of us made no attempt to challenge his obvious embellishments, particularly since Sheila and Lizzie were clearly enjoying them.

"It must be a mad place altogether," said Lizzie. "Our store here's been overrun with *eejits* of every class and color, buying what they need for the diggings. They'll pay any price they're so wild with excitement. They're convinced they'll come back rich!" She looked around the table. "And maybe they're right."

"Do you ever think you should join them?" I said.

Sheila laughed aloud. "Not at all! Sure we're sitting on our own goldmine beyond at the emporium. We're not depending on luck at all. And we'll be here long after this madness dies down."

"So you're going to stay in Bathurst, then?" I asked.

"Aye," said Lizzie. "We're going to build a proper shop—you know, bricks and mortar—and we'll be respectable citizens."

Sheila smiled. "Aye, and maybe we'll even open a branch in Sydney!"

"But without the leprechaun!" I said, laughing.

Phineas clapped his hands. "Brava, my dear ladies, brava!"

"And what about yourself, Patsy?" I asked. "Will you be opening the coffee shop after all?"

Patsy glanced at Phineas before she spoke.

"No, Kate. I did a lot of thinking out there at the diggings. And I've had some long talks with Phineas. Now that we have this money, we're thinking about building a hotel here in Bathurst. A nice one, built of weather board or sandstone. And it will be for women only! It'll be a clean and cheap place for them to live, and I'll employ a few as housekeepers who can live rent-free. I'll have rules on 'entertaining guests,' and they'll be encouraged to learn other skills so as they can escape their old way of making a living."

Phineas was bursting to chime in. "Patsy and I will be partners in the enterprise," he declared. "I, of course, will oversee the design and construction of the property and my dear angel here will manage it."

"But what about Malachy?" I burst out.

"Arrah, leave me out of it," said Malachy. "The only building I'll be looking for is a wee house where meself and Phineas can put our feet up beside a cozy fire. 'Twill be a grand change from living in tents, so it will!"

Phineas stuck out his chin. "As you wish, Malachy, but *I* am not yet ready to retreat from society!"

I thought as I watched them that, for all their differences, they belonged together. I was delighted that Phineas would be helping Patsy, but when he grew bored of that, he could always go home to Malachy. As for Patsy, was she really giving up her old life, or would her hotel for women just be a nice name for a brothel?

Later that night, I took a chance and posed the question to her. I'd expected an angry response, but instead she gave me a thoughtful answer.

"Listen, I know you're afraid I might go back to the streets, Kate. But why would I? I have money now. More money than I could ever have dreamed of. And that's because of you." She paused and drew a deep breath. "While I was nursing Phineas back to health, we dreamed aloud about what we'd do if we struck gold. I told him I would change me ways, and I would help other women in the same boat as meself." She smiled. "You know, Phineas was a great listener and he made me feel that I was worth something. Besides you and himself, very few have ever done that."

I nodded. "That's true, Patsy."

She leaned closer to me. "I know better than anyone what it's like to be out on the street with no choice but to sell yourself to whoever's willing to pay for it. I know what it's like to be looked down on by so-called 'respectable people.' And I know how you begin to believe people's opinion of you—that you belong in the gutter. Not everyone has someone like you or Phineas to care about them and encourage them. So, if I'm able to do that for . . ."

She trailed off. I leaned over and put my arms around her. We were both in tears and there was nothing left to say. I silently thanked God for her decision, and thanked Phineas for caring about her. And I prayed that her dream would come true.

The next morning I took a tearful leave of everyone, promising to stay in touch, and boarded a private carriage bound for Sydney. As we drove away from Bathurst towards the Blue Mountains, I closed my eyes and let my mind wander. I should have been over the moon at my good fortune, but my heart was heavy. So much was still unresolved. I wasn't the same girl who drove off with Luke the previous October. Back then I was an inexperienced eighteen-year-old, alone and fearful of the future. Now, I was no longer that naïve girl. I'd overcome hardship, disillusionment, and trauma. I'd taken responsibility for my decisions and had the strength to face the consequences—good or bad.

My thoughts turned to Nathaniel. How would he react to the changes in me? Would he still expect the young girl who turned to him for explanations of everything that was new to her—the girl who was in love with him? Would he want this new, experienced Kate? And, more importantly, would I still want *him*?

I thought of Luke, too. I had forgiven him for betraying me. In the end he had tried to make things right. Still, he'd left me in a complicated situation. Legally and, according to the Catholic Church, I was still a Kinsella. I desperately wanted to be a Gilvarry and have a chance to start again.

I forced myself towards happier thoughts. I would soon see my dear friend Bridie again, and sweet, young Mary. But most of all, I would finally see my brother, Paddy. It was a miracle that after four long years he was here in Sydney. I couldn't wait to embrace him, to feel the presence of my own flesh and blood filling up that empty corner of my heart.

My return journey over the Blue Mountains was much easier than the first. Many more inns had sprung up along the way, no doubt a result of the hordes of people traveling to the gold diggings. I was well able to afford indoor shelter at night this time, instead of sleeping in a tent, or under the stars. I no longer needed to build a fire and roast salted pork or make damper. When we finally descended into Emu Plains, I stayed at the same inn where Luke and I had stayed, happy and excited for what lay ahead. I shed a few tears for the wishful dreamers we had been.

My excitement rose when I finally saw the outskirts of Sydney ahead. Every mile after that seemed like a hundred, so great was my desire to reach the city. At last, the driver stopped at the entrance to the Emerald Isle Hotel and Tavern. I climbed out of the carriage and raced inside.

I saw Bridie immediately. She stood with her back to me, absorbed in inspecting crates of wine.

"Bridie!" I shouted, as I ran towards her.

She dropped the ledger she was holding, her eyes huge with surprise.

"Mother of God! Is it yourself, Kate? Sure you're a sight for sore eyes!"

She hugged me tightly, then drew back to inspect me. "You're looking well," she said, "a bit thinner maybe, and not as pale as before. Time in the Outback has done you good!"

"Aye, maybe," I said, "but time in the gold diggings has done me even better."

Bridie's eyes grew wide. She took my arm, led me to a chair, and sat down across from me. "Tell me everything," she said. "I just last week got your letter from Bathurst before you went to the diggings. Did the girls all go with you? Did youse find gold?"

I took a deep breath and told her the whole story in as much detail as I could recall. "They're all staying in Bathurst," I finished up. "Sheila and Lizzie's store is flying with business and Patsy intends to build a women's hotel. My friends Malachy and Phineas are staying there, too. And I told you about Lizzie's wee girl, Sabine."

Bridie nodded. "Aye, isn't that grand. What's the child like?"

"Ah, she's a wee *dote*, Bridie, beautiful and bright as a button."

"And the gold?"

I nodded. "More than enough to do anything we want."

Bridie took it all in and I saw no hint of jealousy. Instead, she seemed genuinely happy for all of us.

"Youse have done well, thank God. Even Patsy. I wish her luck."

"And how are things with you, Bridie?"

She stood up. "I've helped make the Emerald Isle a big success. And Mr. O'Leary is very grateful, as he should be."

"But you still won't marry him?"

"Why would I?" said Bridie. "Sure things are grand as they are. And did I tell you I have a permanent contract with the Royal Theater to sing there every Sunday night." She threw out her chest. "I have a great following and it's growing every week."

I was suddenly very tired. I stood up and took Bridie's hand.

"I should go on up to bed," I said. "I'm wrecked from the journey. I'll see you tomorrow and we can talk some more."

Bridie wouldn't let my hand go. "Tired or not, there's something you need to do first. Come with me."

She led me out of the room and into the adjoining tavern. It was still early evening and just a few patrons were scattered around at the tables. A tall, young man stood with his back to us dusting bottles on shelves behind the bar. Bridie led me towards him and then backed away.

"I'll just leave yez to it," she said, and left.

I was confused at first. Then, as I watched him my heart leaped in my chest. I would have known him anywhere.

"Paddy!" I cried. "Is it really you?"

He turned around at the sound of his name. He was more masculine than I remembered—no longer a boy—but his dark red hair and bright blue eyes were the same. He stared at me for a moment and then a broad grin crossed his face. He dropped the cloth he was holding and rushed out from behind the bar.

"Kate!" he shouted, his arms outstretched. "My God, 'tis yourself. I never thought I'd see you again."

I walked into his embrace and threw my arms around his neck, making no effort to hold back the tears that demanded release. I buried my head against his chest and wept, our hearts beating in harmony as all the pain of separation ebbed away.

We eventually moved out of the embrace, both of us grinning, but still not taking our eyes off each other. It was Bridie who broke the spell.

"Are yez going to stand there gaping at each other all night? Away with you now and talk in private. Paddy, take the night off and be with your sister."

She thrust a room key towards me. "The coachman's after delivering your bags, and there's tea and maybe something a bit stronger waiting in your room. So away now with the both of yez."

Paddy and I stayed up half the night talking. My earlier sleepiness had disappeared in my excitement. I hadn't felt so happy in years. We reminisced about our childhoods, recalling stories that brought Maeve and Christy momentarily back to life. We wondered what had happened to Da, although we both believed he was dead. Then we wept over everyone and everything we had lost. We talked about his life since the day he had left for Liverpool. He'd apparently done well working on the boats for a while, and then he'd settled in Liverpool where he worked at odd jobs.

"I should have gone home sooner," he said amid tears. "I might have been able to stop Christy from running away and you from going to Australia. By the time I got there you both had gone, so I went back to Liverpool. If it wasn't for your man Nathaniel, I might never have finally found you."

I nodded. I wasn't ready to talk about Nathaniel. Instead, I changed the subject. "Well, you're here now and that's grand. Have you thought about what you want to do here?" I raced on. "I applied for a grant on Luke's settlement, Tara, in your name. It turned out to be a bad place for farming, but the boys who are running the farm next to it are planning to turn their land over to sheep grazing. You could join up with them if you have a mind to."

He nodded. "That's good of you, Kate. Let's wait and see. And what about yourself?"

"Me? Ah, well, I hope to start a free school for immigrant and Aboriginal children."

I made no mention of Luke or Nathaniel and somehow Paddy knew better than to ask.

"There's more I can tell you about my life here," I said, "but it'll have to wait, Paddy."

We bid each other goodnight and hugged again at the door. Then I slipped into bed. My dreams that night were filled with images of our old farm at the foot of Slieve Gullion mountain and they were all happy.

Bridie woke me the next morning with a hot cup of tea.

"Ah, there you are. 'Twas lovely to see the two of you last night. How long since you've seen each other?"

"Four years," I said. "Thanks, Bridie, for taking him in and giving him a job."

"No thanks needed. Sure he's a lovely lad, and hardworking. Mr. O'Leary is very fond of him. Anyway, 'tis not me but Doctor Harte you should be thanking. Paddy wouldn't be here if it wasn't for him."

"I know," I said.

We sat in silence for a moment. "So," said Bridie. "When are you going to see himself? There's no time like the present. I brought you his address. Your friend Lucy Foster came to see me. Lovely woman. She's working as his nurse. Funny how things happen, isn't it?"

She thrust a piece of paper at me, then left. I sat for a long while staring at it. Part of me wanted to race over immediately to find Nathaniel and part of me wanted to put it off as long as possible. I finally decided that Bridie was right. No time like the present! I put on the blue day dress I bought in Bathurst, brushed my hair, and reached for my matching hat and gloves. I examined myself in the mirror, wondering what Nathaniel would think when he saw me. Then I shrugged my shoulders. What did it matter what he thought? I was a different Kate now, shaped by all the experiences of the past years. There was no going back to the naïve Kate who sailed on the *Sabine*, nor did I want to. Before I could change my mind, I picked up my bag and Bridie's note with his address and set off.

Lucy Foster jumped up from her chair the second she saw me come through the door. "Kate! How wonderful to see you!" she began. "Your friend Bridie told me you'd be coming to Sydney but she wasn't sure when. Nathaniel—er, Doctor Harte—has been looking forward to seeing you. He said you were great friends on the ship. He's out on a call just now. Isn't it a coincidence that I'm working for him? And a fine doctor, he is."

I was surprised at the way Lucy chattered on. She seemed nervous, not like the Lucy I recalled, although she looked the same, if not younger than when I had last seen her. "Do you think he'll be gone long?" I asked.

"There's no telling," she said. "He spends a lot of time with his patients. But come on into the office. We've no patients waiting now. I'll make tea and you can tell me all about what's happened since I last saw you."

Reluctant as I was to go over the story again, I took the tea and tried to get the story out with as few details as possible. "The others stayed in Bathurst," I finished, "and I came on to Sydney."

"And what about Luke?"

"Luke? As far as I know, he's still working at the sheep station up north."

"I wish him luck," said Lucy. "He's a fine man."

I nodded and changed the subject. "And what about you, Lucy? How's Poppy and Maria?"

She appeared to relax. "Poppy is enrolled in school and enjoying herself," she said, smiling.

"And Maria?"

Lucy leaned her head back and closed her eyes for a second. "I was greatly blessed to meet Doctor Harte," she said, "and he welcomed Maria with open arms. He has several Aboriginal patients and Maria is a great help in communicating with them. Because of her, they've learned to trust Nathaniel—er, Doctor Harte."

I noticed that was the second time she'd slipped into using Nathaniel's first name and quickly corrected herself.

"Anyway," Lucy went on, "things have worked out very well for us here in Sydney. My boys have been here to visit. They've bought a few sheep and begun turning the farm over to grazing."

I seized on the change of subject. "I put in a grant application for Tara in my brother Paddy's name. I finally saw him last night and I told him about your boys. I thought it might be nice if they went into business together. Let me know when they're back in town so I can introduce them. I'm staying at the Emerald Isle Hotel."

"And what are you planning to do?" Lucy asked. "Now that you're a rich woman I suppose the world is your oyster. Will you go back to Ireland?"

"No, I won't be going back," I said, "I've no family left there. I'm thinking of opening a free school for children of immigrants and Aboriginal children. I was thinking maybe Maria would be interested in working with me."

Lucy hesitated. "So you'll be staying here," she said at last. "Well, I wish you all the best."

I stood up. "It was nice to see you, Lucy. Please let Doctor Harte know I was here. I will come back another time."

By the time I got outside, I could hardly breathe. There was something odd about Lucy's behavior that I couldn't understand. She was far from the same calm, confident Lucy I had known in the Outback, the Lucy who had nursed me after Sparks's assault, the Lucy in whom I had confided about Luke's and my marriage. I waved the waiting carriage away because I needed to walk to clear my head. I was probably making more of things than necessary—after all, people change. Maybe I had expected too much of a welcome from her. Maybe she really *was* jealous of my good fortune. By the time I reached the Emerald Isle Hotel, my mind had cleared.

I was finishing dinner in the tavern that evening when a shiver crawled down my spine. I stiffened. I knew immediately that he was behind me.

"Kate? Kate, is it really you?"

His voice drifted over my shoulder and at the sound of it all my doubts drifted away. I swung around, my heart beating wildly. He stood before me, his blue eyes shining, his mouth slightly open and his face flushed.

"I ran over here as soon as I heard. I'm so sorry I missed you earlier."

He held out his arms. I rose and walked into his embrace. We stood together without speaking, only the thudding of our hearts breaking the silence. At last, he pulled away and gazed at me, his eyes moving from head to toe and up again, finally resting on my face.

"Nathaniel . . ." I began, unable to form words amidst the tumult of emotion that had overcome me.

He reached for my hand. "Let's sit down."

We sat without taking our eyes off each other. A server came to the table to ask for his order but she may as well have been a ghost. Neither of us answered her and she retreated, shaking her head. Then Nathaniel's gaze shifted to my finger which still bore my wedding ring.

"How could you have married without telling me, Kate?" he

asked, his voice raw with emotion, his eyes glistening with tears. "How could you have left me to hear it from Bridie?"

I was taken aback by his sudden accusation.

"But I *did* tell you, Nathaniel," I said. "I wrote you a letter the night before I left Sydney. When I finally received your letter telling me about wee Christy, I realized you never got it. I'm sorry."

He bowed his head. "So am I, Kate. But I suppose it makes no difference now." He looked up at me and I couldn't read his expression. "And where is the lucky man? Why isn't he here with you?"

There was a sharp edge to his tone and I could feel my temper rising. I tried to control it. But it was no use.

"What was I supposed to do?" I cried. "I never heard from you after you went back to England until I was already in the Outback. I was all alone here once the Pitt House was sold, with little hope of another indenture. Besides Bridie, Luke was the only friend I had. He offered me a way out and I took it."

"So where is he?" he asked again.

"Working at a sheep station up north, not that it's any of your business."

I felt I was being backed into a corner, having to defend myself. Yet I realized that every angry word was piercing him like a knife. I could see the pain on his face and I reached over to touch his hand but he pulled it away.

"I'm sorry, Nathaniel," I said, choking back tears. "I was never in love with Luke and I told him so." I hesitated. "I was always in love with you, and I still am."

There, I had finally said the words I'd been holding back from him. "The marriage was never consummated," I went on, "and I'll be seeking a divorce in the courts and an annulment from the Church. Luke will not be coming back."

He stared at me, a range of expressions passing over his face.

"If only you'd told me how you felt, I would have waited for you until doomsday. But now . . ."

A shiver of fear ran through me. "But now, what?" I whispered.

"Now it's too late. I'm engaged to Lucy Foster."

"What? But . . ."

I could force no more words out. All I wanted was to get away. I jumped up, knocking over my chair and pushed past Paddy, who had just appeared. I raced to my room and shut and locked the door behind me. I sat down on the bed and began to sob. When I could cry no more I set my anger free. At first I blamed Nathaniel. Wasn't he the one who told me to live my life without him? Wasn't it he who never wrote, those first two years? Why had he done this to me? And with Lucy Foster of all people? Wasn't she much too old for him? I thought back to my conversation with her earlier in the day. No wonder she had seemed so nervous. No wonder she wanted to know if I was here to stay. Then I turned the blame on myself. If only I'd written to him sooner. If only I'd had the courage to tell him how much I loved him. If only I hadn't married Luke.

I was exhausted by the time I lay down to face what I knew would be a sleepless night. There was no point praying that Nathaniel would change his mind. God had let me down so many times before, why should this time be different? Apart from Paddy, I was about to be alone in the world again and I would have to make my own way.

From then on I did my best to put Nathaniel out of my mind and get on with my own business. Securing the divorce and the annulment was easier than I thought, helped no doubt by the fact Bridie and Mr. O'Leary were on good terms with magistrates and bishops in the city, many of whom frequented the Emerald Isle Tavern. I presented the court with the letter Luke had signed, acknowledging the fact that he was aware his wife was still alive in Ireland when we married. I realized then that by admitting such a thing he was guilty of bigamy and could well be prosecuted if he ever came back to Sydney. It made me even more grateful to him that he had put himself in such peril to make up for his deceit. The magistrates granted my divorce in relatively short order.

It was a more delicate task to persuade the Catholic authorities to grant an annulment. I argued that my marriage hadn't been consummated but they were skeptical of Luke's letter confirming the situation. I was nervous they might expect me to undergo a physical examination, which would have been humiliating. Time and again, I silently thanked Maria for stopping Sparks before he could abuse me further. In the end the bishops didn't require such a process, but they left me on tenterhooks for several months before approving my request.

Freed at last to return to being Kate Gilvarry meant I could start my life over again. I began searching for a suitable building in which to open my school. My idea of a free school which would serve immigrant and Aboriginal children was not met with enthusiasm by many property owners in the city. But I stuck to my guns. In the back of my mind I knew that I had enough money to buy or construct a building if all else failed, but leasing an existing space would be much faster.

I finally secured a building on Pitt Street that had space downstairs for classrooms, and an upstairs apartment where I could live. The irony of the location was not lost on me—one, that it was on the street named for Major Pitt's family, and two, that it was not far from the brothel where Patsy had lived. Once I had the building secured, I set about remodeling it, although it was hard to find laborers since so many had left Sydney for the goldfields. I also began advertising for teachers and was overwhelmed by the responses. Many of the applicants were young immigrant women who had been governesses in England and who had sailed to Australia in search of a better life. Many of their stories reminded me of my own experience and were not that different than what the Irish orphans had faced. I hired three of them and put the others on a waiting list.

My next concern was to find a teacher from one of the native tribes. I wanted Maria more than anyone else but I had not attempted to find her. Nathaniel's medical office was the last place I wished to go. I had no desire to run into either him or Lucy Foster. In the end, it was my brother, Paddy, who went on my behalf and came back with the news that Maria was very eager to work at the school.

I had been so busy with all my preparations I hadn't noticed how time had flown by. But 1852 had slipped into 1853, taking winter, spring and summer with it. Now it was May again and a year since I had left Tara. I thought of it now, and how, if all had gone well, Luke and I might have been waiting to celebrate the miracle of harvesting seeds that had grown into healthy wheat crops. It was only the good moments of those months that shone in my memory. The rest—the long, cold, lonely nights, the downpours and disappointments, the hard physical labor, and the constant terror of predators—lay hidden in shadows. I suppose that's what happens with all memories eventually, except for those few experiences so profound they can never be hidden no matter how great the desire to do so.

"Happy birthday to you! Happy birthday to you! Happy birthday, dear Kate! Happy birthday to you!"

Mary Timmins's sweet voice rang out in the small, private room at the Emerald Isle Tavern. I thought I was imagining things when I saw her enter, carrying a birthday cake adorned with lit candles. Instead of the young woman in a nun's habit, I saw a girl with curly blond hair, blue eyes, and the face of an angel.

"Come on in, girls," called Mary, looking behind her.

I stood stupefied as in walked Patsy, Sheila, and Lizzie, all of them singing, and wearing the bonnets we'd been given in our travel boxes. Feeling faint, I reached for the nearest chair. How could this be? Was I imagining it all? I was sure I was back at the Newry Workhouse on my sixteenth birthday when Mary and other orphans had come to the dormitory, bringing a cake and a homemade greeting card and singing to me. At the time I had imagined they were a choir of angels. Now I had the same feeling, that I was surrounded by angels again.

I looked at Bridie, who was grinning broadly as she put on her orphan bonnet. I put my hand to my head. For no reason I could explain, I was wearing my own bonnet with the crimson ribbons. She'd invited me over to the tavern for a "special treat" but she hadn't given me any details. The date was May 15 and it was my twentieth birthday but I hadn't put two and two together. I stood up and hugged each girl in turn, holding back tears. Before I could speak, the door opened again and in came Phineas—and Malachy, who was holding wee Sabine by the hand.

"We bring most glad greetings, my lady," said Phineas, who was dressed to the nines in a tailored olive-green coat, a cream vest, and white cravat. On his feet were polished, black leather boots, and a diamond ring glittered on his finger. I rushed over and hugged him, which took him aback. As he dusted off his coat, I turned to Malachy, who was not so grandly dressed, and hugged him, too, kissing his whiskery cheek. Then I picked up little Sabine, who was wearing an adorable pink frock with matching ribbons and kissed her on her plump cheek.

I looked at Bridie. "How on earth did you—" I began.

She waved her hand. "Sure didn't I arrange grander affairs for herself, Mrs. Pitt? This lot weren't too hard to persuade."

At that point my brother, Paddy, came in carrying a tray of drinks, and everyone began to speak at once.

"Don't think we came just on account of yourself," said Sheila. "Lizzie and me's ready to open a branch of our emporium in Sydney. So we thought we'd kill two birds with one stone."

True to form, I knew she was just trying to get a rise out of me.

I was certain, in my heart, that they would gladly have come just so we could all be together.

"We were hoping to see Doctor Harte here too," said Lizzie, "and make it a proper reunion. Is he coming?"

I swallowed hard. It hurt my heart that he wasn't there. Maybe Bridie hadn't invited him.

"He said he'd try, but he was very busy," said Paddy, "but I brought Maria."

I seized on the chance to change the subject. I went over to where Maria stood in a corner near the door and drew her by the arm into the center of the room.

"This is my friend Maria," I announced. "We met in the Outback. She's going to be teaching at my school." I turned to her. "You remember Malachy and Phineas, don't you?"

A smile lit up her face as Malachy approached and gave her a hug. Phineas greeted her in a more formal manner, and wee Sabine ran up to her and hugged her around the knees. Maria bent down and picked the child up and Sabine began laughing with delight.

As the evening progressed, so did the merriment. Bridie entertained us with songs, while Phineas, who was full of surprises, accompanied her on the piano. Mr. O'Leary joined us along with two Irish musicians and a few of the orphans who'd been at my wedding. Soon there was dancing—jigs and reels—reminding me of the nights on the *Sabine* when lessons had finished and young orphans danced, their feet tracing ancient Celtic patterns on the wooden deck.

I could stay there no longer and I slipped quietly out of the room and out of the tavern into the coolness of the night. I looked up in the sky for the North Star, even though I knew it wasn't there. I remembered the night on the *Sabine* when Nathaniel had explained to me that the North Star—which my da had always said would guide me when I was lost—wasn't visible in the Southern Hemisphere. I remembered how sad I had been to hear that and how comforting Nathaniel's words had been. How I longed for the sound of his voice now!

"Kate? What are you doing out here in the cold?"

It was Nathaniel. I couldn't answer him. Instead, I just shook my head.

"They've been asking for you," I said at last. "Everyone's here."

"I came to see *you*."

I waited. Someone opened the tavern door and the sounds of music and singing drifted out. When silence fell again, I looked at Nathaniel. I couldn't see his face clearly in the shadows but I could feel his presence with every inch of my being. Suddenly, his hand was on my arm.

"I'm sorry, Kate."

"So am I."

"Can you forgive me?"

"Yes," I said, knowing that I truly had.

He pulled me into his embrace, but I fought to free myself.

"No!" I cried, more forcefully than I meant. "No, we can't do this. We mustn't."

His voice was hoarse with emotion. "Yes, we can, Kate, and we must!"

He backed away. "I am hopelessly in love with you, Kate. I always knew it. And, after I last saw you, I knew that would never change. Lucy eventually came to accept it too. She knew she had to set me free and, in the end, she did so. We must thank her for that, just as we must thank Luke for setting *you* free. We're meant to be together, Kate." He drew closer again. "Take all the time you need," he said. "I know I've disappointed you in the past. All I ask is that you love me, Kate."

All pride and fear left me the moment his lips met mine. A sensation of exhilaration and joy I'd never known before surged through me, along with a feeling of blissful contentment and I knew I had found home.

"I can't promise I'll be ready to marry again anytime soon," I whispered as we finally stepped apart, "but I *can* promise you from the bottom of my heart that you are the only man I will ever love."

I couldn't see his face, but I knew he was smiling. He put his arm around me and led me towards the tavern door. "Come on, then, let's have a proper reunion. I can't wait to see all my brave and beautiful orphans again."

Epilogue

COME HERE TO ME AGAIN NOW, 'TIL I FINISH THE
STORY—

In the autumn of 1873, Bridie O'Sullivan held a farewell concert at the Royal Theater in Sydney. She invited our "mess"
group from the *Sabine* and as many famine orphans from Sydney
as could attend. News of the event spread by word of mouth and
through a notice Bridie posted in the *Sydney Morning Herald*. Ad-
mission was free to each woman and her guest, the only stipula-
tion being that the orphan wear the bonnet she had been given at
the start of her journey from Ireland.

That evening, I walked hand in hand with Nathaniel into the
foyer of the theater to find a noisy throng of women, most of
whom I didn't recognize since we had all arrived on different
ships. It was an amazing thing, though, to see us all together. I
hadn't realized how many of us there were. The women wore
bonnets, some well pressed, some ragged and tattered, but all,
like mine, embroidered with the name of their owner and the
name of the ship they had sailed on. As recognition dawned
among them, they rushed to hug one another, squealing like the
girls they had been when they first arrived in Australia, even
though now they were middle-aged women.

Some had come alone, others with husbands. Together, they
sipped drinks, nibbled on finger foods and marveled at the grandeur of the Royal Theater, which most of them had never set

foot in until now. When a bell rang signaling that the performance was about to begin, they edged their way through the ornate double doors and into the interior of the theater. Some rushed towards the plush, red velvet seats, vying to get as close to the stage as possible, while others made for the upper gallery. In no time, seats were filled, leaving latecomers to stand crammed together against the back wall.

Nathaniel and I made our way to the box nearest the stage, which Bridie had reserved for us and the rest of our "mess" and guests. I was transported back to our last reunion, twenty years before, when Nathaniel and I had at long last pledged our love to one another. I looked at him now. His brown hair had begun to gray, and he wore metal-rimmed spectacles, behind which his blue eyes still sparkled. We had been married for sixteen years and were blessed with two children: a solemn, studious son we'd named Michael, who wanted to be a doctor like his father, and a daughter, Grace, who was by contrast outgoing and full of mischief. We had left them in the care of Maria, who still taught at my school and assisted where needed in Nathaniel's growing medical practice. His reputation as a researcher and practitioner of hygiene-based procedures meant he was called upon frequently to speak at medical associations throughout New South Wales. I was proud of him for this but, more importantly, for the fact that over the years local Aboriginal tribe members had grown to trust him with their care. As for me, my school continued to thrive, although it had been rough going in the early days when citizens picketed in front of our building protesting the education of Aboriginal children. In time, the furor died down, and we went about our business.

"Well, would you look who's here!"

I didn't have to turn around to know it was Patsy.

"Aye." I laughed. "And how's the *craic* with you, Patsy?"

She let go of Phineas's arm and rushed forward to hug me, grinning from ear to ear. No one seeing her for the first time would ever have guessed she was the same girl Bridie and I had visited at the brothel on Pitt Street. Her gown and hat were expensive but tasteful, as was her jewelry. She stood straighter than in the past and her Belfast accent was reduced to a subtle lilt. I put these changes down to Phineas's influence and the confidence he had instilled in her.

"Are you still giving the politicians what for?" I continued. "I see your name in the papers now and then."

"Aye, sure they're calling me the second Caroline Chisholm," she said, referring to the English social reformer who had fought both in the British Parliament and colonial forums for increasing support for women immigrants, including convicts, back in the 1840s. Patsy had taken up the cause of women like herself, who'd been left with no option but to fall into prostitution, robbery, or drunkenness on the streets of Sydney. Like Caroline Chisholm, she argued for more support from the government for them, the kind of support she offered at her hotel in Bathurst. At first, she'd been laughed out of meetings, but her persistence and ability to state her case logically and forcefully was winning the day.

The stage curtain was still closed as Nathaniel and I took our seats next to Patsy and Phineas.

"How's Malachy doing?" I asked Phineas.

"Fortune has not smiled on our dear friend, madam. He was too weak to make the journey to Sydney for dear Bridie's festive occasion. But he sends his good wishes to everyone." Phineas accompanied his words with an exaggerated sigh and flourish of hand, but, beneath his dramatic gestures, I saw sadness veiling his eyes.

The hubbub of the audience in the stalls and gallery rose and fell, the women's bonnets bobbing and shaking as they talked. I looked down from the box, excitedly awaiting the rest of our group. As with Patsy, I heard Sheila before I saw her.

"Will ya not dawdle like an oul' feller, Andy," she cried as she climbed the stairs to the box, "sure the feckin' show will be over before we even sit down!"

"I'm coming, lass," said Andy.

Sheila had married a well-off Scotsman and had three teen-aged sons who were studying in England. She had moved to Sydney after selling the emporium in Bathurst. The box seemed to shake as she stomped up the stairs, her husband behind her. She had always been a buxom girl, but now she was almost as round as she was tall. In a scarlet dress, and extravagant jewelry, she looked the very image of a Sydney matron. While she was well into her forties—she and Lizzie had always lied about their real ages—her skin was smooth, her cheeks burnished by a heavy application of rouge, and her small hands dimpled as a baby's. Her husband, Andrew McTavish, a Presbyterian Scot, who owned an import-export business, was as plump as Sheila, balding and bowlegged. From what I heard, he doted on her, which was fortunate given that Sheila loved to be the one giving orders.

"Hello, Sheila," I said, standing to hug her. "How are you, and how are your boys?"

"Och, them three," she sighed. "They'll be back from England any day now that the school term is over, and I'm dreading seeing them, so I am. Their bloody English accents give me the pip. You'd think they were swallowing marbles when they talk. Andy here says it's what we're paying the school for—to make them into proper English gentlemen so they can come back to the colonies and get positions in law or government." She paused for breath. "I think he's full of shite. Didn't I do alright for meself, Belfast accent an' all!"

She bustled into the row behind us, pulling Andy in beside her.

"Any sign of Lizzie and Sabine?" she asked. "Lizzie's not been well. I hope Sabine can coax her out."

I nodded. Lizzie's story had not turned out as well for her as for the rest of us. I had been worried from the first time I learned that she had signed her baby girl over to the couple to which she was indentured in Moreton Bay, only to escape with her and Sheila to Bathurst a year later. I wondered at the time how long it would take the authorities to track her down. Almost three years passed until her employers arrived with the police at the emporium in Bathurst and snatched the protesting Sabine out of Lizzie's arms. Lizzie was arrested and brought before the court in Moreton Bay on kidnapping charges and, even though Sheila, Patsy and Phineas had pleaded with the magistrates on her behalf for clemency, she had been sent to prison for fifteen years. When Sabine turned eighteen, however, she ran away from her adoptive parents and made her way to Bathurst to find her mother, whom she still remembered. After finding out that Sheila had left for Sydney, along with a recently released Lizzie, she followed them and set up house with her ma. When Sheila sold the Bathurst store, she put aside half the profits for Lizzie to live on when she was released. The strength of their friendship had impressed me from the day I met them on the *Sabine*, and I wasn't surprised that their bond endured, and would probably last a lifetime.

A sound on the stairs caused me to swing around. Without meaning to, I stared at Lizzie in alarm as she slowly climbed, tapping her cane as she went, one hand resting heavily on Sabine's arm. I hardly recognized her. She looked like an old woman, her gray hair sparse, her cheeks sunken, while her dress hung lifelessly on her thin body. Patsy jumped up.

"Here, Lizzie, take my seat in front. Phineas and I can move back beside Sheila."

I squeezed nearer Nathaniel and helped Sabine settle her mother in the vacant chair next to me. Sabine smiled at us. "Hello, Kate, hello, Nathaniel, it's nice to see you."

"And you, Sabine," I said.

She had grown into a beautiful young lady, tall with long, dark hair like Lizzie's used to be, large brown eyes and full lips. I wondered how it had been for her living with those people in Moreton Bay—the ones Lizzie had told me punished her constantly for her "sin." I wondered how much they had punished Sabine for it too. The miracle was that Sabine had never forgotten her mother and had been determined to find her once she was old enough to leave.

The only one of our "mess" still missing was Mary. I no sooner thought of her than she came rushing up the stairs, her long habit rustling about her ankles.

"Sorry I'm late," she breathed.

Of all of us, Mary was the one who still looked like the young girl who had left the workhouse all those years ago, but she bore no traces of the fearful uncertainty that had filled her then. Now, her beautiful face was serene and kindness radiated from her large blue eyes. I had seen Mary often over the years since she spent much of her time tending to the needs of immigrants in poverty-stricken communities around Sydney. In fact she had encouraged many parents to send their children to my school. I smiled when I saw her blond curls poking out of her bonnet.

She put her hand to her head and blushed. "I know." She laughed. "Bridie wanted us to wear our bonnets," she said, "and I couldn't disappoint her. I had to get permission to go out without my veil, but Mother Superior just laughed and told me to go ahead. It feels kind of odd, though!"

She squeezed past me and knelt in front of Lizzie, taking her hands in hers.

"How are you, Lizzie?" she whispered.

Lizzie put her hand up to her head. "Ah, I don't have me bonnet anymore," she said, her voice thin and hoarse. "They took everything away from me in that oul' place."

"It's OK, Ma," said Sabine, reaching into a bag beside her and bringing out two brand-new bonnets. Here," she said, handing one to her mother, "Bridie left these by for us. She made them herself. One for you and one for me. Look, they have our names on them, and the name of the ship, the *Sabine*. Bridie said I deserved one because I sailed on the *Sabine* the same as the rest of you."

Lizzie took the bonnet and put it on while the rest of us applauded.

At that moment, the lights dimmed, the curtains slid open, orchestral music filled the theater, Bridie O'Sullivan stood center stage, a spotlight illuminating her diaphanous aqua gown, and threw up her arms in greeting.

After twenty-five years of public performances at the Royal Theater, Bridie had told me that she was retiring.

"I've had a good run at it," she said one evening at the Emerald Isle Tavern. "'Tis time I was putting me feet up!"

"But you're still a young woman, Bridie," I said, "and still in fine voice."

"Arrah, will you whish't, Kate," she said. "If I keep going, in a few years I'll be as hoarse as an oul' crow. No, I want to step down while I'm at me peak. Anyway, Mr. O'Leary and I have plans for the next few months. We're going back to Ireland to visit what's left of our families after the oul' famine."

I looked at her in alarm. "But you're not going for good, are you?"

She laughed and patted my arm. "Not at all," she said, "sure this is my home now, but I might come back with a surprise for all of yez."

I waited, my mind racing with possibilities.

Bridie grinned. "I might come back as Mrs. Terrence O'Leary!" she announced.

I was blindsided. "But you said . . ."

"I know what the feck I said. 'Tis only the oul' biddies back in Ireland would be scandalized if they thought him and meself were living in sin all these years."

I smiled at my dearest friend. I didn't for one minute believe her reasoning. The Bridie I knew never cared what others thought of her, and certainly wouldn't do anything that important just to please the old ladies of Ireland. No, our Bridie wanted to get married but, after all these years of saying she wouldn't, her pride wouldn't let her admit her real feelings. I reached out and took her hand.

"I wish you and Terrence all the best in your marriage," I said, adding, "and I can highly recommend it."

I'd thought about Luke then, and our ill-fated marriage. I bore him no ill will for his deceit—he had, after all, tried to make things right. But I realized that we'd entered the marriage without the essential ingredient of love. Love is what nourished my marriage to Nathaniel and would nourish Bridie's too. My brother, Paddy, now a prosperous sheep rancher, married to a sweet Irish girl named Rose, and the father of six rambunctious children, would occasionally mention if he'd seen Luke in his travels. From what he told me, Luke had never remarried. I never stopped hoping that he would, one day, find love.

I hoped the same for Lucy Foster as well. Paddy, who was in business with Lucy's sons, saw her often.

"She's a strong woman, Kate," he'd said once. "She bears you no ill will about Nathaniel, and wishes you nothing but happiness. She's happy as can be managing one of our sheep stations up north. After all her years in the Outback, she found she was no longer suited to city life."

After greeting the audience, Bridie waited for the cheers and applause to die down. The spotlight dimmed and she began to sing "The Last Rose of Summer," a lament of loss written by Irish poet Thomas Moore, accompanied by a lone harpist. As she sang, the audience grew silent, each one of us orphans no doubt lost in our own memories of loved ones lost to famine. But before long, Bridie stepped up the tempo and soon feet were tapping, hands clapping, while some of the latecomers at the back of the theater broke into dance. Jigs and reels were followed by Australian music hall favorites including "South Australia" and other popular sea shanties celebrating Australia's seafaring history; and "Click Go the Shears," a lively song about sheep shearing, which the audience sang with gusto.

Later, the room grew silent again as Bridie sang another lament, this time in Irish—the one she had sung at young Jamie's burial on the *Sabine*. I squeezed Nathaniel's hand as she sang, and when I looked at Mary, her head was bowed. Patsy and Sheila sniffed noisily and Lizzie began to cry aloud. When Bridie had finished, the room remained silent.

It was time then for some hearty Irish anthems. The audience joined in with the likes of "The Wearing of the Green," and "A Nation Once Again," and I had an image of young girls in horse-drawn carts singing their hearts out on the way from Newry to Dublin on a cold August morning. Back then, the songs had been sung with defiance; now, it seemed, the defiance had softened from resistance to a simple joy in our heritage. When Bridie began "The Wild Rover"—the song Patsy had sung on our way to the gold diggings—Patsy stood up and belted out the words, much to the amusement of Phineas, who kept shouting, "Magnificent, brava, my angel!" while the rest of us laughed aloud.

At the conclusion of the concert, Bridie asked everyone to stand and sing, while the musicians played the first few bars of "The Parting Glass"—an old Irish song about emigration.

> *"Of all the comrades e'er I've had, they're sorry for my going*
> *away*
> *And all the sweethearts that e'er I had, they'd wish me one more*
> *day to stay*
> *But since it fell into my lot that I should go and you should not*
> *I'll gently rise and I'll softly call, goodnight and joy be to you all*
> *So fill to me the parting glass and gather as the evening falls*
> *And gently rise and softly call, goodnight and joy be to you all!"*

The memory of that reunion of 1873 will stay forever in my heart. It was the only time I joined so many other famine orphans gathered in one place, and the first time I saw clearly how we had grown from fear and uncertainty to the security of knowing our place in this new world. It was then the realization dawned on me that we had become Australians. Our children were Australians, our futures were Australian futures. Yet, in our souls we carried the memories of that land in which we were born, memories joyful and tragic, memories softened by the gentle music and poetry that flow through that ancient island. We are emigrants and we exist in two worlds, one past, one present, and we are nourished by both.

That night, as I lay beside a sleeping Nathaniel, listening to my children murmur in their dreams, I gave thanks to God for guiding me on this journey.

Author's Note

The Famine Orphans is a work of fiction based on the true story of the Earl Grey scheme, under which 4,100 female orphans of the Irish Famine, between the ages of fourteen and nineteen, were shipped from Irish workhouses to Australia between 1848 and 1850. The girls' participation in the scheme was voluntary although most, facing a bleak future in Ireland, agreed to go. The scheme's official purpose was to combat the shortage of domestic servants in the growing colony. However, at the time there were also thousands of unmarried male convicts there as a result of England's program of prisoners' "transportation" to Australia, which had been deemed a penal colony. In the 1840s, colony administrators were anxious to build settlements and, for those to be successful, they needed the convicts who had served their terms to then marry and settle down. The Earl Grey scheme was, therefore, seen as a win-win for both sides—Ireland would be freed from the burden of famine orphans in overcrowded workhouses, and Australia would benefit from an influx of single young women to perform domestic duties and eventually marry many of the convicts.

While official information on the orphans' experience is still sparse, reports indicate that seventy percent married within three years of arrival, to both Irishmen and Englishmen, nearly half of them men with religions different from their own. Records also suggest they married older men, had large families, and often endured early widowhoods. Some remained in Sydney, Melbourne or Adelaide, while others joined their husbands in the interior of the colony to pursue farming or accompanied them to the gold diggings near Bathurst and elsewhere to seek their fortunes. In recent years, many of their descendants have embarked on their own genealogical searches, which are enriching the historical mosaic. Amidst this new interest in family histories, the orphans are often referred to as "the Mothers of Australia."

The orphans arriving in Sydney were lodged in Hyde Park Barracks while awaiting indentures as domestic servants. While most of the early arrivals were hired quickly, later ones were often left waiting at Hyde Park Barracks. This was a result of vicious press reports vilifying the orphans and fueling anti-Catholic and anti-Irish discrimination. Those orphans not hired often turned to prostitution and thievery to survive. The power of the press and the consequent avid opposition by the public, resulted in the scheme being halted in late 1850.

In telling this story, I used numerous resources to convey the orphans' experience as accurately as possible but, where necessary, have injected my imagination for the sake of the story. My account of the Irish Famine and conditions at Newry Workhouse reflect published and anecdotal research. My account of the voyage to Australia is based on actual ship diaries, journals and data from historic sites. The stories of my fictional orphans are imagined but woven around information gleaned through research. For example, while twenty-one ships sailed to Australia carrying orphans between August 1848 and April 1850, the *Sabine* was not one of them, but still similar to the others in many respects such as dimensions, voyage route, and daily routines. My accounts of the orphans' reception in Sydney and elsewhere are taken from articles which appeared in Australian newspapers and from documented dispatches from legislative hearings at the time.

I have drawn upon other documentation from Australian historical sources such as: National Library of Australia (Trove), University of New South Wales and State Library of South Australia, Museum of History of New South Wales, and the Irish Famine Memorial at the Hyde Park Barracks, in order to render an accurate description of Sydney during the period—including critical dates of road development over the mountains into the

Outback, dates and descriptions of the gold rush, and political and economic developments which would have affected the orphans' lives.

While my previous works of historical fiction have all tied my characters to significant historical events in Ireland, England and America, *The Famine Orphans* is my first novel based on a true story. For this reason I felt a greater obligation than ever before to get the story "right." After all, I was born and raised in Newry and it was easy to put myself in the shoes of Kate Gilvarry. I owed her, and the other orphans, the courtesy of telling their stories with as much honesty and accuracy as possible. I hope I have achieved that.

Acknowledgments

As always, I am indebted to my agent, Anne-Marie O'Farrell of the Marcil-O'Farrell Agency, for her unwavering support, encouragement and friendship over the last fourteen years. Her excitement for me when I have finished a manuscript, and her patience with me in times of creative drought, have sustained me throughout my writing career.

I also want to thank my editor, John Scognamiglio, at Kensington Publishing, whose consummate ability to focus quickly and directly on where a manuscript can be improved, has always resulted in a better story. My appreciation also to the Kensington staff for their careful attention to all aspects of the production of this book.

Also thanks to my dearest friend, and "first" reader, Bernard Silverman, whose "platinum level" editing saved me from embarrassment, and for giving so generously of his time. Also, I want to remember one of my previous first readers, David Hancock, who is sadly no longer with us.

Additionally, I want to thank Hugh McShane, historian and author of the Hugh McShane History series, who hails from my hometown of Newry, Ireland. It was his passion for the story of the Famine Orphans of Newry Workhouse that encouraged me to write this book.

Thanks also to everyone who has cheered me on during the writing of this book—The Lucky's Gang; Pawley's Sisters; and the Wonderful Women of the Warrington Book Club. I am so grateful to have all of you in my life.

And last but not least, a shout-out to my beloved family in Ireland, who keep the flame of Ireland burning as a constant source of creativity for me and upon which I draw for each and every book I write.

THE FAMINE ORPHANS

ABOUT THIS GUIDE

The suggested questions are included to enhance your group's
reading of Patricia Falvey's *The Famine Orphans*!

Discussion Questions

1. Would Kate have stayed in Newry had her mother not died? If so, what do you think her future would have looked like?

2. Do you think if the orphans had known about the discrimination they would face in Australia and the expectation that they would marry convicts that they would still have chosen to go?

3. How did the orphans change, if at all, on the sea voyage to Australia?

4. What did you think of Kate and Matron's decision to include Patsy at the last minute? Were there more deserving girls?

5. Do you think it was appropriate for fourteen-year-olds to be included in the Earl Grey scheme?

6. What did you think of Kate's struggle with Lizzie's attempted abortion? Did you agree with her decision to let each of the other orphans decide for themselves?

7. Was Nathaniel justified in advising Lizzie to take the indenture in Moreton Bay even though it meant giving up her child?

8. Was Mary's decision to join the convent a result of a true calling or her attempt to hide away from the world?

9. What did you think of Kate's decision to marry Luke? Was it true that she had no other options?

10. What did you think caused Sheila and Lizzie to have such a close bond?

11. What was it about Bridie's character that made her emerge as such a strong character?

12. Did you believe Patsy would give up prostitution? Was it the influence of Phineas, or her own strength of character that made her successful?

13. Do you think that Luke deserved Kate's forgiveness?

14. Overall, do you think the orphans were better off as a result of the Earl Grey scheme?